SLEEPING
UNDERWATER

Laird Ryan States

SLEEPING UNDERWATER

Laird Ryan States

Coffin Hop Press

COFFIN HOP PRESS LTD / CANADA

LAIRD RYAN STATES

Coffin Hop Press Ltd.
200 Rivervalley Crescent SE
Calgary, Alberta Canada T2C 3K8

www.coffinhop.com

info@coffinhop.com

Publisher's Note: This is a work of fiction. Names, characters, places, and incidents are a product of the author's imagination. Locales and public names are sometimes used for atmospheric purposes. Any resemblance to actual people, living or dead, or to businesses, companies, events, institutions, or locales is completely coincidental.

Book design © 2019 Coffin Hop Press

Cover design © 2019 Coffin Hop Press

Cover Art © 2019 Guillem Marí

Lyrics to *"Love Love Love"* by John Darnielle used with permission from the artist

ISBN: 978-1-988987-15-6

CONTENTS

Foreword

King Saul fell on his sword when it all went wrong
And Joseph's brothers sold him down the river for a song
And Sonny Liston rubbed some Tiger Balm into his glove
Some things you do for money
And some you do for love, love, love

Raskolnikov felt sick, but he couldn't say why
When he saw his face reflected in his victim's twinkling eye
Some things you'll do for money and some you'll do for fun
But the things you do for love
Are gonna to come back to you one by one

Love, love is going to lead you by the hand
Into a white and soundless place
Now we see things as in a mirror dimly
Then we shall see each other face to face

And way out in Seattle, young Kurt Cobain
Snuck out to the greenhouse, put a bullet in his brain
Snakes in the grass beneath our feet, rain in the clouds above
Some moments last forever
But some flare out with love, love, love

—John Darnielle, *Love Love Love*

FOREWORD

Most novels begin with an idea for a story, a character or a theme. The novel you're about to read began with a place. In 2006, Ryan made his first journey to the island of Sel Souris in an online journal called The Irresponsible Journey.

Ryan told the story of his own trip to Sel Souris, an island south of Spain and north of Africa, little known to outsiders. I was fortunate to be among the few friends invited to join him through posts and updates about his trip.

Our small group came to know and love a place that never was, a mysterious paradise that shared its genes with ancient myths and the golden age of the pulps.

Sleeping Underwater grew from those first journal entries and it's probably fair to say that Ryan didn't invent the story so much as he heard it around a campfire one night, on a Sel Souris beach.

His love for the island and its people is obvious and inviting. He doesn't see them as lesser for not being real. His devotion to his characters and their stories makes it easy to slip completely into their world the way Carter, one of the heroes of this novel, slides into a warm bath until not even the tip of his nose is showing.

The island loans its magic to the book's stubbornly real places, making London shift like a dream from the familiar to the impossible and back. It's not so much that nothing is what it seems as that everything is what it seems and another thing besides. The book is a mystery and a pulp adventure, a false document and a true story.

Most of all, it's a memorable (and occasionally irresponsible) journey.

Enjoy your trip.

- Gayleen Froese, September 2018

PART ONE

SLEEPING UNDERWATER

T his is not a mystery novel, though I'd understand if you mistook it for one. In a mystery novel, there's a detective, a mystery, and there's a solution.

I am, or rather was, a detective.

Once, I had a partner, a brilliant and complicated man. Under his employ, I participated in many of those sorts of adventures. This story isn't one of those. My apologies if that's what you were hoping for. I think most of those, in hindsight, were probably contrived.

The truth, insofar as I believe in truth, is that actual mysteries do exist. For the interesting ones, however, there are no solutions. Real mysteries are puzzle boxes that open up to stranger and more terrible mysteries. You can seek answers, but you'll only end up with more questions. I've made peace with that.

You might also call this an adventure story. I cannot deny that there are many exciting things in it, and a great deal of violence and risk. So, if you think of that as adventure, then you may be right.

I consider it, if I'm being honest, nothing more than the story of several strange events that led me to the man I love. The vast and unknowable clockwork that runs the universe and sends us where we need to be at the times we need to be there. I no longer look for answers about any of these things. I have forsworn adventure, and that no longer bothers me one bit.

The story you are about to read takes place in the late nineteen-eighties. By then, my excessively brilliant partner Andrew was dead, or so I believed, and my last great adventure with him long done. Honestly, it felt as though the only interesting part of my life was over, and I was dragging out a long denouement until death claimed me.

I'd kicked around London for a few years since the big finish, mostly taking dirty pictures of unfaithful spouses. The closest I got to interesting work was the occasional missing persons case. Unlike what you see on the telly or at the cinema, it isn't exotic work. It's depressing. You either never find a trace, discover the person's run off on purpose, or you find they've died. The nasty photos are the nicer way to spend your time. Missing persons cases can damage your soul.

It seemed impossibly glamorous back in those days when I realized that rock journalism was not for me, just as nothing else I'd ever tried had been for me. Part of that, of course, was that I believed I had fallen in love with Andrew.

I took the job out of curiosity, and thinking it would make me as cool and exotic and mysterious as he was. My curiosity was soon satisfied. I was never in my wildest dreams half so cool as he was. Not until the day he died. On that day I was positively cold.

Since then, my earnings were barely sufficient to meet expenses and I'd frequently considered abandoning the job altogether. Poverty and free time on the dole were more appealing to me than the bleakness and the boredom of it.

I'd supposed I would get out of London for a start and live cheaply until I put together exactly what I ought to do with the rest of my life. I was, in fact, about to ring the licensing board. I wanted to see about a partial refund on my fees and insurance when somebody knocked on my open office door.

"You Niles Townsend?" he asked, and I looked up. He was small and frail but god-awful handsome, in jeans and a David Bowie t-shirt that clung tightly across his chest, and a beat-up leather jacket studded with pins.

"Yes," I said. "Can I help you at all?"

"I'm told you're the finest dick in London," he said to me with a cheeky little bastard smirk on his face like he'd known me for years. Somehow it came off as charming, but the hairs on the back of my neck stood up, intimations of trouble coming off of him on a low frequency.

"I haven't any idea where you've heard that, but you've been severely misinformed. I make no promises as to quality work. I am, however, relatively inexpensive."

"How inexpensive?" he asked. "Because to be honest, I'm skint."

I smiled. "We ought both to be careful. This much honesty in a room can be dangerous."

His eyes twinkled and he came forward to offer me a hand. I stood to shake it. There was that odd sense of years-knowing, and more of the same feeling that a storm stirred silently in the distance. If I was a dog, I'd have lain my ears back against my head and looked for shelter.

"Name's Carter," he said to me. "Carter Bennet."

I blinked. "Sincerely? And you're skint?"

He looked uncomfortable and shrugged as he sat in the chair across from me.

Carter Bennet had designed the Museum of Industry in Liverpool three years ago, and became something of a celebrity when Prince Charles spoke out against it, calling it a carbuncle. The consensus in architectural circles was that it was a remarkable building, especially for a man so young, and that he was the proverbial "one to watch".

"I would have thought you'd have people banging your door down."

"Did have for a while, but I quit."

"Quit what?"

"Architecture. I got bored with it, thought if I were smart, I could live off the money I'd been putting by for donkeys' years. Didn't work out that way, sadly."

"Bored? Are you mad?"

He shrugged. "People've said so. I don't know. I just lost interest."

I looked him over and wished very badly I could be him. I don't know how it is that certain people can walk through life with such calm assurance and reckless disregard for common sense, while the rest of us get an acid stomach just trying to decide which bloody shirt to wear. Life must be such a pleasure cruise for the lucky people who don't agonize over every detail.

"Look," I said, "seriously, why did you come to me? Whatever your problem is, it's likely above my level. I take photos of cheating wives all day, and then crawl home to a flat that would look like home to a Tibetan monk. I can refer you to an actual detective if you'd like."

"I liked your advertisement in the book."

My advertisement in the book was a tiny one-sixteenth of a page bargain spot. It had my name, the words "Consulting Detective" and my phone number. That was the lot. I cocked an eyebrow.

"You didn't make any claims," he continued, "and you didn't spend much on it. It made you seem mysterious and competent, you know, like you didn't need to advertise."

I believe it was at that moment the process whereby I fell in love was completed. That makes me seem extremely shallow, but it's not as it sounds. There is enormous pleasure in being understood by a stranger. There is an equally deep pleasure for a man approaching middle age to be flirted with by a person at least a few years younger.

Also, I am extremely shallow.

I let out my breath in a slow sigh.

"Marry me, would you?"

He laughed.

"Carter," I said, "if you like, you can tell me what's going on and if I think I can help you, you can be my official last case. If not, I'll tell you straight, all right?"

"Fair enough." He nodded, and he started to lay out the story.

Very shortly, I'd agreed to take his case, a simple missing property affair, with the reservation that I felt it better suited to a police investigation. There was a strange moment when we didn't know how to end the conversation. We didn't really want to. We'd resorted to awkward pauses that went on for far too long to be anything but embarrassing.

Finally, I asked him if he wanted to grab supper at a place down the street, and we headed there, settling into a booth in the back. The waitress knew me by name and winked when she saw me there with Carter. I tried not to blush. I blush far too easily.

The two of us engaged in small talk as we waited to order. Music we liked, the latest in the litany of atrocities by the Thatcher government the usual. Then we ordered and talked some more.

"So," he said. "Why are you quitting?"

"Got bored. Anyhow, figured I could get by for donkey's years on the money I'd put by," I said, in a passable imitation of his voice.

"Piss off with you and don't tell me, then."

"It's a really terrible job," I said, "and I'm shit at it. I got into it a long time ago, when I'd nothing better to do. I've begun to hope that possibly I might now find something." I left out the parts about Andrew, and how that ended. It felt like swallowing a lump of something unpleasant but necessary.

He nodded, making eye contact and then looking away.

"So, what's that then?"

"I have no ideas. Just hope. Comics are out, tried that for a bit when I was nineteen. Music journalism is out. I did that for altogether too long. As jobs go, they were almost as ugly as what I do now."

He smiled at me as I spoke, not amused exactly, but oddly fond. "You've a lovely voice. You could be a newsreader, or sing or something."

I looked at the table, waiting for the chips I'd ordered. "You're teasing me," I said quietly, and trying not to blush at a simple bloody compliment, knowing if I saw his eyes and a trace of sincerity, I'd glow like the setting sun.

"I'm not," he said, hurt at the accusation. "I don't. I don't ever do that. It's ugly."

"So, what about you?" I said. "You can't just quit being an architect after having such success. That's mad."

"I guess I'm mad then, because I've quit."

I shook my head.

"Look," he said. "If you're not enjoying life, you need to change something, don't you? That's just sensible. And I wasn't enjoying it. None of it. I'm sure I'll figure out something."

"Braver than me," I said, my tone making it quite clear that it was a meagre challenge.

"Not really. You're quitting, too."

"Yeah, well, I've not been famous for it or anything, nor have I exactly made my fortune."

"Fame's not much."

I looked at him as though he were speaking Latin.

"It's not," he said evenly and calmly, not trying to persuade himself. It felt like an apology.

I shrugged instead of him doing it, just for a change.

"It's nice for about ten minutes," he said. "You get a lot of free things sent to you, and the money is all right. Then people start wanting things back. You have crazy people who send you death threats."

"Some of whom are heirs to the throne of England, I'm told."

He laughed. He had the sort of laugh that catches.

"You laugh now," he said, "but the truth is that His Royal Parasite is just one of thousands of rich idiots who take it all very seriously. I had to hire security, which was nice in that I made some good friends, but it costs dearly. You read about those people who win the pools, and it's gone in a year, and you think they're fucking tossers, but they're not. You just don't realize until you're in the middle of it. It's expensive to be rich and more to be famous. I was only half of each, but it was the wrong half of both."

"Well what'll you do now?" I asked, leaning back.

"Teach, maybe. I dunno. Hadn't figured it out yet, and then all this nonsense happens with my things."

"Right," I said, "Well, the good news is that it doesn't sound like the crime of the century. So, I'm reasonably sure we'll get them back. Especially if you're right about the hiding place."

"I am," he said. "I'm bloody positive."

I wanted to tell him again to call the police. But I didn't. Any excuse, at this point, to look at his pretty, dark eyes.

I nodded.

Our meals came. We ate them. He looked nervous.

"Look, mate," he said. "When I said I was skint, I wasn't speaking in hyperbole or anything. I'm actually skint. I've not a dime right now and I shouldn't have ordered."

As he'd ordered a cup of tomato soup, I wasn't all that worried about the cheque.

"Don't worry about supper. It's on me."

His eyes registered disappointment that he hadn't ordered more, a charming lack of guile I found irresistible. I didn't extend the offer because I don't reward that behaviour, however sexy it is, and also because I didn't honestly know if I could cover too much more myself.

"As for my fee," I said. "You've promised once you get your things back, you'll be able to pay me, and your promise is good enough."

"You don't even know me."

"We're both Englishmen, are we not?"

SLEEPING UNDERWATER

It was his turn to decipher the dead language I seemed to speak.

"You're not serious," he said.

"I'd like to be," I said. "I wish I were. It would be nice to live in such a world."

There was a moment of quiet at the table.

"I'll pay," he said. "Got to, now. Jesus."

"This reminds me, I need to thank my mother for teaching me manipulation through guilt."

Carter coughed and laughed at the same time. I pretended not to have made a joke.

"Yours too?" he asked.

"I think it's a standard option on mothers, actually."

"Yeah," he said. "I never really picked up the talent."

"I had sussed that out," I said. "You've mastered, instead, the art of looking like a lost kitten."

He looked at his soup, took a sip.

"So where are you from, originally?" he asked.

"Manchester. You?"

"Liverpool."

I nodded, I'd sort of figured that out, as one does.

"You don't sound like you're from Manchester."

"I do in the mornings, and when I'm drunk."

"I can't imagine," he said, "seriously."

"With some luck, you won't need to imagine."

He smiled, looking me in the eyes for just a little longer than either of us meant to keep at it.

"How does someone become a detective?" he asked me.

"I don't know. I would imagine my situation was not typical."

"Well," he said, leaning forward, "now I have to know."

So, I told him.

It was one of those dreadful music industry parties that I kept being invited to because they wanted me to write shiny cock-suckingly glowing tales of the beautiful people. I rarely did, because the beautiful people were rarely either. In those days, I was shy and even more pale than I am now. I wore black mascara and a lot of sheer and gauzy blouses. Half the time I wore a skirt, but not in a cross-dressing way. I was lucky enough to have a kind of David Bowie androgyny. I was also quite convinced that I was a straight man.

Ah, youth.

I didn't know, like, or get an interview with the band whose album release we were celebrating. I spent most of the night drinking martinis with some of the other music press I had come to know.

One of these was Janice. She worked for the same rag as I did. We'd dated briefly until she'd told me she suspected I was gay, and I'd told her to go to hell. After a few weeks we had reconciled, didn't speak of it again, and spent all of our time together as we usually had done.

"Niles," she said, grabbing my arm in a shaking gleeful frenzy of starfucking joy. "There's someone here you need to meet."

"Janice," I said, "I'm nearly certain there isn't."

"You positively must," she said, jerking me to my feet. I looked at my mates apologetically. I pulled my arm free and shook out the gauzy fabric so it hung right over my paisley slacks.

"God, woman, you're a nuisance. Who is it, then?"

"There's a man over there in the corner who is an honest-to-god private detective. He found Danny's little sister last year."

"Danny?"

"The lead singer..."

"Oh, right, of the band, right."

She rolled her eyes.

"You're the worst bloody reporter in the world."

"Yes, I really am."

She kissed my cheek.

"Oh, come on, I was kidding, love."

She wasn't. We both knew that I was on my way out of the business and that it was a dead heat between a firing and me quitting.

She dragged me over across the dance floor, where spots and coloured lights swept and weaved. The music, and the smell of pot, and the lights, and my usual sense of complete non-belonging made me feel dizzy and distant.

She was talking to me, but I couldn't make out her words under the din. I mostly felt her talking to me through the vibrations of her hands. She led me into a side room and the noise died down to where I felt I could breathe.

"...eyes you could die in, and so glamorous," she said.

"Sure," I said.

We moved over to the table. Danny, the lead singer, was there. I recognized him now. He was talking to a man who had his blond head turned so that I couldn't see his face.

Janice tapped the blond on the shoulder and said something I couldn't hear.

He turned around, a little annoyed at being interrupted, as she pulled me in close.

"Andrew," she said, "this is Niles."

He looked at me with clear, cold, amused blue eyes that moved up and down me with quick precision.

"Well," he said. "Someone is sexually confused, isn't he?"

I blushed, and he smiled apologetically.

"Sit down," he said. "Janice has talked my ear off about you."

"Has she now?"

"She's quite completely in love with you. Bit pathetic for her, no?"

It was clear that Janice couldn't hear what he said to me, because she was smiling and nodding like a fan.

I looked at him. "Listen, mate, who the hell do you think you are talking to me, and about her, like that?"

He stopped smiling and nodded. "Good. You'll do."

"I'll what?"

"You'll do."

He handed me a business card. It read, "Andrew Matheson, Discreet Investigation" and had a number and address.

"Can you come by tomorrow at noon? I'd like to speak with you on business."

I nodded vaguely.

"Good. Now get the hell out of here and go do something you enjoy, won't you? You're a bloody glutton for punishment. Why are you still at this party? You can't stand anyone here."

I smiled, uncertainly, feeling a little dizzy, and stood back from the table.

"Isn't he marvelous?" she said to me, and I had to admit, he had something. What it was, I'd no idea. I still didn't know if I wanted to talk to him again or just punch him in the nose.

I couldn't stop thinking about him for the rest of the night. The next day I showed up to see him.

His office was all glass and steel, with dark blue carpet and a black steel desk. He was sitting behind it, dressed in a shiny grey suit with a pale pink t-shirt underneath. He wore glasses to read and seemed a little young for that. He hadn't noticed me come in.

I was dressed in a black t-shirt and jeans and carried a briefcase
I'd bought at a jumble sale a year or so before. My ears were still
aching from the night before.

I stood halfway in and halfway out of the open door,
awkwardly, and then he noticed me.

"Oh, hello," he said. "Niles. Come in, please. Have a seat. I'm
just going over something here. I won't be but a moment."

I sat down, and realized, to my horror, that he was reading a
comic book I'd written. That comic was on top of a stack of my
comics, and a pile of the music magazines I had written for. The
tips of my ears were hot, and I tried not to squirm, to blush.
Goddamn my blushing.

After a few minutes, he looked up.

"And so," he said, tossing the comic aside, "you went into
journalism."

"Er. Yes."

"Why is it, do you think, that your comics were so terrible?"
He asked the question with such an even-handed tone that it really
couldn't be heard as insulting.

"Well," I said, "there's only so far you can go with stories of
people in costumes striking one another in the face."

"Pretty far," he said. "Further than this, to be sure."

"And there were editorial restrictions, and the fact that the
things came out in eight-page chunks weekly, which made it
impossible to pace the bloody things."

"And yet."

"I was nineteen, and I didn't know what I was doing. And it's
a shit business."

He smiled, genuinely amused.

"And so, you decided to write for this…" he gestured at the
magazine contemptuously, "…piece of tripe."

"It's a job. It pays, and I meet any number of charming and
delightful people."

I batted my eyes coquettishly, sarcastically, my goat gotten,
my cock's comb rising.

He chuckled.

"You don't like me, do you?"

"I don't even know you, but you're failing to win me over
thus far. Look, why am I here?"

"Well. I'm wondering if you'd be interested in a job."

"Where?"

"Here."

"I don't know anything about investigation."

"That's probably true, but you know research, and believe it or don't, that is a large part of the work. Besides, I think you'll come to learn I have a remarkable sense of people. It's my singular talent. I think you have one as well. For example, you don't like me at all."

I shook my head, frustrated. "You've been a complete twat to me so far. What other impression was I supposed to take away?"

"Beats me. Yet, I think you'll also come to see that most people seem to find my manner charming, for some reason. It's always been this way for me."

"What do you need an employee to do?"

"Well, that's a bit tricky. I simply, at this point, need one. It's a permanent position. You are bondable, with no criminal record. I've checked. You had a few incidents in your teenaged years, but those have all been suppressed. If you take the position, I will pay twice what you make at the magazine. Within ten years, if you want them, the business and the clients will be entirely yours."

I blinked.

"How's that then?"

"I intend to return home, and, at that point, I'll have no need of any of this. I'm vain enough that I would like to leave my legacy here. This place."

"Where's home?"

"Find out. You've three days. If you pull it off, we're in business. If you can't, or don't feel like it, then it's been a treat to meet you."

I leaned back in the chair grinning.

"Is this a prank?" I asked. "Have my mates put you up to this?"

"No," he said.

"Look, you don't know me at all."

"I've researched you and talked to you twice. I already know more about you than anyone you've ever slept with."

I blushed.

"You're right," he said. "Bad example, in your case. I know more about you than your own mother, then."

"So, you're sending me on an errand, testing me like in some boys' adventure story and, if I pass your test, you'll train me to be a detective and hand your business over to me?"

"In time, yes."

"That's madness," I said, laughing.

11

"Yes," he said, looking me in the eyes, "isn't it though? It's mad and impulsive, and I promise you that every day of your life can be this fabulous. You can have the kind of life you've fantasized about since you were a child. You can be a hero and adventurer. You can be so fucking cool that it makes your teeth hurt. All real, not pretending."

I blinked.

"Well," I said, "you're not English, though your accent is passable. So that's a start."

He smiled thinly.

"Root hog, or die," he said. "I'll see you in three days."

I got up and went out to the little car I drove back then, held together, literally, by baling wire and drove straight to a phone directory so that I could find the municipal records office.

"Oh my god," said Carter. "That is the coolest fucking story I've ever heard. This really happened to you?"

I smiled, a little embarrassed. "Yes."

"Apparently it all worked out for you then, yeah?"

"Apparently," I said. "It likely sounds cooler than it was."

"It sounds very cool, mate."

"Well. I'm sure that, as you get to know me, I will seem significantly less cool."

"Usually this is true," he said, smiling.

"So," I said, "what's the life of a glamorous young architect like?"

"I wouldn't know," he said, shrugging again. "Mostly there's a lot of time hunched over a piece of paper drawing things and ignoring other people until they get really angry with you."

"Sounds fab," I said.

"You have no idea," he said. "Then there are the autograph hounds."

"The interviews with the architecture magazines for teens, and the photo shoots that you do for them. Five Gothic Cathedrals Carter Can't Stop Talking About."

"Right," he said, carrying on. "You can see where a man would want out."

"Oh, certainly," I said. "That's probably why Frank Lloyd Wright faked his own death and toured the States for the rest of his life as a Frank Lloyd Wright impersonator."

"That was Antoni Gaudi who did that, actually."

"I stand corrected," I said.

We looked at each other for a long pleasant moment.

By this point, we'd had six cups of tea each. We both knew it was time to go and kept putting it off. It was a replay of the afternoon, though it was near on 8 p.m. now.

I knew full well why I was putting it off. I'd no idea why he was.

"Well," I said at last, "I really need to get on home."

"Yeah, right," he said, "course you do."

We both stood up.

"So," he said, "I should give you my number."

"Right," I said, legitimately stunned I'd not asked so far.

"Except I've not got one right now. But I'll call you to keep checking in."

I paused before speaking.

"All right."

"Well then. That's me," he said, "Night."

He stepped outside and I shook my head and followed after.

"You've got no place to go, have you?"

"No. Not as such."

I sighed.

"Right, if this is going to work, whatever this is, you need to stop playing coy with me. If you want to stay at my place, just ask me. Don't just sort of hint and look hangdog."

"I wasn't," he said, a little put out. "Why would I even dream of that? You don't even bloody know me. Why would you let me stay?"

"Do you want to?"

"Yeah."

"Well, come on then."

He stared at me, with it not registering. "Bloody superhero, you are."

"You've not slept on my couch, yet."

We walked out into the now dark and slightly blurry street.

"Can you afford the tube?" I asked.

"Yeah," he said, a little embarrassed.

"Good. Let's go."

13

We walked in companionable silence to the station and waited.

"This is really nice of you."

"Well, actually," I said, "I'm a sex murderer, so the joke's on you."

The joke sounded funnier in my head than it did out loud, but he laughed.

"So, how'd you pass the test?"

At first, I was a bit lost as to what he meant, and then it dawned on me. "Oh...Andrew's test. It's not a very good story really. Sort of an anticlimax."

I had hoped he'd let it drop at that, but he didn't.

Two days into my investigation of Andrew I realized I had still come to nothing useful. I suspected that he had changed his name at some point and that had buggered everything else past recognition. So, I called Janice, which was probably something I owed her.

"Niles," she said calmly, without much investment.

"Hello Jan," I said. "Sorry. I should have called, but I've had a really shit week."

"Of course."

"How long have you known Andrew?" I asked her.

"Oh, about an hour longer than you, and you've seen considerably more of him."

"Did he say anything about where he was from?"

"No," she said, as though it were preposterous. "Why on earth would he?"

I nodded, but of course she couldn't see me.

"Yeah," I said, "I expect you're right, yeah."

"What is going on?"

I laughed. "He's offered me a job, if you can believe it?"

She snorted. "Rent boy?"

"Hanging up now, bitch."

"Oh, poor baby, don't run off mad."

I hung up. Ah, Janice.

I decided to spend the day in a more productive way. Sometimes you need a sword to untie a knot.

SLEEPING UNDERWATER

I went down to the market and got myself a roll of good sturdy butcher's twine and a Stanley knife. I rifled through my closet at home until I found a balaclava. I put it on with a pair of bulky army surplus pants and a black sweater from a charity shop until I looked just like every thug I'd ever seen in a film. I went to Andrew's office and I waited across the street in my little car until I saw him leave. I followed him home and kept seeing him look back and forth as though he felt my eyes on him. That made me hold back a bit.

I waited outside his flat until I saw him go out again. Then I waited around the front door until someone else was leaving and snuck up to his door. He had his name on the buzzer box. It wasn't until this exact moment that I'd realized I'd absolutely no idea whatsoever how to break into a place.

I tried the knob, hoping he was one of those.

He wasn't.

I started to panic, pulled my balaclava on again, and proceeded to kick the hell out of his door. Kicking a door in is not like they show in films. It all depends on the door, of course. In some places it's easier than you'd think. This wasn't one of those places. After a good couple of kicks, one of his neighbours opened her door to look outside. She screamed her guts out at the sight of me.

I turned to her and started to apologize but she slammed her door shut. I weighed my chances of kicking the door in promptly against how long it would take the police to show up for a man in the uniform of the IRA.

I left immediately, drove around for a while, and thought. I decided to hide in a cluster of hedges near the door. I would wait for Andrew and then, at the appointed time, I'd jump out and abduct him. With fear on my side, I was guessing I could get him to talk, and it was the sort of bold move I imagined he would want me to try.

An hour later I was in the back of a police car and on my way to a holding cell. I will admit that I cried. I had, despite a youth of wild excess, been raised with a terrible fear of being arrested. The idea filled me with shame and horror. My entire ride was filled with haunting imaginings of my father's sad disapproval, and my mother's ceaseless weeping.

I told the police the truth, basically, that it was a practical joke on a friend, and that I'd meant nobody any harm by the thing. I felt they more or less believed me, though it was clear that nobody was amused in any case. It likely helped that I was crying, and that I provided every piece of information they asked for. I did not ask for a lawyer, because I was young and stupid. I answered anything they asked without hesitation or internal censor.

I eventually asked if I could make a phone call, and I dialed the number on Andrew's card.

His answering service picked up and I spoke to a young girl whose name, I still recall, was Lia. She was very calm and reassuring, and she could tell I was in a lot of distress. Some people in this world are kind beyond belief, god love them. She put me on hold, and in a few minutes, Andrew came on the line, sounding annoyed.

"Yes?"

"Oh, thank god," I said. "It's Niles. Look, I didn't know who else to call. I've been picked up by the police."

"Was it for kicking in my door?"

"Yeah."

He made a small noise, undecipherable in intent.

"Fantastic," he said. "That was an interesting strategy to gain my favour."

"I can explain, though, if I'm being up front, it's probably still quite stupid."

"I expect so."

"Can you please come down here and speak to them?"

"Fuck. All right. This is partly my fault. I shouldn't have expected common sense from a child."

That stung and I hesitated to speak.

"Thank you," I said, meaning it.

I sat in the cell with a number of drunks and angry, bloody young men who mostly let me be, probably because I was dressed not unlike them and entirely unlike myself. I stared at the floor, not making eye contact, and a long time passed before I was let out.

Andrew was waiting in the lobby.

"They've agreed to release you to me, on account of my excellent reputation, and on account of the fact that this is your first arrest and that you are clearly a twat instead of a public danger."

"Thank you."

"Don't thank me," he said. "Thank the constables."

I did so, though none of them bothered to look at me.

SLEEPING UNDERWATER

"There will be a court appearance and all of that," Andrew said.

"God," I groaned. "I am such a spastic."

"Come on."

He turned and left the building. I hastened considerably to follow him, and I got in his car.

We drove in silence for several minutes.

"All right," he said. "I am now calm enough to hear your explanation for this."

"Okay," I said. "Three days wasn't enough to get access to all the departments I needed to speak to. There was no record with anyone of your immigration, and so I assumed you'd changed your name. The change of name people weren't all that cooperative in tracking down your original name, at least not in a hurry, so I realized I couldn't get it done."

He nodded.

"Not all that bad," he said. "Keep going."

"So, I thought I'd talk to your friends, but I didn't know anyone who knew you except Janice, and she only met you the same night as I did. With nothing left, I thought I'd try a daring ruse. I bought this hard looking outfit and some twine, and I thought I'd hide in your place and surprise you and tie you up and get you panicking and try to get it out of you that way. Pretend I was a thug sent by one of your enemies."

Andrew looked at me with actual astonishment.

"My sweet bleeding lord on his knobby cross," he said, "That is the very worst plan I've ever heard."

I hung my head.

"Yeah," I said. "I admit I'm less enthusiastic about it now than I was at the time."

He turned his head because he did not want me to see him smile.

"Oh lord," he said.

"I know, I know," I said. "You're very kind to come and get me, and I swear I'll bugger off out of your life. Believe me, I quite understand."

He laughed hard, as though he'd been choking on it. This went on for some time, and my face burned with shame. Tears welled down my face. He stopped laughing sharply and went pale.

"Don't do that," he said, tenderly. "I'm sorry."

"Fuck you."

"Niles. I'm sorry. You'll look back on this fondly some day"

I never have. Telling the story, even painting myself in a slightly better light for Carter, I still felt the blush of shame. I am prone to it, shame, and to blushing, and I hate both.

"Look," he said, pausing to make a right hand turn across two lanes, "That was a terrible idea, but it was awfully brave and, um, creative, it cannot be denied. You made a very common mistake is all. In addition, naturally, to the huge ones in judgement."

I wiped my eyes with the palms of my hands.

"Yeah," I said, "what was that then? Tell me how I'm stupid."

"You never phoned me up and asked me where home was."

"I...when I asked the first time, you told me to find out."

"You ought to have asked me again. And again after that. Or bargained if need be. You were always right next to the certain truth and you went elsewhere looking for it. That's poor thinking."

"Well I came back to it, didn't I?" I asked angrily.

"Oh yes. Undeniably. You just overcomplicated, which is, honestly, the only difference between a genius and a very bright person. And one can learn to stop."

I said nothing.

"You're hired."

"I don't want it."

"Of course, you do. Stop sulking."

I continued to sulk for the next few days, and then I showed up at his office.

When I walked in the door, he smiled at me as though I were an old friend. I almost cried with relief, and with happiness that I'd not blown it, and that he was actually, sincerely pleased to see me return.

Carter stopped laughing eventually, about halfway through the tube ride to my street. I was grateful. He leaned against me a little as we got back to my place, tired out, complaining his stomach hurt. His casual use of body contact was either genuinely a part of him, or genius flirting.

My flat wasn't much. It was on the second floor. It might have charitably been called four rooms – the bathroom, my bedroom, the living room, and a semi obscured kitchen. The water heater was crap, so I made steady use of a well-trusted kettle left to me by my gram. By habit, the first thing I did on entering the place was to set it up for a boil on the gas stove, which was older than me by about Carter's age. That was somewhere between 5 years and a million, I supposed.

"Oh my god," he said with genuine warmth as he walked straight in and embraced the wall that faced toward the street. His fingers gripped the edge of the window, curling slightly, and he ran his other hand over the bare brick.

I turned back from the kettle to see him on his knees, examining the mortar between the bricks, fascinated. I raised an eyebrow.

"Tea?" I offered. "Or I have some instant coffee, if you prefer."

"No thanks," he said running a hand between two rows of bricks,

I sat and watched him make love to the wall, bemused. I might as well have been invisible. I was jealous of my own flat for a moment, which made me feel rather silly.

"Is this the original flooring?" he said.

"I dunno," I said back. "From the bloody looks of them it could be."

"Deep runnels," he said, as he lay on the floor to examine them from a better vantage point.

"Worn out and ragged," I said.

"That's a lousy way to look at it," he said, sitting up. "You don't know what you've got here. This place is amazing. I mean, yeah, it's a bit run-down maybe. I imagine the plumbing and wiring are both nightmarish."

"You've got that right, mate."

The kettle began to whistle, and I got up.

"Gas seems fine," he said.

"Yeah. Only thing that works."

As if on cue, the lights dimmed low and yellow. London glowed outside my window, strange and huge and unfathomable in every direction. For three long seconds, we didn't speak.

"The plumbing and electrical were probably added years later, and wedged in. The gas was put in when they built her. And she is a gorgeous thing, she is."

"Well you can have her, then." I shook my head. "I've had it."

"I mean, I get it," he said, "it's probably a bit trying to live here. Probably your landlord could give two shits about fixing her up but, in the right hands, this could be a really perfect place."

He was right. I could give two shits. I owned her, for what that mattered. Selling the place was the second part of my plan on getting out of London.

"I'd prefer something built this century, with hot water for the bloody shower," I said. "Or even a proper shower."

His eyes went wide, and he ran looking for my bathroom. I heard him gasp.

"Oh. My. God."

"Well, all right," I said. "I have to admit that's a bit nice."

He had climbed inside my seven-foot long clawfoot tub and stretched out so he could lay invisible. "This is bloody perfection, right here."

"Be better with a proper shower instead of that tacked on hose thing."

"Well, you could fix that."

I laughed, because it was funny. The very thought of my attempting home improvement made me laugh again.

"Look," he said, suddenly very serious, "I see where you're coming from, but you need to stop that right now. I won't have it. I won't. This flat is a bloody masterpiece. If you could still build places with this kind of craft and materials, by god, I'd probably keep doing it."

I opened my mouth to object, but he held up a hand.

"You're an ignoramus. Sorry. Your opinion stopped being relevant around the time you said you'd prefer something built this century. You're like a fat old man who dumps his Nobel prize winning wife for a beauty contest winner because that's like, better, or something. For all you know this place was designed by Nicholas Hawksmoor..." He looked at the place where the walls meet the ceiling. "It wasn't," he continued, "I think he only did churches, but there you are."

I smiled. "There I am, indeed."

He looked horrified. "I'm sorry. God. That was rude. Sometimes I get excited and..."

I leaned in and kissed him.

I pulled back. He pulled back and we looked at each other.

"So, you are gay," he said.

"Yes," I said. "Surprise!"

"Leave off," he said quietly, embarrassed.

"And you're gay too," I said.

He shrugged, which I found charming in some insolent, closeted way.

"I'm sorry that I kissed you without asking first," I said. "That was rude."

He shook his head. "I liked it."

"Me too," I said. "Very much."

"Good."

He looked away nervously. Wondering, I could see, if he'd got this wrong, if he was expected to be in my bed in exchange for the place to stay. My stomach dropped.

"Oh god, no," I said, stammering, "No, it's not what you're thinking. I didn't ask you here for that."

He nodded, relieved or something.

"I'm not rich enough to keep a rent boy," I said smiling.

He smiled back. "And you'd want one built this century, anyway."

"Oh, pack it in, you're not old."

He nodded, and something passed over his face for a second before the smile came back to life. "I'll be thirty in two years. I shudder to think of it."

"Yes," I said drily. I was thirty-five. "I'm sure."

"I think I'll stop talking now," he said.

"That would be best," I said fondly.

He nodded. "All the best conversations in the world happen in the loo with one person in the tub and the other on the pot," he said.

"I can't say I've had many since moving out of home."

"Comfy isn't it?"

"You're really very odd, Carter Bennet."

"You're really very handsome, Niles Townsend."

I blushed, as nobody had actually ever called me handsome before. Smiling, I stood up.

"Well," I said, "here's me then. I'm off to bed. The door is open. You are under no obligation. The couch is yours, should you wish it."

"I'm going to sleep right here, if I can cop a pillow or something."

I laughed and went to the closet. I handed him the pillow and an old quilt. Our hands brushed and he looked in my eyes. "It's not 'no', Niles," he said. "It's just 'not tonight.'"

I smiled. "Okay. We've a long day tomorrow. Best to rest."

He cocked a mischievous look at me. "Woo. Right. You think pretty highly of your own performance, don't you?"

I tossed a roll of bog paper at him. "You're losing your appeal," I said, and flicked the loo light off, heading to my room.

But he wasn't.

The next morning, I woke up first. I stayed in bed for the better part of an hour because I was afraid of waking him up. Eventually, I couldn't do it any longer. I get restless in the mornings and have to move around, or I go a little mad.

I got out of bed and put on a robe. I wanted to shower and shave and get dressed, but that would have meant going in and disturbing him. Furthermore, it would have meant resuming our conversation from the night before. I was rather muzzy to try and seem witty and warm and wise and sexy.

Instead, I crept into my kitchen and ran some water into the kettle for a brew. I looked out the kitchen window at the pigeons on the ledge, and I thought about cigarettes the way people think of their first lover. Tears nearly stood in my eyes as I remembered the taste and feel, and how very bad for me they were. I remembered how young I was when I smoked them and how pretty I was back then, though I'd no idea. Now I was narrow and lean, clean looking at least, age starting to show at the edges of my eyes. My hairline had begun to move back a little further on my forehead of late. I was vain enough that I'd started avoiding the sight of myself in mirrors.

I am told that, for most people, three in the morning is the loneliest time of the day, the time when they stare at their ceiling and slowly dance with all their regrets and fears to the same terrible song again and again until exhaustion drops them back into sleep. For me, the loneliest time of the day was waiting for the kettle to boil. I stood waiting, feet cold, half dressed, for that first dose of caffeine I so desperately needed to get through the day. I thought of all the crowded family tables with well-scrubbed children, everyone eating a hasty breakfast in a noisy rush, and looked ahead at the stretch of solitary breakfasts that stood before me. I wondered what the point was of getting up at all.

I loathe children, and I'm not all that wild about noise and tumult in general. I'm even fond of my time alone, most of the time. It's not what I want, to be straight and normal and working the factory job. It's not.

But between 7 and 8 in the morning I sometimes wished I was loved.

It's not that I actually lived the life of a monk, to be clear. I'd had my share of gentleman callers. Many of them even stayed the night. Several of them were still on friendly terms with me. One or two were even what I'd call lovers, for a time. Mostly, though, it was a series of friendly blokes with whom physical intercourse had been pleasant, but with whom I'd no more a chance for intellectual intercourse than I would with an affectionate Afghan Hound.

The breakfasts with these people consisted of awkward attempts to find things to talk about. Often that turned out to be football, god help me.

On very rare occasions, my evening callers were women. I did this from time to time in the dark desperate hope that I would like it. Sometimes I even did, but not in a way I'm proud of, and not in any way could ever share with the women in question. It was an infantile need to be held, I think, by a surrogate for my mother.

I should mention, for those who haven't yet sussed it, that I will never be Philip Marlowe. The sound of water splashing on the hardwood floor interrupted my sad clichéd British gay self-pity.

"The fuck?" I said, the epitome of wit, as always. I walked over to the door to my loo. "Hello? You all right?"

"Yeah," he said, "Just getting up."

I stared at the door, not sure how I ought to reply.

"Niles," he said, "are there towels in here?"

"Yes," I answered, "in the narrow closet by the sink. Feel free to borrow a razor as well."

"Cheers," he said, and I heard the sound of his dripping.

I walked back to the kettle, added loose black tea to my grandmother's Doulton teapot, and poured the water in to steep. I opened the fridge and found a slice of lemon still cello-wrapped. I dropped it in the pot as well.

In about three minutes, Carter walked out, dressed in the clothes from the day before. His hair was still wet, and he had not shaved.

"You should have woken me up," he said, "I hate to think I kept you from the shower and all that."

"I've not been up long," I said. "No call to worry."

23

"I could murder a cup of that," he said.

"Help yourself in a second," I said.

He made a happy noise of assent and sat at my little table. His fingers were wrinkled and pruny. He rubbed his hands together. I sat opposite him.

"I didn't hear you run the bath this morning at all," I said.

"I didn't. I ran it last night at around two a.m. I couldn't sleep."

I nodded, mulling that over, sort of rolling it around my brain a little.

"Carter," I said, "hypothetically, if I had walked into my lavatory to rouse you this morning, would I have found you asleep in a full tub of water?"

He smiled.

"You could have drowned," I said, "and left me to deal with that, thank you very much."

"Nah," he said. "I do it all the time."

"You're mad."

"Yes. It's been said. By you."

I shook my head slightly and poured the tea.

"It's a lovely tub," he said. "Best I've ever slept in."

"I can never tell when you're taking the piss."

"I told you. I don't do that. I didn't care for it in school, and I don't like to do it to people."

"Right then," I said, "I think I'll perform my morning ablutions so that I feel sane. Please do help yourself to the fridge. It's not a very generous offer, I'm afraid."

I stood up. He put his hand on my wrist. "You're not cross with me, are you? I don't mean to be a bother."

I looked him in the eyes. "Carter," I said, "one thing you will soon learn about me is that I'm not shy about being cross. I'm not. You're a very strange person but, as it happens, I'm rather fond of strange people. Don't ever apologize to me for who you are. If I seem to be asking questions, it's because I don't understand why you do what you do. I would very much like to. It's my nature. Hence why I stuck with my job as long as I've bothered."

He looked at me for a moment and his eyes got a little shiny. He looked, hurriedly, at his tea.

"Okay," he said.

"Okay," I said. "You'd best still be here when I come out of that room or I will be cross."

He looked up at me like I had telepathic powers.

SLEEPING UNDERWATER

"Oh yes," I said, "I'm on to you."

He blushed and took his tea in both hands to sip.

I walked to the loo and prayed the shower had some hot water. It did.

Carter was, happily, still there when I came out of the shower. I was dressed in a shiny grey suit with a narrow black tie and freshly polished black shoes. I topped off the look with a grey fedora. I am pleased to say that a man of narrow frame, such as myself, can carry off this look without seeming too precious.

I walked over to the kitchen table where he sat, with a soft smile, flipping through an old Rupert annual from my shelf.

"I used to love these," he said, his hand moving gently over the pictures.

"Why'd you stop?" I answered.

He looked up at me.

"I...suppose I haven't. I just hadn't thought of Rupert in years. I had a teddy bear that looked just like him."

"You and every boy in England," I said, pointing to the top of a bookshelf where mine sat in a quiet place of honour.

"You're very cool," he said.

"No," I said, "I'm not. It's childish, really. I just don't care to let go of childhood. I liked childhood, you know."

"I don't, actually. I hated being a kid. Told where to go, what to do, constantly being beaten on by the other kids."

"Oh yes, all of that. I do remember. I'm not one of those prats who thinks of childhood as a blessed state of paradise. It wasn't. It was just new. Everything was new. I was constantly learning things, and finding hugely interesting things. And I didn't feel the need to question bloody everything. That is worth holding onto."

"I'll take freedom, mate."

"Fair enough."

I drank a glass of water.

"So, given the meagre leads you've provided me, I fear I've quite a day ahead of me. I need to get on the job. You're free to hang around here, read my comics, all that."

He nodded.

"One more thing, Carter," I Columbo'd, "You said that your things were taken from your flat. Were you lying about having a flat in the first place, because you were embarrassed, or was there some reason you didn't want to go back to it last night?"

He fidgeted in his seat and looked uncomfortable.

"Make no mistake here," I said, "you have five seconds to answer and then you become my houseguest, but not my client. And then I go over to the phone and resign my lic—"

"I didn't want to go back."

"Why?"

"Because they broke in the first time, right? So, they could just walk back in again, couldn't they?"

"All right," I said, "That's fine."

"Are you angry with me?" he said, looking up at me.

I smiled. "No. I'm sorry. I don't mean to turn 180 on you like that, love. This is me wearing my professional hat."

I pointed at my hat, wryly.

He relaxed visibly.

"I think we're friends now, Carter, and, when I'm not on the job, you'll find me a different person. Right now, though, I am on the job, and that means you're a liar, not to be trusted, and I will have to treat you like a bloody client."

He laughed. "You rehearse that?"

"Oh, fuck you," I said. "Yes. I have done."

"I'm sorry," he said, "but it just sounds so silly in real life like that."

"People lie to me on a daily basis. Or if they don't, they occlude the truth. Mostly I am polite enough to let it slide. Occasionally my professional responsibilities demand that I be rude."

"I'm not lying to you, mate. I swear."

I clenched my jaw. "Say that again, if you think you dare. Look me in the eye as you do so."

He declined.

"Right," I said, fixing my tie. "Give over your keys."

He reached into his pocket and gave them to me without a thought.

"Stay here," I said. "Read. Listen to records. Watch the video player. Clean the place if you like. Do whatever calms you. I'm going to see what can be seen, and I'll be back before it gets dark."

He nodded.

"There is half an ounce of pot at the bottom of my sugar canister. Feel free to indulge. Do not drink my scotch."

"God, as if," he said.

"Will you be alright?" I asked, professional demeanour slipping a little.

"Dunno, really," he said. "Hurry back."

I frowned slightly, not sure exactly what it was about his behaviour this morning that filled me with such grave concern, but it was something. I wanted to believe he was just a strange, pretty man, coping poorly with the after effects of a break in. People tend to take them much worse than they think they will. We all live with a false sense of security when it comes to our homes. To lose that shakes you up.

I'd pegged him as coming from a middleclass home, one of a number of siblings. He was smaller than most of the other kids, and he was still smaller than most people as a grown man. I had pegged him as gay, thank heavens, and as closeted about it for one reason or another. I suspected that he had suffered a loss in the recent past, and that the loss had brought about his sudden change of behaviour, and a willingness to toss his old life over the side. In addition to that, I thought he might be a drinker. It was possible that he was a victim of some kind of abuse. He had a way of flinching and reacting strangely to even mild annoyance that worried me.

I loathed my ability to see these things in people, to be so detached about it. It strengthened my need to quit this lousy business in which it was an asset to see and predict the worst of what people need, and what they'll do. It was a skill, I expect, that life would have taught me eventually. The job, and my former employer, had taught me much faster.

That was when it struck me. Carter reminded me just a little of Andrew Matheson, my former employer, my late lover.

Whom I had more or less eventually murdered, as it happens.

I smiled, playing the part.

"I'll be back as soon as I can, love. I'll bring curry."

Which, I thought, I will likely pay for with a credit card, because I want to look flash.

The thing about lying is that everyone can do it, and everyone does. This does not exclude me, and never has. I had told Carter that I'd be following up on his case today, checking his leads.

This was, at best, a partial accounting of my planned activities for the day. You see, the one thing about this case on which I was in absolutely no doubt was that Carter wasn't telling me the truth. This didn't make him the bad guy, and it didn't mean that he shouldn't have been helped. All that it meant was that something about all of this either scared him or would paint someone in a bad light. This could have been him, or it might have been someone that he was fond of.

The average person doesn't engage a detective to find the sort of things that Carter said had gone missing from his flat. They just shrug, move on, and replace them. Conversely, it must be said, the average thief wouldn't steal them, either. This is what engaged my interest, frankly. He'd also told me that, once returned, he'd be able to pay. Nothing in the hasty summation of assets missing led me to understand how that was so.

The simplest answer to this was that Carter was lying. Something else, something of interest, had been nicked along with the chaff he'd listed to me. William of Ockham is an investigator's best friend.

With this in mind, I was planning to thoroughly go through Carter's flat. I had his keys and everything. I'd asked, and he'd given. This probably meant that he didn't think he had much to hide. It might have meant he was just too distracted to say no.

His flat was on the sixth floor in a much nicer part of town than that in which I lived. This was to be expected and I'd a suspicion he owned it. I opened the front door and went up the stairs. The front door was painted white and had a number of deadbolts on it. His keys were not numbered, so it took me a few tries before I got in.

The first thing I noticed was that the floor just inside the door was covered in envelopes. Bills mostly, but also some letters from various architecture and design firms. I didn't open them, having some claim to ethics. I stacked them neatly on a wrought iron table that sat by the door.

The place was covered in a thin layer of dust. He hadn't been there in a while. Aside from that, it was immaculate. The furniture was sparse. He lived alone, and it was clear he didn't entertain often. There were a few low shelves, but the main living area was dominated by a set of three large cylinders of a smooth blue-gray plastic. I went over to them and found that they spun around on their base with a nearly musical sound of metal on metal. There were a series of hatches that opened on these cylinders, in the same way that some cassette players opened. If you pushed them gently, they unlatched and pulled quietly up and out of the way.

All of his things seemed to be in one compartment or another. His books in a few of them, a decent sized TV and video-player in one, a lot of albums, and a stereo that made me want to weep with naked envy. When he was done with any of them, he could slide the hatch door back and it was gone.

The same arrangement worked on a smaller scale in his kitchen and bedroom and loo. There was no clutter, not a bit of it, except in three places. He had a tangle of things on his kitchen table, a similar tangle on a bedside table, and on the back of his toilet tank was a scattering of change and ticket stubs.

I was a bit flummoxed. He had struck me, to be honest, as the sort of man whose flat would look as though the Northern Irish took regular exception to its contents. This place was a sort of wet dream fantasy for anally fixated obsessive compulsives. It was, of course, quite stylish in a way the magazines would find sexy. It just didn't feel much like a place he would love to live in. I remembered him embracing the old half rotted bricks of my hellhole, and his almost carnal love for my clawfoot tub, and I asked myself why he would live in such a place.

I was about to theorize when I nearly stepped on something small and round and blue. I knelt to pick it up. It was a tablet of something illegal. I looked at it, nodded, and promptly flushed it down the toilet. I fucking hate pills.

The ticket stubs on the back of the toilet were for clubs with all night dance parties. In light of this, it wasn't surprising to find this poison in his flat. While it was a cheap enough drug, it was an expensive habit for a man with no job, but not likely an indication of addiction, thank god.

I walked up and down the hall of the place, feeling like I was in a rather swanky airport lounge, trying to decide which of his privacies to invade first, when I realized that this place was a beard. He was a prize-winning architect. This was the sort of place where he was supposed to live. It certainly didn't look as though he spent much time here.

He wasn't shy about staying over at strange men's flats. I happened to know this for a fact.

As I mused on all of this, I made a connection.

Carter had mentioned that the items stolen were in three cardboard cartons. The one thing I didn't see anywhere in this flat were cardboard boxes. He simply didn't store his things that way.

I searched again, looking in closets for cartons, and did not find a one.

How the hell, I wondered, would a junkie thief find anything in this place? How would they even know what to look for? To the naked eye this place was empty, filled with large strange sculptures. Your average drug addled bastard was apt to be very disappointed. I could not imagine that Carter would have just left cardboard boxes lying on the floor to become a crime of convenience for the first drug fiend to wander in.

The thief had been here before, and Carter knew them. They were not the strangers he'd indicated. This came very near to being my first lead.

Why the hell had the cartons been here at all? It wasn't how he lived.

A cartoon lightbulb appeared above my head and I realized that the cartons maybe weren't his at all. He had just been hanging onto them. They belonged to someone else. The someone else Carter had been trying not to talk about.

It was only a theory, but it felt sound.

I obviously needed to talk with Carter again. Before I did that, I needed to do some looking into him. The most important thing I had ever learned from Andrew was that the best way to get the truth from someone was to know it in advance.

I went to the library to do some looking into Carter. He was the youngest son of five. He'd grown up in Liverpool. He was the son of a sailor. His mother taught Sunday school and music lessons. None of his other siblings lived remarkable lives, though the family seemed relatively free of strife. He was the only one to go to university and was the first member of his family to receive a degree.

He had been very successful almost immediately and, being young and good looking, he'd had his picture taken a lot. For all of that, the pictures were rather flat. He looked shy and unhappy in most of them, even as he smiled gamely. The interview I found, though brief, painted a picture of a young man without any malice or ego, but also without much joy. He came off much posher and more well-spoken in the interview than he tended to with me and I wondered which, if either, were the artifice.

SLEEPING UNDERWATER

The photos were all much alike. Shots of him in front of one building or another shaking hands with someone, or candid shots at parties. He did not seem to ever have an escort and the accompanying articles, in a rare show of restraint, did not comment. Perhaps he was well-liked by the press. It has been known to happen that some people simply get a pass based upon charm and decency.

The photos and the interviews stopped altogether about a year prior, which matched up well with my own hazy memories of when I stopped seeing him mentioned. There was, as near as I could tell, no article about his retirement. It may have been just as simple as his being the flavour of the week, quickly famous, readily forgotten. Architecture, it must be said, is a niche interest.

The articles fleshed out my understanding of him somewhat, but left me no hints at all as to who the stolen cartons belonged to, or who had taken them. No paramours had made themselves known, nor enemies. His narrative lacked any apparent drama. This was inconsistent with my understanding of humans. Humans have drama. Inherently. Andrew had once told me that, when examining the life of a person, once you have eliminated all obvious sources of passion, you will have to look at the hidden and the minute. The hidden passions and those passions wrapped up in matters of no consequence are the deepest and most dangerous of all human feelings.

All I had to go on, at present, was his conviction that they had been taken to a warehouse near my office, and that they had been sold for drug money. Carter had told me he suspected the thief was a friend of a friend of his, who had grabbed them up for a quick score. He didn't want the police involved for reasons of privacy, because the items were personal to him.

It was a fishy story, all of it, and I was trying very hard to stay above it, dispassionate but interested. It was complicated because I could still remember the smell of him and the taste of his tongue from the night before. I could still see the lock of hair that kept falling in his eyes when he looked down nervously, a thing he did constantly. I remembered the way my heart pounded when he showed that one moment of passion about my flat and let his guard down. The minute and the hidden, perilous and attractive.

I hadn't felt this way about a person in a long time, not since my former employer.

I swallowed bile, actually, not figuratively, and left the library for a chemists. I chewed some antacid tablets and headed back to my car. There was nothing for it but to talk to Carter face to face. This was always a delicate thing.

Liars, in my experience, do so for a limited number of reasons. Very few of these reasons are malicious. Most of them are based in fear. Few things make people as dangerous as fear does. This is not just because they are afraid of being punished, but because they are afraid for someone they care about. Most dangerous of all, they fear they are not who they'd like to believe they are. People will do or say anything to preserve their image of themselves.

It's not kind to just confront these people in their lies. You can damage them badly, beyond the point where they can be useful in the investigation, or to themselves. You won't get what you need, and it's needlessly cruel. People in horrible situations need to be talked to carefully. You ask questions around the issue. Try to find the truth without making them give it away. Confrontation is the last resort, best used if nothing else is left.

I pulled up outside and gathered my thoughts before going up. I thought about what Andrew would have done, and how I felt about using him as my role-model. Somewhere, in the imaginary dialogue between his opinion and mine, I came to a plan.

When I walked in, Carter was shirtless, and on his hands and knees on the living room floor. He'd pushed the furniture back and was washing the floorboards with a sponge and bucket. The entire place smelled of pine. He'd dusted. Dear lord.

"Oh my god, Carter," I said, "there was no call to do this. I was joking."

"No, it's all right," he said, wiping his forehead. "I got a bit restless in here all day."

"Well, god, thank you. I didn't even know I had cleaning supplies left," I said, setting my keys in their basket. "Oh, hell. I forgot the curry. Dead sorry."

"Don't worry about that," he said. "Besides, I don't think you're up for a curry."

He smiled and pointed vaguely at my face.

"Shit, have I?" I asked, wiping at the corners my mouth for the white residue that seemed to invariably come with those tablets.

He walked up and wiped at the corner of my mouth with his thumb. "That's got it," he said, standing so close to me that I could see the beating of his heart as it made the skin across his belly ripple.

SLEEPING UNDERWATER

I felt my breath catch, and I couldn't say anything, so I quickly stepped back a step. "Excuse me," I said, "just a tick."

"Right."

I went to the loo and closed the door to run water and stare at myself with some measure of disgust. He was a client. Anything else had to wait. Had to. Unless I quit. I flushed the toilet and walked out.

He was putting away the bucket.

"I hope you don't mind. I had to snoop a bit to find this."

"Feel free to snoop if you intend to do it in the name of tidying my flat."

"Feeling better?" he asked, slipping his shirt back on.

"Yeah. Thanks."

"I used to eat a roll of those every two hours," he said. "Until I quit."

"That's awful," I said. "Perhaps it's best you did then."

"Well, I thought so, yes."

I nodded.

"Carter," I started, "we need to speak frankly for a moment."

He looked like I was about to hit him, and sat down. "Okay," he said quietly.

"You've hired me to do a job, and I intend to do it. In order to do this, I have to distrust you, your motives, and everything you say. It's part of the territory."

He nodded.

"This greatly conflicts with my personal regard for you. I'm afraid that I may not be able to effectively separate my feelings for you from my responsibility to your case. With this in mind and, with the notion that I will probably be watching you with a suspicious eye, if I remain on the case, I need you to decide if I should quit, and refer you to someone else."

"I don't want you to quit. You're right to be suspicious. You don't know me at all. And there are lots of things I haven't told you and really don't want to, because I don't think they're important." He stopped, and looked back up at my eyes, "Also because I don't know you yet, either."

I opened my mouth to speak, but he waved me down.

"Look," he said, "I know it's foolish. I don't care. I'm a private person, and that's my bloody right. I like you, and I can tell you like me back. If I have to have an investigator all tied up in my life, I'd just as soon he did like me, really. I'd rather he was

33

worse at the job and cared for me than to be a total cracking whiz who didn't care if I lived or died."

I thought of Andrew, and pushed the thought away. "Okay, if you're sure."

"I'm entirely sure," he said.

"Well then," I said. "Let's run to the shop on the corner and pick up fish and chips, and I will interrogate you."

"That sounds delightful."

I had a tab at the chip shop down the lane, and that was a good thing, because they certainly didn't take credit cards.

The place smelled warm and spicy. Donair kebabs spun on their little stands, and there was the fresh smell of fried everything.

"Hello," said Rahim, the sixteen-year-old son of the owner. "The usual for you?"

"Two please," I said to him, "On account."

Rahim looked at me, nodding, and then at Carter. He seemed slightly ill at ease with it, but showed the good grace to try and hide it.

In what seemed like no time at all, Rahim handed me a couple of bags of full of thick greasy chips, hot crisp fish and some Cokes. It all smelled wonderful. I handed one of each to Carter.

Our breath hung a little in the air, as we stepped out into the night. Carter nibbled a chip out of the bag without using his hands, chewing lightly for it was still very hot.

"It's the best thing in the world, isn't it, a fresh batch?" he asked as he swallowed the last of the first chip.

"It is very nice."

"It's bloody amazing. Do you know it's been actually months since I've had a fry up?"

"Probably for the best," I said, "if we both want to remain so slim and pleasant to look upon."

"Hell with that," he said, "I'll have yours if you don't want them."

I reared back protectively to guard my treasure.

We were laughing as I opened the door and as we headed into my flat. I grabbed up a couple of plates and set them on my coffee table. I dumped mine out onto a plate and nudged the other to

Carter. He shook his head and smiled, holding the bag up to his face and breathing deep.

We ate in a comfortable lull, listening to the radio and not talking. He was not a self-conscious eater, showing no shame in enjoying the experience, not afraid to get a little grease on his face. I smiled as he ate, watching him. I knew I was only putting off the inevitable. I enjoyed watching him, enjoyed small talk with him. He was so funny and so sad and so pretty, and it felt like I had known him for years. It was a shame I was working for him.

"Well," he said, crumpling up the greasy newspaper, "I suppose we should get to it."

"I suppose so," I said, reaching into my coat for a small notebook.

He settled back onto my couch, crossing his legs under him and embracing a throw pillow. He looked comfortable and shifty at the same time, but in an affable way.

"All right," I said. "Let's start over at the beginning. What exactly has been taken?"

"Three cardboard cartons about this big," he said holding his hands about as far apart as a large pizza box and then as deep as a foot and a half or so.

"Do you remember the colour?"

"Cardboardy colour, you know. Brown."

I nodded.

"Okay," I continued. "You've given me generalities, but I must ask what exactly is in the boxes?"

"A lot of things. I don't know what all. It's personal stuff, and not worth anything to anyone but me, as far as I know."

"Can you be more specific?"

"Yes."

"Will you?"

"I don't want to. It's personal."

"How will I know they're the right cartons if you don't?"

They've got my name on them in black magic marker."

"I see."

He smiled and shifted in his seat. "Is that it, then?"

I laughed. "Oh, no. Not remotely."

"I didn't think so."

"The contents of these boxes, do they belong to you?"

"Yes."

"You're not holding them for someone else?'"

35

He paused a moment. "No."

"You had to think about that?"

"Yes."

"Do you keep a lot of things in cartons in your place?"

"No. You know I don't. You've been there, I assume."

"Right. Why these cartons?"

"As I said, Niles, I had some things in a storage locker, but I couldn't afford it anymore."

"Okay."

He looked at me. "Did you like my place?"

"I don't know," I said. "Sort of, in an abstract way. It didn't seem much like you."

He shrugged. "It's a lot cleaner than usual. I've had a lot of free time."

"Well it's certainly planned out to avoid clutter."

"I like to not be distracted. So, when I'm listening to music, I prefer not to have the TV hanging about. And I really like to know where everything is. The world's quite messy enough."

"Well that's true," I said, "and it's an interesting design, but I think you prefer life a little less sterile."

"I like to keep my things in line. I let my friends add the excitement."

"I see what you've done here," I said. "You've turned this around by asking me questions. You're trying to get away from me, by instinct. Your instincts are very strong on that, I think. We'll pause our discussion of your flat for a moment, okay?"

He rolled his eyes. "Okay."

"You said you had a good idea who the thief was?"

"Yeah. She's a junkie named Derek, who hangs around my friend Azif. Azif brought her by one night when he stopped off to say hello. He was polite, but I saw her eyes all over my stuff, and I know that look. She was looking for a fix. When the stuff went missing day before yesterday, I was sure it was her. All of it in boxes right in the hall like that, it would be easy and quick."

"Okay," I said, moving into the crucial part for me, but trying to show no difference in tone. "So, you think she took the stuff to a warehouse near here. Why?"

He shifted. "Not so much a warehouse, really, it's just used that way. Used to be a corner shop, but it's been shut down forever. It's owned by this old guy who buys junk at a shop across the street, like a pawn shop, but he doesn't loan. He's got a building full of crap. He also, like, doesn't ask questions, you know?"

"Would he have bought what was in the box, considering that it's all personal stuff, not worth anything?"

"I don't know. I hope so. He might have bought one or two things, or given the slag a couple of quid just to get rid of her and dumped the boxes in the back."

"Right," I said. "And what if he didn't?"

"Then I'm probably screwed."

"Did you try going by and asking?"

"The guy told me that, if he'd bought it, it belonged to him and, if I didn't like it, I could call a cop."

"Why didn't you?"

He didn't answer.

For a long time.

"Carter?"

"It was personal. I don't want the police poring over everything. I just wanted it back, and I still do. It's mine, and I want it back, and I asked him, and he said no."

"Anything in those boxes that would get you in trouble with the police?"

"I don't know, Niles," he said, getting a little riled.

"You don't know?"

"No. I don't know what the law would think of me, and what I am, and what I own, or what I'm reading this week. God only knows what laws they've passed while I wasn't paying attention. Is it illegal for me to kiss you yet? You tell me."

"I had to ask."

"I know," he said. "I'm sorry."

"Don't be sorry," I answered. "You've every right to privacy. You're the one who's been wronged. Shall I go on, or do you want a break?"

He pushed his hair back off his face. "Go ahead."

"Have you any notion why someone might deliberately steal what was actually in those boxes?"

"I couldn't begin to think why anyone would want any of it. Anyone who would steal those boxes is crazy or doesn't know what's in them."

I nodded, sensing something there, but not sure what it was. I was also sensing that he was starting to get emotional. These were fairly mundane questions. I decided to pull back before forcing him to directly lie.

"Okay," I said, "we're done for now."

He breathed a sigh of relief.

"We'll likely do this again, and soon. For now, it's dark, and I think it's time to do some work."

"What's that?"

"I'm going to go sit in a parked car across from the place and see who comes and goes. If my walking in and talking to the man isn't going to be fruitful, and you've made it quite clear it won't, then I have to catch him with the evidence. I have a camera with a zoom lens. With any luck, I'll get a shot of your things, and be able to get evidence of stolen property. With that, I may be able to persuade the owner to part with it. If anyone other than the old guy is hanging about, then I'll have something even more interesting to use."

I was making up nonsense that sounded vaguely reasonable. I was, by now, certain that the boxes held something of extreme interest, possibly extreme value, but I had no idea what. I wanted to see who came and went from this place and to see if I could determine exactly why Carter was so sure these were the people who had his things. I needed photographs of people, and to get a sense of the place. If I got the chance, I'd try for his things, because that is what I was being paid for. At this point, I was more interested in the story I wasn't getting.

He looked at me uncertainly. "Why don't we just go there, and, I don't know, sneak inside."

"We don't know who may be in there, and how they'd react. Also, it's illegal."

"Oh,"

"I'm not Batman. I'm pretty sure we'll get your things back, but we'll have to be a bit patient. This is the really boring part of what I do."

"Can I come along? It sounds exciting to me."

I leaned back against the car seat and took a sip of cold coffee. He was asleep next to me, his breathing as slow and regular as waves on a still night. He had, it seemed, a rare talent for sleeping anywhere. I was wishing I were asleep, and the sound of his sleep so close by was acting on me as further enticement. I, however, needed to stay awake. I had no idea why he was even in the car.

He could have been at the flat in bed, or the tub if he preferred, rather than tagging along distracting me.

There was a bang from across the street and I was jolted alert with a start. The red painted wooden door of the abandoned shop opened and a man with red hair came out, carrying a few boxes under his arm. A green Toyota pulled around the corner and stopped. The hatchback opened and he put the boxes in. Then he walked around the side and drove off. I took a few shots of his face and, as the car pulled away, I got at least one good shot of the license plate.

"Did you get it?" he said, obviously awake.

"Yeah. I got it."

"So, what do we do now?"

"Well," I said, "I'm a bit torn really."

"Okay."

"On the one hand, I could go back to the office, log on and find out who owns the car. Then we'll know exactly who is responsible here, or at least be awfully close to it."

"Right. And on the other?"

"Well, I think I could pick that lock, and we could go inside and likely find what we're looking for. Which would be illegal, of course, and possibly dangerous."

"If we did the second, that would leave the police entirely out of this, is that right?"

"Oh yes, indeed. By the very nature of the operation, I can assure you that I'd be doing my humble best to avoid the police altogether."

"Right, then. That's the way."

"Yes. I understand that's your point of view here, naturally. I, on the other hand, have my license to consider."

"You're quitting. You said."

"And I'd like to not go to jail."

He shrugged, irritated, and irritating me. "Right, okay. Fine"

We sat in silence for a moment.

I pondered the options. This was the sort of situation I'd always thought looked so cool on telly. This was the sort of quasi-legal, justice over law, kind of case I had used to pray I might again experience. Somehow staring down the barrel of the consequences, I wasn't as sure anymore.

"Oh hell," I said, "You wait here. Are we clear? I don't set a foot out this car until you promise to stay exactly here."

"Okay, man, bloody hell, I promise, right?"

LAIRD RYAN STATES

I looked him in the eye and when I was sure I believed him, I got out. I opened the boot and rummaged for the little black bag in which I kept my tools. It would be the first time I'd used them, shy of breaking into my own flat once two years back. I crossed to the door and looked at it. The door was secured by a padlock at roughly eye level. It was not locked.

Because I am an idiot, I was relieved at not having to take the time to pick the lock. I opened the door and stepped inside, flicking on my torch. The room was full of cartons, covered in dust. They were clearly taken from various places in the middle of moves. I looked around for the cartons Carter had described.

Every second in the place seemed to last hours, and the dust was tickling my throat and nose. I fought a sneeze. Every creak and whisper made my pulse race.

Then I found them. They were at the bottom of a stack of various boxes. I smiled, and started moving cartons until I could get at them. I knelt in front of them and, after wavering a moment, I opened one.

It wasn't, as I'd been half suspecting, drugs or pornography. It was a lot of papers and old photographs. He had given me ample reason to suspect that these cartons were valuable in more than a sentimental way.

I was also wondering who the hell would buy such a thing as this and store it in what amounted to a junk shop. I wondered about the other boxes in this place, stacked in various piles, looking like they were all bound for someplace else, sitting on shipping pallets.

I decided that I could wonder all this elsewhere.

I went back to the door and found that someone had already locked it from the other side.

My heart pounded in my ears as all the reasons why it was dumb for me to be glad to find an open lock flooded in at once. I just prayed that Carter had laid low in the car and would, once they were gone, come and fetch me.

I tried to push the door wide enough that I could take a peek, but had no luck. I listened for voices. Finally, I heard a shrieking noise as the padlock pulled from the wood on the outside of the door and felt some relief that it hadn't been reinforced. Likely this meant they didn't routinely try to intentionally imprison people in this room.

I pressed the door the rest of the way open and saw my car across the road, empty. I rushed across and found a pile of glass on the passenger side, and blood on the seats. I opened the door, tossed the cartons inside, and looked for Carter. He was gone.

I took a number of deep breaths, which a therapist had once advised me to do at the onset of panic. Theoretically, it is intended to calm. In practice, I've found it just allows me to be really alert for the experience of terror. Terror is one of those things that can make you careless.

Another of the hundred thousand things Andrew taught me is that reading trains us to be lazy observers as our eyes move left to right. If you really want to be careful when you're looking for something, move your eyes from right to left. I did that, but if anyone were still present, I did not see them.

Tiny cubes of glass glinted on the front seats along with a couple of smears of blood on the dash and on the passenger door. I imagined that they'd smashed his face into the dash and pulled him out the window. There wasn't enough blood for anything too serious. Unless, of course, he'd died from a whack to the head.

I'd no intention of dwelling on that. I was looking for the camera. I'd left it on the dashboard, and it wasn't there anymore. It wasn't laying on the floor, not obviously. I drove some distance away and parked the vehicle discreetly. It didn't take long to find that the camera had been shoved far back under the passenger seat. The telephoto lens was cracked, but the film was probably still good.

Tapping my hands on the steering wheel, I tried to think as I drove, desperate to remember a place where I could get a roll of film developed at this hour. I found a shop and paced back and forth about the store waiting for them to be done. When they were, I thumbed through the photos until I found the clearest shot of the driver and of the licence plate.

I drove back to the office, headed upstairs, and quietly panicked. I glanced at the phone a thousand times, wanting it to ring. I went over the events in my head a thousand times.

I walked in circles waiting for the sun to come up, wanting to call the police for every second of it. Any contacts I did have in the constabulary were not on duty at this time of night.

At almost exactly 8 a.m. I called a toll-free number for the licensing database. I had a paid subscription to this service. I gave the licence number, and a description of the vehicle. After listening to the woman on the other end type and chew gum, there was a brief pause, and then she gave me a name and an address. The name was Carl Jherek. It was entirely unfamiliar to me.

I had to go there, but I didn't much care to go there alone. I reached for the phone and dialed a friend I'd not spoken to in many months.

"Des?" I said, as someone mumbled into the phone.

"This had better be good then."

Des sounded angry, as well he might at this time of the morning. His line of work kept him up rather late.

"I'm sorry Des, but it's a matter of quite urgent importance."

"Sleep, man. Sleep is of bloody urgent importance."

"I've a client and he's been abducted."

"Call the police then, mate."

"I can't. I mean, I know I should. I just can't, is all. I don't want to go alone. I will if I have to, and I expect you'll feel very responsible, especially in light of how…"

"All right, man, Christ. I'll be over in a little while."

"Good."

He was there in an hour and fifteen minutes, which means that he did actually hurry a bit. I restrained myself from hugging him as he got out of his black Austin Mini. Watching him get out of that car was always like watching a particularly fascinating magic trick. Des was six and a half feet tall, bald, twice as broad as I am and had the cool and menacing look of a Kray brother.

"Should I carry a gun?" He said it in as casual a way as I might ask if I should bring a bottle of wine to a dinner party. It was that exact quality that I needed from him.

"I don't know," I said.

"Well, I'll err on the side of, then. You want one?"

"No. No, thank you."

He shrugged. "Where are we going?"

"House of a bloke named Carl Jherek, for a start."

Des blinked. "How'd you get tangled up with Carl Jherek, then?"

I pinched the bridge of my nose, dismayed that a man in Des' line recognized the name. "You know him?"

"New in town but making a name for himself."

"As what?"

"Oh, the usual. Extortion, bookmaking, murder for hire, Egyptian soul theft, and that."

"You aren't funny."

"You're wrong there. I'm hilarious. Nothing funny about soul theft though. We should maybe hit the road, mate."

SLEEPING UNDERWATER

Des drove, because I don't much care for it, and because I'd been up all night and didn't expect to be at my best. Des held the wheel with one hand, the other gripping a large mug of coffee, as I nattered on about the night's events.

"Soul theft," I said for the third time since the trip had begun. "Fucking ridiculous. I don't believe in any of that crap. The soul is bollocks."

"What did the sheep say when a man reached down its throat and pulled out a little golden bird?"

I blinked. "What?"

"Ba," he said, grinning.

I shook my head. "If I'm supposed to get that, I don't."

"Tch, and here's where I reveal myself as quite learned and wise."

"I'll never tell."

"Who'd believe you?"

More people than you think, I thought to myself. But I don't like to be disabused of my own personal notions of myself, and so I return the favour for others whenever possible.

"The Egyptians, man," Des said, "they didn't think of the soul as one thing. They thought we had seven of them."

"Like different personality aspects?"

"More like different jobs. These people had a really complicated afterlife."

"Okay."

"A lot of Egyptian magic was based in using different parts of the soul, your own and others, and that tradition really spread out. Like into Voodoo."

"So, this guy fancies himself a magician or something?"

Des looked out the windscreen, streetlights passing overhead, considering his answer. "Nah, don't think so mate. He's just a crook with a really weird business plan, and a little learning."

"I still don't get your joke."

"The Ba is the part of the soul that contains your personality. Sort of the core of you and what makes you unique. They drew it as a little shining bird with a human head."

"That is a very poor joke."

"I told you it wasn't funny."

"So, you did."

43

"Look mate, whether you believe or not, you need to understand this is serious business. These people are true believers, and they're dangerous."

"Lunatics often are."

"Yes, they bloody well are, Niles." He said that with heavy finality, and the car was awkwardly quiet. "Have you got any idea how your friend got tangled up in this."

"Not really, no. These people came into possession of a bunch of his things, and he was sort of non-specific as to how and why."

"How nice. I wonder what he knows."

"Hmmm," I answered. "This is going to be astonishingly unpleasant isn't it?"

He laughed his deep throaty laugh and clapped my shoulder with a hand the size of a small ham. "What else is new, son? What else is new?"

Des turned off the headlamps, then rolled to a stop, parking in the street. It felt colder that it probably was. I looked over at Des. He was looking out his window, breathing slowly and regularly.

"I've got to say, Niles," he said, "that I don't like how little we know about what's going on here. It's very possible that your mate has stepped in something he shouldn't ought to've and is now getting what he has coming to him."

"I'll leave aside our fundamental differences of opinion on the morality of what you winkingly call 'criminal justice' and simply say that if Carter is a member of that subculture to whom it applies, I would be more than simply astonished. I would be astonished in a very complex way that would take years to resolve."

He sighed. "Stow that, all right? It's neither the time nor the place. Let me ask you, does he use drugs?"

"I don't know," I said, "I mean, presumably he does. I found some pills in his flat. Most people do a bit here and there. I don't think he's an addict. He's got his issues, to be sure, but I don't believe that's his deal."

"That's as may be. You know as well as I do that most of what the baddies do, they do to each other."

"Carter isn't one of them. He's an architect."

"No mate," he said, "he used to be an architect, and he gave you a pretty blurry accounting of why he stopped."

"He's a pretty blurry sort of thinker, Des," I said. "Which sounds worse than I mean, honestly."

He smiled.

"I am willing to bet you ten pounds right now that he owes Jherek money in excess of a thousand pounds."

"I'll take that bet," I said. "Whatever this is, I'm quite certain it's not about money."

"Everything's about money really. Or the lack of it."

"Yes, yes, Des. I do get it. You are streetwise and cynical and hardened by your years of employment in the criminal underground."

"Amen," he said chuckling.

"Daft bastard."

"Right," he said, "So I think our best approach is to be utterly polite."

I thought about that for a second. "I hadn't considered that option."

"This business is like any other," he said, "Professional courtesy can take you pretty far, as long as it's clear where you're standing."

"If this issue can be resolved with a friendly natter, I am more than fine with that."

He checked his gun to be sure it was loaded and put it back in his shoulder holster. He placed extra clips in a series of custom pockets on the inside of his dark blazer. I stared, fascinated, and found myself wondering again at the injustices of the world. Under the blazer he wore a black turtleneck shirt, smooth and pristine. If I'd tried wearing one, it would have been covered in tiny hairs and crumbs and bits of lint by the time I'd left home.

"I'll handle the talking, then?" he asked.

"I'll speak in answer, but I will follow your lead."

He rolled his eyes and shook his head. "You always say that, mate."

"I will this time."

He looked at me and all the mirth and good humour were gone from his eyes. I felt my balls get cold and crawl up into my belly. I understood, in that moment, why people paid what they did for his services and I loved him just a bit more, because I had so rarely seen it before.

"I'm fucking terrified of this prick, Niles. So, keep schtum. If you open your mouth and turn this one bit uglier than it needs to be, and manage to survive, I swear to god I will put you in the hospital until you're an old man who can't even remember what I used to look like."

"I promise," I said, "Perhaps I should stay in the car, in fact."

"Oh no, mate. No sodding way. Let's go, then."

We got out of the car and walked over to the house. It didn't seem like anything special or ostentatious, not like Tony Montana's huge mansion. Of course, this was real life, I understood.

Des rang the bell by the purple door. Inside we heard strange music. Arabic, I thought, but with bells and stringed instruments I didn't know off hand. It was very odd. A window was cracked part of the way open and I could smell tobacco smoke, which grabbed hold of me and shook me about with desire. It was an amazing, thick smell, pipe tobacco or something related, with a sweet, spicy something else overlaid on it. I heard voices laughing. I put my hand on the railing and pulled it back sharply. Sitting on the back of my hand was a large purple beetle. I shook it, and the beetle fell to the wooden steps, landing on its back. My instinct was to crush it, but something held me back. It righted itself and crawled between the boards.

A man came to the door and opened it. He was tall and broad and Eastern European. I wondered if he were Romani. He was dressed rather like one, in a loose linen blouse and a load of scarves. He wore several earrings and rings on his fingers. One of these was shaped like a beetle. The little hairs on my neck moved slightly. I loathe coincidences. They are signals from the world that something has gone very wrong.

"Yes," he said, to Desmond. "What do you want?"

"Hiya," Des said. "I hate to be a bother, but I'm wondering if we could speak to Mr. Jherek."

"Who the fuck are you?" he asked right away, in an accent more Arabic than anything.

"I'm Desmond Kingston." He inclined his head almost imperceptibly in my direction. "I work for Niles Townsend. He's a private investigator."

"You are not police?"

"Fuck no, mate. I do collection for the Kernaghans mostly. Not here for them, mind you. This is a personal call."

"What do you want?"

"As I said," Des continued politely. "We would like to speak to Mr. Jherek."

"What about?"

"We're looking for a missing person," Des said. "We think he might have turned up here, and we'd like to work things out, so everybody goes home happy."

He looked at Des for a second, then let out a noise somewhere between a sigh and a grunt. "You wait here."

"Of course," Des said, hands relaxed at his sides.

I looked at Des to see if it was okay to speak. He looked back as though he'd no idea, so I kept my silence. We stood on the stoop and it was just cold enough again tonight that our breath hung for a fraction of a second in the air between us. The same man opened the door again. It had become reasonably quiet, and I realized that the gathering, such as it was, been had moved downstairs. I could hear it, dimly, as we stepped inside.

"I will need to search your person," the colourfully dressed man said, and Des nodded, surrendering his pistol politely. There seemed to be no particular surprise or anger from either party involved. I was woefully uneducated as to the etiquette here.

He moved over to search me, but seemingly thought better of it. He had a smell on his breath that reminded me of anise, but that wasn't quite right. Then he sniffed at me. He tried to be subtle about it, but it was still weird. It was so weird that I went all over goose pimples.

He inclined his head into the living room, and I walked in. The whole room smelled of tobacco, wine, rum, and the same something else I had smelled on his breath. "Sit, please. He will be here shortly."

We did so, and he left us alone. I sat on the cheap white and floral couch, and Des in a green armchair. The furniture was laughably out of date for a supposed crime lord. They tended, I was informed, toward being a touch flash.

Des looked at me, and even through his shades I could see he thought this was all wrong. I said nothing but pointed at the wooden coffee table. It was covered in the same glistening purple beetles from outside. They swarmed and roiled over each other. I felt as though I'd walked into a nightmare of some kind, and

47

might have said so, except that my thoughts were interrupted by the entrance of a man dressed in a grey three-piece suit from the 1950s. His face was of the same kind of indeterminate nation of origin as all the others I'd seen here.

He cleared his throat, and I saw that he had his men at each exit. It wasn't a threat, exactly, but it was a reminder.

"What do you want, you English asshole?" he asked, impatiently taking a seat in a high-backed wicker chair. He pressed his feet deep in the green shag carpet and looked completely safe and at ease.

I looked to Des.

"My employer has asked me to come and speak with you on his behalf. We're looking for a client of his by the name of Carter Bennet."

Jherek smiled, not pleasantly, and I saw for the first time that his teeth were stained purple.

"Have you seen him?" I said, and Des let air out through his teeth.

"I have seen him. Was that your car my brothers pulled him out of?"

"It was." I did my best to conceal my anger.

"I'll pay to have your window repaired. Bad business to involve the innocent. Insofar as any Englishman is an innocent."

"Mr., Jherek," Des said, "the window is inconsequential."

It wasn't, and I nearly said so.

"We're concerned for the safety of our client, Mr. Bennet," Des continued, "and we're here to negotiate in good faith for his safe return."

He laughed. "Oh, that will be quite impossible. Bennet belongs to the island now."

"Belongs to the island?" I said. "What the fucking hell does that mean?"

Des let out air through his lips, tensing. He was upset with me. I could live with that.

"It's an old saying among my people," Jherek said, waving a long thin fingered hand out before me. The tips of his thumb and index finger were stained yellow and purple, like healing bruises. Nicotine, and something stranger. He looked me in the eyes, as if he'd only now noticed I was there.

"And what does it mean, then?" I asked in clipped but calming tones, pulling myself back in a little.

"It means that you may ask for his safe return until the sun burns out, but there is no safety for him. Even if it were mine to grant, I wouldn't."

I looked to Des, as if to ask why he wasn't shooting people already. He let no expression show on his face. He turned to look to Jherek.

"Sir," he said, "forgive our ignorance, but I think we're missing part of the story here. Let me be clear in my questioning. Is Carter Bennet here in the house?"

"No," he said.

"All right," Des said. "Do you have him in your keeping someplace else, like?"

Jherek nodded. "Yes. He is quite safe at present."

I let out a sigh of relief and was about to speak. Des looked at me from the corners of his sunglasses and I stopped.

"Thank you," Des said. "May I ask why you have him?"

Jherek considered and then spoke. "He is being kept on a leash because he has shown he cannot be trusted with freedom. Once he returns what is ours and makes good on his commitment to my brothers, he will be free to go, should he desire to. He may not."

My heart sunk. It seemed that Des had been right. It was probably the pills, but who knew? He wasn't the gambling sort, and I was certain he was too shy for prostitutes. That left drugs as a source of debt.

"Christ," I said, "how much is he in for?"

Jherek looked puzzled for a moment, his head wavering slightly as he tried to process.

"What does he owe?" Des clarified.

"He owes my brothers and I the sum of...."

He snapped his fingers and a woman entered the room. They spoke back and forth calmly and quietly, and then Jherek nodded, dismissing her.

"Apologies," he continued. "Bennet owes me the princely sum of 135 pounds in expenses incurred."

Just as I was about to open my mouth to speak, he continued.

"We will also require the use of his soul for a time. And he will return to us at once a certain object that he has removed from my person."

"And what is that?" I asked.

"He has stolen the vision of my homeland."

"Are you serious?" I asked.

"Oh yes." Jherek said. "I am as serious as a heart attacked."

I did not correct him. I liked his phrase better, actually. "What do you mean exactly, when you say you will require the use of his soul?"

Jherek smiled. "Consider it the foolish superstition of a backward people," he said. "I believe that if you can acquire the object and pay the debt, on his behalf, we will both be satisfied. If he chooses to leave with you at that time, he may. I doubt that he will. The island has strong hooks in him by now."

He smiled, and looked me in the eye, taking his gaze off Des for the first time. I almost spoke, but his raised finger stopped me.

"I must advise you," he continued, "both of you, that to cross me or to involve the police in this matter will result in his immediate return, though you may require his dental records to confirm it. Am I understood?"

"Quite," Des said. "Thank you for speaking to us. How is it best to speak with you in the future?"

He produced a thick plasticized business card with a phone number.

"Ring me," he said. "If you come unannounced before me again, I will have my cousins kill you,"

Des nodded, and we both rose.

"You are quite a good deal more polite," Jherek said to Des, "than your employer. I thank you for your courtesy. It is obvious that his passions are invoked, yes? Keep him reined in if you are in some way fond of him."

I almost spoke, felt better of it, and went to the car, where I proceeded to pound my fists against the dash like an angry five-year-old until the silence of Des' stare wore me out.

"Are you quite through, you fucking twat?"

"Yes, fuck."

"You said you wouldn't do that..."

"And then I bloody did, yes. Same as last time and the time before. Beat me if you must, or stash it someplace quiet, okay Des? I am who I am, and you knew that going in."

He sighed.

"Yeah, okay, fine," he said. "You should have told me you were in love with this guy before we went in there."

"I'm not," I said. "I'm not in love with him."

"Suit yourself," he said. "Have you heard anything at all from your client about the...you know...thing they're looking for?"

"Christ no. I believe it possible I might have mentioned that if I had. Provided I knew what the hell he was even talking about. Which I don't. Do you?"

He shook his head. "Have you been through those boxes thoroughly?"

"No," I said, letting out a sigh. "To be honest, Des, I've been so panicked, and it seemed like a load of rubbish. Doesn't even belong to Carter, as far as I can gather."

"What? How can you not know?"

"Carter says it's all his stuff, things he had in a storage locker he couldn't afford anymore. I think he's right in the sense that they are currently in his possession, and even insofar as they might have been in a storage locker recently. But I think he's a lying shit about who they belong to."

"Ah."

"But at least he's not a drug addict."

"Or not much of one."

"Yeah."

"Look, Niles. I'll be honest. I'm your mate, and we have been through some things together, but you're out of your depth here. And so am I. This situation would have been terrifying even to Andrew. For better and for worse, you aren't him."

"I'm aware," I said coldly, "of that. I'm aware I'm not a patch on him as far as all this business goes."

"Yeah," he said, "but at least most people actually like you. I think Jherek did, a bit. He let us walk out."

"I'm fucking grateful," I said, "that my affability has allowed me the freedom to walk unmolested. Besides, people loved Andrew."

"Yeah," Des said, "but they didn't like him one bit."

We were quiet for a moment.

"We'd best check out those boxes," I said.

"Yes. I would fucking say so. You had all night. I can't believe you've not already done so."

He started the car, and we drove off in the comfortable silence of old friends.

We arrived back out front of my flat twenty minutes later. Des looked at me and was clearly working up to saying something. I waited patiently. My body was starting to give out on me. My arms and legs felt hard and strange and far away, and my eyes were sore.

"Niles," he said, "Go upstairs. Get undressed. Fall asleep."

"I can't."

"You can. He's safe. Jherek said so, and he's got no need of lying to the likes of us."

What he was telling me was true, and my body was more or less screaming at me to listen to him.

"I'll come back later. We'll look at what you've got, and figure out what we need to do for your mate, right? You're no good to him right now."

"Sleep," I said, "is optional. I have food upstairs, and that will keep me going."

Des pursed his lips and blew out a long breath. "Look, you sad twat, I already owe you a beating. Unless you want me to put you in the hospital, you'll go upstairs and, on your honour, you'll try to sleep."

I stared at him. "You're bluffing."

"You woke me up at fuck o'clock for something that could have waited until noon, to do you a favour. You don't get to make any more decisions, Sonny-Jim."

"Fine," I said, pretending to fight, and yet deeply grateful. Des knew me well enough to handle me.

"That's a good lad," he said, clapping my shoulder. "I'll be back tonight. You've the cartons here, right?"

I nodded. "Okay, Des. Thanks, right?"

"Yeah, okay, Niles."

I noticed that he waited until I was in the building before he drove away. I went upstairs and kicked off my shoes. My flat was still clean, but I felt an uneasiness as I closed the door behind me, and locked it.

I set the kettle on to boil, instinct working me, as I'd no desire at all for tea. My floors were still shiny from whatever it was that Carter had done to them. I'd never seen them actually shine. It made my stomach hurt with guilt and anger and, strangely, loneliness.

I waited for the water to boil, loosening my tie and dropping it on my kitchen table. I added lemon juice to the hot water and drank it slowly, looking out my window. His coat was hanging on the back of a chair, and I looked at it.

SLEEPING UNDERWATER

"You little bastard," I said. "What have you gotten me wrapped up in?"

The room was quiet, and I felt the silence and exhaustion acutely.

I stood up, undid the top button of my shirt and I picked up his coat, and did the saddest thing in the world. I pressed it to my face and breathed in deeply. It smelled of him.

A large purple beetle fell from the sleeve to my table, and another to the floor.

I yelped and jumped back.

The beetle on the table crawled off the edge to join his brother on the floor, and they crawled toward each other while I watched.

I wanted to stomp them, but instead I dropped Carter's jacket. Three more beetles climbed out into the little symposium on my kitchen floor.

I went to the top shelf of my kitchen cupboard and pulled out an empty jam jar. I punched three holes in the lid and put all of them in, one at a time, suppressing my revulsion long enough to pick them up. They made a soft clicking sound as they rolled together.

I caught my reflection in the glass of my window, and startled. Just for a moment, I thought I saw someone else behind me, tall and blonde, his eyes cold and deep. My stomach lurched. I turned, and saw I was alone.

I set the beetles on my table and I picked up Carter's coat, shaking it.

"What have you done to me?" I asked the empty room.

I went to bed and tried to sleep, the light of the early afternoon making that difficult. Nonetheless, I dreamed.

I dreamed of beetles and tall blond, beautiful private eyes. I remembered the sound of Andrew's limbs in the water splashing, the choking of his breath as he struggled. I heard my own breathing — calm and still and decided. Resolute.

The past has a tendency of finding us in our sleep.

PART TWO:

BOY'S ADVENTURE

I'm Carter Bennet now. I'm bad with time, but let's start here.

I am neck deep, literally, in textbooks.

There is an entire course, one that I am desperately afraid I will flunk, devoted to concrete. How to make it, what it's made of, what it does, how to use it. I couldn't care less. I should care more. They'll be goddamned at this college to release an architect into the world with grand and sweeping designs that will not hold up to the real world. They're quite serious. I understand where they're coming from. I agree, but it's the designs that I love. At night, I dream of buildings. When I wake up, I do my best to sketch them out. They're impractical, beautiful. I wrestle with ways to give them form and function and end up frustrated and behind in my studies.

Time and again I wind up here in the middle of the student centre, in the dead of night, trying to memorize the things I will need to remember to pass an exam I won't need to do the job. I am not interested in being top of the class, but I can't be the bottom of the class either. Either one of these things lead to being noticed. I can't afford the scrutiny. I don't want any attention at all. I want to be invisible.

My parents, this time around, have spent so much money, sacrificed and scrimped to send me here, and their dreams are all wrapped up in my doing well. My own sanity is wrapped up in doing well but not too well. I need to belong. I have to be one of the herd. Anything else will burn like fire.

My eyes move over pages of formulae and charts, hard facts and numbers. The pale, perfect frozen beauty of science on the pages. It may as well be Sanskrit to me, but the facts sink in deep enough that I don't have to look at them. I let the human part of me have them, and I let my own mind roam to pencil sketches three hundred years old, cathedrals I have faint and distant memories of.

Time slides past me, unreal, and the sun is up. My eyes are dry, and so is my throat and I am not alone. A tall man with dark red hair is sitting in a chair and staring at me with bright, almost frightened eyes. There's nothing familiar about him, and I am pulled back to full attention.

"Hello," I say. "Are you all right?"

"I'm fine," he says quietly. "Are you, actually?"

"Yes," I answer, sitting back sharply. "Sorry."

He nods, a smile forming. "What are you sorry for?"

"I don't know," I say, stammering. "I assume I did something odd."

"I was starting to think you were a statue, mate. You have been sitting there stone dead for the better part of two hours. You've not moved a muscle. I'm not sure I saw you blink. I think maybe you could use a break."

I stand up immediately, and my hands start to sweat. "Yes. Right. Of course."

He steps back and offers me a hand to shake. "I'm Victor."

"Carter."

"Carter Bennet?"

My stomach flips. "You know me?"

He laughs. "I know of you. I saw your models when they were on display a few months ago. They're wizard, man."

I blink and laugh in spite of myself. "Wizard?"

"Yeah," he says. "They're not like anything. They're so beautiful and strange."

I shrug. "Won't work though. Not with any materials we can use. Easy to model, impossible to build, full scale. Just a laugh, really."

"Too bad. I'd hire you to do my house. Honestly."

"You're not in the program, are you?"

"No! God no. I'm in journo. God knows why. I'm not at all interested, but it seemed a good way to meet interesting people."

SLEEPING UNDERWATER

I nod. My hands start shaking. He has noticed. My pulse pounds in my ears.

"You really don't look well," Victor says, taking my shoulder. "I know how people get about cramming, but how long has it been since you've eaten?"

"I've been snacking on those crackers."

I point toward the empty sleeve.

"Had anything to drink?"

"I don't drink."

"Water, I mean."

"Right," I say. "No. I guess not. I should."

"You're bloody right. You're dehydrated. Look at your hands. You've got circles under your eyes."

He leads me to a fountain, and I drink while he watches. It's odd. Who is this person, I am wondering, and why does he care?

"Better?" he says.

"Yeah. Thanks."

"Well," he says. "Good. Look, I've a class in like forty minutes..."

"Is it that bloody late?" I ask.

He nods. "Why don't you go home and try to sleep, all right?"

"What time is it, actually?" I ask.

I can't wear watches. It's a problem for other people, rarely for me. He looks at his. "Twenty past eight."

"I've no time to sleep."

He shakes his head. "Oh, Carter."

He remembers my name, and I blink. People don't, usually.

"What?" I say.

"You should have slept instead."

I shrug.

"Well," he says. "Good luck."

"Thanks," I say, wanting to leave, feeling shaky and odd.

"I'll see you around," he says.

"Sure."

He pauses for a second, smiling, and then he turns to go. I finally notice that he's very sweet and nice to look at. I can be slow sometimes when people catch me by surprise.

"Victor?"

He turns back around to look at me. He doesn't speak. He just cocks his eyebrow.

"Thank you," I say.

He nods and walks away.

I go back to the table and I gather my bag and books. Half hunched over, I walk back to my room as fast as I can. My arms and legs feel like lead and my muscles are shaking and twitching when I finally get there. I go immediately to the shower and I stand under it, cool water sliding over me and making all the aches go away. I feel myself come to life.

I don't have his number. I don't have his last name. I have a final exam in just over an hour.

Under the water, the conversation plays out in my mind like I am meeting him for the first time, a small step away from being there, like so much of my life.

And this is how I meet Victor.

As a signing bonus Andrew bought me a number of suits. They were well tailored and stylish. Some were very flash and others rather relaxed and bland. All of them were expensive in a way that made my jaw drop. I'd been living a long time making a working man's salary in Thatcher's England. Andrew threw money about like he'd never seen someone poor. I'd protested at first, telling him to spend the money on some charity or another and he'd simply stared at me until I stopped speaking, and told me to consider it a uniform.

Within a year, I understood the reasons why. A man in a suit can be invisible, or he can be instantly set apart, depending on the cut and the manner in which he wears it. It is a uniform, and people speak to you differently according to which uniform you wear. They have expectations, and you can subvert them. Andrew schooled me in Urban Machiavellia, the thousand ways to look bland while holding a knife behind my back, and how to look dangerous while offering sweets.

I was Eliza Doolittle to his Higgins, and he taught me accents. He taught me how to see the ways that men and women give away their lies. He taught me to hide my own, which astonished me, as I'd never had the slightest luck with that. By the time he'd finished, I trusted nobody absolutely. He taught me the laws on what an investigator can do and what they can't do, and he taught me what they actually do regardless.

He treated our relationship as that of master and apprentice, and I took that ethic seriously. Andrew was the most effective person I had ever met. He was thoroughly competent in every regard, and to spend any time with him was to feel a kind of fearful respect.

I had spent a long life of being nothing very much. I was clever but unremarkable. I was undisciplined, the living embodiment of unfulfilled potential. I never knew what I wanted except that I wanted to be special. I wanted, in fact, to be amazing. Larger than life. Andrew achieved this, and he was teaching me to be more than I was.

Andrew took on work when the mood fancied him, and I knew he must have charged a great deal because he was never short of money. I helped him, at first, on the most minor cases, mostly with research. Other times he brought me along because having an employee made him look more like whatever he felt he ought to be looking like under the circumstances. After the end of the second year, I began to work with him on every case, taking notes, and, in general, being Archie Goodwin to his Nero Wolfe. Except that's not right, because he couldn't bear to stay at home. He was out all the time, and I stood there and took notes. Perhaps I was Watson to his Holmes. By that time, I had lost perspective because I was entirely in love with him.

At this point, it's probable you have an idea of the sort of person I am when I'm in love. It's a mixed bag, but overall, it's not pretty. I hated myself at the time, because of two things. The first is because, despite all my lessons in human deception, I was still trying to fool myself into thinking I was straight. The second was that Andrew had taught me love was the source of all human disasters. He had naked disdain for all things romantic, and believed all love was a self-deception necessary to justify to our rational mind our unfathomable desire to have sex with any single person more than a single time.

For a long time, I'd assumed my feelings were based in hero worship. This was also dishonest. Who knows, ultimately, why anyone loves anyone?

There is no way that I could possibly describe the entire time in which I worked with Andrew, lived with Andrew, and, in the fullness of time, slept with Andrew. Five years is a long time to summarize.

It's books worth. He's not worth that attention.

He wasn't worth five years. He wasn't worth five seconds.

LAIRD RYAN STATES

It is weeks later, and I am in Victor's tiny room. It's little larger than the bedroom I shared with my brother growing up. This includes his bathroom, parceled off inadequately with particle board walls. The sound of the dripping faucet is omnipresent in the beige of it all.

He has no room for a stove, and meals are included downstairs with the family he rents from, but he doesn't like to be a bother. He has an electric frying pan plugged in next to his electric typewriter. He lives on cheese sandwiches the same pale colour of his skin. For variety, he grills them golden brown.

He feeds me every time I come over to listen to records on his old turntable. He thinks I don't eat enough. I probably don't. I'm never very hungry unless I'm with him, and then I squeeze the white spongy corner-shop bread into my mouth to prevent the need for talk.

He has become comfortable with my silences. We listen to music. Sometimes we watch television on a ten-year-old set he borrows from downstairs. We sit on his green hand-me-down couch. It's squalor and furious thought in this place, all tangled up together, and it smells of him.

Nights, when I head back to my room, I sometimes smell his place on my sweater, and it comforts me as I sleep. I am not bored these days because he is a constant puzzle to me. There is nothing familiar about him. His is a face I have not seen a thousand times before. I do not find myself straining to call him by the right name, because his name is always at the forefront of my mind, and it stays there until buildings and design push it back. I am swimming in memory and in synthesis.

Victor is gay. So am I. I think he is in love with me, and I feel badly about this because, while I am very fond of him, I don't love him. I have not, this time around, fallen in love with anybody. I have experimented with men and women, and found that I preferred the flesh of men. I like the strength and the smell of them, but I find, sadly, that I do not like to talk to them. And with men, even more than women, you must talk to them. For all the stereotypes, women understand that communication and sharing can be silent. They know that it can be enough to simply sit with someone, to lean against them. That contact is enough sometimes.

SLEEPING UNDERWATER

Men demand words and solutions and they talk because they fear proximity.

I am no different, right?

Victor does not demand words from me, he is willing to sit still and just be. Even when he does talk, he talks to me about something. He does not just talk to build a wall. He is not filibustering until the sex happens.

But I don't love him. It would be so much kinder if I did. I lay awake nights, and I wish that I could. It might wake me up from this dream I'm trapped in. I feel so far away from my own life, observing it from ten feet up and on a five-second delay.

Victor has diagnosed me as autistic, and I suppose I can understand why he would think so. I'm not. It's stranger than that. He would never understand what I actually am. It would be nice if he did, for he might fully explain it to me.

I am waiting for him to pick me up. I am in my room drinking glass after glass of cold water. I am alone, and it's just as well because, if he could see me down the twelfth glass, he'd goggle at it. He'd say something, or ask a question I couldn't answer, and it would spoil everything.

The water shakes through me. I feel it sing. My skin tingles. I hear voices. I remember pressing my face into the neck of a horse that has run for miles, sweat on its neck. It is a thick white smell, and I remember the blind love that this horse and I have for each other. It's all without words. I don't know when or where I met this horse, but water never lies. All my memories are locked away, buzzing and calling to me at the same time. With water, they settle in me with some warmth and I breathe more easily.

I turn to look at the door and a second later there is a knock.

"Come in," I say, still slightly giddy.

Victor is at the door. He is dressed in a three-quarters length black coat. He has a lemon-yellow shirt and paisley trousers and, with the burgundy of his hair, he looks as though the world itself has set him apart.

He is not alone. With him, slightly behind him, is a man my height with ice blue eyes and blond hair cut short. He is dressed all in black and reminds me of Nazi propaganda posters, except that he is smiling, and his smile makes me want to smile back. He is holding Victor's hand, and I am feeling a sudden sense of something like relief and something like jealousy.

"Hey Carter," he says. "This is Tom Bradstreet."

"Oh, hey," I say, stepping over and nodding to him.

"Hiya," Tom says, in a voice that is wrong for his face. It is the deep and cigaretted voice of a Mississippi blues singer coming from his mouth and I smile.

"I've been meaning for you to meet each other, but Tom's been on assignment, for the Times, in the Falkland Islands," Victor says.

"Really?" I say, because he doesn't look old enough to shave, let alone be on assignment anywhere, "That's really interesting. What's it like there?"

"It's a fucking bunch of little rocks. Not worth it," he says, coming inside in a very comfortable way.

"Not worth what," I ask.

"War."

"War?" I say.

"Oh, Tom's simply convinced that we're headed for a bloody war with Argentina over the fucking place. He's mad."

"We'll see," Tom says with certainty.

"I suppose so," I say.

"Well there's no need to talk about that right now," Victor says. "Let's go dancing."

I smile, because dancing is one of my favourite things in the world, except that I never go anymore because I'm too busy with my studies, too busy learning the ways of concrete.

"Dancing," Tom says, "Christ. You always want to take me dancing."

"It's fun," Victor says. "I think you remember fun. You must."

I am watching them, observing their interaction with the earnestness of an anthropologist. They're flirting with each other by pretending to be hostile. I have seen this a great many times, and have never understood fully how it works.

"Fun. Christ. Fiddling while Rome burns. The whole country shot to shit with that sister to Sauron running it. It's halfway to fucking illegal to hold hands now. War's coming, and mark my words, a plague too. Why not dance, I suppose?"

He means every word, and his anger frightens and upsets me. I see Victor blink twice as fast as usual. Tom softens his face and continues.

"Listen to me. Christ. I've turned into my fucking father just like magic." He snaps his fingers.

He looks up at Victor and smiles, and holds out a hand toward me.

"Come on then."

He looks at me and shakes his hand slightly.

"Come on then," he says to me. "We're going dancing. If we don't, it is obvious to me that your bottled need for self-expression is likely to pop you like a grape, for Christ's sake."

Tears come welling for me, and I don't know why exactly, but I take his hand. It feels dry and calloused and warm, like my father's hand. I remember walks along the beach, where he'd take hold of my hand, and he'd talk to me, his strange quiet son, so unlike the screaming brawling lot of my brothers and sisters. He'd tell me about his life and his beliefs, but the words meant nothing to me next to the sound of his voice and the knowledge that he was talking to me, and choosing me.

Victor smiles, as Tom grabs up my hand, and then he kisses me on the cheek.

"Oh love," Victor says, "We're going to have so much fun!"

"All right," I say, smiling.

"Fun. Christ. What's fun about jumping up and down in place, packed so tight with people you might as well be humping them? Oh. Right. Never mind."

Tom lets loose a rasping metallic chuckle and Victor smiles.

"There's my boy."

Hand in hand, the three of us head to the stairs. Before the street, Victor and I each let go of Tom's hand. He is reluctant to do so, tries to hold fast, then shrugs and lets go as we walk into the night in Fascist England. The air is warm, and not too damp, and the sound of traffic is like flute music slowed down so that a song can last a hundred years.

I was filing and doing busywork. It was half past three on a Thursday afternoon, and I heard the door open. I came around the corner from the file room, and saw a man in his late fifties. He was dressed in a drab blue suit that was about a size too small for him, and not in good repair. His face was ruddy and doughy, his eyes watery. He looked like the classic middle-aged working class alcoholic. He had been crying recently, and he had a brown paper sack in one hand.

"Hello," I said. "Can I help you?"

"Are you Mr. Matheson?" he asked, his accent thick and Northern like mine used to be before Andrew performed his mighty labours.

"Mr. Matheson is away on business," I said. This was, naturally, a lie. Andrew was back in our place sleeping off the previous night's drunken escapade, secure in the knowledge that he had collected a fat paycheque on an insurance fraud case.

"Oh, damn me for a fool, I knew I should have called." He looked like he was about to lose control, fall apart, right before my eyes, and so I stepped quickly in.

"Won't you have a seat? I'm Niles Townsend. I work for Mr. Matheson. I'd be happy to help you."

He sat down, hands shaking. He found the arms of the chair to brace himself as he lowered himself in.

"I need you to find the man who murdered my Sara."

I felt badly for this man immediately because he clearly was not made of money. For him to come here signaled desperation and the failure of the police to find anything at all. This was, and still is, a common occurrence.

"I see," I said noncommittally.

He dumped out the little paper sack and photographs of a girl fell on Andrew's desk. The photos had been taken over a number of years, ranging from her infancy to what seemed to be her college graduation. She had grown into a tall thin reed of a woman, blond and pale and big-eyed. She was too gaunt to be actually pretty, but she looked very smart.

"How long has she been gone?"

"Six months now. She was such a beautiful girl."

"I should tell you, Mr..." I paused, as I'd not yet heard his name.

"Cooper," he said. "Frank Cooper."

"I should tell you, Mr. Cooper, two things. The first is that private investigators are very expensive and, unlike in films, they do not ever work for free."

He started to speak and protest, but I calmed him with a motion of my hands.

"The second thing is that, after a couple of months have gone by, it's practically impossible to ever find out anything about the killer. The trail is too cold, and the police don't tend to share information with us. Mr. Matheson would surely love to take your money but I must admit I would feel badly about it."

He nodded and then sat up straight, trying to add an air of dignity to his tattered body.

"You're a kind lad, and I do appreciate it. Money is not a problem. The missus and I have rather come into it."

He reached into the inside pocket of his suit and pulled out a carefully folded cheque. He slid it across the desk to me, and I opened it. I did as I had been taught and managed my face, though what I wanted to do was stare at the cheque goggle-eyed and stammer nonsense syllables for an hour or two. It was a cheque for a million pounds and change, made out to a Wendy Cooper, dated over five months ago.

"Good heavens," I said, sliding it back to him. "How long have you been carrying that around in your pocket. You ought to deposit that immediately."

"She doesn't want it," he said, "The wife I mean. I don't either."

"Why not?"

"No joy in it. My girls used to play the pools together, they did, chipping in on a ticket every week. I used to tease them. This was their last. They won the Treble Chance, lucky shot. A week after she died, Wen found the chit. Broke her in half all over again. Whoever finds the man that killed our girl can have the whole bleeding rotten dirty thing."

He lowered his face, and tears fell in his lap.

"I'm very sorry about your loss, Mr. Cooper. I will discuss this with Mr. Matheson later today, and we'll doubtless have questions for you. I should say again that the chances are very slim we'll find him. The trail has gone cold by now, and..."

"It was never properly investigated," he exclaimed, with some small anger that was not directed at me as such. "He'd killed four others. One just two days before."

"I beg your pardon," I said.

"He's another one of those bloody Jack the Rippers, but you don't hear about it on telly, because they don't want the general public to go mad about it."

I looked at him. It was clear that he believed what he was saying.

"Do you have the names of the other girls who died?"

"Yes, sir. Grab your pencil."

I did so, and a yellow pad.

LAIRD RYAN STATES

"Lisa McCabe, 22. Ellen Darrow, 21. Alice Larson, 19. Karen Millerton, 24. All of them, tall and blond, like my girl. All of them cut up into mince and left in bins like rubbish."

I began to wonder why I'd not heard of this. If it were true, and not the mad delusions of a grieving father, or the wholesale imaginings of a lucid but delusional madman.

I took down his personal information, helped him up from his chair and to the door. I promised that we would get back in touch with him the very next day.

After he left, I sat back down and looked at the list of names. It was then I noticed he'd left his cheque behind. I locked it in the office safe. I'd talk to Andrew later. The pause was fine with me, because I had to find a way to talk him out of the case. There was no hope of success and to fail at it would bruise his ego. He did not do well at failure, each occasion of it left him miserable and overly sensitive. In a case like this, I knew that even he would feel for these parents a little. I did not want him to feel the hurt of letting them down. I also knew that he would cheerfully deal with that hurt for a million pounds, but I did not want to take away the money from Mr. and Mrs. Cooper.

I loved Andrew. Andrew loved money. Looking back, I should have been prepared for a disaster.

It's another club on another night. I am breathless and covered in sweat, in a tank top and jeans. The music is pounding through me. Tom and Victor are on the dance floor. I see their heads flicker in and out of view in the crowd as I sit with my arms and legs cooling.

I take a drink of vodka, and let myself relax into the chair. I close my eyes, and hear my own heart beating in my ears like counterpoint to the insistent music. I am poisoning myself to feel this good, a trick I've learned from Victor. For short moments I am not drowning in myself. I am floating in an amber pool of some other sort. I hear the voices of the people in the club. I smell them, the mixture of their colognes and sweat. I hear the whisper of lips on lips, snatches of laughter. Then there is the beat the beat the beat, and then there is just my heartbeat.

Which stops.

SLEEPING UNDERWATER

I open my eyes and I am standing in front of a building with a glorious upswept roof, angles I've never seen before. It's almost human, as though the whole building has curled to throw itself into the sky, straining to touch the sun. I am standing on grass so green that it seems to catch on whatever it touches, and the sky is the colour of melted gold. I start to cry and fall to my knees.

"Carter," Tom shouts, his voice still quiet against the din, as he shakes me, apparently back to the table now. "Are you with us? Christ."

Tom turns to Victor who is looking concerned. I open my eyes all the way and grab a napkin.

"GIVE ME A PEN!" I shout, my voice ringing so clear through the din that people on the dance floor turn to look. I don't care. Tom steps back startled and fishes in his coat to hand me a biro, which I proceed to use on the napkin. I am trying to remember the lines of it, the texture. I move the pen on the napkin furiously. Tom is watching me with curiosity, Victor with frustration. He wants me to dance with him. It's all he ever wants.

For a period of time that I lose track of, my whole work is on the napkins. Tom is there. Tom is not there. Someone refills my glass. Victor swears at me. Tom is there again. Then I am finished all that I can do. The sketch has taken six napkins, and is not a patch on what I meant it to be, on what I'd seen, what I'd imagined. The napkin blots the ink. My heart hurts, and I feel sick.

The club is quiet. Tom is off talking to a man in the corner. Chairs are on tables now. Victor is asleep in his chair face down on the table. I am aware of where I am, but everything else is slow to return to me. I am a little frightened, and my head begins to throb.

I need water, badly.

Tom comes over, looking amused.

"What time is it," I ask him.

"Three thirty in the morning," he says. "Are you, at this point, finished?"

"Yeah," I said. "I'm sorry. Are we in trouble or something?"

"No. Christ, don't worry. I'm friends with the manager. I just had them sweep around the two of you."

I look at Victor, see how far gone he is and smile.

"Is he all right?" I ask.

"No," Tom says. "He's a barely functioning alcoholic. I suppose he'll live."

I start tucking napkins in my pockets and Tom stops me.

"Hold on, will you? I'd like to see what we're all held up for. Put them back will you?"

I place the napkins back on the table, rearranging them to the right position, and I sit back trying to look calm and detached. He starts to look at them. For a long time. I start to move in my chair.

"Carter," he says. "Did you just, like, create this? From nothing, like?"

"It's nothing really," I say, trying to divert attention.

Tom pounds his clenched fist on the table. "No. Stop that. Stop it right now."

I flinch and move back. He turns and he grabs my arms, His big blue eyes are wet and welling.

"That is not nothing," he says to me. "That right there on those napkins is bloody inspiration. You made that."

I shake my head, dismissively and he grabs my face in his hands.

"No. You made that out of whole cloth and genius, and I won't sit here and watch you pretend that its crap because it isn't."

"I," I start to say something, and he lets go of my face.

"D'you know what I'd do for talent like that, Carter? Christ, you've no idea."

I look at the floor.

"Victor is a smart guy, and he'll probably end up working for a newspaper someday. If I play my cards right, I'll stay employed, but Carter Bennet, as God Himself is my witness, you'll be spoken of long after all three of us are dead and gone."

My stomach is churning and pitching and my cheeks are hot, my eyes dry.

"I don't want that," I say.

"Well, you've got it. You'd best learn to live with it. Christ, come out of your shell and learn to live altogether, in fact."

Victor rouses himself slightly, letting loose a moan and lifting his head. A beer mat is stuck to his face and he looks at me in deadly earnest.

"Have you finished with your stupid building, then?" he says, and yawns.

"You've got a beer mat stuck to your face, you sybaritic arse," Tom says.

I laugh a little as Victor brushes it away.

"I fell asleep," he says, "Not my fault we had to sit about waiting for your spell to end."

"Sorry," I say. "You used to think they were interesting."

"Well that was before they happened every Friday night, you brilliant fucking master-class killjoy."

Tom steps in, and helps Victor to his shaky feet.

"We'd best head home, lads," Tom says. "Before they throw us out, or God Himself whispers to Carter Bennet again, or Victor passes out. We'll crawl to my place. It's nearest."

I pick up the napkins, not done with them, ashamed and proud and very confused. I want to lie in a cold tub and sleep without dreams. Tom smiles at me, and something cracks in the deep parts of me I don't often look at, and I smile back,

"You all right?" he asks.

"Yeah," I say, "just tired. My hand hurts."

"Of course your hand hurts," Victor says, grabbing it up and kissing my wrist with surprising tenderness. "Maniac."

I brush his hair back behind his ear. "You're not upset, are you?"

"Nah," Victor says. "This is who you are."

The thought that this was okay had never crossed my mind. I find it strangely appealing but largely just strange, as though it were an inalienable truth for other people.

But not for me.

Nothing else of note transpired in the office that day. I cut out early and headed back to the flat Andrew and I now shared. As I made it up to our floor, I could hear the music coming from our place. It was one of those loud Italian operas he loved. Even six months earlier, the neighbours would have called the police by now. At some point, Andrew had gone next door and talked with them. They never complained again. I unlocked the door and went inside. On the other side of the door, the opera was a din. Andrew was stripped to the waist and his bare skin was shining with sweat. He wore grey sweatpants and was moving rapidly from one foot to the other, shadow boxing. As he punched and ducked from invisible punches he was singing with the aria, his voice loud and strong and sweet. Muscles moved under his skin in the same way that silk moves in a soft wind. My breath quickened and I stood quietly until the aria ended.

"Hello," I said, "you astonishingly sexy creature."

He turned and smiled at me, grabbing up a towel and mopped at his chest and underarms. "How long have you been here, you astonishingly quiet creature?" He lowered the slider switch on the wall that controlled the volume.

"Long enough to become aroused."

"Just a few seconds, then," he answered, waggling his eyebrows.

I went in to give him a quick peck on the cheek. He tried to embrace me and I shoved him back.

"Expensive suit," I said. "You're all sweaty."

"We'll buy another," he said and went for me again.

I ducked under his arms and backed into the kitchen.

"I like this suit. Go and take a shower. We've business to discuss, seeing as how you failed to come into work."

He blew a raspberry at me. "I needed a vacation from the world," he said. "You wouldn't understand. You miss nine-tenths of it because you're too distracted by mirrors."

As he headed to the bathroom, I yelled over my shoulder at him. "Please! I'm not the one singing opera half naked in front of an open window."

He didn't answer and shortly thereafter I heard the shower running. I took out a long loaf of bread from a sack, and also some pasta and sauce, and began preparing a quick supper. The entire flat smelled of fresh basil and oregano. I warmed the bread in the oven, made a soft garlic butter and a salad. The opera played on in the background. When it was at a lower volume it was a good deal more tolerable. It was, I think, Puccini. I'm not an expert, nor a fan.

"Mmm," he said, "I remember why I keep you around now. It's a tragedy. I've so many talents, yet cooking isn't one."

"Nor self-assessment," I said. "Keep stirring this. I want to change out of this shirt."

He took the wooden spoon and began stirring. He was dressed in cream coloured cotton slacks and a loose burgundy shirt, and going barefoot. He smelled of some expensive cologne and I kissed his neck before I went to change. I felt a good deal more comfortable when I came back out dressed in a Sex Pistols vest and jeans. He rolled his eyes.

"Good lord," he said. "It's nice that you clean up well."

"I do. Give the spoon back."

I took the wooden spoon from him and he gave me a squeeze from behind, his chin on my shoulder.

"Thank you for taking up the slack. I really couldn't face the day."

"Well as it happens, very little of interest happened. I did a good deal of filing. I reconciled the books. I answered some of your correspondence, and a man offered us a million pounds to find his daughter's murderer."

He pulled away from me but left his hands on my shoulders for a second and let out a sigh.

"Lovely segue, Niles, my love."

"Sit down. We'll talk over dinner."

He set the table as I finished up.

"Did you do anything here at home except exercise?"

"Just the music."

I nodded, set the food on the table, and dished out some pasta and bread for each of us.

"So," he said. "Do tell."

I told him what had happened, omitting nothing. He watched me impassively, his blue eyes fixed on mine, and he did not interrupt. At this point we had worked together five years, and we had a routine. I knew precisely what he required from a summary, and so he did not feel the need to ask questions. When I finished, he cleared his throat.

"We'll take the case," he said, "naturally."

"Are you serious?"

"Yes. There's no question."

"We don't stand a bloody chance in hell of finding the killer. You know this."

"First of all," he said, "you've informed him of that, and he's responsible for his choices. Secondly, we shall be clear that we will not guarantee success, and we will charge our standard rates for as long as he is willing to pay. We will not just take the money on contingency. What he decides is up to him."

"He's not in his right mind, clearly. He's lost his daughter. It's exploitation."

"It's not. He has money, and he feels spending it will soothe his guilt over it. We all benefit. It is not my business to advise men how to recover from grief. This method is as good as any. Men have bought indulgences for hundreds of years to expiate guilt."

I shook my head. "You're the boss, I suppose."

"I am, yes. We'll meet with him and talk. If I think that he's a lunatic, we'll turn down his money and let him pay some talentless hack instead. How does that sound?"

"Fairly awful."

"Yes, and this is my point. If he's compelled to do this, I'll take the money. I stand as good a chance or better of finding the killer as anyone does."

"I suppose that's true."

"It is."

We ate in silence for a few minutes. Andrew used the remote to dim the lights.

"This is wonderful," he said.

"I'll tell the shop."

"You're sulking," he said, half asking.

"No."

"I see."

"I'm not sulking. Truly. I'm bothered. I feel bad for him."

"Don't get ahead of the facts. For all you know, he did it. He's quite certain the same man is responsible for all those other girls, yet there don't seem to have been any since his daughter. These killers don't usually just stop you know. Also, I've not heard word of any serial killers in the last while. Considering my excellent connections, I think that I would have."

I let out a held breath quickly. "That man did not kill his daughter. You're just being dark for the sake of seeming clever. Save it for the cheap seats, right?"

His eyes darkened and he glared at me. "Don't speak back to me on matters of my work. Don't mix up our home life with our work life. If you're incapable of doing so, then don't discuss my work at home."

"Our work."

"You know full well what I mean."

"Don't I just?" I said, standing up and leaving the room.

I sat in my room reading Warrior and wishing I were still in the comic business. It seemed that it was suddenly possible, in England, to create comics that meant something. I had burned those bridges forever. My temper often did that for me.

There was a knock at the door.

"Which Andrew are you?" I asked. "The asshole, or the one I'm fond of?"

The door opened a crack.

"Same fellow, unfortunately," he said. "May I come in?"

I shrugged insolently.

"Look," he said. "I won't lie to you and say that I'm sorry."

"Well, then," I said, "turn around and walk."

"Niles," he said, sitting in a chair next to mine. "I'm sorry I snapped at you, but you know I hate it when you raise your voice."

This was true. "Yes. I do."

"Perhaps you're right, and he didn't kill his daughter. Conversely, perhaps I'm right, and he did. If he's hiring us to find out, then we'll probably find out. Can we just forget we started yelling? You're upset, and I'm still a little drunk, and I don't want to fight anymore."

I looked at him and could tell he was sincerely sorry we'd been sharp. He was depressed, and had managed to keep it hidden, even from me, until now. He looked tired, and to be honest, a little closer to his age. When he got down, it was as though all the small wrinkles appeared from nowhere - as if he normally kept them hidden by sheer muscle control. Perhaps he did.

"Oh, all right," I said. "I'm just upset because of the way he spoke to me. I really don't think he was deceiving me. He was a wreck."

"Well, we'll see."

He offered me a hand, and I took it. We sat in silence.

"I'm depressed," he said.

"I had noticed, yes. You should take your meds."

"Hm."

He wouldn't. I knew it. He knew it. Like many brilliant people, he refused to take his meds. He confused his illness with his genius.

Perhaps he had his reasons.

It is later and dark. I'm in a room that smells of Indian cigarettes and pipe tobacco. It also smells of sweat and skin and sex. My head is resting on Tom's chest. He is sleeping, his breath slow and steady. Victor is on his side, his front pressed along my back. I feel his cock pressed against my hip, warm and sleeping now with the rest of him. His cheek is soft and unshaven on my back. I am still awake. My clothes lie on the floor in a neat puddle of fabric. I look at them, the napkins still in the pockets, and try to remember the shapes that make up the whole form of it. I hear the beating of Tom's heart, and I turn my head slightly to plant a small kiss under his right nipple, and I taste the salt sweat of him.

I want to move but dare not because I want them to sleep and I want to feel them sleep beside me. They are calm and quiet and, pressed between them, I am held in place, pinned down in space and time. I am fixed. I am here and now, and not lost in memories of other times and other lives. Their sweat is cooling on my skin, salt water holding only their own memories, and tiny chemical reminders of who they are. For as long as this moment lasts, I am here. I close my eyes and let my nose do the work. Victor lets loose a sigh in his sleep. A small waft of wine rises over my shoulder. I smile.

I taste first communions on his tongue, and he's the only Protestant in this bed.

We three share this bed and have never discussed it, and never needed to. It's the one easy thing in my life. It makes sense.

There is a sudden loose rattle in Tom's chest, and he coughs hard. He smokes too much. He coughs again, a softer refrain, and settles back down, never fully waking up.

His hand moves slightly and rests in my hair. I turn my face into his palm, feeling his rough skin on mine. I hum slightly and softly, feeling my breath on his hand, the vibration resonating in the micrometer between us. He makes a sound in his throat and rolls over slightly and I lift my head to free him and adjust slightly forward, finding myself able to move slowly and gently from the bed.

Victor burrows against Tom's back by instinct. I smile and watch for a moment.

I rifle through my own pockets, pulling out napkins, and place them on the floor, staring at them. The building looks like Atlas, struggling to hold the sky. I can see curves that remind me of strong thighs. I walk around the drawing in a circle, wondering who on Earth would build such a thing. I have never once cared about that. I'm changing, and I'm starting to notice.

My instinct when it comes to sex is to pour myself into one person. I have never had two who poured themselves into me. They are filling me from outside, whereas usually it is me becoming emptier next to someone who needs me, needs more than I can spare.

SLEEPING UNDERWATER

I feel old ghosts slipping into the room, and so I pick up the napkins and put them back in my pockets. I head into the washroom and fill the tub with cool water. I lay down in the water so that just my bent knees and my face stick out.

With my head under the water I can hear all the hidden sounds that buildings make. The sounds of the pipes, the faint groaning movement of joists and beams. I close my eyes and float into the secret language of structures. Tom's building was built in the 1960s, but it sounds older, badly built, complaining softly through the pipes.

I breathe in and out evenly, putting pieces of my building together in my head. I feel the texture of the exterior wall, sleek and pebbled in alternation. A material I don't know in life. Probably not real. I feel a frown.

I open my eyes and stare up at the cracked plaster ceiling. I realize that I am troubled by this building because it wants to be built. The others have never cared. Why is this one different, and why so very persistent? Maybe, for the first time, one of my own really will outlive me.

The room fills with a loud roar and I sit straight up in shock. The water splashes to the floor, and Victor shouts, genuinely terrified. The toilet is still flushing. Then he turns and starts to laugh.

"Jesus," he says, and sits down on the floor beside the toilet, one knee up, the other down. There is no modesty in him, and it charms me. "Are you trying to kill me?"

"Sorry," I say, "I fancied a bath."

"Like hell," he says. "You were sleeping in that tub again because you're so very weird."

"It feels safe," I say, "and I can think."

He shrugs. "We all have our weirdness. I don't need to understand you to love you."

"You love me."

"Yeah, course I do."

"Thank you," I say.

"You're quite welcome, you weird little person."

He crawls forward to kiss me and I pull him in close in an embrace and kiss him back. His skin is hot against my cold wet chest. His tongue plays with mine, and I open my eyes to see his eyes are open and I feel my cock press hard against the porcelain. I laugh and I pull him into the tub on top of me, both of us giggling and splashing. I know that Tom will skin us alive for the mess but I don't let it stop me. We kiss and splash with groping hands and our breath quickens, and hands quicken and then we are still for a moment as hearts slow down, and kisses turn soft and slow and hands move over skin in the peaceful moments after. We sit up and wash each other clean with a damp washcloth and rise from the tub.

He holds my hand and doesn't talk. He leads me to the bedroom, and back to bed. I get back in and he puts his arms around me. I feel safe and warm and sated, like a cat lying in the sun.

Frank Cooper was wearing the same suit when I next saw him. It was probably the only good suit he owned, despite what he was now worth. I tried to understand this, and be sympathetic, though I did not yet understand the mindset that money could be tainted.

He was sitting with his hat literally in his hands. I was sitting at my desk, ready to take down notes on the conversation. We were, both of us, waiting for Andrew. Andrew was not, this time, hung over. He was late, and I admit I was a little concerned. I didn't see any advantage for him in being late to this meeting.

All in all, he arrived forty minutes late, and without saying hello. He removed his blazer, sat at his desk, and leaned back in his chair. He pushed his blonde hair back and let out a sigh.

"Gentlemen," he said, "my apologies for being late. I had a mechanical failure on my Jaguar."

"Again?" I asked.

"Yes, I know. It's punishment for vanity."

I said nothing but did smile.

"Thank you for waiting, Mr. Cooper. Again. I'm sorry."

"It's fine," Cooper said. "My own car is a bit off. I'm always up to my elbows in it."

Andrew nodded. "A man of your resources, Mr. Cooper, could afford a new one. And should."

Cooper shifted nervously. "I've explained to Mr. Townsend..."

"Yes," Andrew said. "He's made your intentions clear. And he did, I'm sure, a fine job explaining why it's a foolish and sentimental mistake."

"He did say something to that effect, yes sir."

"Please. Call me Andrew."

Cooper responded by looking at Andrew as though he'd spoken in Swahili.

"I must reiterate," Andrew said, "that, after a few weeks, the trail runs very cold. Nobody will share the physical evidence with us, and any witnesses will have next to no useful memory. Memory is fickle when fresh, and a fable after a week. I must tell you I rank our chances at five percent. If that."

"I don't expect you to solve Sara's murder to the confidence needed by the courts. I'm sure you're right, sir. I'm sure it can't be done. I believe what you've both told me. I do."

"Well then," Andrew said. "Your contention is that the murderer may kill again, and you want us to somehow stop him from doing so. You realize this amounts to the same thing?"

Cooper shook his head, "Something with the other poor girls will point the way. The police never even looked at the connections."

"Niles did mention your theory to me. What reason do you have to believe it?"

"He's called and told me."

My hands froze above the keys of my typewriter, and I stared open-mouthed. "You might have mentioned that the other day," I said.

"You're right," he said turning to me, "and I should have, but I was afraid it would make me sound daft."

"Have you told the police?" Andrew leaned forward.

"I have," he said. "They told me it was a prank caller, and to think no more of it. They told me the murders were not connected. But the gentleman has called back several times since and I believe him, sir."

Andrew leaned back in his chair, his fingers templed together under his nose. He closed his eyes and then opened them and I saw Mr. Cooper shift uncomfortably in the silence.

"All right," Andrew said. "We'll take the case. Under conditions. Are you prepared to hear them, or shall I offer a referral?"

"Please," Mr. Cooper said,

"We will not take the full amount of your winnings upon success. Should we succeed, you will over pay. Should we fail, we earn nothing. And I will, under no circumstances work for free. You will cash your cheque, and we will charge you our very expensive regular rates. This is the fairest available option to all of us."

I handed Mr. Cooper his cheque, and he folded it into his wallet. Andrew continued.

"Under no circumstances do I expect we will incur a million pounds worth of expenses and fees before declaring we are defeated. If you wish to honour her with the winnings, donate the remainder to a charity that would have pleased your girl. Are these terms acceptable?"

He thought about it for a long time, and then quietly said, "Yes."

"Good, then. If you'll excuse me, I need to pop to my mechanic and make sure they don't bruise her. I'll leave you with Niles for the time being."

I shot Andrew a quick look. "Sir," I said, "may I consult with you before you leave?"

He nodded. "Quickly." He turned to Mr. Cooper. "Do excuse us."

We went into the adjacent file room.

"What the hell, Andrew?" I said quietly. "I've no idea where you want to take this, or what I'm to do."

"I've no firm notions myself, love. He's not lying. He's getting the calls. I find it odd the police dismissed them, and that's where I actually mean to start. In the meantime, just have him fill out the paperwork, and all of that drab business. Get whatever you can on the phone calls. Dates, if he recalls them, and as much of the conversation as he can recall. Descriptions of the voice and any background sounds that might be distinctive. The good news is that if the killer is calling him, and if he is still at it, our odds are better. It all depends on the motives of the police in this incident."

"Okay," I said. "Is your car actually fucked?"

"Is it a Jaguar?"

I nodded. "Why on earth did you get that thing? You don't even know how to change a tyre."

"I do so," he smiled. "I just never ever would. God."

I smiled back. "You're a cat in human form."

"I try," he said. "Best be off."

He gave me a quick peck and we went back out into the office.

"We'll talk to you again, and soon, Mr. Cooper," Andrew said, offering a hand to shake, which Cooper rose to take hold of.

Andrew managed his face, but found it hard to control his distaste. I noticed a slight stiffening to his spine, and an increase in his blinking.

"Thank you, sir," Cooper said.

"Andrew," he said, pulling his hand back. "Really. We're going to talk awfully often. It'll be best all around."

Cooper managed a sheepish smile. "I'll try. I will."

"All I can ask, right?" Andrew looked at his watch. "Dash it all. I told them I'd be back in half an hour with my information."

Andrew left in a flurry of coat and wallet and keys, leaving Cooper and I alone. Andrew could get away with saying "dash it all" in the real world. I still had to marvel.

"He's an odd one, isn't he?" Mr. Cooper said to me quietly.

"Geniuses usually are," I said. "He's half mad. I won't lie. He is awfully good at his job, though."

"That's what I hear, yeah."

I nodded. Andrew had made the news a few times, but most of our cases were kept quiet at the insistence of the people hiring us. Information control was a large part of what Andrew did.

"From whom did you hear it?" I asked, honestly curious what connections this man might have.

"From the killer, sir," Cooper said, "He said only Andrew could stop him, and he begged me to call on him."

I cleared my throat. "No offence, Mr. Cooper, but you're sort of an odd man yourself, you know."

Tom is away. He is often away, because he is a grown up person with grown up responsibilities and a grown up job. He is off someplace exotic, and probably dangerous. I can't remember where. He has been there for months, now. Victor and I are playing a careful game called "Don't Talk About The Empty Space In The Bed." It has made us closer, because we share in missing him so much when he is gone. Victor takes it harder than I do, because time moves so slowly for him, whereas I have a hard time keeping still in those waters. I feel myself slowing down to an almost human life on some nights. Victor is missing lectures and drinking, and taking too many drugs, and I don't care for it. I tell him that, but he dismisses me because he is invulnerable, and what do I know about people anyway? He can be very cruel when he drinks, but I grew up with a drunk in my house, so it does not bother me as it should. I stop listening until he becomes the person he wants to be again, instead of the person he fears he'll one day become.

I spend most evenings at the drawing table that Tom and Victor pitched in on. It's big and expensive and gorgeous, and when they gave it to me just before Tom went away, I cried for an hour. They laughed a little, because they'd never seen me cry, and it frightened them a little bit, even as it made them happy. That's usually why we laugh, because we like to be frightened sometimes. On the drawing board is my course work. There are also drawings of Tom, and drawings of Victor. There are drawings of all of our acquaintances, too. I draw constantly, because I need to express my ideas with more clarity. Words can only do so much, and nothing at all for architecture.

Mainly though, there is the building. It is, I realized a while ago, a museum. For what, I don't know. It doesn't matter, for my purposes. I have drawn it now from a thousand angles. It walks up to me in the street in my dreams and demands to know what I'm up to, daring to sleep. It is that insistent. It promises to make me famous if I build it. I laugh and say that if it wants to persuade me, it had best go another way. But I want to build it, even if I have to be famous as a result. I want it as badly as it wants to be real.

Victor and Tom have said to me, each on their own, that the only thing that could make them stop loving me would be if I put the design in a drawer and started drawing banks with Roman arches. Victor doesn't care about the building, but he does want me to be famous. He wants everyone to be famous, for he seems to feel it is the natural goal of human progress. He would prefer to live in a world where everyone was young and fabulous and famous. In this world, he wouldn't have to try and be as smart as he actually is. This worries me great deal when he talks about it.

I lean over the table, and in the chaos of tiny black splotches on the backing board I see a pattern that reminds me of Cassiopeia. I know why the ancients made pictures of dots in the sky. It was a desperation to bring order to such vast and empty madness as the night sky brings to bear. We tamed our minds to tame the world.

We still do, I suppose. I find myself clearer now, the fuzzier that Victor gets. The further away he gets, the closer and harder I have to look to find the pattern in him that makes him whole. There is nothing you can do for a person on drugs, and nothing you can do to stop loving them. When Tom comes home, he'll sort it out. He has a gift for it.

I am all but done my courses, and I have been offered a number of jobs. My reputation is good. I am told again and again that I'll go far. Nobody tells me where I'll be going. Nobody asks me if I want to go in the first place. I don't. I like it here, wherever this is.

Victor is asleep, and, for the moment, the building is resting deep in the place where it is growing in me. He is lying on the couch in jeans and a t-shirt. It is New Year's Eve 1983, and it is ten seconds to midnight according to the TV that's on with nobody watching.

I tiptoe over and lay my body on top of his, burying my face in his shoulder as the world celebrates on television and I feel him warm against me. His head lolls on his neck with a loose ease, and he is so deeply asleep he does not know I'm there.

I feel my heart start to beat in time with his.

"Happy New Year, Victor," I say softly, and kiss his skin, tasting salt. I see the bottle of gin wedged between his side and the back of the couch. It's more than half empty. It was bought to celebrate. He started early, and I never bothered.

He stirs under me and slowly puts his leg over mine gently, like a small unconscious embrace, the way coma patients will sometimes squeeze your fingers. It lets me know that he's in there, and I am so grateful. I cry again.

"Careful," Victor says, softly, raising a hand to my cheek. "You may rust."

I press my face into his chest, and quietly say, "You drink far too much, and I'm tired of feeling lonely. I miss him. Is it really fair that you have to make me miss you as well?"

He strokes my hair.

"I'm sorry, Carter," he says. "It's not just Tom gone. It's Uni. It's not what I thought I wanted, I guess. I'm at a bit of a loss, you know. Tom has his very glamorous job jetting all over the world writing about it, and that bloody building of yours is a like a time bomb of fucking fame for you, but what have I got?"

"Tom and me, to begin with."

He draws in a ragged breath. "Is that me, then. Am I to be forever the hanger on, famous for my association with you two, a rent boy to the stars?"

I punch him softly in the chest. "Stop."

"I always thought I'd be someone amazing, you know."

81

"You are. Famous and amazing aren't the same."

"Yes. I'll be the most amazing man to flunk out as a Journo this year."

"It's likely."

He kisses the top of my forehead. "You're sweet."

"You'll find your thing, soon enough. You just can't see it right now because you're trying too hard. What do you expect? You're blind drunk half the time."

There is a silence between us.

"Tin Man," he says, "did you just make a little joke?"

"Yeah."

"It was awful. I could barely tell. But good for you."

I sit up on his belly and bounce my bum once. "Shut up, you."

"Make me," he says looking up at me with the same tender smile and intense questing eyes that made me pay attention the first time.

"No. You reek of gin. I'll not reward it."

I get off him, quite serious. I can see the tent in his jeans, and I feel a bit cruel but, as much as I love him, and love the feel of him on me and in me, I will not indulge him to drink and drug and get away with it by being charming. Being charming is half his problem in life, I think, and I like him in spite of it rather than because of it.

"Happy New Year," I say, sitting back to work.

"Bloody animal, getting me worked up and then flouncing back to your drawing board. I shouldn't wonder."

"No," I say, looking at him in all seriousness. "You shouldn't."

He opens his mouth to respond, sees my eyes are quite angry, and he goes, sheepishly, to wash his pickled self as clean of his sins as he can manage.

I was staring at photos of dead girls for the third straight day in a row. For some sick few, I supposed, this was entertainment. For my part, I felt ill. Andrew had laid them out on the table in pairs. A smiling snapshot of a young girl, and beside each, her destiny, hacked and pale blue, with smears of dirt and twigs. In each case, the head had been severed nearly, but not all the way, off. The limbs had been severed and placed in a neat pile on the torso. Their eyes were open and staring up at the lens. Before and after.

"I think we can agree, can we not, that this is the obvious work of the same man?"

"Yes," I say, with more than faint impatience. "It very obviously is."

"And yet, there was no word of that in the papers."

"No. It is as Mr. Cooper told us. Indisputably."

"So the police are keeping it back, also as Frank says."

"So you're calling him Frank, now?"

"Keep on track, love."

"Yes. Yes, I can't think the police had missed it. Look, as my only function here is to repeat back affirmations of your own obvious thoughts, would you mind if I just left my coat on a broomstick and snuck off for a pint?"

Andrew raised an eyebrow. "It's no fun at all that way. To continue..."

"Fuck. Andrew, seriously. I'm going soul blind from looking at these. I can't stand any more. I'm either going to sick up or get used to it, and honestly I don't fancy either, okay?"

"Why would the police keep this quiet? And how?"

"Fucking sorcery," I suggest. "If I were this girl's father, I'd be talking to every fucking reporter in town."

"As would I! My point exactly. There's holding details back for sound criminological purposes, and then there's this. Not only why the hell, but how the hell is the question. What are they telling these people, and why have they not told Frank Cooper?" He slammed a hand down on the desk theatrically.

I looked at him. "I don't know."

"Me either," he said, taking a seat. "And nobody is talking to me about it. Even my best mates on the job have gone mum on me."

"I expect there's a good reason, and I don't know I like us mucking around in it."

His eyes went wide, and he stared at me. "Cor' Charlie, look at you," he clucked like a Cockney faggot.

"Stuff it," I said. "You're not even English."

"Oh come on," he said, "Listen to yourself talking about the police as though they know what they're doing and aren't a bunch of crooked jackbooted thugs. It's the reach of our beloved Führer in this, as sure as anything. That bitch wants no more Yorkshire Rippers on her watch."

"You are such a misogynist cunt, Andrew!"

"Oh please. You're defending Thatcher now, are you?"

"No, she's fucking dreadful. I just can't stand the reasons that you hate her for."

"Well the country got what it wanted, a stern mummy to tell it what to do and when to wash."

I sighed.

"It's the same with any woman in power. Women are inherently fascist. If you don't believe me, eavesdrop on a women's studies group sometime."

"Right. And Mussolini? Big set on her, then?"

"I'm just saying this nonsense about the peaceful, nonviolent loving woman is nonsense. It's no better with a woman in charge, because they're every bit as daft and violent and four times more ruthless and vengeful. And we can't say boo to them because it isn't polite."

"No, you're saying that Thatcher is a fascist because she's a woman, and I'm telling you, at this point, that even women want nothing to do with her."

"They're lying."

"Shut up."

"Nice comeback. You argue well."

"There's no point in debating you. You don't care what anyone thinks about anything."

"I care what Thatcher thinks. How about you?"

"I care what these parents think. I'm going now to interview them, and see if they've been getting calls. I am doing this to get away from you for a few hours."

He smiled. "Right then. I'll stay here and have a drink, consider the evidence, and maybe call in a consultant."

Feeling faintly used, I grabbed my coat and headed out.

I drove around town. Driving was still new to me, and I didn't care for it, but I needed some time to think. All of this, the whole thing seemed utterly wrong to me. Every last bit of it, but I lacked the words to wrap around my unease. Frank Cooper was acting oddly. The way he doled out information was nonsensical and contrived.

I knew from first hand experience how far from normal behaviour people can get while grieving, but it wasn't right. I couldn't think of a reason for even Thatcher to just hush up a serial killer without a hell of a reason in any case. And Andrew.

SLEEPING UNDERWATER

He was always dark, always whimsical, but only cruel when he needed to be for a strategy. Not in years had he been deliberately cruel to me. Yet he had just deliberately made me so angry that I stalked off to do a job he didn't want to do. He could have just told me to do it, and I'd have done it. He chose to be a prick about it. I didn't know why, and I didn't like any of the vague theories that brushed up, half formed, against my mind. I need to be clear here, so as not to be misunderstood. He certainly meant all that he said about women, and about Thatcher, whatever she was, but he also knew better than to talk to me about it, especially when I was already upset.

I couldn't justify in my own mind how he'd trot out his misogyny at the same table he had me working to solve a series of sex murders. If he was being a cunt, it was beneath his usual level. If it was a cunning lesson in his own brand of the Socratic, I was missing the point. I was tired and upset, and all I could do was imagine my own sister hacked to death and laying in the rubbish for having the right look to her, and the right sort of genitals.

Andrew, being Andrew, knew all of this, and yet he still took the piss, still worked me up. I tried to shake it off. I tried to get professional as I headed out to visit grieving parents to ask horrible questions about midnight phone calls.

Four hours later, I'd been cried on twice, and threatened once. None of them, not a mother, nor a father, had received a call like Frank Cooper had. Not one of them was lying about it either. Not one of them seemed a bit aware that any other girls had turned up the same way. I did my best not to let it spill. If the killer had chosen to call anyone else, it was clear that Frank Cooper was the only one who picked up the phone.

I began to wonder if Frank Cooper had, either. The phone company had not released his incoming call records to us. They would not release them to Cooper either, which we both found questionable at best. Until we decided to call the police in on that, we could prove nothing. Andrew had decided not to, yet.

Why Cooper? Why would the killer confess to Cooper, ask for help from Cooper? Had he grown remorseful and called the family of his last kill? Did he want to be caught before he succumbed again? Perhaps. If not for these calls, the logical assumption for the police would be that he had died. Many serial killers take their own lives in a moment of clarity or regret. Why would he not call the others, as well, though? Did he feel some kinship to Cooper? Did he not, perhaps, know how to find the others? Had he known more about Sara than his other kills?

The more I went over everything, the more convinced I was that Andrew had been right in the first place, damn him. Cooper had killed his own daughter. Hiring us was a cry for help. The story about being called at home was a clear confabulation and a metaphor. It was the quickest thing he could come up with when asked a question he couldn't answer. His behaviour, his remorse, his quick memory of the other names, and his knowledge of the connections. All of it made sudden sense.

Perhaps the other girls were rehearsals. Girls who looked like his daughter, perhaps quelling the need to kill, but only for a time. Having finally broken his last tabu, he was probably dissociative about it now. It was the simplest solution, and these were usually correct.

And it was, in this moment, clear to me that Andrew had sussed this out already, and had spent the last three weeks passing time in a kind of game, earning a wage to solve a case, waiting for Cooper to confess or be caught. The police clearly suspected him, and that was why the phone records had not been released.

Andrew had known, and he had let me talk to Cooper, feel for him, stay up nights trying to think of something or anything to do that would help. He had known and not told me.

Me, who he supposedly loved.

He would tell me, I supposed, that he wanted me to come to it on my own, that it was part of my education. He would smile grimly as I explained it to him. He would say, "Just so," with faint satisfaction, but I knew that was a lie.

It was cruelty, and it was betrayal and it was unwarranted. I began to cry with anger, and I pulled over the car and pounded the wheel.

"Stupid, stupid, stupid!" I said.

He'd told me to trust nobody. I had trusted him.

And nothing was ever more important to him than teaching me his goddamned lessons.

Upon my accreditation with the Royal Architecture Society, Tom sends me a congratulatory cable from Johannesburg. Victor, though I've no idea where the money has come from, takes me to dinner to celebrate. He's dropped out of college completely and while he has cut back on drinking and drugs, he's not completely free of them. We are lucky in that he can ill-afford them now. He is working in a record shop. I sometimes hang out there in what suddenly feels like a flood of free time.

I have spent a month considering job offers, none of them very appealing. I know that I don't have the inclination or ability to run my own business. I will have to take a position someplace, and I know full well that junior architects do not start out on museums. My mood is dark and my behaviour probably appalling.

I spend my evenings building a model to scale. The materials are cheap and soft, and I am learning new skills as I go. It is starting to take shape in three dimensions. Time seems to mean nothing, and I have most of it to myself, because Victor works nights and Tom is around the world mostly. The smell of model glue has started to cling to me like a lover's cologne. Victor teases me that I smell like a mannequin, and that I'm about as responsive. I twit him, though I know he's right. With nothing else to occupy me, the museum has taken firm residence in the now.

We are in bed, halfway to sleep, when Victor speaks.

"I know he wishes he could have been with us tonight."

"If he did," I say, "he would have been. He loves what he does, and where he goes."

"I'm sure he'd have wanted to be here."

"It doesn't matter. I'm not upset. Tom is here sometimes, and other times he isn't. It's got nothing to do with love."

"What does that mean?"

"Nothing bad."

He rolls over a bit, and makes a frustrated noise. "Do you suppose he really does love us?"

"Yeah," I say, "course."

"Hmm."

I turn and press my face into his back. He is like a child. When something is out of sight, he has a hard time believing in it. I kiss him between his shoulder blades.

"I know you miss him," I say.

"Don't you?"

I breathe in and out. "Not really."

He pulls away from me, and rolls over to look at me, faintly horrified. "My god."

I roll my eyes and smile. "Oh stop. I do wish he were here, but I want him to be happy."

"And he can't be happy here?"

"Not all the time, no. It's who he is."

He sighs a ragged pre-crying sigh. "I'm sorry, I'm just feeling a bit sentimental, I imagine."

"He does love you, Victor. He loves you enough to have me in this bed."

"Oh, Carter, no. It's not like that."

"Okay, that's true. It was to start. It's not now." I say. "I never minded. I was just happy to be asked."

He kisses my face. "It must be very lonely to be you, Tin Man."

"Never," I say. "I have you and Tom and, if I didn't, I wouldn't know any better."

"You would."

"I didn't."

I reach over to the bedside table and I take the keychain in my hand. They gave it to me at the accreditation. I hold it between thumb and forefinger up against the light, and squint at it. "Not so much, is it?" I say. "Not really."

"The keychain, no. The rest of it is though."

I toss it back onto the table and laugh. "We'll see, I suppose."

He smiles slightly. "I was reading the paper today, love, instead of doing the ordering, and I saw something in the classifieds that you might be interested in."

"What's that?"

He gets out of bed, naked, pads out to the kitchen, and rummages around. He comes back in with his wallet and opens it, pulling something out of it, and then tossing the rest of his wallet over his shoulder casually. It's a folded scrap of newsprint. He hands it to me and my eyes go wide.

"Fuck," I say.

He grins. "I was gonna leave it on the table for you to find, like I'd forgotten it or something."

"This was in today?"

"Yeah," he says. "Is that normal? That they put ads in?"

"It's a formality for government jobs. They have to put a public call out. Never happens though. They always have an architect practically hired and all of that. Still."

"You'll be doing it, of course?"

SLEEPING UNDERWATER

I look at the paper again. It is a call for designs for the Museum of Industry, to be constructed in Liverpool in 1985. I meet the criteria. The submission date is for a week from now, and this is part of the trick. Nobody can ready a submission in time. Except I've finished. I've blueprints, and half a model.

"Nah," I say. "It'd be daft. They already know who's building it. They don't care. They'd just be annoyed, really,"

He looks at me like I've slapped him, a mixture of anger and fear. He steps back and I see him swallow hard.

"Bollocks," he says. "I won't have it. I won't."

"Victor," I say, "You don't understand. It's a legal formality. They don't want to hear from me. They'll be annoyed. It could actually hurt me later."

"You shut up with your damned reasonableness."

I laugh, because that is the first time in any life that anyone has said anything of that sort to me, and it makes me feel as though I could float away, I've become so much larger than I was. I immediately deflate when I see how angry he actually is that I laughed.

"Don't you laugh at me!" he says and he slaps my shoulder. "You think you're just so bloody clever. You don't even have the sense to.....*nnngnh*"

He waves his hands in the air and turns his back on me as he walks into the kitchen shouting.

"What the fuck is wrong with ME!" he continues, picking up a glass and hurling it into the wall with a shatter.

I startle and get up. The floor's cold and I'm naked as I head into the kitchen.

"Calm down," I say, trying to sound reasonable, and he wheels on me.

"Where is he?" Victor yells, taking a step toward me that is so determined I take one back. "Can you tell me that?"

"Johannesburg," I say.

"Johannesburg," he parrots, mimicking me rather better than I find comfortable. "I know his bloody location. I mean where is he when I need him?"

"He..."

"He wouldn't even stand for this from you! He'd slap you silly for talking like this."

"Like what?"

"Like that bloody museum I've been three quarters of a fucking widower over for two years now isn't exactly meant for that ad. It's pre-ordained fucking destiny and you know it. A museum of fucking industry that looks like that?" He gestures vaguely at my work area, at the lines of effort and muscle in stone. "It's a fucking triumph, and you know it."

"I told you that they..."

"I know what you told me. I'm neither deaf nor daft, despite what everybody seems to think of me."

"I don't."

He turns away and leans on the kitchen counter, all the long smooth muscles that make up the back of him are tensed.

"You realize, of course, that you're a bloody Liverpudlian, right? A local. With that design, no less. They fucking can't not say yes. They'd be stoned to death in the town square. If you don't put that in submission, I swear to god you'll never see me again. Or Tom. I know he'd feel the same way."

I blink. "You're bluffing."

"Try me, Carter Bennet. See just how strong I can be, why don't you?

I turn and go back to bed in silence, and within five or six seconds, I no longer exist to the waking world. Goodnight world.

For eighteen hours I stay like that, not caring who it worries, and not wanting to face anything. And not having to.

Apparently, I had reached my limits. Apparently, I had them.

If Andrew was testing me and training me to be his replacement, then so be it. I would comport myself accordingly. I stopped off and had a quick lunch of brioche and baked brie. I reviewed my notes to check and double check to see if there was anything there that would change my mind about Frank Cooper. I didn't find anything.

I found myself thinking about an interview I'd read with David Berkowitz, and cross referenced that with my conversations with Cooper. There were some similarities that made me uncomfortable, but Berkowitz had a much flatter way about him, even in his expressions of remorse. The banality of these killers was horrifying, and the scariest thing about them was their own detachment from their own experiences. As I understood it, that was part of what drove them to kill again, for those brief moments of vivid experience. They needed to chase that feeling over and over.

I was under no apprehension that I was trained for this, but Cooper did not feel like a serial killer to me. Not one in the way it's usually meant, anyway. He seemed to feel real remorse. His affect was too emotional. There was a sense with him, when you spoke to him, of real connection that I am told is absent with the actual sexual psychopath. Still, I was sure that he had killed these girls, and his own daughter. I had no understanding of what could push a man to that. I didn't have any wish to know. I just wanted to stop it, and I wanted to do it in the way that would provide the least amount of satisfaction and reward to Andrew Matheson. He had lost his privilege to be smug.

I left the restaurant and went to the library. After about fifteen minutes of research I found the person I was looking for. Dr. Tabitha Featherstone was a name that seemed to come up over and over in connection with multiple homicide cases that had been successfully solved. She was a behaviourist. Serial violence seemed to be her specialty. She used to teach, but now worked full time on consultation. It took some time to track down a number I could reach her at.

I went home and once I was confident I was alone, I rang her number. After a suitable number of transfers for a bureaucracy, a woman answered the phone. She sounded like she smoked, and was perpetually amused.

"This is Tabitha."

"Um, hello Dr. Featherstone. My name is Niles Townsend, and I'm wondering if you might spare a few minutes to help me investigate a series of murders?"

"Are you with Scotland Yard?" she asked.

"No," I said. "I'm a private detective. I've been hired by the family of one of the victims. He seems to feel the case has been given short shrift by the police."

She sighed in frustration. "Wouldn't be surprised. Is this a serial killing?"

"Well, that's the thing. I'm not quite certain. If it isn't, we're certainly meant to think it is."

"I see."

"I have photographs of the murder scenes, and I would really welcome your input. On all of it, really."

There was a pause on the other end. "Are you all right?"

"I've been looking at these photographs for a week. I'm starting to get used to them. So no."

"I understand completely. Do we have any suspects at all?'

"I'm not sure," I said. "Would I be able to come by and show you these things?"

"Yes. I'm at home, and you can come by. Please bring your credentials, if you would."

She gave me her address, and I told her I'd come by directly.

I drove to her house, which was all the way across the city, but at least still local, and parked the car. The first thing I noticed was that there were three closed circuit television cameras aimed at the doorstep and front yard. I'd never seen such a thing in my life. They tracked me as I walked up the steps and must have been fabulously expensive. Instead of a doorbell, there was an intercom with a hand-lettered sign instructing people to use it.

I pushed the button, and then I heard her voice.

"Hello," she said.

"Hello. I'm Niles."

"I see. Could you show your credentials to the camera please?"

"Of course."

I stepped back and opened my wallet to show my licence.

There was a sudden buzzing noise, and the door opened slowly and automatically.

"Please come in," she said, "and wait in the foyer."

I stepped into the foyer. It was a small room painted white, including the floor, and it had no furniture. There was another camera in the corner of the room. A few moments later, a white door clicked and opened inward, and she was standing there. She was very small, five feet or just under it, and kept her hair cut close to her skull. Her skin was dark brown, with eyes of a slightly lighter shade that drew immediate attention to her calm expression. She was dressed in a white blouse and black crepe slacks.

"Sorry about all this," she said. "I have what you might call fans."

"How lovely that must be for you."

"Yes," she said with a pinched, bitter smile. "Please come in, Mr. Townsend."

I went inside. It was just like the home of every professor I had known, a complicated filing system of books and papers that appeared to the naked eye like total chaos.

"Pardon the mess," she said. "I hate to clean."

"It doesn't bother me."

"Did you bring the pictures?"

"Yeah. Where is best to lay them out?"

She beckoned for me to follow her to a side room. It was a dining room table. I started to lay the photos out in pairs, before and after.

She took a pair of big blue framed glasses out of her pocket and put them on and leaned over the pictures. She stared at them, her eyes moving back and forth from image to image like the eyes of a raptor.

She looked up at me. "Who hired you?"

"The father of this girl. Sara Cooper," I said, pointing.

"Is she the most recent?"

"Yes."

"This is murder by rote."

"I'm not at all sure what you mean."

"This is not the work of a sexual psychopath, but it's most definitely the work of a person who wants to seem like one. The serial killer is excited. His work can be precise, but there's passion. He's often experiencing orgasms. These strokes are too steady. The killer was being careful, staying calm. It's dispassionate." She removed her specs, and tucked them in her pocket. "God help me, knife wounds are like brush strokes. They speak volumes."

"You're sure of this, then?"

"Positive. Is there any connection between the girls, aside from a similarity of appearance?"

"No, or at least not one we can see."

"I think you'll have to look harder."

"Right."

"It was the father of the Cooper girl, you think?"

"Um. Yes."

"You're very probably right. He's covering for his guilt. It's surprisingly common."

"So I would imagine." I began to pick up the photos.

"Does this help you at all?"

"Oh yes," I answered, looking at her. "I'll be firing the client for sure."

"Or Andrew will," she said quietly.

I looked at her open-mouthed. "Oh god," I said, with the sharp wit of a seasoned professional.

"I made some phone calls before you got here. I apologize. As I said, I have fans."

I nodded. "Does Andrew know?"

She shook her head.

I breathed out a slow sigh of relief.

"Andrew Matheson gets no favours from me."

I looked at her, shocked to hear anyone speak ill of him. Andrew, the beloved. Andrew, the feared and respected.

She looked back at me. "You do see it, don't you?"

"Yes," I said, not sure what I was talking about, but knowing what the answer was just the same.

"You be careful," she said, putting a hand on my wrist.

"Of Andrew?"

"Yes. Whatever it is he does to people, whatever power he has over them, I've never felt it. He's a mean-spirited gloating ass. And yet, all I ever see are people shaking his hand with great big smiles. He terrifies me. I can see in your eyes that he may have begun to terrify you. Whatever charisma he possesses, you're just as I am. Immune. I imagine you'd have to be to have any personality of your own left at all."

I finished packing the pictures up, and put them in my dossier. I did not reply to that. I'd no idea whatever to say.

"I have to be going," I said, not wanting to talk to her about Andrew anymore. This little taste had been enough. "Thank you so much."

"Yes. You're welcome. Be careful."

I did not look at her, and moved to the door. She showed me out quietly and put her hand on my back before I went out.

"I'm sorry, dear," she said, and I nodded, heading out to my car and driving back to the office in silence.

What wakes me is the strong smell of tobacco and a familiar weight on the bed beside me. I open my eyes blearily, and blink. It's nearly dusk again already, and I have a heaviness to my flesh that comes to me with too much sleep and not enough water. I turn over and I see Tom sitting on the bed with his knees up, smoking a cigarette. He has not yet noticed I'm awake or that I am looking at him. He is looking across the room. His skin is deeply tanned, and his blond hair is sun bleached. He is wearing a white linen shirt with the cuffs rolled back, and khaki trousers. He looks so much like a character from a film that it makes me smile. It dawns on me that I must be dreaming, and so I reach out and lay my arm across his lap, and breathe in the smell of him.

He strokes my hair, and I make a soft noise without meaning to.

"So, you're awake?" Tom says.

"Yes," I whisper, my throat dry and scratchy. "Is this a memory or is this happening right now?"

"How should I know?" Tom answers. "Christ, the way your mind works."

I don't know what happens next, so this must be happening now. I smile and sit up. "What are you doing here? You're supposed to be in Africa."

"Yeah," he says, "you've got that right."

I press my face against his. It's smooth, and I wish I knew how he did that. It's so hard to shave that well. I've always got a trace of stubble, especially in the hinge of my jaw.

"I'm glad you're here," I say. "Victor's insane when you go, and I've missed you."

"You're glad to see me, are you? Christ, I don't think you've thought this through."

I kiss the side of his neck and run my hand along his side, the warmth of him through the linen warming me in turn. For a lapsed Catholic, Christ weighs heavily on his vocabulary. I've missed it.

"No," he says, taking my hand up in his to give it a light little friendly kiss. "None of that."

I cock my head, more surprised than anything, and I look at him. "Is Victor here? We had a fight, but I don't want him to miss you."

"He's gone down to the shops to pick up groceries. We've spoken."

"All right."

"You pong, you filthy bugger. I've been in slums that smell better than you do right now. That's to be expected considering you've laid about here for god knows how long."

I smile. I love the way he talks, the way everything in his life and mind is just a bit more vivid than real life is.

"Are you asking me to have a shower?" I say.

"I'm telling you to have a shower, mate."

I kiss his lips and go into the bathroom, and lie down in the cool water. A thrill of relief comes through me at once, life pouring back into the desiccated fibres that weave around each other and make up my body. There is the silence, and I am too excited to listen to the sounds behind the silence. I let myself come awake and alive, and then I wash and shave.

I go back into the bedroom and dress. Tom is reading something he has in a notebook. He is reading it as though he is reading it over and over again. I pay no mind to what I actually put on, but it is comfortable. The sweater has a hood I can pull up, and I do, because my wet hair is freezing me half to death.

"Are you sufficiently hydrated to speak too?" Tom says to me, and I hear the knife's edge in his voice.

"Yes," I say. "Thank you for remembering."

"How could I forget? Christ. As if your bizarre assortment of quirks and fetishes has ever strayed far from my mind."

His rumbling, cigarette stained voice is still strange and beautiful and frightening, like seeing a child speak with it would be.

"Are you hungry?" I ask him. "I'm starving."

"Well," he says, "I could murder a Liverpudlian."

I blink for a second, trying to remember if that is a sandwich or something I've forgotten. He means me, I realize, and I don't know whether to smile or be angry.

"What did I do?" I say, and walk to the kitchen, where I start eating a handful of leftover chips from the fridge. I like them cold.

"I should be in fucking South Africa, right now. Would you like to know why I'm not?"

"Of course." I pour a glass of milk and start to drink it.

"I'm here, you fucking tosser, because Victor called me and told me you were about to heave your life into a rubbish bin and, after some discussion, I found, to my commingled surprise and horror, that the drunken clot was right."

My eyes narrowed. "Victor's working on the drink, okay? Without your help, I could point out."

"Right," he said, "Let's make this that sort of conversation from the start, shall we? Christ."

"Well look," I say. "I understand it's your job and everything, but if you're going to be halfway around the world all the time, then I think you might want to consider how much right you've got telling us how to live when you're gone. It's not easy for him, you know."

SLEEPING UNDERWATER

"Do I ever, Christ? It's not like I get much of a chance to forget it. It's not my fault that he wants someone to tell him what to do all the time, any more than it's your fault you're crap at it."

I recoil as though he's slapped me, finding that very hurtful without knowing why. "You've clearly come all the way across the world to hurt my feelings, so why don't you just get on with it?"

"Christ," he says, "if all I'd wanted to do was yell at you, there's the telephone isn't there?"

"Maybe you should have used it," I say, "and spared us all the pain of refreshing our memories as to what you look like."

He raises a hand as if he is thinking of slapping me, and then he clenches his fist and slams it into the wall. I try not to let my face change, but it does, from fear to concern. I can't keep from my own face what is going on in my head, and never have done.

He pulls his hand back, and his knuckles are split.

"Fuck," he says, and he heads to the sink, and lets the water run out in a measly trickle to clean his hand. He takes the dish towel and wraps it around his hand and doesn't speak to me for several minutes. He sits at the kitchen table and smokes, trying to calm himself down. I stand by the fridge as though I am rooted there, and I drink cold milk.

"You've got to do it, son," he says to me. "You and I both know it, and even Victor knows it. Come on and be sensible will you?"

"Stop riding Victor."

He turns to me. "He's not here. Look, I love Victor. Christ, if I didn't would I be so angry? You know full well he's lost his mind, and I fucking refuse to take responsibility for that. He knew I worked the international desk when this all started, and I thought that having you here with him would make it easier when I was gone."

"Yeah," I say. "Guess I wasn't quite good enough."

"Stuff that. You know just the same as I do what's wrong with Victor. And you know full well it's nothing at all to do with either of us. He's only happy when he's being told what to do every moment of every day. I don't want to do it, and you bloody can't. And neither one of us should have to in the first place"

"He's trying, Tom. You haven't been here."

"People don't change. Christ."

"I have."

"Yeah. Okay. You have."

"But I'm not people."

"No. You're not. God only knows what you are. People isn't it."

There's nothing but love in his words, and that's all that keeps my heart from shattering as I nod.

"I don't like ultimatums," he says. "But Victor's right. If you don't submit your design for this thing, then, as God is my witness, I don't want to see you anymore. I couldn't bear it."

My eyes well up and I look downwards. "Well, goodbye then. Nice knowing you."

"Oh so that's it, is it?"

"I guess so."

He stands up and comes over to me, putting his hands on my shoulders. I squirm back and look up at him angrily. "Don't you touch me. You're a fucking bully."

He drops his hands to his sides. "I'm not bullying you."

"Yes," I say, "you bloody are."

"I'm being honest. If you don't submit, I couldn't bear to see you again. I couldn't bear to see you having rejected your fucking destiny because you're a coward."

"Coward? What would you know about it? You're so scared of everything you can't stay in one place for more than a fortnight."

"That's not why I travel, you know that, and, as comment, it's beneath you."

"Fuck you."

"And also unto you."

I turn my back on him. I walk into what passes for the living room and stare out the window.

"You don't know what it's like to be famous," I say. "You don't."

"I don't care what it's like," he says. "It's what you're going to be. You can't change that."

"I can," I say, and turn back to look at him.

"Well," he says. "You decide what you have to decide. That's your choice, and none of mine."

"I love you."

"I love you, too," he says, "but I love the idea of you even more. If you kill that idea, then I'll have no use left for you."

I hate him, and I hate Victor, and I remember in a rush all the reasons why other people are not worth the time and trouble of getting to know. Most of all, I hate my building. I hate every line in every drawing and I hate myself for having made it. I hate being different, and I hate being talented, and what I want more than anything else is to go back to bed.

I cry, and Tom puts his arms around me.

"I'm sorry," he says. "I wish it weren't true, but it is. Your talent, Christ. It's so much bigger than three people in a flat in London, and I'd be committing a crime against God to let it stay here with just us."

"You commit a crime against God every time you kiss me," I say to him.

"Not my God, love. Mine's a right bastard too, but this much he understands."

I cry into his shoulder, wanting him to stay here forever, but I know this time next month he'll be in Haiti, and Victor will already trying to figure out what he'll wear to the ribbon cutting ceremonies.

I decided on one more stop. I wanted to meet Wendy Cooper. Thus far I had dealt only with Frank Cooper. Frank had made it clear to Andrew that he wanted his wife kept well clear of the whole business. As he was the client, and as we'd seen no pressing reason not to, we'd obeyed. As far as I was concerned that obligation was meaningless now. I drove to the house. Frank was still at work at this time of day, and that was what I wanted. I knocked on the front door, and I waited.

A few moments later, a nurse answered the door in a pink pastel uniform. I smiled my very most charming smile.

"Mrs. Cooper?" I said.

"No," the nurse answered. "I'm Leanne. I'm Wendy's home care nurse."

"Of course. May I see Wendy?"

She looked askance at me. "Who are you, then?"

"I'm Niles Townsend. I'm a private investigator. I've been trying to find out who killed Sara. I thought she might have some information."

I was a little nervous and felt exposed having revealed this much truth.

"Oh god," Leanne said, pushing her salt and pepper hair back from a broad strong face. "Isn't that fucking horrible, what happened to our girl?"

"Yes," I said.

"You won't get much out of Gwendolyn, though. Mrs. Cooper has been in a coma for months now."

"What?"

"This poor family. I do not know how Frank will get on. I don't really."

"Is she expected to recover?" I asked.

"No. To be honest, Frank should sign the order to let her go. He can't afford this, and I feel a bit crap every day I come in and collect a wage."

I had no idea what to say in response to that.

"Thank you," I said. "Can I ask you something personal, off the record?"

She nodded.

"What do you think of Frank Cooper?"

"I don't know what you mean, sir."

"I mean, personally. What do you make of him?"

"I don't know sir. He's a good man, but losing his daughter did something to him. He's gone all empty, I think."

"Empty?"

"Yeah. Used to be he'd watch TV or read a book. Sometimes, he'd read to Gwen. Now he gets home and he just sits and stares into space until I remind him he should eat something. It's sad. Just the same thing every day, like a bloody robot. I keep hoping he'll snap out of it."

She sighed. "I need a new situation, really. This place is breaking my heart, love. I don't mind telling you."

"Do that," I said to her. "As soon as possible. In fact, today. You seem like a good person, and you don't deserve to be wrapped up in this."

"Wrapped up in what?" she said, her voice amused or worried. I don't think she knew which herself.

I said nothing. I just turned, got in my car and turned the corner in it. I was waiting for Frank Cooper to come home. He got off his bus a few feet up the street. I spotted him. I pulled up beside him and got out.

"Mr. Cooper," I said, "have you got a moment?"

He looked at me for a moment with no recognition. Then with a near audible click, he started to talk to me. "Niles?"

"Yes sir."

"Have we found out who killed my daughter?"

"Yes, I think I have sir."

He looked at me with no trace of worry.

"Good," he said. "Have you contacted the police?"

"Not yet, sir. I wanted to talk to you first."

"All right, then."

"Mr. Cooper? Your wife has been in a coma. She hasn't asked you to hire anyone. Are you going to tell me what is actually going on?"

He started to walk again. His gait was wavery, like a man after strong drink. I followed along beside him. He was reaching for something in his pocket and I kept a safe distance even as I tried to keep up with him, well from arm's reach.

It takes a lot less time and effort for a man to cut his own throat than you'd think. It needs to be said also, however, that there is more blood than you'd ever guess.

The straight razor fell to the pavement an instant before the rest of him did. I put my hands against the wound, trying to keep the blood in, and screamed for someone, anyone, to call an ambulance. It was no use, of course. I felt the last pulse of him slip between my fingers and as he died, there was the smell of shit that nobody talks about.

It was all too real to be borne.

What wakes me is the strong smell of tobacco and a familiar weight on the bed beside me. I open my eyes blearily, and blink. It's nearly dusk again, and I have a heaviness to my flesh that comes to me with too much sleep and not enough water. I turn over and I see Tom sitting on the bed with his knees up, smoking a cigarette. He has not yet noticed I'm awake or looking at him. He is looking across the room. His skin is deeply tanned, and his blond hair is sun bleached. He is wearing a white linen shirt with the cuffs rolled back and khaki trousers. He looks so much like a character from a film that it makes me smile. It dawns on me that I must be dreaming, and so I reach out and lay my arm across his lap, and breathe in the smell of him.

He strokes my hair, and I make a soft noise without meaning to.

"So, you're awake?" Tom says.

"Yes," I whisper, my throat dry and scratchy. "Is this a memory or is this happening right now?"

"How should I know?" Tom answers. "Christ, the way your mind works."

I remember the fight to come, and I realize this is only a memory this time around. I blink my eyes and stare at the ceiling, and Tom is gone. For weeks now.

He's moved his gear into a storage locker, and the place is starting not to smell like him anymore. Every day I am forced to breathe deeper.

Victor is asleep on the bed beside me, arms and legs sprawling, lying on his belly. He has not shaved in over a week. I don't know when the last time he ate. He and I had sex last night. I could not call it making love. He would not look at me. He barely speaks. We are alone again, as always. Nothing is different this time, except that everything is. Every time he has flown off to some deadly place I've been forced to make peace with the fact he might not come home. Victor never has, but that's how his mind is built. He doesn't believe in the possibility of death. It's something that happens in the papers and on telly. He doesn't really grasp it.

I do. I've been there. I remember dying. I remember the slow shallowing of breath and the letting go. The terror and the strange feeling at the very moment like a rush of warmth, like drowning, and then nothing until being pressed out of the warm and throbbing water into the world again, screaming because the peace is over.

It's not to be feared. Not really. Loneliness is much worse. There's a lot worse that life has to offer you than death.

This time, if Tom returns, he'll come as an old friend, and nothing more. Perhaps we'll make love. Most likely we will not. I think that would be more painful for all of us. In this relationship, this bed, there are just the two of us, now. Victor feels Tom's absence much more deeply than I do. I had gotten used to Tom as a presence that came in and out of my life at random. I was always happy to see him. I loved his face and his voice and how he advocated fiercely for the people he loved, and how it turned every conversation into an argument you wanted to lose. There was so much anger and love in him, twisted together.

He loved us. He loves us now, and that's why he quit. He didn't want to hurt Victor anymore, and didn't want to keep disappointing me. I told him he wasn't disappointing me, and that's when he got really angry. I shouldn't have said that. I should have realized.

He is in Haiti now, one of the deadliest places on Earth, because it's where he belongs, a half-inch from the end of things. He stayed a half-inch from the end of us for three years, and felt he owed us a finish. Owed himself too, I imagine.

Victor blames me, because if he hadn't made Tom come home to yell at me, Tom wouldn't have left us. The logic of his argument is inarguable in the way that nonsense often is. He needs someone to blame who isn't Tom. Tom has no flaws in Victor's eyes. Victor believes that if he had been somehow a better lover that Tom would not have traveled.

Victor is, these days, less grounded in the world than I am. This is a prospect that should terrify him, but it doesn't.

I hold him in my arms while he sleeps restlessly.

"I love you," I whisper at him. "Truly."

I have sent in the design. I have not left this flat since. Victor goes to work, Victor comes home. It is quiet either way. My loans are running out. I will take a job soon, but, in the meantime, I am luxuriating in my precious obscurity. I want nothing more than to stay in this bed and lie next to him. I only wish he did not want so badly to escape it.

Victor squirms out of my grasp, still asleep and still angry.

I punch him in the lower back, frustrated. "Jerk."

I roll over and try to sleep. I can't. The sun is coming in the window, aggressively cheerfully, like my mother on every bloody school day ever. I give up. I get up. I shower. I do not lie in the tub. I don't linger. Numb is how I want to feel right now.

I cook a pan full of scrambled eggs and eat them from the pan. I look at the paper to see what is going on in the world. It's hell as always. I look for news of Haiti, and I find nothing. No byline from him. Just as well.

I go to my drawing board and mean to start sketching some ideas I had for an office building, but the pencil moves of its own and I realize I'm drawing Tom. He is looking out the window next to my table here. He is smoking, of course. His shirt is off, and in his hands. We can only see the back of him, lean and lined with the deep scars his father left him. I am crying.

I remember Victor warning me about the scars, because it seemed as if things were headed into sex that night, and he didn't want me to be shocked.

I remember kissing them, my face moving over his back, kissing each lash mark while Tom and Victor made furious love. I was so shy, but I wanted to express it, express something so dim and so poorly understood to me.

It's painful to remember how little I had to give. It is more painful to think how much more I wanted to take.

When Victor comes out, my head is down across the sketch and he picks me up and sets me on the couch, and puts an arm around me, holding me and kissing the top of my head. I love it when he carries me, though I know I should find it shameful to be so small. I love it because it makes him stronger, and he needs that, needs to feel it. He needs to control something. If not his own life, then let it be me.

"Hold me tighter," I say. "Squeeze."

He squeezes me tighter, his strength surprising, and I love it.

"More," I say, my voice demanding, and he wraps tighter around me, until I cannot breathe. This. This is what I wanted. I feel myself stirring, growing hard against him, and I hear breath catch in his throat. I press my face to his neck and bite him hard. He moans. I am feeling faint and dizzy, black spots in the corner of my eyes.

"More," I whisper, almost inaudibly and he lets me go, the oxygen slams into me by instinct and I fall back on the couch. He takes me in his mouth and begins to bring me up from the dark. I feel my heart shake me as it beats. I arch into his soft questing mouth and I lose all track of myself and him.

I come and, with that, comes a scream of pain and need.

He lies atop me and holds me, kisses me, and I feel as though I'm leaving the water for good. He is holding me and making me breathe. Five fingers, five toes. Angry, frightened, and knowing nothing.

Yes. All in order.

I spent several hours talking with the police about the suicide. They made me sit in a small room, my suit soaked through with his gore, and asked me the same questions over and over in different ways. As blood dries, it contracts a bit, making my shirt uncomfortable and pulling the tiny hairs so that they pinch and make me want to scratch. Then I'd have had him under my nails.

SLEEPING UNDERWATER

The thought of that was even worse. They let me sit there, playing the games they play, while I said nothing. They did this despite the three witnesses to his suicide. I asked for my solicitor and then said nothing else, as one simply must do, and nobody ever does. The drying blood began to smell faintly of rot, and still they harangued me. They wanted to believe I'd murdered their suspect. It was less horrible that way.

When my solicitor arrived, he congratulated me on my silence. He told me there'd be a dear price paid for them forcing me to sit about in bloody clothes. I didn't care. I wanted to leave.

Within half an hour, I was released without charges. As I was leaving, a detective with deep furrowed lines in his olive face came over to me, his eyes hard to read, but not violent.

"How'd you do it, then?" he asked. "Off the record, like."

"Nothing is off the record," I answered, my solicitor nodding slightly.

"Did you talk him into it?" the detective said. "The crazy bastard."

"No," I said. "It was remorse, I expect."

He laughed. "These monsters don't feel remorse, son, and I think you know it."

I shook my head.

"Well, good for you," he said, "He's done fine with you, Matheson has."

I looked at him with what I'm sure was anger. "What do you mean by that?"

"If he thought it would save him a court date, he'd talk a man to death. I'd like to see it, personally. Cheers."

I swallowed and shook my head. He clapped my shoulder and walked away. I briefly considered what would happen if I bashed a police official with a chair. The complications spiraled on in my already dizzy mind. I let it go.

I wanted nothing at the moment but clean clothes and a shower. Any conversation with Andrew could wait. We were going to have one, and I was going to ask him some very pointed questions, but I would do so once I was clean and impeccably dressed.

My solicitor dropped me at my car, which was still behind the police cordon. I showed ID to get it, and I started the drive home.

I was sure Andrew had heard of this by now. He had friends everywhere. He hadn't come by, nor had he sent his solicitor. Either he didn't think there was any trouble, or he was angry.

Probably he was angry because I had stopped the money train. I hoped that he was angry enough to give me the cold shoulder for a while. That would give me the time I needed to be sick, and then crawl my way back to civilized and dapper junior detective from blood-soaked soul-weary ape. As I turned the corner into the car park, I was happy not to see his Jag out front of our place. I was rather more troubled to find a stack of boxes from a professional mover on the lawn out front.

I got out of my car, came closer, and saw they each had my name on them. They were labeled by room and given numbered stickers, as they do. There were forty-one of them, and they seemed to hold all that I owned. The packing date was for that day. I stared at them.

Fuck this grand-standing nonsense, I thought, and I headed in. My key still let me in the building but, when I went up the stairs, I saw that he had had new knobs and deadbolts installed. The smell of sawdust was still in the hall. I tried my key anyway, for some mad reason. I needn't have bothered.

I rooted through the boxes on the lawn to find clean clothes and threw them in my back seat. I drove to the office so that I could clean up. I was furious, and hurt, but the day had been so shocking and so full of adrenaline and fear that I was too numb for it to register. I was simply doing whatever it took to get clean and dressed, in a dreamlike, single-minded way.

I parked in the underground car park and took the elevator to our floor. When I got to the office, the doors were locked and chained. A piece of A4 was taped to the door with a handwritten note that told casual readers the agency was closed for the foreseeable future. I sat in the hall, leaning against the door. I put my elbows on my knees and my head in my hands. I ran my fingers through my bloody hair and took deep breaths, trying to figure out what, if anything, I could do.

I was roused from this moment of reflection and peace by the gentle nudging of an enormous black leather shoe against my leg. I looked up and saw a tall, dangerous looking man with short dark hair, and a broad build. From my vantage point he looked to be a hundred feet tall. Six and a half at least.

"You Niles Townsend, then?"

"Yes."

He offered a hand to help me up and I took it. He pulled me up with a frightening casual strength. "Andrew asked me to deliver a message to you."

I answered without changing my face in any way I was aware of.

"He says that you and he are quits. He says you are to stay away from him and his business from here on out. If you don't, he intends to have me kill you."

I stare at him.

"Tell him he's an asshole, and that I'll be talking to him very soon. As for you, what is he paying you?"

"It doesn't matter," he says. "It's a matter of professional ethics. He hired me first. I'll have to kill you if he calls for it. It's not personal. It's my job."

He shrugged innocently, as though making friendly small talk, and I found it pleasant in an odd sort of a way.

"Oh," I said, feeling I might have offended. "Well, of course. But do deliver the message, if you would."

He sighed and put his hands in his pockets. "Must I really? You seem a decent bloke."

"I am. Top notch. I do have to insist, sorry."

"Well, I expect I'll be seeing you then. Cheers."

He nodded and offered me a hand to shake. I shook it.

"Name's Des," he said. "Lay low. I'm really awfully good at what I do."

"Will do," I said as he left, and I wondered if I should go down to my car or not, what with Andrew only a phone call away. I went out the back staircase and into the alley, my heart pounding, and I headed to the street, where I flagged a taxi. My clean clothes were still on the seat of my car. I started to cry softly in the back seat hoping against hope the cabbie didn't look at me very closely. He didn't. He did ask me where we were going. I didn't know. Finally, I gave him Janice's address.

When we pulled up outside Janice's house, I paid, and staggered to her front door, filthy and soaked in the middle of the night. I rang the bell, and I waited patiently. The cab pulled away, the sound of its engine fading into quiet night. I waited long enough that I feared she was out. Then I heard the faint sounds of motions from upstairs, and then feet padding and the snuffling sounds of her sheepdog on the other side of the oaken door. She opened it, looking worried and cross, and then she saw me.

"Oh. Oh Niles. Look at you, you're just miserable."

I opened my mouth to say something, but I wasn't able to.

"Are you hurt?" she asked, immediately mothering me and I had to bring my hands up gently to keep her from getting Jack Cooper's remains all over herself.

"I'm fine," I said. "It's not mine. A man killed himself next to me. I need to shower, Jan. I'm sorry. I have to shower."

She didn't ask why I was there, nor did she fuss me at all. Home is the place where when you go there covered in human remains, they let you use the shower.

"Of course. For god's sake, come in."

I went in carefully, leaving my shoes at the door. I knew where the shower was. I'd crashed on her couch many, many times in the past. I went in and locked the door behind myself, and proceeded to get undressed. I left my clothes in a pile on the pink porcelain tile. I looked at the mirror on the medicine cabinet, and the small plaque of a kitten playing with a roll of bog paper. I turned on the shower and let the water run a moment before getting in. Once I stepped in, the tub immediately looked like a video nasty. So much blood in a man, and so much of his on me.

I soaped myself again and again under the hot water until I was pink from head to toe and the water ran clear. I turned off the water, got out, and used a towel from the basket of towels she kept for guests, god love her. God love all women, actually. I looked at myself in the mirror. What are you, I asked myself. Are you sad? Are you tired? Are you scared?

No, my face answered, this is anger. You might not recognize me.

But you will.

I swallowed and knocked on the bathroom door.

"Janice," I called. "Have you got a robe or something? I've not got any clothes."

She laughed, with a mixture of delight and lechery, and I smiled in spite of myself.

I had been a shitty friend to her for years. She was still a good one to me.

I am wearing a suit, sitting in an office high above the ground. There is me on one side of a table and, on the other, an assortment of terrifying people also in suits. We are discussing my future. This future includes overseeing the construction of the Museum of

Industry in Liverpool. I will have a staff to handle a lot of the practical details, which is to the good as I know nothing about actually supervising anyone. The very idea seems foreign to me.

I will be moving to Liverpool. There's really no other choice, though I swore I would never go back.

My salary will be a lot more money than I had expected ever to make. It will persist for the next several years, until my part is finished. At that point, the firm will most certainly want to offer me a position as a senior architect.

I accept and shake hands. As I'm leaving, I overhear them talking about how shy and quiet I am. This is rare for architects, it seems. Happily, they don't seem bothered, only curious. I am fine with that. Victor is waiting outside in the car. He is dressed in a suit, for some reason. I have an excuse.

"So?" he says, "What happened?"

"I got the job. They're building the museum."

"Oh my god!" Victor giggles like a child. "They know you're just a crazy person, right?"

"I assume it was obvious."

He kisses me and gives me a hug. "I can't believe it. Tom is going to shit himself!"

"I hate that expression."

"He will, though!"

"The world should be so lucky that dysentery be caused by success. There'd be less of it."

"We have to call him."

"Yeah," I say. "We will."

He starts the car, and proceeds to drive us away. "Dinner is on you, Mr. Soon-to-be-world-famous-architect."

"Sure. Why not?"

"Oh god. Champagne. We're having champagne."

"Look, Victor," I say. "It's not all good news. I can't stay in London. The museum's in Liverpool."

He laughs. "Who gives a shit for London? We'll live in Liverpool. All the boys have your sexy little accent there. I'm sure I'll be quite happy."

"What about your job?"

"Sod the job. As if what I bring in matters a toss. I'll stay at home and cook and clean and all that. I'll be your perfect little housewife."

"Complete with the valium and alcohol problem," I add, and he thinks I'm kidding.

"Oh, of course. The madness and boredom sneaking up on me so gradually that all are surprised when I walk into the Tesco with a gun."

"Ha ha," I say, and he thinks I'm laughing.

He bounces in his seat and nearly drives into the oncoming lane.

"Jesus, drive will you? Christ!"

He laughs again and looks at me. "Yes, Tom. All right."

I flip him off, smiling. "Look, Victor. I want you to come along. I do. But you'll have to find a job. It's not the money. I couldn't give a damn. It's for you. I don't want you at home all day. I want you back in university or something. Okay?"

He shrugs noncommittally. "Yeah, okay."

I take this to mean exactly what it does mean. He will think on it, but he will not think hard. I let it go. It's a series of small battles with Victor. And I love him, so what else is left to me but to fight them. It's possibly been good for me. And he's gone to considerable effort for me, hasn't he?

"Tom is going to be so proud of you," he says, and it's good to hear him speak of Tom with fondness instead of as if we were speaking of Satan, the great betrayer.

"I don't think he will," I say. "I think he'd just be disappointed if I'd done less."

Victor shrugs. "Who knows what he'd think? The cranky, faithless bastard."

I laugh. "It's possible you need to move on, my love."

"Fuck that. Moving on is for suckers."

"I'm starving," I say. "Take me to a restaurant and stop talking to me."

"With pleasure," he says, and he turns the radio up loud. The Smiths fill the car with indulgent self-pity, and we drive on laughing like a pair of idiots.

Janice stared at me across from breakfast once I'd finished telling her the entire story. She was having a vodka and orange juice for breakfast. This was a cornerstone of our friendship, actually, that we both liked to drink a great deal and never took the piss out of each other for it. That sounds much more horrible than I mean. I mean that judgement, actual judgement, rather than mockery for the sake of fun, was not a part of us.

"That's all really strange and horrible, but I don't understand any of it." She looked at me and leaned back in her chair slightly.

"Don't look at me," I said. "You can play Dr. Watson all you like, but it won't make me Sherlock Holmes. I'm sure I've seen any number of clues, but I'm fucked if I can piece a coherent narrative out of any of this."

She nodded. "Do you at least have any idea why Andrew is so very angry? I mean he's got a reputation for having a temper but I can't believe he'd hire a man to kill you. It must be a joke or something. I mean, he's got a reputation hasn't he? He's one of the good guys."

I looked her in the eyes. "Why, exactly, are you so fond of him?"

She hesitated for just a moment and then smiled. "Well for heaven's sake, why wouldn't I be? He's tall and blond and gorgeous."

"And gay," I added.

"Naturally," she said rolling her eyes in mock frustration. "And he's mysterious and brave. Have you heard the story of how he got Danny's sister back? It's bloody amazing, and he's got loads just like them. Quite literally everyone loves him."

"You needn't tell me. I loved him too. I'm aware that he has considerable charm and charisma, and he can be very kind, but I can't be the only one in the world who's noticed he's a bit of a shit to people?"

"Oh that," she said, waving her hand dismissively. "He's so obviously playing the part of the curmudgeon. He doesn't mean it. You can tell."

"No," I say, "Really. He means it. I swear. He can't stand people. He hates people. He doesn't trust anyone. He's never trusted me in all the time I've known him. He was just managing me. We shared a bed, damn it."

"And aren't you the lucky devil there?"

I shook my head. "Janice, he's threatened to have me killed."

"Oh, it's probably part of one of his tests. That's all it is. He's training you. He probably wanted to have you figure it out on your own."

"No," I said. "He's fucking about with me. And somehow he's responsible for Frank Cooper's death. Somehow."

111

"Niles," she said, exasperated, "That's ridiculous. You'd all but confronted him for his crime, and he took the easy way out of it."

"No. That is not what happened. It just isn't." I didn't go on to explain that there didn't seem to be anything easy at all about the way he'd died.

She shrugged. "You're distraught. It's to be expected. You've been traumatized. The man died in your lap. You're also probably upset because you'd been feeling sorry for him. Maybe you still do?"

"Hell yes, I felt bad for him! My God, even if he did do it, I feel pity for him. What could drive a man so crazy that he'd go and do all that he's done?"

"Ah Niles, my sweet romantic boy. Perhaps he was just an evil shit."

"Evil," I said evenly.

"Yes."

"Big 'e' Evil?" I followed up.

"Mm," she said nodding.

"There is," I said, "no such fucking thing. There's weak and strong. There's selfish and there's giving. There's no good, and there's no evil."

"We'll have to agree to disagree, there, my love. I'm not a religious woman, but I've seen enough of the world to believe in evil. Most of the time, you're right, people do terrible things for stupid reasons. Sometimes, more often than I'd like to think, though, someone is just evil, or something just takes a hold of them."

She stopped suddenly, and looked at me. She frowned and a little crease formed above the bridge of her nose. "Never mind me. None of that matters. What matters is that you stood right next to a man who killed himself. You're not going to be quite right about that, or much of anything for awhile, and that's all right. We'll muddle through. We always do.

She reached a hand across the table and I took it.

"I'm sorry, Jan," I said. "I know I've not been much of a friend of late."

She waved a hand dismissively. "Pish. You've only just recently found your first love. It has a tendency to make one into a bit of an empty presence for awhile. I'm sorry it didn't work out, but you're one of the good ones, and you'll find someone who deserves you, if this all turns out to be an actual breakup and not just, you know, one of those things."

I squeezed her hand, and smiled. I loved this woman, and I wished I could be in love with her. At one point, I think she'd have wanted that. I think she'd moved on by now. I hoped she had. In any case, I did love her.

Her phone rang, and she squeezed back, and then let go. "Must get that, probably work."

She crossed across her kitchen, and lifted the phone. "Janice P—"

She stopped abruptly. She held the phone to her ear with her left hand, and her right arm seemed to go slack. I could hear a faint buzzing as someone spoke to her on the other line, and I took a sip of orange juice.

She set the handset next to her phone on the counter, and crossed over and opened one of her drawers. From it she took a large knife, and then, before I could react, raised it and swung it down across the tip of the index finger of her other hand. The tip flew through the air like a bit of errant celery and hit the floor.

Her eyes were fixed on a point on the wall behind my head, empty and calm. She did not scream as her blood spurted across the formica counter.

I screamed for both of us, as her dog nosed uncertainly at the piece of her mistress. I grabbed a tea towel off the counter and began to wrap her hand in it, demanding she hold it tightly. She looked at me with empty eyes and a fixed dreamlike smile on her face.

I needed to call the ambulance. I picked up the phone, and Andrew was on the other end.

"Hello, Niles," he said. "I got your message from Desmond. Keep well the fuck away from me, or next time, I will have her slit her own throat. You don't have enough friends left in the world to spare one, do you?"

I made a choking noise in the back of my throat, and the line went dead.

I stared at the handset for a couple of seconds, and then did what needed doing urgently.

I called an ambulance while she stood and stared at me. I was wearing a white terrycloth robe and some underpants belonging to one of her endless string of younger boy toys. The terrycloth was very absorbent and I was covered in blood. Again. I held her in my arms until the ambulance arrived, and just before they pulled her to the gurney she whispered in my ear.

"And another thing, Niles," she said, sounding uncannily like him. The sound of his voice coming through her lips seemed to startle her as much as it shook me. She twitched as though coming out of a trance. "Get your shit off my lawn," she screamed in a panic, and then sobbed and screamed in pain as if feeling it for the first time.

They pushed her into the back of the ambulance and told me where they were taking her.

I went back in the house, and tried to clean up. I threw the tip of her finger in the trash, not sure if that's what one did. I wiped up blood. The dog paced and watched me nervously.

Her telephone rang again and, at first, I barely knew what to do. In a haze I picked it up.

"Janice's residence. This is Niles Townsend."

"Ah, you are there," another familiar voice said.

"Des?" I asked.

"Yes. I'm afraid so."

"I should very probably run away right now, shouldn't I?"

"Yes," he said. "I've one of these car phones."

"Right. Kind of you to call."

"Not really," he said. "Wanted to be sure. Everyone answers the phone. Everyone."

I heard an ambulance on the other end of the line, and my heart lurched into my throat.

"Christ," I said, "What have I done to deserve this?"

"Nobody deserves what I do, mate. See you soon."

"Ta," I said.

I hung up the phone and ran upstairs to throw on a pair of jeans and a black t-shirt. I had no chance of running. I had to make a stand of some kind right here and now, and in another man's clothes. I stood by Janet's bed and looked for something useful. Her cigarettes were by the bed, on her reading table. There was a silver Zippo lighter with inset mother of pearl, her initials engraved upon it. I grabbed a can of her hairspray and assessed my situation.

I heard his car pull up outside and laid down under Janice's bed, trying to breathe softly and evenly. I tried to remember the breathing exercises Andrew had taught me. The key to success in a tactical situation was to be the least adrenalized one involved.

SLEEPING UNDERWATER

The front door was still open, and I could hear Des walking around downstairs. He was calling my name softly, inviting me to come out and make this quick. He seemed to mean it. He was a very polite sort of psychopath. I stayed put. Eventually he'd come to me.

I heard him come into the bedroom. His foot nudged the terrycloth robe. I lit the lighter and he heard the click, or smelled the fuel, and he froze. I reached from under the comforter and sprayed the hairspray at once. A jet of flame sprayed with it. The bedding caught fire and the flames burst past it, over the carpet and over his legs. Des screamed in shock and pain. No matter how well trained you are, it's surprising to be on fire.

He dropped his gun. Tossing the can away, I rolled out and across some hot melted carpet to get it, burning myself, too. I hoped it was more painful than deep, and just tried not to look, and to keep moving, grabbing up Des' gun while he kicked and slapped at his legs. Standing up, breathing hard, I pointed the gun at him.

"Surprise," I said, looking at him.

His eyes were full of tears and I could see through the holes in his trousers that blisters had already formed and burst. His charred flesh was running and he could not manage to speak as he fell to his rear end, landing away from the melted carpet.

He closed his eyes and tears ran. He looked like a child, so surprised now that it was real. My stomach churned at the stink, and I threw up on the floor. He leaned back against a chest of drawers. He was in shock. I put the safety on the gun, and tucked it in the back of my jeans, pulling my shirt over it.

"I'll call an ambulance," I said.

I did so, setting the phone on the counter as the operator tried to confirm that we needed a second one. I filled the dog's food bowl. Then I got in my car, and drove straight for my flat. Andrew's flat. I let the terror take over on me, and the horror. I prepared myself mentally to put every bullet I had at hand into Andrew. If I had the stomach for it, this gun was an opportunity. It would never end up traced back to me. I wasn't sure I did have the stomach, mind you. I had no real idea just what I was going to do.

115

LAIRD RYAN STATES

Every time I see my picture in the paper, or I am recognized by strangers in the street, my stomach aches. I have taken to abusing antacids. I carry rolls and rolls of them in my pockets and eat them constantly. The corners of my mouth are usually flecked with lemon yellow smudges as a result. My co-workers tease me about them as if they were a little flask of gin that I kept in my coat pocket.

In the last six months I have been introduced to everyone in the United Kingdom. I have been forced to shake hands with most of them. I have met the royal family. The Prince of Wales smiled politely at me, and engaged me in small talk. The next day he slagged the Museum off in the press. He called it a carbuncle, and a shameful example of the death of dignity in modern design. I have never liked princes. Not one of them has ever taken to me. They see some hint of what I am and it makes them nervous.

Victor is delighted by the money and the attention I'm getting. He is less delighted by the fact that he can come to none of these parties. In this place and time, there is no way that our love could be a matter of public knowledge. The tabloid press has not prodded or probed, and I have found that curious. Perhaps Tom has called in favours, or, just as probably, the powers that be cannot afford to let it be known what I am until this building is entirely finished and open for business.

At least Victor does not blame me for it. He is the first one to make sure nothing interferes with my success. He spends his days at home, collecting articles, and acting as my personal assistant. He books my interviews and appointments and makes sure my clothes are laid out for me.

I lie in bed beside him at night, my tongue chalky and sour and my body bone tired. I am soul sick of being known. The building leaves me alone in my dreams, doubtless because it takes up my every waking moment now. He strokes my hair and whispers kind words to me as I try to sleep.

During the days, I work on new projects. They are banks and office buildings, mostly. I am called upon to design a skyscraper to be built in Kuala Lumpur. It is supposed to be the tallest building in the world. That is all they have asked of me, that it be the tallest. My stomach churns to think of it. I study the newest building materials, and I read book after book on Malaysian architecture, and I wonder why it is so important to make it tall. Why is tall all that matters to them?

SLEEPING UNDERWATER

Tonight, I have left work and got on a motorcycle. I drive to the docks. I rent a small boat and I take it out of the harbour into open water, surprised how much I remember of boat-craft from my father. I lie on the deck and stare up at the night sky. It is a clear night and the heavens open up before me and show me, to my great comfort, just how very small I am.

I remember lying on my back on ancient Mediterranean evenings with a teacher in a boat like this. He would point out each of the stars to me, and tell me their names. In those days, we took the stars very seriously. Their motions influenced our behaviour without question. Astrology was science them. The interaction of the spheres was ground upon which reliable decisions could be made.

Now, it is the laughable pursuit of sweet minded flakes like my Victor. He reads the paper every day and must read me my horoscope, for he takes it very seriously. He does not understand that Astronomy killed Astrology like Science killed Magic. I remember so many lives where magic was a real thing, and the lives of men were lived at the mercy of gods and demons. It was not better. It was much worse, but it was simple. It was necessary that we move on. We killed our gods with reason, and took command of our destiny.

Astrology assumes that the interactions of celestial bodies are favourable or unfavourable to certain courses of action. How can we ascribe any predictive power to them now? We have put so many bodies of our own in orbit. Thousands of glittering little soda cans in space bleep and hum and spin and spin around us. We believe we have done this to help us talk to each other, and to see things with more clarity. In actuality, we did this to shield ourselves from the influences of the spheres. We surround ourselves with static and interaction, and we tell the stars to mind their own business. We will choose our own good and bad days now.

In this modern age, it is best not to be seen at all, for everything that sees you influences you. Quantum physicists seem to agree with me.

There are so many people looking at me all the time that I don't know what I am anymore. I lie on my back and stare at the stars, and tears flow down the sides of my face to the deck. I hear the motion of the waves and the distant clanging of the directional buoys. The stars are the same, just the same as always.

Victor is at home, worrying. I get up and turn the boat around. I don't want him to worry about me. He is my lover, and I am all that he has in the world now. This doesn't please me, because he should have more in his life than just me. I have so little to give him now. The world keeps taking and taking from me. I feel like an Ayn Rand hero, all righteous indignation at being used. My cheeks flush with shame at the thought that I might be seen as agreeing with her greedy, self-interested, hateful donkey shit of a philosophy. I don't. I am just tired, and it is not the world's fault that I am ill-equipped to handle fame.

I owe the world something for being allowed to walk it, as do we all, and any whinging is just the childish moans of a tired animal.

I arrive home at one in the morning. Victor is asleep on the couch in front of the TV. He has gone through a bottle of wine, so it's little wonder he's already out. I pick the bottle up off the floor, set it up on the table, and I turn off the television.

The phone rings and my hands shake as I answer it. Late night phone calls terrify me. I worry that my sister is calling me to tell me my mother has passed.

"Hello," I say.

"Hello," Tom says, quietly. I blink in shock. I've not heard from Tom in over a year.

"Tom?" I say, needing to be sure.

"Yeah," he says. "Sorry. It must be as late as hell."

"It is." I say. "It's all right. Where are you? How are you?"

"I'm in New York," he says. "It's everything they say."

"That's marvelous," I say. "Is everything okay?"

"No. Christ, Carter, you and Victor need to go and get the test."

There is no need to say which test. We all know there is only the one.

"What?"

"I've got it. I don't know how long, but I was in Haiti for Christ's sake, and we haven't, you know, since. You're probably safe. Still, you need to go and have the tests. Just in case."

I find myself thinking life is an unmerciful bitch. I should be used to losing my friends one at a time after all these lives, but as my memories return, I am more offended by death, not less.

"Oh my god, Tom. I'm so sorry."

"Well don't be sorry for me yet. I might just have taken you to hell with me."

"There's no one I'd rather go with."

He breathes in harshly on the other end of the phone. "Cheers, mate. All's well for you otherwise?"

"It's fine," I say, my own words sounding strained and thick.

"Good. I see they're building your museum."

"Yes," I say wanting to change the topic. "Tom. What're you going to do?"

"I'm coming back to England," he says. "I've no choice. I'll be in London in a fortnight."

"You should come to Liverpool," I say.

"So that you can take care of me? Christ."

"Yes."

"Forget that. I'm not dragging the both of you into this. Unless you've got it yourselves. Then we'll all stick together. Barring that, you live your fucking lives, both of you, and let me sort out me, all right?"

"I can't promise that. Don't make me."

"I'm telling you. End of argument. You're building your masterwork. I refuse to interrupt that. God would have my skin."

"Fuck your God," I say, upset.

He is smiling as he answers. "Just keep building your churches, Carter."

"I don't build fucking churches."

"Oh, my love," Tom says. "That's where you're wrong."

The line goes dead and I put mine back in the cradle. I sit down hard on the floor and cry my guts out. My sobbing rouses Victor. He sits up blearily and looks at me. His eyes sharpen at once and he comes over to kneel in front of me.

"Oh my god, Carter. You're crying. What's wrong?"

I tell him.

Two weeks later we are told we do not have the plague.

Three weeks later, I have bought a flat in London.

I parked outside the building and waited for Andrew, cautiously filling the car with what remained of my things, most of the boxes having been carried off by who knows what passersby. Sitting in the driver's seat, I felt oddly shielded and cozy as I waited for a sign of Andrew, any sign at all. None came in the four hours I waited. I checked into a motel and stashed my belongings. I showered and changed. I shaved and soaked and thought long and hard about everything. My side and arms were red and sore from my roll in melted nylon. Lying in a cool tub made me feel much better. I applied an aloe lotion and bandages to my burns.

I looked carefully at the gun, noticing where the serial number had been filed away. I counted my bullets. There were five. The clip held thirteen if you had one in the chamber. I wondered why Des had been carrying it half unloaded, but trying to understand his motives was beyond me. I had lost the faith in trying to predict why anyone did anything. Possibly I'd been far down his "to-kill" list.

In retrospect, it's a little shocking how quickly I'd just taken it as a matter of fact that Andrew, my lover and employer, had simply rung up Janice and talked her into cutting herself, and giving me that last little message of his. I should probably have just been grappling with this, trying to find evidence they were in collaboration, that this was a put on. But I'd cleaned the blood. I'd thrown away a piece of my friend. I didn't question it. I didn't have time for doubt.

I was focused instead on immediate matters of survival. Des was not likely to come for me again any time soon. Andrew was just as likely to send someone else after me, assuming he knew where to do so. He'd not had anyone camped at the boxes of my things, which would have been what I would have done.

Right now, he had no idea where I was. The chances he'd find me in this motel were slim. My car was his best shot. I made a mental note to trade licence plates with someone after dark.

It was my intention to abandon defence altogether in favour of a good offence. Andrew was a creature of habit. He liked the things he liked with a strong passion. He was not, in my experience, particularly interested in self-control. He would follow his usual social patterns soon enough, the cocky bastard. That was how I'd find him, and before I put an end to him, I'd sure as hell find out why he'd turned on me so suddenly and why he'd led me through the garden path to hell in the process.

True to my plans, I snuck out once the sun went down and I swapped my plates with someone else. Then I drove around his usual haunts, looking for his Jaguar. He had a number of clubs he favoured, and friends he often visited. I saw no sign of his car anywhere. If I were him, I might be going by taxi right now.

Still, I wanted to wait until he was good and cocky.

I headed back to the motel room, and went to sleep. I had no dreams. It was the kind of sleep where you close your eyes and are simply absent from the world for a while. I woke and turned over to put my arm around him, absent-mindedly, and felt a nearly physical sense of having fallen. I broke into a sweating gasp. It took me several minutes to calm down from the horror at actually missing him.

I nipped to the lobby and picked up a newspaper and read it from one side to the other. There was nothing much of interest in it. Nothing about Janice. Continuing coverage of Frank Cooper's death revealed that he had kept a journal of his murders, detailing a man ill at ease with his horrible compulsions. It sounded like bollocks to me. There was no mention of Andrew in it, or the fact he'd hired us. There was no mention of me.

He'd no doubt persuaded Mr. Cooper to endorse the check over to him prior to this point, during one of the private meetings they must have been having all along.

I was in a black mood. There was no need for any of this. If Andrew's entire plan had been to pilfer this money from a mad killer all along, I don't think I'd have been very hard to convince. I wanted to know why he'd done this. Was he simply tired of me, and planning to take the cash and run? Would he have done this all along? Was he setting me up to get killed? Was he setting me up to catch Cooper and to cement my own reputation before he left London? He had always more or less meant to leave London.

Why was he so angry? Why would he do what he had done to Janice? Not how, you'll note, had he done what he'd done to Janice. I didn't think about that. I couldn't face that yet. I hated him and I loved him, and I was young and confused. I sat in the motel room trying to put it together. I remembered each conversation with Mr. Cooper, and my stomach tossed and churned as I picked up the threads of guilt I should have noticed then.

I remembered the dog sniffing at Janice's fingertip. I thought of her dog at home alone. I thought of her alone in the hospital. I wanted to go and see her, but I couldn't bring myself to do it. I could feed her dog. This much I could do, even though it was a terrible idea.

I drove to her house and let myself in with the key she'd given me that morning. The dog was gone. The house smelled of smoke and there were footprints on the carpet. Big boots. I went to her phone, and I called information to find the number for the RSPCA. They had Janice's dog safe and sound. My shame burned in my eyes as they told me the firemen had picked him up when they'd come along with Desmond's ambulance.

I told them I would pick up the dog if Janice was not out of hospital soon, and made it clear that they were to destroy the dog under no circumstances whatsoever. They promised to call me at the motel long before that time came.

Reassured, I got back into my car. I returned to the motel, and paced the floor nervously, feeling angry and upset and restless without fully knowing all the reasons why. The phone in the motel room rang around four in the afternoon.

I answered it because I was, apparently, incapable of learning.

"Hello Niles," Andrew said on the other end of the phone.

"How the fuck did you get this number?"

"I've had an illegal tap on Janice's phone for years. You're really quite predictable, love."

"Don't you fucking call me that."

"I'll call you just exactly what I choose to call you, sweetheart. I will do exactly what I like."

"Really?" I said, barking a harsh laugh through a tightened throat. "So will I."

"Threatening your life really was pointless. I should have known."

"I have some questions, you mad bastard, and I shall have answers."

"No," he said, "you shan't. It's nothing personal, Niles. You were a fine bed partner, and you've the makings of an excellent detective if you can shake your pathetic naiveté and your need to find the best in everyone. But it's over, and I am moving on now."

"Fuck you," I said, "and fuck your clever posturing."

He laughed gently. "Niles, if you leave off all of this right now, I'll call off Des. I'll be out of England in a week and we can both have our lives back, all right?"

"Fuck you," I said. "Des is out of the picture. I put him in the hospital. He's badly burned, and there's no fight in him. I want you to tell me what's going on here."

"No," he said. "Behave yourself. That's a shame about Des. Nasty trick. I suppose I'll have to persuade you another way. If I see you, or hear from you, or even have the slightest hint that you've been looking for me, not only will I make sure Janice swallows her own tongue, I will make sure that Janice's dog is bumped straight to the gas."

I swallowed. "You're a fucking monster."

"That's what my mother said right before I talked her into slashing her wrists, Niles. We both know now that I can do this, and we both know you won't let that happen to your friend. Nor should you. It was a kindness to you that she only lost a fingertip. I'm not without sentiment, entirely."

I started to cry like a scared child, and I hated myself for showing that kind of weakness in front of him.

"You've driven me to this," he said, with as much kindness as he could muster "I'd much rather we'd parted differently, but you went behind my back and I can't have that. You very nearly ruined everything. Goodbye Niles. Live well."

I hung up the phone and sat on the bed. All the anger had been whipped out of me, replaced by a sick cold clammy fist in my stomach. He had found my control switch. I couldn't let him kill Janice. Or the dog. I knew with absolute certainty that he would, if pressed. In fact, one would be the same as the other to him. He didn't care for dogs, and little more, maybe less, for women.

So I did nothing. I sat and wept and fell asleep sitting up.

When I woke up, I was not alone.

Des sat on my bed. He had a very large gun pointed at my face. He was wearing a pair of grey cotton gym shorts that did not go at all well with the long black coat and black t-shirt he was wearing. Neither did the long white patches of gauze on his leg. The bandages that were showing spots of dried blood and dark yellow. He was sweating, and his crutches lay on the floor.

"Good morning sunshine," he said. "Hope you don't mind that I let myself in."

"Not at all," I said.

The new flat is by the Thames, and is very spare, but posh. At the moment our belongings are still mostly in boxes. We left the furniture in Liverpool. I called my Mum, and had her portion it out to my hundreds of cousins.

LAIRD RYAN STATES

I have been sketching a design for the place, with modular storage and the ability to put things out of sight when I don't need them. Victor is less than enthusiastic about the sketches, telling me he doesn't want to live in a library AV room. I smile and tell him it won't be like that, and to have faith. It doesn't matter. He has already as good as moved out. I am just waiting for the end. It hurts, but I've started to make peace with that pain, because I know I will have to. Perhaps I'm even ready.

The flat will get me in the magazines when it's done, and the idea might catch on, though it is expensive. I will have to have some of the units custom made by a plastics manufacturing company I've used before. Thinking about all of this in great detail, and deciding on the colour scheme for the blinds and bins, keeps me from thinking about death and loss and people moving on and outgrowing me. I don't spend time thinking about Tom's insistence on living alone and coping alone. I don't see the growing mania in Victor, or his contempt for what he thinks is my retreat from the world. I don't think about the tiny little virii that may or may not be swimming in my blood waiting to tear me apart from the inside.

I ought to be condemned.

I am at the drawing table, which I did bring, and I am sketching my vision of the bedroom. I am deciding what size of bed I will need. I stare at the page, thinking over my options. Left to my own devices I like a small bed, even if I'm sharing it, but Victor sprawls.

He comes into the living room and sets a bag of groceries on the counter. His eyes are animated and intense. When he reaches into his pocket to find a tissue, I can see his hands shaking. I think he has been taking speed, unless he is a manic depressive and I've failed to notice. I believe I would have. I don't know the last time he slept properly, but it might have been in Liverpool.

He puts away the groceries. He doesn't look at me. He still hasn't forgiven me for not putting him on the phone when Tom called us. We have not spoken to Tom since. He wants to deal with this on his own and though it is a little awful, I respect him. Who am I to tell him how to live, or how to die? There can be dignity in doing either one alone. We all do the last one alone.

I pay closer attention than Victor does and I know that Tom isn't even still in London. He's in Spain, for some reason, and he filed a story on the Basque and their struggle for recognition. This is why Victor has not found Tom at any of his old haunts. I'd tell him that, but he hasn't asked me.

I sketch in a single bed with light penciled lines, then rub it out. I consider if I might want a hammock to mimic the feeling of being held tightly as I sleep. I think that might be too eccentric, though it can be taken down and put away in the morning. I then consider the problem of blankets and where they'd go in the daytime, and, less lightly, continue to sketch in a single bed.

"Anything of note in the shop?" I ask, trying to make conversation.

"No," he says. "Bread, milk, the usual."

"I keep hoping for something really exciting and new. Never happens."

He smirks unpleasantly and keeps putting things away. I keep drawing the bedroom. The flat is silent except for my pencil, and the sound of his breathing and cupboards opening and closing, and the myriad of tiny sounds buildings make when they are nervous.

"I'm onto you," he says.

"What's that?" I say, not looking up.

"He's in Spain."

"How does this mean you're onto me, love?"

"You've known for ages, haven't you, without seeing fit to tell me?"

"Victor, you maniac, I've known for five days. I saw his name on the story in the paper. That's as long as you could have known if you read them and paid attention."

"Fuck you," he says. "You're so clever aren't you?"

"Victor, don't."

"Don't what?"

"Don't be crazy."

"Oh what would you know about it? You're a freak. You turn your feelings on and off like the sodding light switch."

"That's unfair."

"Fuck you and fuck fair."

I look back down at the drawing, and I draw in the bed with darker angry lines until it starts to dominate my vision of the room. This is a design for a man who lives alone. No question.

He is yelling things at me, things about Tom and my criminal lack of concern for him. He lists all the things in the world I love and do not love. It becomes clear to me that he doesn't understand me at all. I keep drawing. I do not look up.

He demands to know what I think about what he's said to me. He demands that I tell him Tom's phone number. I don't know it, and wouldn't betray it if I did. He stamps his feet. He throws one of my books of sketches across the room. It's his storm, and I'm not in it.

"What do you have to say for yourself, you miserable, heartless, fucking thing?" he shouts in my face.

I turn the sketchpad around, and show him what I've been thinking.

"What do you think of the bedroom?" I say casually.

He drops silent and steps back as though I punched him.

"You bastard. It's apparent that you don't love him at all, and equally apparent you don't love me."

"Apparently," I say, "you'd know better than I."

He turns on his heel and walks out. He does not slam the door. There's some dignity in that.

Once he is gone, I get up and I go to the bedroom. I lie on the futon mattress we've been using in the interim, and I imagine that I've died. I lie still. I slow my breathing. I imagine the warmth of surrounding waters, suspended in nothing at all but the rich purple heartbeat of god. I do not fool myself.

I am alive and famous and utterly alone in London. I didn't even want to come here. I came for Victor, in the hopes it would keep him with me. Keep him stable. Keep him from going mad with anticipatory grief. It didn't. He loves Tom still, after all of this, with a passion our easy friendship cannot touch. A living Carter is no match for a dying Tom. What could be more exotic or fashionable than to be young and pretty and dying?

Almost anything. Sweet, stupid Victor.

Salt water floods the hollows of my face in heat and bitter memory. This flat will be my tomb, filled with tall plastic sarcophagi. All my belongings will be in their place, catalogued and ready to go with me on my passage to the afterworld.

If he can die alone, so can I, and the hell with him if he wants to die of the plague with Tom. The quest for self-annihilation isn't a race. Everyone gets there in their own time. It's elegance of form that matters. I'll show him how a man dies. I will show them all.

In the next life, I will be smarter than to tie myself to the emotional equivalent of mayflies.

I stand up, go into the living room, and I pull big sheets of paper to the floor. I start to sketch the place in more detail. I am sketching furiously, almost in life size, how this place will be. I begin to sweat, and I take off my shirt and trousers and sketch and sketch into the night and into the welcoming dawn until my hands and elbows ache and I lie sleeping on a bed I've drawn for myself.

A word on guns, if I may. I'm not an American, but like everyone, I've been exposed to an enormous amount of American films and TV shows. This can lead one to a kind of blasé attitude regarding guns. They are so omnipresent in American culture and, one presumes, American life, that they seem to be little more than a prop indicating the possibility of violence. They have become a comfortable shorthand for the idea of hostility carried out at a remove. One person pulls the trigger and the other is taken out of the story. It's a bloodless manipulation of plot.

It is not, I need to say, like this in real life. Des pointed his gun at a spot cleanly between my eyes. The barrel was so close to me that I could not fix my eyes on it properly. This was fine, as I did not wish to. Des held himself to be a professional killer. I began to doubt the truth in that, as I could not conceive of a single reason why I would not be dead if it were true. A true professional would have just pulled that trigger and I would be so much meat on the floor.

My gun, which is to say the gun I stole from Des earlier, was in the bedside drawer. There was no sense in even trying to get to it. Even if I did get it, and he did not shoot me just for trying, I doubted I would be able to pull the trigger.

"Can you tell me," Des said, "why I haven't shot you in the face as of yet, you daft cunt?"

"Well, I was just considering that. Is it because you don't have the nerve?"

He smiled thinly. "Niles. I don't think you should taunt me. I've a gun in your face, I'm in pain, and I'm very highly motivated to shoot you."

"Then please go ahead. Honestly. I'm completely exhausted with deciphering people's motives. I'd take it as a relief."

"I'm going to set this gun down for a second," Des said. "If you make a move, I'll make you sorry for it. Believe it."

He set the gun down, and did not take his eyes off me. I stayed still. He reached down and scratched at his bandages, letting a little relief escape his lips.

"Des," I said. "You know you should still be in hospital right now. If you won't do that, then please, I speak now out of concern, don't bloody scratch it. You'll get an infection or something dreadful."

"They're already infected, thanks. Hard to avoid that with a burn this big."

"Yes," I said. "That's probably so. In my own defence, you were there to murder me."

"I'm trying quite hard to keep that in mind, mate, honestly," Des said through clenched teeth.

"That's decent of you."

"It is, actually," he said, an edge creeping into his voice. "I have been discharged by Mr. Matheson, so that you know."

"I see."

"So, I'm not here on business at this point."

"I see."

He picked up his gun, and put it away in his pocket.

"The hell of it is," he said, "that if I killed you now, it would just be bad for business."

"Yes," I said. "Best you don't."

"Oh stop," he said, standing up shakily. "Just stop. You have a near fatal love for sarcasm, don't you?"

"You've not seen me at my actual best, I'm afraid."

"I suppose there's truth enough in that." He took a couple of hesitant steps to the door, shakily.

"How the hell did you get here in this state?"

"Taxi."

"Look," I said. "I understand that you might have felt a need to come by and get revenge, all things considered."

"Shit," he said, turning back to look at me, "it's nice to be understood."

I stood up, the muscles in my lower back twinging. "As a result of Andrew and I resolving our little differences, I am being forced to lie low for a short while. Can I drive you back to the hospital, or to your home, or wherever?"

He looked at me, his eyes widening slightly.

"Are you serious?"

I nodded. "I really want you to go back to the hospital. Seriously. I did what I did to save my life. I don't want you to lose your legs because you feel a need to prove how hard you are."

"Gosh, that's swell of you," he said, fed up. He reached for his gun.

I kicked him once in the shin, lightly and he went down screaming. I stood over him and watched as he cried.

"If you ever pull a gun on me again," I said to him softly, "I will end you. I don't want to, but I will. Instead, I think we should make friends. Now I'm going to help you up and drive you home."

He let me help him up, and looked at me with watery eyes. "Take me back to the hospital. I can't fuckin' stand it."

"All right."

We hobbled outside, and I helped him into the car. I tried very hard not to laugh as I got in. In the passenger seat, he looked small and tired. I drove us in silence for a few minutes. The car was thick with the smell of his burned legs, sweet and unpleasant.

"Can I ask you something?" I said to him.

"Why not?"

"Where did Andrew find you?" I asked. "Because I need to be honest. I think you're not a professional."

"I am now," he said. "I've been paid to kill you."

"Fair enough. I assume I'm your first, then."

He nodded.

"Got to start somewhere," I said.

"Yeah."

"So where did he pick you up?"

"I bounce at a club. I've seen him around loads. And a few days ago he just comes up to me, and offers me a contract killing."

"That's a strange thing to do."

"It is," he said, with an odd tone to his voice. "Isn't it?"

I let him sit with that for a few minutes.

"So," I said, "Do you actually want to do this for a living, or was this just a passing fancy?"

He didn't answer right away. "I've been," he said, "I dunno, thinking about it for years."

I had no answer to that.

We were quiet again, and then he started to shake slightly.

"You all right, then?" I asked, looking nervously at his legs.

"No, mate." He said. "I'm not. I think I'm really sick."

"Yeah," I said. "Okay."

He was sweating heavily and leaned back in the seat whimpering and making wet choking noises.

"Steady on," I said. "We're nearly there."

He nodded and closed his eyes, breathing raggedly.

"Do you have any medication you should be taking?"

He shook his head and said nothing. I could see his lips moving as he silently counted through the pain.

"You keep on counting," I said, getting a little hysterical in my own empathy.

He didn't seem to hear me. I could see he was right on the edge of fainting. I pulled up into the ambulance bay of the hospital.

"I can't come in," I said. "Best of luck. If Andrew comes to see you, be careful."

He opened the door and got out, walking five steps through the automatic bay doors, and then he fell. Two nurses began to move toward me to ask what had happened. I pulled out far too quickly to provide answers. They stared after me. I saw them in the rear view, looking confused.

I drove back to the motel. I took a walk, stopping at a shop for a cup of coffee to warm my hands. I felt faintly sick about the long-term consequences of burning a man's legs. I also felt faintly sick at the growing realization that Andrew had clearly done something else to him as well, though I did not know what. It was becoming impossible not to wonder precisely what kind of monster Andrew actually was. I had a lifetime of indulgence in trash novels and superhero comics to support wild theories of all sorts. These theories collided in my thoughts in a tangled muddle, leaving me with no answers and sick to my stomach.

The theories didn't matter. He had powers, whether magical or something else, over the minds of people. The more I remembered his dealings with people, and the ways in which they fawned over him, and bent over backwards to help him, or the times he'd barely meet a person and immediately knew their motives, the more foolish I felt for not realizing it all along. I'd thought he was brilliant and charismatic, and that I'd been missing something. He was actually a monster the whole time.

I should have felt vindicated, somehow, to know that he wasn't just a better grade of person than me. I'd spent years, even as I grew to love him, feeling like the ugly older sister. I had learned a lot from him on how to get by in this world, and this line of work, but I knew I could never be him, so perfect and utterly persuasive and insightful.

I should have felt, as I said, vindicated. I wasn't.

The things he could do, or seemed to be able to do, were not possible in any rational world. It's all well and good to fantasize about magic and ghosts and monsters and rot like that. It's quite another to stare it in the soul, and to feel it stare back.

It is an uncomfortable and chilling realization. If one of the monsters is real, then maybe they all are. Maybe there's no reason left in the world at all, and no safety to be found from what might be under your bed.

Tom and I are sitting in a restaurant not far from my flat. He has lost weight, and he looks tired. His eyes are sunken in and there are permanent shadows there. He called me an hour ago and asked me to see him, and so naturally I came. I am surprisingly happy to do it. Compared with what I'd imagined, he looks quite good, really. He is wearing a long pea green scarf, even now that he's hung his jacket up on the hook on the end of the booth. The waitress takes our orders, and he and I enjoy a moment of companionable silence.

"You look really good, all things considered," I tell him, and he snorts derisively.

"That's shite, and I think we both know it, but you're very kind."

"It isn't," I protest. "I expected you to look like some kind of skeleton person."

"I'm feeling relatively well right now. Christ. I'll take it, you know."

I nod. "I'm glad you called."

"Had to," he says. "I don't know who else to talk to about this."

"About what?" I ask him.

"Can you please get Victor to stop?"

I blink. It's been near on a year since I've spoken to Victor at this point, and I'm a bit startled at the notion I've got any control over him.

"Tom, Victor left me ages ago. He doesn't call. He's really, really angry with me. I don't even know what you want him to stop doing, though I'm imagining I could guess at it."

Tom barks a little laugh. "You haven't heard from him in months?"

"No, honestly."

He leans back. "You're serious?"

"Yes," I say. "Not a word. He stormed off in a huff."

"I'm sorry about that. Christ, I really did a number on the two of you, haven't I?"

I shrug. "I don't think it was going to work out for us for the long term no matter what any of us did."

"Still."

"Well it's nice of you to feel sorry about it, but you've got more on your mind than that."

"Not really. I'm too tired to travel so much as I used to. They've got me on some pills, Christ, and that doesn't help."

"So what's all this about Victor?"

He shakes his head. "He won't stop bloody bothering me. He's on the phone with my editor demanding to know where I am all the time. Apparently, he's twice tried to hire a private investigator by the name of Townsend to find me, but the fellow said no, and called me both times to tell me I might want to engage the police. Good for him."

"Why'd he do that?"

"Says that it's unethical for an investigator to take a case from somebody he deems to be unwell, and that furthermore he felt an obligation to let me know about it."

"He sounds all right. I can't think most of them would go to the bother."

"He does seem a good bloke. Told me I ought to contact the phone company and make sure they log calls from Victor's number."

"Is it that bad?"

"Christ. You've no idea. I don't answer my phone anymore."

I sit back in my chair. I look at him, and shake my head. "I knew he was upset, but I have to admit, this all seems a bit odd."

He lights a cigarette. I consider nagging, but decide that if I were him, I'd indulge whatever vices I chose.

"It wasn't so bad for the first few months. He was just, you know, trying to check in, or half pissed and looking for sex."

SLEEPING UNDERWATER

Victor has never called me half-pissed and looking for sex. I doubt that it would be dramatic enough with me. He would not likely catch a fatal disease from me, and so what would the point be, actually? I nod at Tom meaningfully, prompting him to continue.

"But he's gone straight off the bloody tracks now. He's convinced himself he has a cure for this, and that I need to go with him to the island."

"The island?" I ask, a cold feeling rising in my gut, dim memories of past lives slowly rising to the surface

"Place called Sel Souris," he says. "Have you heard of it?"

"Not in ages," I say. Not in lifetimes, I think to myself.

"Nobody has. It's a little piece of rock in the Atlantic, populated, since the 18th century, by a bunch of European and Middle Eastern castoffs. They don't care much for visitors, and their chief exports are implausible rumours and weird tales."

"And Victor thinks they have a cure there?"

"Who the hell really knows what he's thinking right now. Christ. I'm not bloody going to Sel Souris with him. I'm not going by myself either. That island is too fucking dangerous to visit."

I blink, and he smiles.

"Yeah," he says, "Think on that."

"You mean to tell me this place is worse than Liberia?"

"Christ, there's no contest at all. At least Liberia pretends to have a government and tries to make tourists think they might be somehow safe."

"Wow."

"According to what they have for law in that place, it is illegal for Europeans to set foot on the island under penalty of death."

"I think I might remember hearing something about that," I say, memories of fire and screaming drifting hazily and unpleasantly across my mind's eye. "Have you ever been?"

"Yes. I did an article on the place. I was there for 14 hours on a forged American passport, and I spent the entire time I was there terrified of speaking. My accent, and all that. Never again."

"I don't understand your job."

"Few men do," he says with a mock John Wayne twang. His blue eyes sparkle and I remember all of the reasons I love him.

"I've missed you, Tom."

"Yeah. Christ, me too."

Our drinks arrive. His is a scotch, and mine is a club soda with cranberry juice.

"Should you be drinking?" I ask him. "I don't think it's probably all that wise for a person on medication."

He sips the drink. "It isn't."

"Ah."

"Carter, can I ask you a question some might deem very personal?"

I shrug, because it's ridiculous to me that he would think I'd object to such a thing from him.

"Sure," I say.

"How closely do you watch your money?"

"Not very," I say. "Though I may have to start, now that I've quit."

"Quit?"

"Being an architect. At least for awhile. I need a break."

He lets out a sigh.

"Fair enough," he says.

"Why d'you ask me that?"

"I think you need to take a look into it. I assumed Victor was with you because he has been to the Island six times now, he says."

"I don't follow you."

"He can't afford that working at a bloody record shop."

"He must have another job now."

"He doesn't. Look, when you were living together did you have a joint account?"

"Yeah, course we did. It was a pain in the arse otherwise."

He puts his face in his hands. "Carter, please, please, Christ, please tell me you took his name off."

"No. I never bothered."

I shrug.

"Carter," Tom says, explaining it to me very slowly, "He is paying for his mad trips, his private investigators, and god knows what else with your money."

I think about it for a moment. "Yeah," I say, "you're probably right."

"Are you not angry about this? At all?"

I think for a moment and examine my feelings, which are really very calm. "No. He's doing it because he loves you. And I love him. If this is what he needs to do to make peace with all of this, then it is. It's only money. I have all that I need."

"Well, that's very sweet of you," Tom says with a tight smile, "but would you for Christ's sake take the loaded gun away from the infant. You're writing a blank bloody cheque for him to destroy himself and to fucking drive me out of my skull."

"Yeah," I say, "okay. You're right. I'll take him off the account. I'll call him and tell him, and then I'll do it."

"Fuck that, you daft asshole. Take him off, and then tell him."

I nod dismissively, and he relaxes. "Look, Tom," I say. "Is there any possibility at all that..."

"That what?" he asks, cutting me off.

"That Victor is right about the cure?"

He looks me in the eyes. "Victor's been taken in by a bunch of con artists. These people have made a living out of being fucking weird since the 1960s. It's just bullshit."

"You're sure?"

"No!" he said, slamming his hand on the table. "I'm not. Christ, of course I'm not. For all I know I could fly there and some magic fucking witch doctor could wave her hands and I'd be right as rain. But if I listened to every idiot fucking hopeful cure that floated my way I'd do nothing else. I'm dying, Carter. I've made something like peace with it. God can take my life, but he won't make me fucking dance all over the world for his amusement."

"Okay."

"Christ," he says, "I'm sorry. You've got my interests at heart. I have to stop bloody yelling at people."

"It would be nice," I say, and put my hand on his.

He lifts it and kisses it. It is unmistakably a goodbye kiss. "You're one of the good ones," he says, as he gets to his feet.

"You have to go?"

"Yeah," he says. "Bone tired."

I hug him goodbye, and I realize that under the bulky army sweater he really is a kind of skeleton person. I press my face into his chest and get a good smell of him.

"You take care," I say to him.

"You too," he says. "And please, please pay more attention to your life."

I smile. "Why would I want to do something like that?"

"Fair point. Christ."

I watch him walk away, out the front door and down the street through the front window of the place and then I realize he's left me with the bill.

I laugh and laugh, and sit down in the booth and finish my drink.

The next day, I went and I got the dog. I snuck him into my motel, left him with food and water, and then went out again for the day. I called the hospital to see if Janice was still there and what time visitors were allowed. She was being kept on suicide watch, in fact. When I arrived, she was crying. The nurses explained she had been doing this more or less since her arrival. I sat at her bedside.

"Hullo sweetheart," I said, "How're you feeling?"

She looked at me and seemed to need a few moments to recognize me. "Niles?" she said blinking with reddened, sore looking eyes. "Is that you?"

"Yes, Jan," I said, leaning in to kiss her cheek. "It is."

"Tell them," she said. "Please tell them to stop giving me drugs. They think I'm crazy."

"I know," I said quietly. "I know you aren't."

"Niles," she said quietly, "Please tell me the truth. They say I've chopped off part of one of my own fingers. Is this true?"

I nodded.

"Isn't that strange?" she said. "I can still feel it, and it feels like I'm rubbing it on warm velvet. It's lovely."

"I'm glad."

"What about Bentley?" she said in a sudden concerned panic.

"I've got him, Jan. He's just fine."

"Oh good. Worst thing about living alone. I worry what will happen to him if I fall down or something."

"He's just fine."

"I don't remember doing it at all, you know. I just remember picking up the knife and then suddenly I was in so much pain and you were grabbing at me. It was awful."

She spoke the words with a calm and relaxed way about her, like polite card table conversation. I suspected equal measures of morphine and terror had granted her this terrible placidity. The sound of her voice made the hairs on my arms stand up and I wanted to burst into tears of horror. I didn't want to frighten or upset her. She had enough trouble to cope with thanks to me.

"Why would I do such a thing to myself, Niles? I'm really quite happy."

"As well you should be, love," I said. "You've a lovely home, an excellent career and throngs of young male admirers."

She slapped my forearm gently, and giggled girlishly. "Oh you. Stop it."

I looked her in the eyes, and felt tears coming to them. She looked back with warmth and love and no anger.

"You're my best friend in the world, Janice. I'm so, so glad you're all right," I said, my voice cracking a bit.

"I'm fine," she said. "What's a fingertip really? Could have been worse. Best I stay here for a while until they figure out why I did it."

"Psychomotor epilepsy," I said. "I'll bet you anything."

"Epilepsy runs in my family, you know."

"I do," I said. "And psychomotor epilepsy sometimes causes strange behaviour."

"I remember something about that."

I nodded, and leaned in.

"If they decide that's what it was," I said quietly, "don't take the pills. Promise me."

She looked me in the eyes and said nothing.

"I swear to you Janice, by whatever it is that I still believe in, that you are fine. Whatever they decide is wrong with you, smile and nod, and fake your meds."

She nodded slowly.

"You know?" she said, her eyes filming with water.

I kissed her forehead. "He'll never hurt you again."

"I thought I was mad," she whispered back to me.

"No," I said, "I was. I thought he loved me."

She stroked my cheek with a bandaged hand. "Oh dear."

I held it gingerly and kissed it. "I have to go. When this is all over we'll talk. You do what you have to do in the interim. You're a tough old bird. I expect you can manage."

"Stiff upper lip," she said, "All that."

I nodded, and left the hospital room.

I wandered to the burn ward, and asked after Desmond. When I went to his room he was asleep, and looked peaceful. I decided not to wake him up.

Instead I went to a pay phone, and I called my sister to see if she'd be willing to take custody of a sheep dog for a few days. She said she would, and didn't actually ask too many questions as to why. Once I told her Janice was in hospital, she practically jumped at the chance to help. My sister still held out the distant hope that I would marry Janice one day. This sometimes made me smile, and other times made me furious. That day, I went with grateful.

I bundled the dog up into the car and dropped him off, and he seemed happy enough, with the kids, and another dog to run around with. Considering the distance between myself and my family, I suspected everyone was safe and happy for a good long while. I didn't take chances by hanging about waiting for trouble.

Desmond in hospital, Andrew believing me cowed, and the dog being safe, I left my car in front of the motel and walked some distance to a carpark where I stole the least conspicuous car I could find. I swapped the plates with another car, and started the motor with a hammer and a screwdriver. Then I went to the one place I truly believed Andrew would stop off sooner or later, his bank.

I parked across the street, wearing a baseball cap, which I would never normally have done. I wore a pair of sunglasses I purchased at a filling station. I watched the front door in a good old fashioned stakeout.

Stakeouts, unlike guns, are one thing television gets right. You sit and stare and stare, and try to look like you're just reading a paper. You try very hard not to fall asleep. You sing along to the radio. You cross your legs and squirm because you have to urinate, but you're terrified that the three minutes you take off will be the exact time your quarry comes and goes. Desperation sets in. You eventually use a bottle, and it smells bad, but you don't really mind because you are sweating and miserable and the whole car already smells bad anyway. And then precisely at the moment you think you may die of the boredom and stiff legs, the person you're waiting for just shows up after all.

In this case, Andrew arrived in a taxi. He was alone and wearing a long leather coat I'd not seen before. He had dyed his hair a rich dark brown, but I knew it was him right off. The taxi waited outside, and after around half an hour, Andrew came back, got in the taxi, and pulled away. I followed the taxi knowing this was my point of maximum vulnerability. Andrew, being paranoid to a potentially superhuman degree, could well spot me, or even, God knows, sense me somehow, and the game would be up. I could see him talking to and laughing with the driver. He seemed not to notice me, or possibly not to care.

SLEEPING UNDERWATER

I expected the car to head for one posh hotel or another, but was instead very surprised to see it turn onto a residential street. I stopped at the corner, and watched Andrew get out. If he saw me, he gave no sign. He walked up to the door, knocked, and after speaking with a woman I could barely make out, he went inside. The taxi pulled away.

My heart was pounding as I realized he intended to stay here for at least a while. I had no idea who the people in this house were, or why he'd chosen it. I wanted to walk up and pound on the door, but I didn't have enough information. I was still mulling this over when the entire family suddenly trucked out the front door, carrying suitcases, and got in a car. The expressions on their faces were calm and expressionless. The three kids, all between four and eight were not joshing or quarrelling as they got in the back in the most orderly of fashions. The car started, and they drove off.

They did not come back that night. I pulled the car in a little closer, and even grabbed some sleep.

When dawn awoke me, their car had not returned. Andrew, being a professional sybarite, was surely asleep. I got out of the car, closing it quietly, and walked up the lane to the house. I tried the door carefully, and when that didn't work, I checked the back door. It was also locked. The back yard provided me cover to take out my lock pick and open the door. It was not dead-bolted. I took off my hard soled shoes, and stepped inside carefully. The gun was in my right hand as I went into a family kitchen. Empty bottles of wine were sitting on the table and a pack of his cigarettes as well. I kept walking and, to my left, there was a hallway. The doors were all open except one. I swallowed and turned the knob trying to muffle the click, and entered. He was asleep and he was, to my shock, not alone. I stepped closer and I saw the young man in bed with him.

He looked very much like me. Brown eyes, sandy hair. He wore it longer, as I had when I was younger. His cheeks were well defined, without seeming gaunt.

I wanted to throw up.

I walked over very carefully and put the gun to Andrew's temple. As the metal pressed to his flesh, his eyes opened. He had the good sense not to panic.

"Well," he said quietly. "Good show."

"Thank you," I said. "Who's your friend?"

"Do you like him?"

"I'm guessing not."

"He's very cooperative," Andrew said. "Nothing like you, really."

"Tell me, why'd you bother with me at all?"

"I wanted to try having a real friend for a change," he said calmly. "But I should have known it would get stale."

I felt my finger squeeze a little on the trigger, but I didn't pull it. "My heart bleeds for you, you fucking sociopathic animal."

"I'm not," he said, "a sociopath. I'm not doing anything you wouldn't do if you were as persuasive as I happen to be. After a while, the temptation is more than you can bear."

"There's where you're wrong."

"Well, go on," he said. "Shoot me then."

"No. I'm not a killer."

At this point, his friend woke up and jumped for me in one sudden terrifying motion, all teeth and fingernails. I turned on instinct and pulled the trigger twice. The boy fell bleeding to the sheets, and I tried my best not to scream. Andrew was laughing.

"I could have told him to stop," Andrew said, and stared into my eyes, and there was a strain on his face.

When I was a small boy I once deliberately stuck my finger in a light socket that was turned on. If you have ever felt this sensation, that is the best I can do to describe this one. I felt it in my spine and arms, and I could see my hands start to move all on their own, the gun coming up. I realized he was trying hard to make me shoot myself now. I pulled the trigger again and the bullet struck him in the shoulder. His eyes closed and the electric feeling stopped just that suddenly. He moaned and clutched as blood streamed through his fingers.

"You need to really focus for that, don't you?" I said, a little scared at exactly what I was feeling. The boy was dead, and I'd done that. He'd forced all of this. My hands shook with rage. "For some people your voice is enough. But you need to look at me to really force it. Don't you?"

I took care of that problem with my thumbs, quietly grunting as I pushed his eyes back into his skull. It was physically easy to do. I could deal with the emotional part later. His screams stopped short when I punched him in the throat. I wrapped duct tape around his mouth and around his shoulder, under the armpit as tightly as I could, to slow the bleeding. Then, I wrapped his legs and wrists. At that point he could do little more than whimper.

SLEEPING UNDERWATER

His blood was all over me. I had been soaking in one puddle or another for days. I'd lost the ability to feel ill about it. I wanted a shower more than I wanted any other thing in this world. It was an insane thing to do, having killed one man, and blinded another, but I did it anyway. I took the fastest shower of my life, and then dressed in some clothes I found in the closet and, while Andrew lay passed out and bleeding badly, I considered what to do next. There had been three gunshots. Someone had called the police for certain. They'd be here about instantly.

I went, fetched the car, and hauled him out to the back seat while the neighbours gawked. When I pointed the gun at one of them, it was amazing how quickly they shut their doors. I drove away, switching cars twice in parking garages, and headed back to my motel. I waited for my moment, and then took him inside where I could think.

I'm not sure what I am avoiding or why I am frightened. Victor, for all that is wrong with him, doesn't scare me. I know him too well and love him too much to think he'd do me real harm. Perhaps it is just that I hate to deny him anything, even though it is for his own sake that I do. I manage to find his number by asking around in the club like I've just mislaid it. It's the nature of the culture to be so scattered, and nobody has questioned me.

Alone in my place, I have been drinking for an hour, not to excess, but just trying to calm my jangled nerves and to build courage enough to ring him up. It is now half past nine and I hold the phone to my ear, breathe deep, and dial.

"Hello," Victor answers, sounding for all the world like he was born and raised in Boston. "Kevin Clark speaking. How can I help you?"

"Hello?" I say, feeling half mad.

There is a telling moment of dark silence.

"Carter?"

"Yes. Victor?"

"Yeah," he says. "It's me."

"What the hell was that?" I ask.

"It doesn't matter," he says. "What do you want?"

141

I am suddenly angry, but I don't want to let him feel he's got a rise out of me. I swallow it.

"I've had a really good look at my bank statements."

"Our bank statements," he says.

I have no response to that. "What?"

"It's a joint account. As much mine as yours."

"That's crazy."

"That's as may be. Your crazy, though, and not mine."

I sputter for words, and come up with nothing.

"Is that it?" he says. "That everything?"

"No," I say. "Would you mind explaining at what point you went completely mad?"

"Let's see," he says. "Oh yes, I remember. It was right after I realized that the both of you were involved in a conspiracy to sit back and let Tom die."

"A conspiracy."

"You heard me. The two of you can lay back and let him end, but I won't have it. While you both wallowed in your indifference, I went out and I looked for a cure, and I found one. You know why? Because I'm fucking clever and I'm fucking alive."

"There's no cure, Victor. There just isn't."

"How would you know?"

"Well," I say, "you've got me there."

I laugh slightly, half wanting to scream my guts out.

"You'll see. I'll bring it home, and he'll take it, and then you'll both fucking beg for the privilege of apologizing. Both of you."

"No," I say. "This is all over. I'm putting an end to it. You're not going to that island again. It's crazy. We both love you and this is stopping now, right? Do you hear me, Victor?"

He laughs sadly. "Oh Carter, you sound so very normal these days. That's sad. I'm sure we'll see each other very soon."

He hangs up. When I try to ring back, there's a busy signal. Fine. If he wants to be this way, he can leave the phone off the hook. I pace around the flat, my body refusing to lie still. All of the emotions I am not good with are running through my blood like a disorganized guerrilla army, until exhaustion sets in like lead.

I sleep fitfully. Dreams and memories of the island and his sweet face tangle and dive like hawks for mice in my thoughts, and I wake before the sun. I shower and dress, and call for a cab to take me to my bank. I arrive out front, and I go to the teller to close the account. She is shy and nervous, and as she investigates my records, her skin goes red.

"That can't be right," she says. "Just let me check this, sir."

At this point I am certain I am too late, but I let her do the job so that she may feel she's done all she can.

"Sir," she says, "The account seems have been closed by the other party last week.

"Ah," I say. "Good. Thank you. I didn't realize he'd been in."

"Sir, have we displeased you in some way? Your business is of the utmost importance to us."

"Oh no," I say. "Not at all. My investment accounts will remain here. We're simply transferring some funds to an island bank if you follow me."

She nods. "Oh I see," she says, and then smiles. "I follow you."

I wink at her and leave the bank. My stomach aches. He's left me in a very bad place. I am not penniless. I do tend to keep a large amount of cash on hand because I am always worried about banks. I do have investments that I can cash in, but I am not wealthy now. The truth is that it has been long enough since I checked the account that I may have been in this situation for some time.

I decide to go by his place, the address easily tracked down when you have the phone number and access to a phone book. At first I find nothing, and then I check the listing for a Kevin Clark with the same number. I jot the address down, and I take the car there. The address belongs to a large townhouse with a "to let" sign on it. His car is out front, and there are boxes being loaded into a moving lorry.

I head up the walk and find myself face to face with him. He is surprised to see me. I do not stand out of his way, but directly into it.

"How much of this did you do just to hurt me?" I ask him, not able to look him in the eyes.

"Very little," he says. His tone is injured and angry. I believe him.

I look up at him. "Is this what you need to be happy?"

He drops the box he's holding and he takes me by the shoulders. "I promise you, if I go there to that place and do this, Tom will live. He will."

143

He believes it. This much I can see for myself. His eyes are tired, and there is almost no anger in them now.

I put a hand on his face, and he turns to kiss my palm. I pull it back. "Oh Victor. I wish it were true."

He stiffens as I pull my hand back from him. "How can you act this way? It blows my mind, Carter. How can a person be you, do the things you do, be the way you are, and still be able to stand there and tell me there's no magic in the world?"

I look at my feet. "I was there when it died."

He rears back. "When what died?"

"Magic," I say. "It died slowly, a long time ago."

"No," he says, smiling and mussing my hair like a father and son. "I'll show you. You'll see. Magic isn't dead. It's just quiet. It's hiding."

I look at him and realize I'm crying. "You don't understand magic. If you did, you wouldn't be giddy about that at all."

The corners of his mouth turn down, and he steps in close. "Oh, I know," he says quietly, "sometimes the magic shoes make you dance forever."

"Forever and ever. You've no idea."

He kisses my forehead. "It doesn't matter. You look me in the eyes and tell me what you wouldn't pay to keep Tom in the world."

"You," I say and rub my eyes with my own forearm. "I wouldn't trade you for him."

He looks away and steps back a couple steps.

"Tom is my friend," I say. "I love him, and I always will, but this was not about him, Victor. And never was. There was always you in my life. You woke me up and pulled me in close. You warmed me long enough to let me hatch. And Tom? He'd never have you risk life and limb for this either."

"Carter," he says, and he stands stock still. "I'm doing this for all of us. It'd be the same if you were sick."

"I know," I say, wishing it were true.

"I'd give my heart if it meant his would keep beating. I'd give him my blood if he needed it, and I'd give my eyes to see him grow old."

I hear the clicking of beetles for some reason. It frightens me, and tears start to flow. "I can't talk you out of this?"

He shakes his head.

We stand there for a few minutes and look at each other. I want to ask him to take me with him, but I know his mad plan is probably not flexible enough for that. I stand on my tiptoes and I kiss him goodbye. "Come home safe, and promise me if this doesn't work that you'll join us back in the land of sanity."

He laughs and looks me in the eyes. "You'll see me soon. I promise."

I sob, and I head back to the car, crying as the driver pulls away. When he turns back and waves, it is the last time Victor ever sees me.

Andrew was dressed in pyjama bottoms and blood. He'd passed out but was breathing shallowly in the bathtub where I'd left him, hands and feet still bound together behind his back. I checked myself for obvious signs of blood and, again, found none. I needed to look my best. I shaved and put on the best suit I could find and that I had taken care to press with the iron provided en suite. I looked very good. I looked over my shoulder at Andrew. He was still out. I'd be lucky if he lived, even though I'd packed gauze in his eyes and properly bandaged his shoulder.

"Be seeing you," I said to him. "Don't die on me. Yet."

I got in the car and I drove to the hospital. I stopped at a florist and picked up a nice bouquet. I went into the hospital and signed in, carefully signing in about two hours earlier than I actually arrived. The guard didn't check. They never do. I headed to Janice's room, and she was flipping through a magazine.

"Hello, love," I said, brandishing the flowers and putting on a show.

"Oh they're lovely."

I leaned in to kiss her hello and I lingered, whispering. "I can't stay, love. If anyone should ask, I've been with you since very early this morning, all right?"

"Of course," she answered, sounding frightened.

"Good."

I pulled back, and she and I had some obvious small talk before I ducked out.

I meandered carefully to the burn ward, and to Desmond's room. He was awake, also reading a magazine. He looked much better.

"Hello," I said.

"Hello," he said, looking at me suspiciously.

I sat down in the chair and looked at him. Once I was satisfied we would not be immediately interrupted, I said, "Don't shit me, Des. Do you know what you're doing in this chosen career of yours? For real?"

He nodded. "I need your help. The work, such as it is, is completed. I need your help in dealing with consequences. I don't anticipate any strenuous work. I can pay you."

He looked me in the eyes, slightly amused.

"You?" he said, dragging his finger across his throat and inclining his head to indicate the unspoken Andrew.

I nodded quietly. "He's not quite finished, but he's contained."

He whistled. "The fee isn't cheap."

"I know, but I'll pay it."

He looked at the ceiling and then back at me.

"Yeah," he said. "Okay, fine."

"Are you up to checking out?"

He nodded.

"You don't have to," I said. "I'm sure I could consult with you just as well here."

"To be honest, I'm keen on seeing this."

Still cold inside, I gave him a slip of paper with the motel address, a tenner for the cab, and I left.

I drove back, stopping at Tesco's for rubbish bags and gloves and an assortment of sharp knives and gauze, and I acquired a lot of other things to make it seem less peculiar, and then I waited for Des to arrive.

The taxi pulled up and Des got out with two canes, walking slowly but with less obvious pain than before. That's what intravenous antibiotics and morphine will do for you. I welcomed him into the motel room, smiling for the benefit of onlookers.

"How're the legs?"

"Quite badly burned," he said. "Thank you for asking."

"Look," I said, "I don't mean to be a bother, but are you going to whine about this forever? You were trying to slay me."

"Fine," he said, raising one hand defensively. "Fine. So where's the body?"

"You mean Andrew?"

"I mean the body. If you snuffed him, we don't have an Andrew. We have a body, mate. That's it."

"Well," I said. "By whatever reckoning you hold to, Andrew is in the bathtub."

SLEEPING UNDERWATER

Des hobbled over to the door, and opened it. He made a short surprised noise, and then closed it. "What kind of a fucking psychopath are you? Have you been fucking torturing him?"

"No," I said. "I blinded him. He left me no choice."

Des closed the distance between me and grabbed me by the shirt front. "You'd best explain that mate, because I'm not buying it, and I have some fucking ethics, right?"

I slapped his hand off me. "Save it. I'm not the one who decided to do this for a living."

"I never decided to gouge out people's eyes for a fucking living, you sick fuck. If I'd have done you, I'd have done it clean and quick, right? Not for the sheer fucking joy of it, as you seem to've done."

"You don't get it."

"So explain it to me, right?"

"I'm trying."

He took a breath and sat down in a chair, and looked at me expectantly.

I laid out the story for him, the same way I'd have done for Andrew, leaving out no details. When I was done, I stood and stared out the front door of the little window at the top of the door.

"So if he's some kind of monster, and he can make people do things, why did you not shoot him right there?"

"Because I'm not a killer," I said, and then, to my horror, started to sniffle, remembering the blood that ran down the sheets from the holes I'd put in that boy. "I wasn't until he forced me to be one."

"So you don't intend to kill him then?"

I turned to look at Des. "You believe me?"

"I believe you're telling me what you think is the truth. And that his coming to me the way he did was a bit off. That's all that I need. The idea of being an assassin is based in being able to remove a person from the world without the burden of needing proof, yeah. Your sincere conviction is all I need."

I shook my head because none of that mattered to me. "Fine."

"But why didn't you kill him? You're not a killer, but you'd have me do it? That's morally hollow, mate. First year philosophy."

I stared at him. "I don't want to kill him. I want to remove him from being a danger. He needs to talk to do what he does, and his eyes, sometimes, if people are resisting. So I want to remove both and then leave him to be found."

"It's a noble fucking idea as long as you're willing to go to jail for it. In which case, why call me? Frankly, from what you've told me, I think you're fucking half-nicked already. Pointing a gun at the neighbours and dragging him out into the street is not smart. His disappearance will draw media attention, and you're the very best suspect there is."

"Yes," I said, "I was sort of thinking along those lines. The way I see it is that all I can do is be smarter from here out. Between you and Janice I think can demonstrate an alibi. It'll have to do."

"Well," Des said, "Hope springs fucking eternal. Your best hope is that you, like most people, just bloody get away with it, you know?"

"Yeah."

"So. I'm gonna be honest. Your plan is shit. He's going to find a way to finger you at this point if you let him live. You could scramble his fucking brains and that would do the trick, but then why not just snuff him in that case?"

I thought it over. Anger and fear and sentiment had clouded my judgement. "What now?"

"We wait until it's dark. You're lucky he's not been screaming his head off. He's probably shocky. Have you got something we can wrap him in? We'll place him in the trunk, and we'll head out of London, find a nice little lake and sink him properly."

"That's your plan? Fuck, I could've done that one myself."

"It's a classic for a reason. Besides which, it's a job easier for two."

I felt sick to my stomach, sitting there and planning a murder so coldly. I remembered the way Andrew could rub my shoulders and almost literally make all the tension melt. I locked those memories into a small box and pushed it away from me.

"We've got a while to wait," Des said. "Fancy a bite?"

I nodded and we went to lunch and got to know each other a bit. He was surprisingly interested by the fact I used to work in comics, and that's mostly what we talked about. Secret identities, and the whole morality of vigilante heroes seemed surprisingly relevant.

We went back to the motel and watched some television together. Once the sun went down, we wrapped Andrew in plastic bin bags, and dumped him in the trunk, ignoring his mumbling and faint struggles.

SLEEPING UNDERWATER

We drove out of London and kept on for a few hours. We found a little pond with a small stone bridge across it. The moon was bright and the night was filled with stars. It was so beautiful and I realized that it had been years since I'd really seen the stars. My reverie was interrupted by the slam of the car door.

"Let's make this quick," he said. "In and out."

We dragged him up to the middle of the bridge. I gathered some heavy stones from the ground near the pond, and duct-taped them to the package. When it was done, neither of us could doubt he would sink. We stood there on the bridge, breathing hard.

"You ready?" he said.

I nodded and we lifted and heaved. Andrew began to flail and struggle but tied up, as he was, he could do nothing but go down.

That was when I felt the sudden electric shocks in my arms and legs. I felt the urge to jump in and save him. I was fighting, but I feared I might give in. I was distracted by the sound of another splash. I turned to look for Des, and he was gone. I just saw him hit the water. Des began to scream in agony as the water soaked his burned legs. He tried to swim towards Andrew, as if to save him, but his movement was so hampered that he kept going under.

"Des!" I said, shouting his name without realizing how dumb that was.

I could see Andrew struggling weakly, clinging to life with frightening will, and I tried to keep my eyes on Des. His arm slapped out to me for help.

I ran to the shoreline and grabbed up an oar from a rowing boat tied to the jetty. I waded in and offered the oar to him

"Take the oar," I shouted.

He lunged for it and took hold. He was still panicking and pulling back into the water.

"I've got you," I said. "Stop fighting me."

I remembered my years of swim lessons and was suddenly grateful for my mother making me go all those years as I got him back to shore, even as he struggled against me in panic.

We flopped over, both of us panting.

I crawled to my feet. Des was babbling at me, but I barely heard. He pulled himself up and stood in front of me, still in pain but grateful.

"I've no idea why I did any of that. You're right. He's not human. Thank you."

I pushed him slightly away. "Excuse me," I said, "but can you stand to one side? I'm watching him drown."

He breathed hard beside me as Andrew had vanished deep under the surface of the water. I was watching the bubbles rise, waiting to see them stop. They slowed, and then the water went still. I waited there until even the ripples from our thrashing about had stopped, and the surface was like black glass reflecting the yellow moon.

I nodded then, and turned to go.

"Christ," Des said. "You are a hard one, aren't you?"

"No," I said, quietly. "I just had to be sure, or I would never sleep again."

Tom and I are at a cafe in Gibraltar. It seems that nobody remembers what happened to Victor but us. This is just one more bond we share, but it does not make us love each other any more or any less. We are family, but to see each other is a little painful. Our eyes are like mirrors in which we can see our own failings and the ways in which we both let him down. A part of Victor had stayed behind on Sel Souris, and we have every intention of getting it back and taking it home to England. We've spent hours and days discussing exactly how we mean to get to the island, and then off the island with the hope that nobody sees us.

The beach where we will find what we're looking for is accessible from the sea, but it's not a place anybody goes. The French tested poison here a long time ago, and now nothing grows. They say it's dangerous to even walk there. That prospect is not a worry for us. Tom is a dead man already. The prospect of walking through some toxin that might shorten his life a little is much less frightening than what already lies in store for him. He volunteered to do it. If he hadn't, I'd have asked him to.

We both believe the plan will work. We tried asking politely for them to give Victor's eyes back to us, and we were told they would never be returned. They feel they've made their point now, and that the English people will stay the hell away. Certainly Her Majesty's Fascist Government has done nothing to help us. They've made a sternly worded statement to Sel Souris by letter. They've sent letters to France, and to Spain, both of whom deny the island as their territory, though each have claimed it in the past.

All in all Victor was mentioned for two days in the press, and everyone spun it the same way. A lunatic barged into what amounts to a rogue state where he wasn't welcome. He was punished for his crime, and what was left of him was returned home. It was tragic but, since the fall of the Empire, the average Briton clearly felt that he got what he deserved for leaving the civilized world.

They might be right.

It doesn't matter. Tom and I have loved him since we were barely adults, and we need to do this. We let him down, because we never believed he'd really follow through. Once we knew he would, it was too late. He'd gone there for us, and we would go there for him, that was that.

The boat is waiting, and the four man crew knows the way, though they seem baffled that anyone would want to go. Tom and I have spent almost all we have left to pay them enough money that they will do it. We leave the cafe, and board. It is night when we ship out. We stand on the deck, as the boat heads out. The night is still and warm and we hold hands, staring out into the night. It's lit by the moon and a curtain of stars that Victor will never look at again. He used to love the night. He used to tell me about it, and sometimes we'd lie on the beach at night and count stars together like silly children.

He'd never tell me anything ever again, either, and that kept going through and through me like the soft lapping of the waves against the hull.

It takes near to five hours of sailing, though it is still dark when we get there. We see the island at first as a purple glow in the water. Tom tells me the island is new, and encrusted with phosphorescent algae, and that's really the prettiest thing about the place. As we get closer, we come along from enough distance to approach from the western side. He tells me to look for a gap in the glow. We see it, and as we get closer, we see the beach, barren and shocking, like a scar in the greenery.

"Not even the algae grows here," he says. "A hundred years, Christ, and it's still ruined."

He spits over the rails. I look at the coastline and feel a deep sense of loss and horror that I can't really understand.

The ship pulls up close along the shoreline, but the crew is nervous, and they don't want to stay. Tom is yelling at them in

Spanish, because they are trying to get out of the bargain, but he seems to be winning the argument. I look at the island and I keep trying to remember nothing of it. I push the memories down. I will let Tom be the authority on this place, and I will agree to his version of the events, because that is the most practical thing to do. Being here, this close to the maimed heart of the island, makes me physically ill.

I feel, for a moment, the flutter of a soft wing on my hand, and I look down with hope. It's just a dragonfly. It must have lighted aboard the ship in Spain. There are no dragonflies on Sel Souris.

I brush away a tear, not wanting to cry in front of the Spanish sailors. I suck in a lungful of air, colder out here, and it braces me slightly.

Tom seems to have persuaded them to wait a half an hour.

"They're worried about pirates. Apparently, the locals love to come out to boats they spot and, if they don't have the right permits, they kill everyone on board and go straight to salvage. Christ. Fucking barbarians."

"Well, let's not be here very long then."

He laughs. "Too right."

He jumps into the water and starts to swim to shore. He moves quickly and easily. He's strong right now, though God knows what he might catch from the water. I try not to think of it. He crawls up on the shore, and then I see him dart over to the monument. He stays there for a while, and then I see him running back. He is swimming back out to us, and he is swimming more slowly now. I begin to worry about him. I gesture to the crew using the little Spanish I know, and what I remember of the hand signs my father used to use on the fishing boats and I try to get them to move in closer, and they do, just a little bit.

We pull him back up on the deck. He is grinning like an idiot. The crew start barking at each other, and the boat tears away, headed for France, where we have agreed to disembark. He is laughing and lying on his back.

"We did it," he says, his voice giddy, "Christ! We did it! Sod you, you wankers."

He thrusts two fingers up with glee, and here sitting behind him, I see the V for victory, whereas they, if they were looking would be getting quite the opposite. I also laugh, even though I'm worried. I see the prize sticking out one end of his oilskin rucksack. Without looking, I tuck it back, and fasten the sack. I can't bear to see them, to look at them and not be seen by them in return.

I stroke his hair and look at him, so giddy with triumph, after so many months of being in bed off and on.

"You're freezing," I said, "We've got to go down below and warm you up."

He puts his hand on my face. "Oh Christ, Carter, sometimes, life is so fucking amazing."

And he is right, of course, though we sometimes forget. Though terrible things happen, and people are unfathomably cruel. The world is harsh and dangerous and beautiful, and so are we all. And every moment of it, however terrible, is a fucking miracle of confluence, coincidence, design, and madness. I hold him on my lap as the boat takes speed, and we head into the night on this last adventure.

Obviously, I did not go to prison, nor did Des. When Andrew dropped out of sight and none of his friends or other contacts heard from him in over a week, there was some attention focused on me by the police. I was questioned thoroughly, but never charged. I never seemed, actually, to be under suspicion.

Dr. Featherstone, notably, did call me. She asked me if I thought Andrew would cause any further problems at this point. I told her I believed he was gone for good, probably moved to Australia or something. She made a phone call to Scotland Yard, I later discovered, and, for reasons I didn't even wish to know, all suspicion of my part in things evaporated. God knows what she told them, and god knows what they had already known.

A short while later, papers reported that Andrew had been murdered overseas. I do not know how or why this was done. I presumed that Dr. Featherstone was involved with this. Her connections to Scotland Yard seemed extensive. Again, I didn't want more information.

The boy in the house, and the family who lived there, were numbered among the many unsolved deaths that happen every year. His parents were found in their car, seat belts still on, at the bottom of a canal. I surmise that Andrew had asked them to drive in, and who could refuse a reasonable request from a charming man with such lovely teeth.

As it turned out, he had made me his beneficiary some months before his disappearance. I stood to inherit several million pounds now that he was dead. One of those million, I presumed, had once belonged to Frank Cooper.

The true story of what precisely had happened to the Coopers and how, exactly, Andrew was involved in it, I never discovered. I have theories, but that is all they are. In the end, the answers are not important to me. The killings were over. Andrew, probably even more dangerous, was gone from the world, seemingly with the tacit approval of the Home Office.

I left his life with my soul callused, my hands bloodied, and my bank account increased. I had, as it happened, made a friend for life in Desmond, though I was not, and might never be comfortable with his work.

Thus ended the Great Adventure.

And what came after?

I bought a new car. I left myself a modest amount in my savings account. I leased a new, much smaller office and bought a flat. The remainder of the money was disbursed as follows:

One million pounds was anonymously donated to the surviving siblings of the dead boy I had shot. His younger siblings had been on a week's trip to Blackpool with their grandparents. It didn't make me feel less guilty, but it was something

One million pounds was disbursed for the upkeep of Mrs. Cooper.

One million pounds was disbursed to the London Opera. That was for whatever good had remained in Andrew.

One and a half million pounds was disbursed to a non-profit organization that counsels victims of violent crimes.

All of this did much to make the few remaining suspicious souls believe I'd nothing to do with killing him. I like to think it was only a small part of why I'd done it.

Des would not take any money from me. He viewed what we had done, in the end, as public service, and he couldn't be seen taking money from me. It might look like I'd paid my way out of his contract.

I then rejoined the world.

Janice and I still saw each other, but she gradually became more distant. I was a reminder of a nightmare she'd sooner forget. I understood completely. We loved each other in the way that only old friends do, but that did not make it easier.

SLEEPING UNDERWATER

The sort of exciting cases Andrew had attracted, and, I've come to think, largely created through his manipulation of people, soon vanished. The job had no real appeal. It was just another job. Photos of cheaters, finder of lost cats. Occasionally, some good would come of what I did. Usually not. Usually it was just one unpleasant and unhappy person, out for an advantage over another.

I ate alone, lived alone. Occasionally I dated.

I was more cynical, more educated and more aware of what people, including myself, were capable of, and perhaps this was to the good. Common wisdom states that the key to happiness is to know yourself. I'm not so sure of that. It must depend upon what you find out.

With Andrew gone from my life, so too had fled the magic. I was entirely at peace with that. I was no longer a hard as nails secret agent man. I lived my ordinary and unexciting life.

I was, and you'll pardon me for saying this, just like any one of you. Just myself, once more.

Until I met Carter Bennet, I suppose, and magic woke up the killer in me.

PART THREE:

PAST LIVES

The blonde man awoke face down in the sand. He was cold and wet and dazed. He sat up to look at himself.

He was naked, except for scraps of leather on his feet and a peculiar under clout that had been so ruined by salt water that it barely hung together. It was blue, where not encrusted with salt. It had a strange elastic loop that clung to his waist and held firm there. Similar fabric encircled the places where his thighs met his torso at each leg hole. There was a peculiar arrangement of fabrics that concealed an opening by which he could extract his penis and urinate without removing the under-clout. This fascinated him with its cleverness.

His skin was a paler blue, as though it had never seen the sun, wrinkled from soaking and covered in small bites. His hands shook. He breathed in deeply, and he wondered how long it had been since he had last drawn a breath. A tension in his body faded, and corners of his mouth pulled up into a smile.

The sun came out, then, from behind the clouds, and he turned his face toward it, in the way that flowers do.

He laughed out loud, startling himself with the sound of his voice, deep and warm. He blinked his eyes and saw the blue of the sky and the pale green of the water and looked for the place where they met. He knew that somewhere in that imaginary place where sky and water meet was the place he came from. He knew he had always existed in that imperceptible, yet boundless area in many times and places.

He fell on his back and kicked his legs and moved his arms, like a baby testing out its body, rediscovering how it worked with a kind of joy. He was giddy with the simple pleasure of breathing, kept sucking in lungfuls of it until he made himself dizzy. The ground spun under him, and slowly stopped. Tears ran down his face. The ocean inside him tried to escape, as he had escaped the vast one at the fringes of the beach.

He saw a girl nearby, a small child, no more than eight years old. She had deep brown skin and wore a simple tunic dress of startlingly iridescent pink. She was staring at him as though he were a crazy person of some kind. He could not blame her. Here was some strange, and all but naked man, kicking and flailing and laughing in the sand. It was a wonder she had not run for the nearest hills. If anything, the girl had edged closer. Her dark eyes were wide and curious.

She spoke to him, and though he could seem to grasp a word here and there, he couldn't understand her meaning at all. He sat up on his own calves, on his knees to face her. He showed her his palms, face up, then turned them over to show they were empty.

"Don't be scared," he stammered, the words coming haltingly.

Her eyes fixed on him, and she knelt down beside him, cocking her head like a curious dog. She put her hands on his, comparing the size.

"Do you understand me?" he asked, and she seemed to silently mouth what he had just said.

"I understand some," she said, and then looked to him for some kind of approval.

He nodded. "What language are we speaking?"

She blinked and laughed. "Latin."

"Latin?" he replied. "When and where did I learn that? When and where did you learn that, come to think of it?"

"School," she offered. "Nobody speaks it anymore."

"Perhaps. You speak it very well for someone so small."

She blushed, slightly, and it was not the usual pride of approval, but something closer to worry. He felt as though he had misspoken, and patted her hand to reassure her. "What is your name?"

She put her hand on her chest. "Marya. What is your name?"

He put a hand on his own chest, and found he had no answer. No name at all sprung to his lips. Not even a whisper. "I don't know."

She was worried now, and put a hand on his forehead. "You look very sick, and your skin is very pale."

"I feel fine, and I will feel better, in time."

"Should I get a..."

She struggled for a word she did not know. He smiled.

"Le docteur?" she finished, her brow furrowed.

"He recognized the word, again, not certain where he knew it from, and he nodded.

"Are you catching?" she continued in French.

"No," he said, also in French. "I have been in the water a long time. I think, possibly, my boat sank."

She nodded. "I will go and get him."

"Wait," he asked. "Where am I?"

"Salt Mouse," she answered, running off.

He did not know if that was the name of the place, or if she had meant to call him a name. He laughed again, and braved standing up for the first time. He looked in from the coast he'd landed on and toward the rolling green hills inland. He walked from the sand to the grass. The wind carried a smell of roasting meat to him and he salivated like a starved animal. He was, he realized, a starved animal. He had no idea how long it had been since he had eaten a morsel. Nor where he had been. The grass was soft and damp and cool on his feet. He sighed with pleasure.

He could hear the running of water, louder than the waves lapping the shore, and ran toward it as awkwardly as a newborn colt, falling over twice. He came to a small stream that fell over a short drop into a small pond. He lowered his face to the falling water, which was fresh and sweet. He lay down, with a hand still dipped into the pond. He felt as full and happy as a house cat by a fireplace.

Marya returned some time later, with several people in tow. Many of them were as dark skinned as she was, and dressed in the same bright colours. One man stood apart. He was pale, nearly as pale as he himself was, and dressed in formal clothes that looked strange. The man wore eyeglasses. He recognized them, but they seemed old fashioned. Quaint.

The formally dressed man had a black satchel, and knelt down beside him cautiously. A man with long, kinky hair offered him a purple wool blanket. He took it and smiled, not sure what to do with it.

"Cover yourself, sir," said the doctor. "There are women present."

"Of course," he answered, wrapping the blanket around himself.

"Your French is very odd," said the doctor. "I do not know the accent."

"I am not very surprised," he replied.

The man nodded without comment, and looked at him as though attempting to determine his species rather than his ailment. The blonde man found that amusing, and he smiled. The doctor's expression softened also.

"I am Dr. Georget, the Governor's personal physician. May I look at your injuries?"

"Please," he replied. "Something must be wrong with me."

The doctor took out a stethoscope and listened for a heartbeat. He recognized it as a stethoscope, but it seemed large and unwieldy, the earpieces larger than they needed to be. It was still cold against his chest.

"Breathe deeply, please."

He did so.

The doctor nodded, put away his tools, and touched him lightly, feeling for sore spots and for broken limbs. He leaned in and looked at the little sores that ran up and down the sailor's skin.

"Am I well?" the blonde man asked.

"Aside from the work that crabs seem to have done to your skin, you are very healthy. Or so it appears at a glance. You show no signs of serious injury. Your skin is over soaked. The salt will itch you soon without a bath; but your eyes are clear, your heart and lungs are strong. Do you have any idea what has happened to you?"

The blonde castaway closed his eyes and tried to remember. Flashes came to him, and he shook his head in frustration.

"There was some kind of struggle. A man, very angry with me. Something happened to my eyes, and then I fell into the water." His features twisted into a frustrated grimace. "I am sorry. I cannot recall more, and it is infuriating."

"You have been through something traumatic. Your memories may return with rest. You are safe now, at least." The doctor furrowed his brow. "You should be badly burned from a long time at sea without shelter. You should be malnourished and dehydrated."

"I feel as though I was underwater, I think, for perhaps a long time."

The doctor laughed. "I must disagree."

Marya drew closer, peering at him, and putting a hand on his shoulder.

"Are you hungry?" she asked him.

"Very much so," he said to her, smiling.

"May I give him something, doctor?"

"Yes, my dear," the doctor said. "Thank you for asking. Sometimes it can be very dangerous for a sick person to eat. Good girl."

Marya frowned and nodded, a very serious girl. She pulled out a pear and handed it to the castaway.

"Thank you," he said, and took an immediate, all too hungry bite. Juice ran down his chin, and he sighed with pleasure. "Oh, that is good. Thank you, little girl—Marya."

Marya nodded, and looked away all too quickly. The castaway politely looked back to the doctor.

"I remember living in a city," he continued. "Paved roads. So much loud music. I remember—oh, just little things, damn it."

"Well," the doctor said, helping him rise, "Again, do not strain to remember. I reiterate, my friend, that you are quite safe now. You have washed ashore on the island of Sel Souris. You may consider yourself a guest of the French."

"I have never heard of Sel Souris."

"Few have." said the doctor. "Although that is likely to change soon. It is unique and remarkable."

"I look forward to discovering so."

"You must still be famished."

He nodded sharply, and the doctor started to lead him up the hill, past the onlooking eyes of the locals.

"One moment," the castaway said, as he gently pulled free from the doctor.

He walked toward Marya, who was flanked on each side by women who must have been family to her. He stopped respectfully and bowed deep at the waist with as much grace and decency as he could muster, wrapped in his blanket.

"Thank you again, Marya. You have been both kind and brave."

Marya smiled, and he took her hand gently and kissed it.

161

"I salute you," he said in Latin.

One of the women, her mother he presumed, pulled her back protectively. He made eye contact with the woman, seeking conciliation.

He walked back to the doctor, who offered an arm. It seemed a strange gesture, but he was in no position to judge the etiquette of the time and place. He took the offered arm and they walked up the hill together. Georget stiffened as they walked past the crowd. They parted for him with some fear and distaste.

"You do well to placate the locals thus," the doctor said quietly. "They are a pack of mixed breed savages, by and large. The refuse of Europe, washed ashore to breed and fester here."

There was not a trace of irony realized by the doctor.

"I've been charmed by them thus far," he said, "and seem to find myself in their number."

"You'll see the other side of them soon enough, I've no doubt. Troublemakers all – Pagans, Mohammedans, Hindoos. If there is a primitive superstition or ungodly heresy in existence, you will find a practitioner here."

The castaway nodded vaguely, trying to be polite.

They came to the crest of a hill, and across the valley was another hill. On that hill stood a large purple house of remarkable size and opulence. He knew at once that whatever authority ruled here must live in that house. His skin crawled with some distaste. He had an inkling, whoever he was, that he did not care for authority.

"You do not recall your name?"

"Yes."

"We shall have to call you something."

The castaway smiled.

"Call me, shall we say, oh…Nemo. It suits me."

The doctor laughs at this little joke. "More Latin. You had best exercise caution, my strange friend, lest you gather attention on this island."

"I am not remarkable enough," Nemo said.

Carter's three cardboard cartons were on the floor in front of my sofa. Des and I were looking at them and not speaking. Neither of us actually wanted to open them. The boxes probably held what amounted to a solution tied up in a bow for us. Whatever Jherek wanted so badly was in the boxes and we needed it to trade for Carter. It seemed to me, and I knew Des well enough to be reasonably sure we were in agreement here, that this meant what was in there was trouble on a level we didn't even want to touch.

"Okay," Des said after the longest pause. "Fuck it, I'll go first." He grabbed up a box and opened it, His expression didn't change. "Clothes," he said, and set it on the floor beside him.

"Hold up, Des," I said. "Let me see."

Des handed the box to me and I took out a shirt and held it up. It belonged to a tall man, taller than me, and I was positive that it didn't belong to Carter.

"Not his?" Des asked.

"No. Not his."

"Well, that confirms one part of the theory," he said. "Handily."

I looked at the clothes in more detail. They weren't the sort of thing Carter would wear. They were the sort of things I'd have worn back in the day, flamboyant and light, mostly silk.

I took up the second carton and opened it. It was full of cassette tapes and video cartridges. Most of them were store-bought, but some were mixtapes and the cartridges looked like home videos.

"Shit," Des said. "That looks like a bunch of work to go through, doesn't it?"

"It rather does. But it looks like a bunch of music and that's all."

"Unless it's computer programs on those tapes or something."

"I don't think so. Could be wrong."

"I vote we don't get into them unless we have to."

We looked at the final box. I nodded and then picked it up.

I lifted the flaps, and, at first glance, it looked like more clothes. When I rooted around inside I found a photo album. I opened it and I saw it was full of photos of Carter. He looked more serious in the photos, and more shy than I was accustomed to. He did not seem to like the camera, nor to be photographed. In some of them, Carter was with a short blonde man with blue eyes who seemed never to stop smoking. There was something faintly familiar about him, but I must have known a dozen men who met that description.

163

In a very few there was a third man, and this one I remembered. "Des, I know who these other two blokes are."

"Really?"

"Yes," I said, pointing to our third man, a very tall redhead with bright green eyes. "This is Victor Mayhew. And the blonde man here, his name is Tom. Tom...something or other. I can check into my files later."

"Your files? Seriously? You worked for these guys?"

"No. But the ginger nutter here tried to hire me. He wanted to track down his ex-boyfriend. That's Tom, here. Tom had contracted AIDS and had decided to be on his own for whatever reason. Victor here didn't seem to think that was for the best. He was much too persistent, and I had to turn him down a few times. It's a fine line between helping someone find a missing loved one and assisting them in organized harassment. He had leapt wildly across that line."

Des shrugged.

"Anyhow," I said, pre-empting any argument on the ethics of paid human-hunting, "I did find Tom and give him the heads up that Victor was looking to hire me. He seemed entirely reasonable, and free to make his own decisions on who to see and not see."

"And they're obviously both chummy with your boy," Des said.

"Yeah. This, I suppose, explains why of all the offices in all the world, he had to walk into mine."

I heard the sadness in my own voice, as I realized Carter had lied to me a little about how he'd chosen me. It surprised me, and hurt my feelings. Worse than that, it made me angry. I tossed the photo album lightly onto the couch beside Des.

"Well, this is all bloody interesting," Des said, "but I have no idea what Jherek needs with any of that. Unless it's the tapes."

"Yeah," I said. "Fuck. I hope its tapes of people talking or something. I know nothing at all about computers. I don't think I've the right player for these videos either. I've got Betamax."

"Well," he said. "I can beg, borrow, or steal the other. No worries."

I smiled. "Anyone else would mean that as a figure of speech."

"So do I, y'twat."

I chuckled and reached my hand into the box for a last go over and felt something hard. I grabbed it. It was a piece of heavy plastic or glass, wrapped in a dark and shiny purple silk scarf. I lifted it from the box. The end of it poked out, and was rectangular. Other than that it felt like the prisms I'd played with in school. Same weight and texture. I pulled the scarf off, and inside the plastic were two golf ball sized white spheres with thread trailing off.

Des looked at me like he was going to throw up.

I was about to ask why and then turned the thing around in my hands. I wound up staring into two bright green eyes encased in the lucite brick I was holding in my hands. One pupil was small and perfect. The other had dilated strangely and unevenly. The threads I thought I'd seen were the remnants of the optic nerves.

"Peek-a-boo!" said a nasty voice in my head, and I clenched my jaw to keep from dropping the thing or screaming. I flashed back on the feeling of my thumbs sinking deep into Andrew's face, and tasted bile rising in my throat.

"Those are fucking human eyes in glass," Des said. "For real."

"Yes." I said nodding. "I've no idea how they did it, but that's what they are, all right."

I couldn't stop looking at them, and waiting for that voice to taunt me again. It didn't happen. I just kept looking, and holding them up at eye level as though I expected them to blink. I honestly don't know how long I held them up there.

Eventually, Desmond took them from my hands, and set them on the table. "Niles?"

"Yeah?"

"Talk to me, man."

"Nothing to say."

"Impossible," he said, trying to lighten the mood.

I stood up and went into my kitchen and stared out the window. Des watched me from the couch, and left me alone. I poured myself a glass of water and drank it down. It tasted like blood and sand.

"Eyes," I said. "Window to the soul."

"Yeah," Des said. "That's so."

"Also a common substitution symbol for the testicles. Blinding has always been a metaphor. Eastern European gangsters are obsessed with it."

"This is also true," Des said, and let that hang there a moment before asking "Are you okay?"

I looked at him, forcing half a smile. "Not in any way. Those are fucking eyes. In glass. I don't know who goes to that kind of effort. It can't be easy to do, or cheap. That is a lot of anger."

"Or a museum piece," Des said, "I mean, if we want to avoid the whole jumping to conclusions."

"Look at the ginger bastard closely."

He leaned over the photo album, and then at the eyes, and went the ashen gray I'd come to associate with impending vomit.

"Shit," Des said.

"Yeah."

I paced back and forth in the kitchen, not looking over in that direction, trying to come to some notion, any notion what to do next.

"Well," Des said, "This Victor bloke must have pissed off the wrong man eventually. I'm thinking safe money is on Jherek, you?"

I nodded, "Yes. 'His country's vision', he called these. He wants this chunk of glass pretty badly, I think. The usual mobster bullshit reasons of honour satisfied. All that. I'm thinking Carter swiped them back somehow, in the name of his friend here. Sentiment."

Des nodded. "That makes sense, yeah. So, let's take the eyes to Jherek and put an end to all of this crazy shit, and you can get back on with your life. Neither one of us wants any more excitement than we already have. Okay?"

"No."

Des blinked.

"Have you ever put a man's eyes out, Des?"

"No."

"I know. Oh, you've laid some beatings in your line of work. You've likely killed by now, but I don't think you've done that. I don't think you have it in you."

"You never know," he said flatly, "until the time comes, and you have to."

I shook my head. "No. Some have it in them and some don't. I do. I'm not proud of it, but there it is. If I have to, if I think the circumstances call for it, I can put a man's eyes out. That is a thing I know about myself. That's the little revelation Andrew left me for a legacy. It's a terrible thing to know, but you're better off knowing it. Knowing what you can do."

"Niles, mate, don't get spacey on me right? You're starting to make me wish I'd stayed home, here."

I smiled, sat beside him, and put a hand on his knee. "Des, you're free of all this. You can go home. I absolve you of further responsibility."

He shoved my hand off his knee. "And now you're the Holy See, are you?"

I laughed. "I have to do something stupid and dangerous and mad, and you don't. This isn't your mess, this time."

"Am I your friend, or aren't I?" he said, looking me in the eyes.

"Always. You don't need to…"

"Then shut it."

I looked at my knees and felt my chin trembling, my eyes getting hot and red, and wet. I hated my own weakness. I hated Andrew for making me do that to him. Making me remember it, teaching me I could do it. I let myself cry.

"What is going on in your head?" Des said, genuinely puzzled.

I shook my head slightly, unable to talk at first. "Carter took back Victor's eyes, Des. I can't undo that gesture. I can't. He wouldn't want me to trade the eyes for him. I know this as fact. I just know."

I wished I could trade my own heart to give Andrew back his eyes, and to simply have put a bullet between them coldly and quickly.

Des clapped my back. "Okay. I get it."

I stood up, embarrassed, and wiped my eyes with my hands. "He was acting sketchy from the moment he showed up. I should have called the police the moment he tried to hire me. I knew it, and I didn't because he was pretty."

"Clock it," Des said.

I cocked my head at him.

"I wondered how long until you'd find a way to take blame, you fucking dim ponce."

I laughed a choked laugh, on the verge of hysteria without really knowing why.

"Whatever this is," Des said, "it isn't your fault. I could throttle that little bastard for dragging you into this."

"I was already in this," I said. "Chains of fucking destiny heavy as lead."

"How do you figure that?"

"Victor came to me, about all this, years ago now, and from that moment it's all been one thing. And this is the last straw, the nail in the coffin, Des."

"What is?"

"The eyes, love. The eyes have it."

He winced and shook his head. "Terrible fucking joke."

"I'm not joking. That's mythic resonance, that is. I've read enough paperbacks to recognize it."

"Niles," he said, starting to try to convince me of something.

"I know I'm mad, Des. You don't have to point it out. I'll be hearing voices soon enough."

"Too right," the voice said.

I nodded grimly.

"So what do you intend?" Des asked.

"Violence," I said. "Copious, terrifying, and simple. I don't know much, but I know what works."

Marya helped her mother bake bread. Her hands started to ache from the kneading. It was hard work, but fresh bread was worth it. This was when she first heard the purple noise. She stopped and stared into space, mind focused on this strange new thing. Her mother noticed the something was wrong and tapped her gently on the shoulder. She was accustomed to her strange little girl, and her strange little ways.

Marya started to knead again, and looked sheepishly at her mother. You couldn't stop kneading bread so soon, or it didn't rise properly. Something changed when you worked the flour. It learns how to be bread. Her mother kissed her forehead softly and went into the yard.

She worked the dough with her small strong hands, softly singing without any particular words. The purple noise came on again, louder than before. She could also hear her mother beating the rugs with a wooden paddle, a strong steady rhythm. She wove her song into it, around the impacts.

There was something in the song that made the dough easier to work. It became softer, smoother, more supple as she worked it with voice and hands. The little strands she could sense in the dough, but not see, changed their shape and the dough took on the texture of satin. She moved the loaf to a stone paddle and covered it with a towel to rise.

Her hands smelled of tiny lives, furiously growing. She held them to her face, breathing deeply of them. Her mother walked in at that moment and told her to go wash up. She did so, watching the water in the basin go from clear to milky. She wondered why this happened, but knew better than to ask her mother. Marya loved her mother, but knew that her mother did not care one bit why anything in the world worked; she only cared that it did.

Marya tossed the dirty water in the basin out onto the lawn, and refilled it with clean before putting it back on the stand by the door. She watched her mother peel vegetables and wondered if she would one day be so pretty. She hoped so. She also wondered if one day she would become so uninterested in wondering about things. This seemed the saddest, scariest part of adulthood.

Her grandmother was nearby, resting in her chair, with a blanket up to her chin. She was watching something that only she could see. She stared into space as though she were looking back in time. Her lips sometimes moved, but she no longer spoke. Marya hazily remembered times when this was not so, when her grandmother not only spoke, but sang. Something had happened inside of her head since then that had taken her away from the world as Marya saw it.

Her grandmother, they told her, had once been a queen of her people. Her family had, in those days, traveled from place to place in Africa and Europe, trading and never stopping for more than a few days. They were hated and it was dangerous. This island had been better for them. The outsiders here had welcomed them, and even married in with them. It was, her mother said, a nowhere place. It belonged to nobody and to anyone who wanted it.

Marya's mother had been born here, and so had she. She had never seen Europe. She didn't want to. It seemed a horrible place, where nobody understood kindness. She'd been told that they burned alive anyone who could listen to the dead. She was certain that they'd have burned her as well for singing to the bread or for hearing purple noises. She doubted that they would have heard the purple noise in any case. They were too busy killing each other over God.

She went over to her grandmother, and brushed her steely hair with an old scarlet handled brush. Her grandmother turned her face slightly, and looked right at her. She mumbled something soft. Marya did not understand it and didn't need to. For a short moment her Grandmother was aware enough to see, and to be seen.

"Marya," her mother said, "Go fetch your father."

Marya set the brush down, kissed her grandmother's hair and put the brush back in its place on the side table.

She walked down the lane to the little building where the men go to sit and drink and argue. She was nearly there when the purple noise stopped her again. It was so strong this time that she froze, feeling a tingling in her limbs, a sense of panic.

She looked down, and felt a lurching need to throw up. She had nearly stepped on one of the little winged men.

She stepped back carefully, looking over her shoulder to be sure there weren't more of them. There weren't. There were only the two that had been in her path. She knelt down in front of them. They were standing, looking straight ahead with their little jeweled eyes, unmoving. They stood with their pale purple wings unfurled and veiny, the tops of their wings touching. They had thin hair like thistledown that moved with the light wind.

She reached out and stroked the edge of one wing, so fragile and soft. It trembled like the surface of a soap bubble, and the purple noise rang in her skull louder than ever.

They immediate closed their wings into hard little shells on their backs, and they looked right at her. They had no mouths and could not smile or frown. They cocked their heads from side to side, as if trying to understand her. They took each other hand in hand, and foot in foot, and walked off into the tall grass with their usual odd gait.

She wondered what it would be like to have feet just like hands, and why any little thing so different from people would look so much like them, and why they would want to hold hands as they walked. She had no answers.

She tipped her head down to the grass where they had stood, savouring the sweet spicy smell left behind. Soon, some of the beetles came and rolled in that same spot, clicking happily as they rolled in it, and over one another in some alien joy. She would have watched longer, but remembered she was on an errand.

She made her way to the tavern and opened the wooden door. Her father was tall, but not a strong man, like so many in this place. These men worked with their hands. Her father worked with his mind, using numbers. He was smart, and respected for being smart. He noticed her coming in, and his eyes looked owlish behind his spectacles. He was happy to see her.

SLEEPING UNDERWATER

"Marya," he said, waving her over to his table.

She went, a little nervously, because he was sitting with some of the Jherek family. They were a family with a thousand different brothers and cousins, or so it seemed, and always they were in trouble. She had listened to her parents argue about this. Her mother agreed with Marya that they were nasty to look at and dangerous to be near. Their eyes reminded her of the eyes of sharks, black, dark, empty, hungry.

She felt, unhappily, like she was taking sides against her mother, as her father swept her up on his lap. She loved it when he did that, even though she was probably getting too old for it. One of his arms held her tightly around the waist.

Bernor Jherek smiled, his breath beery and his teeth shiny white. He pulled out a little piece of boiled sweet and offered it to her.

She took it, saying thank you without making eye contact. His hand felt rough and unpleasant, and she tucked it in a pocket in her apron.

"Don't you want it now?" Bernor asked her.

"Thank you, but Mama does not let me have sweets so close to supper."

"You're a good girl to mind her then," he said, and all the men mumbled assent. Their eyes looked as though she has interrupted something with her presence, and she felt shame, her cheeks hot.

"Papa," she said, "Mama sent me for you. It's supper soon."

"Yes," he answered, "I'd figured that out."

He set Marya down, and shook hands with each of the men at the table.

"We'll talk again soon, Lem," Bernor said. "It's got to be done soon, if at all."

Her father nodded, a little nervously. He took her hand, and they walked back to the house.

"I don't like them," she said.

"I don't like them either, sweetheart. When you're a grownup, you'll find sometimes you have to be friends with people you don't like. The Jherek brothers want many of the same things we do for the island, and we work together as good neighbours must. When I'm gone, I'm sure they make fun of me and my specs. They call me Frog. They need me, though, as I need them, and so they are polite to my face."

"What's a frog?"

He blinked. "You know what a frog is, Marya, from the books. Big eyes, like mine, green pebbly skin, big feet. The boy frogs puff up their necks to show off for their girlfriends."

He puffed up his cheeks, and looked very silly.

"I remember now that you make that face," she said, giggling. "The baby frogs have no legs at all, and look like little minnows?"

"That's right."

"Why are there no frogs here?"

"I don't know dear. The same reason we've not got many animals at all, whatever that may be. This is a strange place, as islands very often are."

They walked into the house together, and Marya's mother clucked her tongue, smelling the liquor. Marya began to set the table as her parents laughed and teased each other.

While Des sat on my couch, wondering if I'd lost my mind altogether, I went into my bedroom and changed into a t-shirt and jeans and a brown leather jacket. I put on a baseball cap, and some black leather gloves and sneakers. I now looked nothing at all like myself, at least not as anyone had seen me dressed in many years. In the mirror, my face was still and slow.

"Do you really think you've the stomach for violence," the invisible voice asked.

"Look," I said quietly, though out loud "I'm done simply hoping you'll go away. Can you at least tell me this? Are you going to make this more dangerous for me, or less dangerous? It doesn't matter, as I'm going to do it anyway. I'd just like to know."

"I'm always here, Niles. Always. You just haven't been speaking to me, that's all."

I nodded. "Anything I can do to return us to that state?"

"Renounce violence and all the ways of menace and danger and intrigue."

"Far from fucking likely," I said. "Welcome aboard. I hope you'll love it here."

I came out of the bedroom. Des looked up at me and shook his head.

"I hope you plan on taking a gun," he said.

"No," I said. "I don't intend to bring a weapon at all."

SLEEPING UNDERWATER

He blinked. "You're mad. The things I hear about these people, Niles, you don't understand. They're not to be fucked about with. Sincerely. They kill people, and seem to enjoy it. It's not just part of their, like, business model."

"I don't intend to bring a weapon. I never said I don't intend to use one. The world is full of weapons laying all over the place. Everything is a weapon if you hold it right. And most of them are hard to trace. Now, you say you've heard things. What have you heard? Start at the beginning and work through."

Des let out a sigh, and leaned back. "It's not much, and I can't swear to all of it, right?"

"That's understood."

"Okay. The Jherek boys showed up out of nowhere about two years ago. Honestly, like out of nowhere. One day they just showed up on the streets and were dealing and shylocking. Resistance and response from the people who currently held the territory was short lived. Rumour is that Jherek had information on some of the right people, and everyone leaves him alone because of it. However, they also leave him alone because his soldiers are insanely violent when provoked and because he isn't getting very grabby. They've kept to their little piece of dirt and haven't been expanding since then."

"What did you mean about Egyptian soul theft?"

"Jherek and his boys seem to be really into the old time religion, they say. One of the things they supposedly did during the turf dispute was to cut up a guy on the other side. They wrapped up each piece and left it where it would be found. Except for the guy's prick. They left a fake wooden one of those."

"That is very eccentric," I said, more annoyed by it than intrigued. I could only tell from the sound of my own voice.

"Yeah, and they let it be known they had his prick, and explained that for as long as they had it, the other side had better behave themselves. They said if they destroyed his prick, this guy would have no protection from the monsters in the underworld. The other side took it to heart, I'm told, because, a lot of weird things started to happen."

"Such as?"

"I don't actually know. Probably like most of this nonsense, you know. They're told to be on the lookout for it, so they start seeing coincidences everywhere. Patterns are perceived that do not, in fact, exist. Who knows? Not me. They do not talk about it. At all."

"Since then, Jherek's only had to threaten. Apparently, a guy was into Jherek for a couple thousand pounds. They let him off the debt in exchange for his Greater Ka. He agreed, went through some ritual with them, and walked away laughing. Two weeks later he'd gashed his wrists open. They found him in an alley. Cats were eating his corpse."

"What's the Greater Ka?" I asked. "The name's ringing a bell, but I've not kept up with mythology or the occult since college."

"Harry down the pub told me it's a sort of guardian angel that looks out for you and channels divine wisdom to you as you go through life. In Voodoo they call it the gros bon ange, he says."

"Harry down at the pub seems like an interesting fellow to get to know."

"Talks to people a lot. Pays attention. I'd hate to play him at Trivia."

"So basically, these people are left alone for the same reasons you'd get left alone in jail after eating your first cellmate."

Des chuckled. "It's like half the people think they're too crazy to fuck with, and the other half are actually afraid of magic."

"In your gut, Des, what do you think? You think the magic is real?"

He shifted uncomfortably. "I don't have an opinion, to be honest."

"I'm asking for your gut feeling."

"I don't have one, right. I don't even know if I believe in that stuff."

I looked him in the eye. "Really now?"

"I know, I know. I've not forgotten about all that with Andrew and that. That doesn't have to mean magic. It could have been something else."

"Fair enough. Do you think Jherek has something else, or is it showmanship?"

He took in a breath. "Some from column a," he said, "some from column b. I'm fucking convinced that he believes in his own shit."

"I was sort of thinking along the same lines, actually. Considering the way he talked during our visit."

Des stood up and walked over to my kitchen window, looking out into the street below. He wasn't the kind of man who was prone to sudden silences. I was torn between interrupting it, and letting it be. I was in the mood to rush into things, and maybe, I thought, I should let him slow me down some more. That might be prudent.

"Niles," he said, "this isn't just one bloke. This is a whole gang of hard men who, I repeat, really like to hurt people. Even with two of us, the chances are very good that we're going to get killed, and that will accomplish nothing for your friend. I hesitate to suggest this, but perhaps you should talk to the police."

"They'll kill Carter for sure, in that case. It's not an option. Does anyone know where this lot comes from?"

"No, they seem to come in all shades and have accents nobody can place. They just talk about coming from 'the island'."

"They're from an island."

"So are you."

I shrugged it off and handed him the jar with the beetles. "I'm sure these aren't from around here. I bet we can find out where, though."

"So what if you do, mate? What good does that do us?"

"I want all the information I can get on where these people came from and why."

"What does it matter where the fuck they're from? Mad bastards with guns are the same the whole world round."

"If I know what they want, what they actually want, it gives me an edge, Des. This is more than money to them, clearly. If I can even half understand it, I might be able to act more wisely."

"Whatever you say, but I don't see how that changes anything if your plan is to burst in guns blazing and get your boy out of there."

"With a few moments of sober reflection, I suppose it's not the entirety of my plan. Sadly, it's still the likeliest place I'll end up at. Anyhow, first things first, I need to find an entomologist."

Des rolled his eyes. "Are you fucking serious?"

"Forewarned is forearmed."

"They're fucking bugs, you daft bugger."

"They're all I have right now," I said, and then stopped. "No. Actually, not quite."

I was suddenly tormented by the sure knowledge that I should already know more than I did. That there was something familiar about this, that should have been right on the tip of my tongue. Then the idea dove back for deeper waters, and I had to let it go. I could only hope it would come up for air again later.

"Niles?"

"Never mind. I'll start with the beetles."

LAIRD RYAN STATES

Nemo sat on a patch in the centre of town. Enough time had passed and nobody, finally, was interested in staring at him. His face had become familiar. Most of the islanders seemed to think of him as simple, because he had lost his memory, but also because he spent so much time just looking at things. He rarely spoke unless spoken to.

Marya was on the other side of the town square, sitting quietly with her friends. She had not paid enough attention to the conversation because she had been watching Nemo, the handsome stranger who had treated her so gallantly when they first met. He still seemed impossibly pretty and exotic.

One of her friends jostled her, giggling. She responded by, very maturely, sticking her tongue out at them.

"Marya loves the stranger," one of them said to her, and Nemo heard it from across the grass, and looked in their direction.

Marya said nothing, and just stared at him as he lay on his side, looking up from book he held in one hand, and then he looked back down at the pages. She stood up, and walked over to him, her friends covering their mouths to stifle giggling, and calling her back in hushed tones.

She was suddenly very aware of the scabs on her knees as she stood beside him. He had fallen into the book so deeply for a moment that he did not seem to notice her. Her pulse quickened at the sight of that intensity of focus. His passion for reading excited her.

"Hello, my brave and gallant young saviour," he said, without looking, without moving his lips at all.

She stepped back sharply. "Hello Mr. Nemo."

He smiled, and rolled on his side. "I wondered if you might hear me."

She nodded uncertainly.

"How marvelous," he said. "Nobody else here has. I keep expecting them to, but they don't. Isn't that strange?"

She barely understood his meaning, and it made no sense to her anyway. Why should anyone hear him at all if he spoke without speaking.

Oh dear, she thought. He is so beautiful. I do love him.

He stood up and mussed her hair like uncles do. She felt her stomach ache at the chasteness, and the intention of the contact.

SLEEPING UNDERWATER

"You think that you do," he said without speaking. "You see a handsome man, with no memories and no life of his own. It's very easy to paint your own desires on this blank canvas. It's very common. You're a very special sort of girl, and, if you think on it, you'll find I'm right."

He turned to go back toward the mansion, book under his arm. "Are you coming," he asked out loud. She nodded, following, considering his words.

"Aren't you sad," she asked him, "to remember nothing? Does it scare you?"

"Your Latin is much improved," he answered, so they could speak in secret. "Have you been studying?"

"No," she answered. "I don't know why it's better."

"I suppose I do."

He offered her his hand, and she took it. They walked around the base of the hill, and to the water where the only sounds were those of the waves, and the distant sound of men mining salt.

"You didn't answer my question."

"You're right," he said. "That's a rude thing adults do to children. I dimly recall that I absolutely hated it."

"Then stop it," she said, a little angry at being called a child.

"No, it doesn't make me sad."

"Aren't you lonely? You must have a family. Perhaps a wife, or a little daughter who misses you."

He nodded. "I might. If I did, I think they may be long dead. I don't think I do. It is quite possible. If you like, you can feel badly on their behalf. I simply don't remember them. This life here on the island is all that I know. That and shadows and dim flashes that make up nothing."

"It sounds terrible."

"It isn't, but I could never explain it to one so young as you."

"Which is another thing that adults always say," she says, tossing a stone into the waves.

"It is, but it's not a cheat, I promise. No word of a lie. There really are things age and experience teach you that nothing else can. I wish, honestly, you never had to learn them at all."

She shrugged, not sure what she thought. "Why do you remember nothing?"

"Because I'm not as other men are. I can hear you in my head, and you can hear me in yours. That's enough to show you that we are more like one another than we are like other people. Is that not true?" He added the rest without speaking aloud.

"I remember everything that has ever happened to me," she said. "Sometimes I think I remember things that happened to other people that I used to be."

"It may not always be so."

Her eyes brimmed with tears. "I don't want to forget."

"You will, one day. If you do, you will be as glad about it as I am."

Their conversation had become completely silent now, as they sat side by side, pitching rocks in turn. Her eyes were sad and shiny.

"How could I ever be glad for such a thing?"

"The older you get," he said, "the more things you'll have done you'll regret doing."

"And more I will be happy about!"

"Losing the memory of those things will seem a small price to pay to forget your regrets, Marya."

She reached out and touched his arm.

"What have I done," he said, "to earn this show of affection?"

"You told me the truth when it was difficult and ugly. I do love you. I don't care if you think I'm silly."

He put his hand gently under her chin, lifting her eyes to his. She felt as though maybe he would lean in and kiss her. He didn't.

"If you love me," he said, "You must love me as an uncle or as you love your friends. There can never be any more between us. I am a million million years old, and if I were ever to fall in love, I would probably fall in love with another old man. It seems to me, my sweet, that I prefer the pleasures of men."

She reared back, confused and wordless. "You give me so much to think about," she said, "that my head hurts."

"You see," he said, "Already you wish to forget telling me that you love me."

"Never," she said, looking him in the eye.

He smiled kindly. "You aren't silly at all. You're only young. You have not learned to temper your emotions because you have not yet needed to."

Her cheeks burned, and she was about to shout at him, when she heard the purple noise. Beside her, Nemo stiffened, and he stood up quickly.

"Best you head home," he said.

"I don't want to. I want to talk."

"We have forever to talk. Right now it isn't safe. Besides, people will think it unwholesome that I spend so much time alone with you."

He winked at her. She suddenly wanted to scratch his eyes out and stomp them to jelly in the sand.

He winced, and she realized he had seen the vivid image just as she had pictured it.

"There's trouble in the governor's house tonight," he said. "I have to go."

He left, and Marya stayed by the water thinking. She wondered if dreams were sometimes memories in hiding. The more she considered, the more questions she had.

Then, for the first time, the purple noise resolved into a voice.

"Help," it said.

I left Des with the task of going out into his community and trying to gather some intelligence on the Jherek organization. I was looking for practical information, like how many of them there actually were, and where they loitered. While he looked into this, mostly to get away from me for a few hours, I went to the university in search of an entomologist. It didn't take me very long. Entomology is not the kind of rock star science that quantum physics is. There are no household names in entomology. I'm not sure why this is so, but it's so. After a few polite inquiries I was put in touch with a Dr. Leonard Somerset, who was an expert on the taxonomy of beetles.

I knocked on the door of his office, and he welcomed me in. I sat down in the chair in front of his desk and looked the room over. On one wall was a tall cabinet full of narrow drawers. I assumed, from what I'd seen on television, that this was full of preserved samples. The desk was immaculate, no pens askew, no ink-stained blotter. There seemed to be a place for everything in the office, and each thing was very carefully in that place.

Somerset was a large man, broad shouldered, and pear shaped with bright lively eyes and full lips. His forehead was high. He moved with precision, with few wasted movements, clasping his hands together on the desktop.

"How can I help you?" he asked with a mild Scottish overtone to his accent.

"Well, I'm a private investigator," I said. "Niles Townsend. I'm investigating a disappearance. A kidnapping, actually. The only piece of physical evidence we have is in this jar."

I set the jar on the table, and he leaned forward to look, and it was clear right away that his attention was fixed.

"These were left behind, I think, by the people who took the victim. I'm pretty sure they aren't from around here."

"You're certainly right, there, Mr. Townsend."

Somerset opened the jar, shook one of the beetles out into his hand, and gently stroked the hard shell.

"Surely not," he said to himself, and then tipped the beetle on it's back, so that its legs kicked and pinioned. The beetle in the jar kept its head pointed toward its brother always. I watched with fascination of my own. That seemed unnatural.

"Not what?"

"Well," he said, "I have a suspicion as to what these are, but it seems unlikely."

"I would say the exotic is a strong possibility here."

"In order to be certain, I shall need to kill this little fellow."

"I understand. Do what you have to," I said, then stopped short. "They aren't endangered or anything are they?"

Somerset smiled. "No, I don't think so. Just not widely distributed."

"All right, then."

Somerset reached into a drawer and took out a sharp scalpel and some very fine tweezers. He took a mandible in the tweezers and used the scalpel to remove it. He held it up to the light and looked at it with a magnifying glass. He made a soft noise of interest. The beetle kicked and writhed on its back, and his brother in the jar tapped repeatedly at the glass.

He set the mandible down and put the tip of the scalpel into the head of the beetle. As the flailing began to slow, the other one in the jar settled down abruptly. I felt queasy enough I was afraid I might sick up, but kept my face calm and expressionless. I neither wanted to interrupt him, nor to think closely about what I was watching.

Somerset cut at the underside of the beetle and pried it open. He took a deep nervous breath and then reached into his drawer and removed something that looked like a jeweller's eyepiece. For several tense moments he slowly investigated the abdomen of the beetle, then gasped and pulled out a small greenish-grey sac the size of a grain of rice.

"How many of these were there?" Somerset asked me.

"Just these two."

"Remarkable. You are likely find more. They tend to swarm."

"So you know what they are?"

"I will know for certain in a second."

He cut the little sac open, and there was a warm spicy smell and a very small amount of purple and silver powder slid out, barely enough to see. Somerset produced a small glass tube and used the edge of the scalpel to tip the powder inside. He capped it with a small cork.

"What is that?" I asked.

"The assumption is that it's a type of pheromonal marker, but the truth is nobody has studied it very closely. These beetles are extremely rare. They're not even formally classified. Frankly, it's a matter of luck that I've ever heard of them. If you'd taken this to someone else, they might have had no idea. It seems impossible, but this," he shook the tube, "is a smoking gun."

"So where are they from?"

"This beetle is from an island called Sel Souris. People there are said to use this powder to induce visions, I'm told."

"And that's the only place they come from?"

"Well," Somerset said, "as far as we know. Beetles are common as dirt. Almost more common. We have more beetles classified than any other kind of animal, and we're certain we've barely catalogued a tiny percentage of the actual number of species that exist. Beetles are the true owners of this planet."

"Well, they're doing a piss poor job running the place."

"Their needs are simple," he said, smiling.

"Do you have any idea where Sel Souris is?"

"I don't know anything, truly, but what I've mentioned, and only because of the beetle."

"Well, I thank you," I said, standing up, and I shook his hand. "You've taken me a lot further than I was."

"I'm glad I could be of service. I hope it all turns out for the best."

"I'd better get back to it."

"Do you mind if I hold onto these?"

"Be my guest."

"Thank you. I've a nephew in Canada who is crazy for insects. I'll make a gift of one."

I nodded, keeping my opinions to myself, and I left his office.

The name Sel Souris was bringing that lost thought back up from the deep, but not fast enough for my liking. I went to my car, trying to place it, with no success at all.

Marya did not know how long she'd been lying there, with her ear to the ground, straining to hear more. There had been no more words. She realized, absently, that it was getting dark outside.

She had given up on town. The noise of the people there had been too loud, and distractions too plentiful. She had run past her still scandalized friends, and straight on down the road, until her feet had ached from pounding into the hard-packed dirt. She made her way to the crossroad that led to the mounds, and laid down there where the roads met.

She knew it was not safe for people to go much nearer to the mounds than this, so she had stopped at that place to listen. She begged in her mind over and over for it to speak, but it had not worked.

Exhausted, she stood up and stretched out, standing on tiptoes. The muscles in her calves felt as tightly wound as a guitar string. She heard a sudden note strike through her body, and the tension faded, her legs no longer ached.

She turned, took a breath and walked toward the mounds. Her parents had told her many times never to go to the mounds. The little men lived in a different world to theirs. The air they breathed was not the same air as men did, and neither could survive long among the other.

As she walked, with every step, the world smelled less green and more purple. She knew from the stories that she would soon hear the chiming of the mounds. Soon after, she'd see the mounds where the little men lived, and from which the beetles crawled in their millions and to which they returned.

She didn't hear any chiming. She heard the sounds of an engine. It clattered, clanked and rattled. Two men were nearby, dressed in diving suits, and she knelt down to hide from them. The men spoke to each other in French, but she could not hear them well. The suits they wore muffled their voices.

A small hand rested on her knee, and she looked down to the little man beside her. His hand felt and looked like the stem of a dandelion. She reached down to stroke the soft blossom like tendrils on top of his head. The little man looked her right in the eyes. She had no idea what he was thinking. She wondered if he was as lost as she was. His face was entirely blank and unknowable.

"Can you talk?" she asked in her mother's tongue, and then again in French. He gave no sign of understanding. The Frenchmen came a few steps closer, and the little man startled, clambering up her arm, and onto her shoulder, She felt the tiny hairs on his arm tickling her cheek. He moved her hair with both of his little hands, hiding behind it.

The men stepped into the clearing, and startled to see her. They turned to one another, speaking quickly, and with their arms. She stood up, frightened. One of the men fumbled at the little window on the front of his helmet, his gloved fingers struggling to undo a little latch. There was a soft hissing as it swung open.

His face was sweating, and he had a large light brown moustache which drooped comically, its waxed tips having melted.

"Do you speak French?" he asked her.

She nodded, her legs trembling with the urge to run, her head swimming with fear.

"Don't be scared," the man said, "I'm no monster."

"I know," she said, trying to sound polite. "You must be very hot in that suit."

The man smiled and nodded wearily.

"What is your name?" he asked.

"Marya."

"I am Napoleon Findeville."

Marya knew of him. He was a friend of the governor, called here to study the little men. He was a scientist, and a writer. Her Papa thought him to be an Imperialist. She looked kind to him. His eyes met hers, and there was real concern for her there.

"It's not safe for you to be here," he said. "You must head back to the road as fast as you can. The air is bad here, and that is why I require this suit to be here. Do you understand?"

"I do. I can't go back yet."

"Why ever not?"

The other man tapped his shoulder, and Findeville brushed it away as though it were an annoyance.

"I hear a purple noise asking for help," she said, not sure if it was wise.

Findeville reared back as if she'd blasphemed, his eyes terrified and disgusted. "That's terrible."

The little man on her shoulder extended its wings suddenly and was revealed. She felt the softness against her face.

Findeville reached out quickly, more quickly than she would have thought he could in the suit, and grabbed the little man in a fist. The purple noise shrieked and keened in her head, the sound seeming to tear apart in threads. He dashed it against a tree, and the noise stopped.

The little man was broken, thick milky liquid oozing from a tear in its side. The little eyes were as wide and expressionless as ever.

She screamed. Findeville looked at the broken little thing in the grass, breathing hard, horrified, looking ill.

Marya ran toward the mounds rather than away from them. Findeville's companion grabbed for her, but too slow.

She ran, the two of them following after her, not half so quickly as she could move. The hoses that fed into their helmets, and the weight of the suits slowed them. Suddenly she saw the mounds. They were nothing like in the stories she'd heard told. She stared, unable to fully understand the sight of them. Her eyes were glassy, as the men caught up to her. There were other men there, with machines, digging. Black smoke poured from the engines. She breathed in the purple tasting air. It choked her, poisonous, wonderful and strange. Her eyes fluttered like the wings of the little men and she fell.

When she awoke, she was in bed, dressed in her nightclothes. A wet cloth was laid across her dry and prickly face. She called for her mother, and both of her parents rushed into her room, in turn scolding her and plastering her face with kisses.

She saw Mr. Nemo standing on the other side of the doorway.

"Nemo," she said.

"He found you near the mounds," her Papa said, "You're very lucky."

She was unable to stay awake any longer, and fell asleep in the arms of her parents. She dreamed of beetles and little men, and machines which dug and pounded into her belly without mercy or reason.

SLEEPING UNDERWATER

I spent the rest of the day at the library researching the island of Sel Souris. By the end of it, I was ill.

My stomach was all acid and dismay and I hadn't eaten anything. I left the library in the early evening, as the sun was going down. I drove back to my flat and was grateful to see Des' ridiculous car parked out front. He got out as I pulled into my spot.

"Where the fuck you been, mate?" he asked me. "We were supposed to meet up over an hour ago. I was starting to worry."

I put a hand on his biceps. "Sorry, Des. Honestly, I am. I wasn't thinking."

"You can't fuck around like that when we're involved in things like this, Niles."

"I know."

I moved to go inside and he followed after me, more than a bit annoyed. He was clearly bothered by more than my lateness. I supposed he had enjoyed his fact finding mission about as much as I'd enjoyed mine. Once I got inside the door I immediately put the kettle on. When I turned back, Des was staring at my couch with an ashen look.

I turned my head at him.

"Oh Christ," I said, "What mad bullshit has now invaded my home?"

Des didn't answer. He stepped back and shook his head. I stepped quickly to him, because he looked like a man about to faint.

"Des, are you all right?"

It was then that I saw that the cushions were crawling with purple beetles. There were at least a hundred of them. I muffled a sound of alarm that came unbidden.

"Fuck me ragged," I said to him.

"Shit," Des said, and he headed to my kitchen sink and ran cold water over his face.

I started to pick the beetles up one at a time and brush them into an empty shoebox, after dumping the current contents, receipts mostly, on my kitchen table. I wound up only squashing a few of them. I put the lid on, put a heavy book atop it, and examined the floor and my clothes for strays. I knew they could be inside the sofa in the thousands. It seemed very important to me to get rid of all the visible ones at the very least. That much would allow me to not flee in revulsion.

I sat on the floor, my elbows on my knees, and head in my hands.

"I think I'm going to lose my fucking head, Des."

"Niles," he said, looking as shaken as I'd seen him since the bad old days, "I've got to tell you something, right? If I do, you have to swear you won't take the piss."

"Trust me, at this point, I don't think anything is ever going to make me laugh again."

"They were crawling there in the shape of letters. It said 'help.'"

I nodded. "You have no idea how much I believe you. These fucking things are…" I paused, trying to find the word, "Uncanny. I don't know what they are, but they aren't just garden variety bugs."

Des looked relieved that I didn't think he was crazy. "How the hell did they get in here."

"Old building," I said, and left it at that, having no better answer in my pocket to produce.

"Kettle's boiling."

"Thanks. Fancy a cup?" I was already halfway to the kitchen to pull mugs and pour.

"Got biccies?"

"Might have. Feel free to root in the cupboards."

He moved to look, and pulled his hand back. "I'll do without."

I checked the cups twice before I poured. We sat at the kitchen table, and had a very civilized and normal cup of tea in total silence.

"Those fucking things have a really strong smell," he said after a few minutes.

I nodded. "Known for it, apparently," I said. "The five people who've ever heard of them, know them for that. And for swarming."

"I don't normally have a thing about bugs, you know?"

"Yeah, I don't blame you."

"So," Des said, "you found out where the beetles are from, then?"

"Yeah. Island called Sel Souris. Somewhere near Gibraltar, but not near enough to matter to anyone. The beetles only live there, so I'm thinking that Jherek and his bunch brought them along for some reason. Fuck knows why."

"Makes sense. They're always talking about the island."

"So I recall."

"Didn't find out as much as I'd have liked to," Des said. "Near as I can tell, it's Jherek and a load of his family. There's maybe twenty of them, people say. That doesn't count the women though, or the locals they hire from time to time."

"They have locals working for them?" I asked, surprised in light of the research I'd done.

"Yeah, but strictly street corner dealers. Weed, opium, some specialty items. They don't track in coke or meth at all. They may sell a little junk, but it's not their line. This might be another reason they've been given a pass from the really big boys."

I nodded, and then realized I was a terrible detective. "Oh hell," I said. "I do know why they brought the beetles. They're product. I didn't twig until just know, but the entomologist told me the locals there use these beetles to induce visions."

"You are fucking kidding me."

"No, I am not."

"I thought Purple Haze was just a street name for like their brand of opium."

"Purple Haze."

Des looked at the box of beetles over on the floor. "Too fucking weird."

I sighed and nodded. "Do we know where they hang out?"

"Well, the house we've been to. Some of Jherek's cousin's have flats of their own. They also own that warehouse you were in. They apparently have a social club above the shop across the road from it. Invitation only."

"Did you get any hints where they're keeping Carter?"

"Nah," he said, "but I'm willing to bet it's the social club."

"Why's that?"

"It's what I'd do. I think it's less of a social club than a drug depot. This means there are always users hanging around and it means they already have people on guard. Easiest way to manage him."

I nodded and poured another cup. "Okay. By the way, you're right. These people are fucking crazy."

"Yeah. I didn't need confirmation. I was confident."

"I tried to find out the history of the island, and see if there were any political situations that would profit from exporting organized crime, and importing the cash. I didn't find any. What I did find out is that these people hate us. The English. The French. Everyone, actually. I'm not sure why. Apparently in the 19th century they revolted and drove off the French governor and went completely isolationist until the Second World War. At that point they had little choice but to run into people again. It's illegal for Europeans to set foot on the island."

"Sod off. Illegal?"

"Yeah. They let Canadians, Americans and Australians visit, on a short leash. Anyone from former European colonial holdings, really, are welcome. A small but steady stream of Indians, Pakistanis, and Africans seem to emigrate there."

"But not the evil Euros."

"It's a strange, angry little place."

"Naturally, we let the fuckers walk around here on our island. That's everything wrong with us in—"

"I did find something really relevant," I interrupted. Des and I did not see eye to eye on immigration. I handed him photocopies of some newspaper articles.

He looked at them, not reading them. "What's this, then?"

"Those are the stories about Victor Mayhew and the foreign office and the Sel Souris incident."

"The what?"

"Yeah. Came and sunk like a stone. I'm surprised I missed it, considering our prior encounters. I suspect that the foreign office might have worked harder to resolve it if Victor weren't a 'self-confessed homosexual'. That's how they refer to him about a dozen times in those articles."

Des ran his eyes over the articles and at the appropriate place his eyes widened.

"They gouged his fucking eyes out and shipped him to Spain on a fishing boat? And we just let that go?"

"Yeah. He broke their local laws, and that was that. The government paid for his flight home, and he went to live with his parents. End of fucking story."

"They gouged his eyes out," Des said, "And they dipped them in plastic for keepsies."

"Yes."

"And so, your boy, Carter, he swiped them back."

"Yeah."

"Christ. Everyone involved in this is totally insane. Top to bottom."

"You have no idea," said the voice in the back of my head. "Just none."

Des stood up. "Okay. So your boy swiped them, and Jherek wants them back pretty badly."

"You say he showed up out of nowhere one day. I'm willing to bet they showed up here right after the eyes were stolen."

Des looked at me.

"You think they came here specifically to get the eyes back? They came all this way for that?"

"For the principle of the thing," I said. "Yes. And they are paying for it by selling their weird specialty drug."

Des walked to the door. "I need a packet of Silk Cut."

I nodded.

"When I come back up here, I hope like hell you're going to tell me what you have in mind next. I'm strongly inclined to think running the other way might be best."

I smiled at him weakly and he left me alone with my thoughts, and a box of angry beetles that clicked and hissed softly through the thin cardboard that kept them out of sight.

Marya felt very ill the next morning. She woke up with dry, itchy eyes, and a rash of raised purple bumps that spread from her shoulder down over the dove-wing shaped bones on her back all the way to the middle of her back, the very place she could not reach to scratch.

She sat up and ground her back against the headboard. Sweet rushing relief came in waves, a guilty pleasure. She knew it was wrong to scratch at a rash, but could not help it. She felt the back of her nightgown become wet and sticky. She felt dizzy. The room seemed to spin around. The slight breeze from the open window was sweet and cool against her face.

She called for her mother, sounding littler than she wanted to. Her mother came at once and pressed a lightly floured hand against Marya's forehead. She murmured something, the words meaning less than the tone, concerned and soft. Her mother left the room, and came back with a cold wet cloth. She put the cloth on Marya's forehead, and moved to turn Marya on her back.

She felt the blood, and jerked her hand back in horror. Marya saw her own blood on her mother's hand, and was scared for the first time.

Marya's mother lifted her to her feet, and pulled the nightie off of her, tossing it to the floor. Marya was naked, and felt the awkward differentness of everything whenever she was naked in front of someone else. Every gesture of her body seemed over-amplified to her, and her skin seemed more awake, more attentive.

Her mother's face was a mask of horror, and Marya was afraid that she would start to cry. She didn't want to cry, because that was for babies. She wanted nothing more to do with childhood.

Her mother ran another wet cloth down Marya's back. She could feel every thread of it. Pain and relief came in immediate succession as wetness hit each welt and bump. The cloth came away crimson, and with black strands sticking to it that looked like fine hairs. The breeze from the window distracted her from her nudity, the relief of the water was fleeting, and the itching returned. She whimpered, her cheeks flushing with shame.

Her mother made a soft cooing nose at her, and Marya had a moment of clarity. She realized how much she and her mother said to each other without ever using any words at all. They spoke, and had always spoken, in a code of facial expressions and subtle touching. Their eyes, and the shapes of their mouths said more that any words, and at times like this, they often abandoned them altogether.

She was laid down on her belly, and her mother left the room for a moment. She looked at the headboard and the bedposts. They were old wood, the varnish scratched and etched by time and long use. It had belonged to her mother before it was hers, and she wondered how many people before that had slept in this bed, called it their own. She had stared at the headboard many times, waiting for sleep to come, trying not to think of nightmare things. She saw faces in the grain of the wood that seemed to shift and change before her eyes. She had noticed that the things she saw were often scarier at night than they were in the daytime. She wondered why this was.

Something, this time, was different. Instead of seeing faces in the wood she was seeing the bed itself, wondering where it came from, and how it worked. When she had seen men building things, they used nails to hold the wood together. She could see no nails in this bed.

It was then that she noticed the joint work, where one piece was cut with a notch, and the other had a tab that fit exactly into it. She realized that the bed needed no nails to stand together.

SLEEPING UNDERWATER

Each and every piece had been designed to hold another piece in place. It was beautiful and she had a fleeting sense of how the entire world worked. The revelation took just a moment, and she was forever changed.

Her mother came back with a ceramic basin and another cloth. She pulled a stool up to the side of the bed and ran the cloth over Marya's back, singing softly. It felt wonderful, and she surrendered to childhood for just a while longer. She was entirely happy to be babied. She was aware of her mother's love, pure and uncomplicated. She closed her eyes and sighed in relief.

She wanted to ask who built the bed, and when, but the alternation of itch and relief were too strong. Her mother kept to the song, and Marya let her mind wander.

She imagined a chair. She could picture it clearly, high-backed, with three slats in the back that looked like strings of brown beads. The slats were held in place at the top by a carved, curved backrest. They fitted into perfectly drilled holes in the backrest and in the seat. She understood why it held together and knew that to break even one slat would cause the chair to all but fall apart. She knew how to build the legs of the chair, and how they should slot into the bottom of the seat. She knew why they needed slats of their own to connect them, and to spread the load evenly.

She took the chair apart in her mind and looked at every piece, turning it around in her head. She marveled at the interdependence of each piece, and how each dark and polished piece had once been part of a tree.

Wood seemed so different from trees that she could barely connect them. Everything that anyone built was built from something that had just happened to be in the world. All of those things were as dependent upon each other as the pieces of the chair. As she stepped back further and further, the immensity of the universe began to overwhelm her. It was all so complicated, everything holding everything together, and all so fragile that she wanted to weep with fear, or with joy.

"She's feverish," her mother said, fear in her voice.

Her father came into the room, and spoke with his wife so quietly Marya could not understand what they said to each other.

She knew she should feel embarrassed to be naked in front of him, but she wasn't. She was too hot, and tired, and spun up in her own thoughts. Then those thoughts stopped altogether.

191

"Help," the purple voice said, and she felt herself wrapped up in a blanket, and lifted in her father's arms. She was carried outside, and between door and cart, the purple noise shut out the world altogether.

Des had demanded a plan of me. I had one, but I didn't care for it much.

Despite riding Des about it, I didn't believe in magic either. I had every reason to, of course, from what I'd been through with Andrew. I preferred, instead, to believe in some heretofore unknown talent of the human brain. This would make it possible to explain with reason, and was, therefore, digestible to me. I was, however, face to face with the total insanity of all of this at every turn: the beetles, my persistent little voice, coincidences upon coincidences.

An argument could be made, of course, that my little voice was just a symptom of madness. I didn't feel as though I'd gone mad, but that meant nothing.

I was grateful to have Des along on this adventure, as much for the simple fact that he was there to confirm some of my observations and to confirm I wasn't simply hallucinating the entire thing.

Also he was large, hard, and terrifying when angry. I suspected that would be useful by the time this was over with. In the end, there was only one real thing I thought we could do to solve this.

My front door opened then, without a knock, and I turned instantly to look, halfway expecting a machete wielding henchman at the door. It was, of course, only Des, still smoking as he walked in. The smell of the cigarette made me want one immediately. I almost asked for one, but decided that renewing an addiction was likely a bad idea, especially at the present.

"Fucking cigarettes, mate," Des said, "are the greatest invention of all time."

"Feeling better then?"

"Worlds better. Almost human. How long do you imagine this smile will remain on my charming and roguish face?"

"Not very long."

"I thought so. Let me bask in this for just a tick longer, then."

"At your leisure."

He took in a deep breath and let it out. "Ready then?"

"I never promised you a plan, really. You demanded."

"I did not demand, either. I just said that I was planning to maybe abandon you."

"I don't honestly remember just what we said. Shall we just agree that we ought to figure out what we intend."

He didn't feel the need to respond. We didn't talk for a few minutes.

"Unless we're willing to trade" I said, eventually, "there's really only one thing we can do. We go to the place we think he's at and we go inside somehow. This will almost certainly require, as I said earlier, copious violence. We then take him out, hope we can survive the engagement, and live with the consequences."

"Niles," he said, "I do not care for your plan."

"I don't either."

"You do," he said, "You want to burst in, shirt torn, and teeth gleaming, and offer him the hand of rescue."

Well, he had me there. "Have you any better options?"

"Sort of."

"Well, by all means, do tell, would you?"

"All right. You go to the place he's at. You get inside somehow, likely involving your demise, and I stay at home and watch Coronation Street."

"Arf. Arf," I said.

"Who's joshing?"

"Right then," I said, "when's the best time for us to go?"

"Whenever the guard is changing, traditionally."

"Do we know when that is?"

"No."

"Well, we should stake the place out and find out then."

"Yes, damn you. That's reasonable."

I grabbed my car keys, and then changed my mind. "We should take your car. I expect they know mine at this point."

"We'll get a car," he said, "in the usual way."

Normally I would have protested the lack of ethics, but not tonight. I knew all the reasons that he was right, and for all he was willing to do for me, I didn't care to press his patience any further.

Nemo and Findeville had been speaking now for several hours, and he did not like most of what he'd heard.

Nemo had met him, in his ridiculous diving contraption, carrying Marya up the road the night she collapsed in the mounds. Nemo had taken her home to her parents himself, angry and worried for her, and wanting to keep Findeville out of it for now. If Marya's father suspected the French were responsible for her condition, it could turn a spark of resentment into a flame all too quickly.

After seeing to her, he had returned to the governor's house, looking for Findeville, demanding an explanation. Findeville had offered one immediately, wanting very much to make it known that he had no part in her injury, that he had, in fact, tried to stop her. For his part, Findeville had asked Nemo to tell him all he knew about the island.

Nemo had told him what little he did know, and one topic turned to another, and to another. The sun had come up at some point during the conversation, and still they had talked on. Findeville had a first-rate mind, and knew how to tell a story with structure and a sense of pertinence. It was a rare thing.

They were interrupted by Georget, who opened the door, out of breath, and barged into the room, Nemo turned to look, and was certain his face must have been dreadfully sour.

"What is it?" Findeville asked, angry at the interruption.

"Nemo," Georget said, "that girl of yours is very ill and asking to see you."

Nemo stood at once. "You mean Marya?"

Georget nodded and struggled for breath. Nemo wondered how long the man had been running. It wouldn't have had to be far to leave him breathless.

"She was taken to my clinic an hour ago, and they called for me at once."

"Is it serious?"

"I've no idea," the doctor said, "She's come over with a strange rash. There's fever and considerable delirium. She asks for you again and again. Her father implores you to come."

"Of course." Nemo turned to Findeville, and rather formally straightened his trousers. "I beg your pardon, but I must go. I found our conversation enlightening and I have more questions. They will have to wait."

"Naturally," Findeville said, also rising. "We will speak again soon. Please let me know how the girl comes along. I fear the worst. She was exposed to the contagion most directly."

Nemo nodded curtly, and shook his hand. He then turned to Georget. "Please, Doctor, take me to her."

Georget led him down the street to the pink and white building that passed for their clinic. The French flag flew from a pole on the scrub grass. Nemo noted that it was, as yet, unmolested. It was early in the day. It would not be there when the sun set. The islanders were growing bolder and more surly with each passing week.

Marya's father, Lem, came out the front door, his huge watery eyes rimmed with red. They were open wide enough that Nemo could see the whites of his eyes all the way around the iris. His skin was pale, empty of blood, and he was sweating freely. Nemo recognized this as the face of a man in a rage, one capable of anything at all. He bore this man no ill will, and let himself be abused.

"What have you done to my daughter, you fucking pig! What did you do to her that you brought her home in a fever, and that now she cries out for you! What have you done to my only child?"

Lem pulled his fist back as though to strike, his hand trembling.

"I plead innocence," Nemo said. "I would never do anything to harm your girl. She has, I admit, something of a harmless crush on me, but I have tried to discourage it. She is a remarkable girl, of whom I am quite fond. She is, however, just a child. I, on the other hand, am an old man, far older than I look. I claim her friendship, but can confess to nothing more."

Nemo put one hand on Lem's shoulder as he spoke calmly and softly. Lem's hand wavered. "Please, sir," Nemo continued. "Lower your hand, and let us speak as friends. You are in a terrible way. I quite understand."

Lem looked at his own hand and, at once, came over horrified, and pulled it down, looking at it as though it were no piece of him. "Please. Forgive me."

"It's forgotten. If I were in your place, I'd be half mad with worry."

"Will you see her, Mr. Nemo?"

Nemo had long given up on asking people to call him simply Nemo. "Of course, if you think it proper."

They went into the clinic, and all eyes turned to him. He was the mysterious stranger still, after three years among them. They whispered as he passed. The clinic was filthy. A woman was crying in some closed room nearby. The place appalled him. Georget was a butcher, it seemed, unless his patient lived in the governor's house.

Marya was on her belly on a high bed with rails to either side. She was draped in a white linen blanket spotted liberally through with blood. Her face was red, and on the exposed skin of her shoulder, he could see welts and hives, purple and angry. He had begun to loathe the purpleness of everything in this place, and his talk with Findeville had redoubled this.

He came to the bed on the opposite side of Marya's mother. Her face was weary with grief. He crouched by the bed until her face was near to his own. He spoke her name.

There came then, at once, a rush of voice and feeling and colour that surged from her to him like galvanic shock, and he fell back. He landed roughly on his buttocks, moaning slightly. Lem stepped toward him to help, but he had already recovered. He got to his knees, and put a hand on Marya's forearm.

Nemo was on the beach again, naked, sand in his hair. Marya stood over him, much older, her eyes dark purple. Her long dark hair was in tangled braids that moved in the wind. Her dress moved likewise, slow, and in strange unison with her hair, like the undulations of seaweed underwater. He knew this was some kind of dream.

"Marya?" His mouth felt smooth and strangely dry, like the pocket of a silk purse.

"This place is the place between worlds," she said. "Words here can be harvested like grain, and turned to bread."

Nemo sat up and looked around. The sky was white and featureless, as clean and fresh as an empty parchment. The sea was dark, like a splash of ink that stretched out as far as the eye could see. He looked at his hands, and pulled them from the sand. The sand was dark and strange. He brought his hands closer to his face. Instead of dark uneven flecks of stone, his hand was spotted with tiny letters, from alphabets varied and numerous. He wanted to read whatever message was there. Words failed him.

"You cannot read here," she said, "Language is still a wild animal, untamed by intellect."

He tried to protest, to tell her to stop this game, but his own words came out in a burbling rush like the droning of madmen and prophets. His heart pounded in his chest, and he stood up, panicking.

"This is where all words come from," she said, her mouth still, her eyes wet and so purple. "Do you see why she ran to you?"

"This is rude," he protested.

The purple sound throbbed in his head like the breathing of a whale, or the heartbeat of God. He hated that noise, hated the insistence of it. He had from the day he first heard it.

"Our intention is to educate. There is a flaw in this interface, but you are the only receiver left. Please help us," Marya said to him. "The child is ill."

He was being shaken by Marya's father, and his cheeks were wet. His neck and jaw ached, as though he had been choked. He gasped to breathe.

Lem was speaking to him, but all that Nemo heard were disconnected syllables, and the buzzing of a great hive. Lem spoke to him again, with urgent eyes. All Nemo could do was pat his hand and leave the room. He had lost his words, and he rushed out to see the sky.

It was blue, thank god.

Murder is only impossible the first time, they say. Once you've transgressed that basic tabu, and especially when you have done so with no consequences, the fear is gone. So is the horror at the thought. It can be done, and done easily. The hand of god does not come down and hurl you to hell in the instant it's done. Like any shock, it fades. I could understand how, for some people, it could be addictive.

I didn't see that happening for me. The thought of violence, even when I'm angry, left me a little weak in the stomach. I knew that I could do it, and I knew that I would recover, but my body rebelled. Some deep animal empathy revolting at the thought of pain.

Des had no qualms in this regard provided he was being paid to do violence. He felt that the money itself offered absolution. He held himself no more responsible morally for the action than a gun could be held responsible. He was a tool rented for job. His only responsibility was his choice to become such a tool. This, I think, troubled him to one degree or another depending on his mood. He believed, or tried to, that there was no other path for him. Like the son of a blacksmith, destined to work the forge, so too was he bred for the delivery of agony. And the occasional ending of it. In his most troubled moments, he blamed Andrew, felt Andrew had changed him into this. Now, it was just what he was. One way or the other, he was a hired goon.

"This is so fucked," he said to me, as he used his tools to break into a Honda. It was exactly mundane enough to draw no attention. He opened the door and got in, leaning across and opening the passenger side for me. Using a key from his belt, he started the car and we drove away.

"I'm certain," I said, "that possessing a key like that is quite illegal."

"So's murder. Shut it."

"Fair enough."

Des said nothing, but shifted angrily and fished in his inside coat pocket for his shades.

"Sincerely, you do not have to come. If you want, I can do this by myself. I'd hate for you to violate your moral code or something."

"Fuck you, twat. I do have one, as you well know."

"Would money make you feel better about it?"

"No. You're my friend. I don't have several of those, honestly. Worse yet, this seems, more or less, like the right thing to do. I don't get to do the right thing very often either. I just. Don't. Like. This. This may fuck up my career."

"You wouldn't want that."

"No. I wouldn't, honestly. Your opinion on the subject of my career is not all that interesting to me. This is my job. It's what I do. Getting on with other criminals is something I need to be able to do."

"Statistically, I don't think the retirement prospects for leg breakers and button men are all that rosy. I think young, hasty, and unpleasant ends are considered de rigeur."

"Speak English, you ponce."

"You know damned well what I mean. You're a good friend Des. I'll miss you when some guy named Luca the Butcher shoots you in the neck."

"That's very nice, Niles, but you're the only one in my career thus far that has injured me in any significant way. You only got away with that because I severely underestimated you."

"And when next that happens?"

"It won't. Try a third degree burn sometime, and you'll find it encourages learning."

"I'm sorry. Again. As I've said before."

"It was good for me. Never underestimate what people will do when they are backed into a corner. That, Niles, is why I hate this plan so much."

"You think I'm underestimating them?"

"I don't think you've even gotten as far as estimating them at all. You've not thought this over enough."

"What's to think over?"

"Whether this is worth dying for."

"I've no intention," I said, "of dying over it."

"Odds are about fifty-fifty that you'll die even with me there. Odds are 100 percent you'll at be, at the very least, maimed without me."

"I think you're grossly overestimating the danger."

"I think that I do this for a living and that you are at best an enthusiastic amateur. You show promise but, in the end, I think you'll find mad desperation and a thirst for human blood can only take you so far in this world of ours."

"I'm not desperate. I'm totally calm. I'm panicky how calm I am."

"You should be terrified," he said. "You should be ready to throw up."

We pulled up outside the spot where Carter had been nabbed, the glass from my window still lying there in little cubes. The door of the back room was locked up again, and the street was quiet. Across from us was the little store, above which perched the alleged den of shame. The windows were shaded, but there was light coming from behind them.

"Doesn't look like much," he said to me, "unfortunately."

"Ah."

"I'm going to scope the place out discreetly on foot," he said. "Wait here. I'll be back."

"You want to split up? Really?"

"You want my help, or don't you?"

"Right, okay. I think the stairway is in back."

He opened the door and got out, walked some way down the street, past the shop, and turned left. I waited for him to walk out around in front again.

After twenty minutes I started to worry. After forty-five, I moved straight on to fear.

I sat in the stolen car and wondered what the hell I would do next.

I started the engine and began to drive around, looking for him. As I passed the place, I saw the door that led upstairs. A tall man stood outside. He was alone. He wore a moustache and a long beard that rested on his worn blue Adidas t-shirt. I did not see Desmond anywhere on either the first or second pass. I was hoping he'd be back waiting where the car ought to be, fussing and pissed off.

He was not.

I parked again, and looked up at the windows for any shadows that looked like Des, or anyone else for that matter. The shades let light through, but seemed to conceal everything else.

I was in a stolen car, in close proximity to murderous thugs who were holding at least one of my friends, and now, possibly two. I had no idea what they might be doing to either one. I was paralyzed. Des was no fool and I hadn't heard him shout out. Part of me hoped he'd simply seen something he didn't care for and bolted. In that case, of course, the only intelligent response was to run away myself.

I was considering this strongly. I wanted to drive somewhere, ditch this car and take the tube home. I wanted to crawl into bed and not get out for a few weeks. I wanted to forget about gorgeous architects, strange magic obsessed gangsters, and glistening purple beetles. I wanted to go back to writing trash for a living. Anything but this.

Instead, I left the car on foot and walked around the warehouse looking for something to use to end a person. In the alley, I found half a cinder block and picked it up in both hands. I kept heading around to the door of the shop walk-up, arranging to come around the guard's corner of the building. I wanted to be unseen until the last moment.

At times like this everything has a way of slowing down. I could see my shadow preceding me on the pavement. I hoped that the guard would assume I was just somebody walking home. Better yet, I hoped he did not notice me at all. As I came to the corner, I could smell him. It was the smell of the beetles, the same smell from Jherek's house that hung on him.

I turned the corner quickly, and the guard turned. He saw the look on my face, and reached for something at the same time as I brought the cinderblock rapidly up under his chin. There was a soft click as his jaws slammed together, the shock transferring up his skull. I saw him go limp and start to fall. I moved to let him fall into me, muffling the sound, and looked side to side, letting him slide down my body.

I brought the block down hard across his forehead and something cracked wetly. I could not afford having this man wake up on me. I opened his jacket pocket, and took out his gun. It was a .45, loaded with nine in the magazine and one in the chamber. It hadn't been fired, but I was fairly sure it would be soon.

I looked at the man I'd murdered. Nothing to do but plunge on, and vomit at the soonest opportunity that was safe.

I entered the walk-up, and closed the door quietly behind me.

After Nemo left, Marya slept fitfully and woke up an hour later. Her throat was scratchy and every breath hurt. She no longer ached, and the world was no longer pitching and spinning. Her back was sore and raw, but did not itch. It was a constant low pain like a sunburn under a rough woollen shirt. She was on her belly.

She made a soft noise, and her father at once picked up her hand.

"Papa?" she said.

"I'm here."

"It hurts."

"I know. You're much better, though. Your fever has passed."

"I'm tired."

"Sleep, then," he said, smiling.

"Can I have water?"

"Of course."

He left the room, and Marya rolled to her back. The pain returned for a moment and then faded to the same dull level. She could hear the ragged breathing of the old woman across the hall.

Her father came back in, and frowned. "You shouldn't be on your back."

He handed her a small tin cup, covered in chipped white enamel. She saw the slick surface and the hint of metal under, and understood why and how such a thing would be done. It was clever. She smiled as she sipped the water. Her mouth felt as though it had come back to life.

"Thank you," she said.

"Sip slowly."

She gulped it down anyway, and burped. She clapped her hand to her mouth, surprised, and laughed. A smile crinkled her Papa's forehead.

He kissed her on the cheek, and rolled her over gently. "Sleep now, Marya. I'll tell your mother you're much recovered. She'll be happy to hear you burp. I promise."

She felt a little ashamed she hadn't asked for her mother, and a little proud that she hadn't. As he left, she turned to look at him, seeing the way his arms and legs hung on his frame. She imagined the inside of his arms, and the machinery inside which was designed to pull and push here and there.

Papa was going to break down someday, and stop working. All machines do, because everything wears out eventually. She too would one day break down, but she was still new. Papa was old, older than her by years and years, more than she could imagine. Many animals didn't live as long as it would take for Marya to be as old as her Papa had become.

She wondered which part of him moved the most, for that would be the likeliest part to break down. Before she could clearly see it, he turned the corner and was gone. Her stomach dropped and quivered.

She paid attention to her own body. Her skin was not working right now, but she'd never heard of anyone dying from skin trouble. She couldn't remember for sure. Lepers, maybe, they might have died of poor skin.

The parts that moved the most were her heart, which was always beating, ticking like a watch in the centre of her, slowly winding down. Her lungs billowed every few seconds. She considered her own brain, which did not move at all, as far as she knew, but which must surely be working all the time. She thought all the time, and the brain made all the rest of the body work.

It would be one of those three, then, that would one day wear out in her father, unless there was an accident of some kind. She pictured him crushed under falling stones, or tripping into the path of a horse and cart, and it made her feel sick. It could happen to anyone at any time, and was no fault of the machine.

Nothing lasts forever.

Her heart ached at the thought of everything, so beautiful and so temporary. Everything is here only for a little while before the world grinds it away. Everything was fragile and beautiful and doomed. She wanted to fix everything she could see.

The purple noise had been with her all this time, quietly whispering under the surface of her thoughts. She had not noticed until just then, when it stopped. She could hear the ticking of the walls moving, and the soft sound of the wind outside.

She wished Nemo were here, because she had questions. She was so tired, though. Her own thoughts seemed to make her ever more tired. Finally she fell back asleep.

She dreamed of beetles and a red-haired man tied to a bed, and of a knight with M. Findeville's face who came to rescue them both.

At the top of the stairs, I could see yellow flickering light that did not seem strong enough for the opaque, flat kind of illumination one saw on the windows outside. I heard people talking in heavily accented English. I took a deep breath and slid my shoes off, leaving them at the base of the stairs. I moved slowly and quietly up the stairs two at a time, heard a radio playing. The hazy light at the top of the stairs was thick with smoke. It smelled of opium, and stranger, but familiar things. It smelled purple.

An elbow poked itself past the left of the door jamb, and then back in, showing me the rough location of at least one man. I looked for my own shadow and saw that it would not give me away. I stopped on the second stair from the top and breathed quickly through my nose before turning and stepping sidewise up the last two. I pointed my gun right in the ear of the dark-haired man leaning there.

"Hello," I said. "Don't let's do anything fucked. I've already killed your man downstairs, so I've really nothing to lose except my temper."

The man in my crosshairs turned to look at me, his eyes widening. His friend across the room turned, one hand reaching for the inside of his coat. I fired a shot over the head of the fellow near me.

"You don't get two," I said, bringing my gun back to the temple of the sweating man in front of me.

The other man raised his hands up and to the side in compliance.

"That's a good fellow," I said. "Now, is there anyone else here on your side? I'd hate to get startled and kill someone."

The man who was almost slightly leaning into my gun shook his head. I nodded.

"Right," I said, looking to the other man. "I'll have you slide off that jacket if you would."

He looked at me, not with defiance but confusion.

"The jacket," I said, "Take it off."

He shook his head uncertainly, and the fellow under the gun translated quickly, stammering. At once, the jacket came off, revealing a shoulder holster.

"Tell him," I said, "to very slowly take his pistol out using thumb and finger, put it on the floor and kick it over here."

He spoke to his friend, who complied at once. I stood on the pistol, not bending to grab it, but wanting to keep track of exactly where it was. I took a look at the room, and saw that on cushions and benches around the room were several men lounging and tripping. Some had hookah pipes, others had purple stains on their lips and tongues. The place reeked of beetles and poppies and sweat. I could see the beetles crawling around, not in the profusion we'd seen them at Jherek's house, but very present, just the same. Nobody seemed bothered or repulsed. Just part of the regular decor. Nicer than rats.

"Where's my friend?" I asked.

The man swallowed and tried to breathe. "Who?"

This was a good question actually. How was he to know who I meant? Even if he knew who I was, there were still two people I could have been talking about.

"Tall man, hard case. Sunglasses."

He shook his head. "I don't know him."

"Ask your friend."

He turned slightly and asked his friend. I watched closely. The other man showed no glimmer either. I nodded. I believed them

"Where is Carter Bennet?"

At the mention of his name, they both looked uneasy. The man across the room glanced quickly at a closed door, unaware of giving the game away.

"I don't know," said the man on whom I held the gun.

SLEEPING UNDERWATER

I pulled the trigger, and he fell to the floor in a sudden slump. A spray of blood and a fine wet powder of bone hit my face and arm, stinging the exposed skin. Most of him ended up on the floor. His mate reached for the gun that wasn't there anymore. It was a good instinct, but he realized his folly and turned to run for the door. I shot him mid-back, and he fell. There was no trying to get up, no crawling. He twitched twice and went still.

Some of the men on the pillows roused and made for the door. I stood carefully to avoid them, pointing my gun in a vague way in their direction. Not one of them wanted anything more than to leave. Half a dozen stayed behind, passed out or past caring. Nobody ran into the room, which showed me that there had been some truth in what I'd been told by the men I'd shot. I also knew that if I were in the back room, I'd stay quiet and shoot me the moment I opened the door. I didn't do that.

I closed the door at the top of the stairs and pushed a bench against it. I retrieved the second gun and put it in my pocket. I piled several more of the benches against the door, and braced two more lengthwise into a cabinet. Nobody was going to open that door in a hurry if I could help it. I kept checking the lines of sight as I worked, watching the back door with special attention.

In the sudden quiet now, I noticed the place reminded me of a dance studio. Perhaps it had been one once, rather than this sad, seedy, dusty nest for addicts. I stood next to the hinge of the door to the back room and tapped the door with the butt of my stolen handgun.

"I think we should talk," I said. "No need for further violence."

I heard the sound of shuffling from inside, and the door opened. I stood behind it, and slow footsteps made their way past the door. I saw Carter from the back, and swallowed.

"Carter?" I asked quietly.

He turned around to look at me. His face was slack, and the hollows of his eyes were the colour of a bruise. There was no more recognition in his eyes than there would be in a pair of glass marbles. His lips were purple, his skin sallow. He blinked at me without apparent interest and then slowly nodded.

"Is there anyone in there with you?"

He nodded.

I clenched my jaw and turned my body sideways against the open door, facing into the back room, looked inside. The room was dark except for a dim bare bulb hanging from the ceiling. The

205

floor crawled with beetles and, against the wall, strapped into a bed was a man. The bed was high enough that I could only see the bottoms of his feet, which were pale and clean and pink like the feet of a baby.

I stepped forward, and beetles crunched underfoot. There was no place to step where you wouldn't tread on them. The smell rose, and my head swam. These fucking things were getting me stoned. I looked carefully and found no other presence of Jherek's men here. I breathed in relief, and turned back to Carter.

"Carter," I asked, "is there another way downstairs?"

He didn't understand the question, but stepped forward, looking at me with wide eyes, and put his hand on my face.

"Je vous connais," he said.

"Oui," I said, "C'est vrai."

He nodded, and I looked at him.

"Are you okay?"

He nodded.

"Is there another way downstairs?"

He looked confused.

"Y a-t-il une autre manière en bas?" I repeated, hoping my French was sound.

He nodded, and headed into the back room. I followed, and I looked at the bed. The man on the bed had red hair, and no eyes. The sight of him was terrifying. His face was drawn and gaunt. It was Victor Mayhew. The beetles crawled in and out of his ocular orbits, and his mouth, open in a vacant grin. His teeth were white and startling. He looked like a mad saint.

"Jesus!" I said.

Carter blinked and looked at the man, and then closed his eyes. "Niles," he said, looking at me. "Did you kill those guys out there?"

"Yes," I said, not knowing what brought his English back and not caring much.

He started to cry, and pressed himself into me, going limp. I had to hold him up with one arm, the other gripping the gun in case I needed to use it. He was utterly silent as he wept, but his body shook so hard I was afraid I'd drop him. He was strong for a man so small. I wrapped the other arm around him, removing my finger from the trigger and held him there for several minutes.

All I heard were soft wet noises. Carter weeping, my own blood in my ears, the raspy breathing of Victor, and the beetles as they swarmed with some alien purpose over everything they could touch.

Marya was out walking in the town. Nemo had noted her going about her daily business, watching from his window. He had not gone out in over a week. He could not speak, nor understand anything anyone said to him. He knew that if Marya had somehow done this, that she could likely undo it. He had no intention of imposing on her until she had fully recovered from her illness.

He had seen her walking twice before, each time with one of her parents watching over her, but today she was alone. He made his way down to the park.

Marya was on the grass, her attention focused on the smallest things, and their connections to each other. She felt as though the world had become a fascinating puzzle. She had not questioned why the grass grew, or why things were one colour and not another, but now she thought about nothing. She found herself overwhelmed with constant sudden understandings.

She realized that she was not alone. At first she simply felt Nemo there in her mind, listening to her. Then she saw him. His mind was stirred up and confused. His face was very calm.

"Hello, Mr. Nemo."

"Epochs and mysteries," Nemo said to her, but in her mind she knew he simply meant to say hello.

She stood up, and came closer to him, feeling his frustration almost physically.

"You came to see me when I was sick. When I asked for you."

He nodded, wanting to avoid words.

"That was very kind. Thank you."

He shrugged curtly, and smiled.

"Above the shop, where the beetles crawl, Findeville kills three men. Desmond has vanished, and the other man has no eyes," Nemo said, meaning to say that if he could have chosen differently, he would have. The words he used made her stomach flip, though she didn't know why.

"Did you catch my fever?" she said silently to him, concerned and fearing the anger in him.

"No," he thought, "Never. I will never hurt you. I know you did not do this deliberately. I think, perhaps, you did not do it at all."

She was shocked, and put her hand on his arm. "What did I do? Tell me."

He reached into her mind, and showed her his vision.

Tears came to her eyes suddenly. Panicked, she turned and ran for the road home, leaving Nemo behind. She pumped her legs hard, feeling each impact run up her legs and back. She was trying to outrun her own mind like a scared animal. Even as she was doing it, a piece of her felt silly. Her body acted on its own, and she was being pulled along unwillingly. She stopped suddenly, fell, and laughed out loud.

She felt as though she had uncovered the most important truth of her life. Tears ran down her face. The salt taste of them reminded her she was a beast, just like any other. She sweated and cried and breathed.

Nemo had caught up to her, and was kneeling down beside her, looking at her lying there, with an expression of concern and confusion.

"You speak French through his mouth a hundred years from now," Nemo said.

What he had meant to tell her, she knew, was that she had scraped her knee.

"I hadn't noticed that," she said, angrily. "Thank you for telling me."

Nemo smiled, remembering dimly some kind of moment from his childhood, how that very tone having passed his lips to some teacher, or father, or uncle. The distance of the memory, the slipperiness of it made him ache with longing for more.

"Blinded ginger men are looping time and trading destinies. It's a dance," Nemo said, pushing her hair back off her angry little face. She was too irritated to pay attention to what he'd meant this time, but his thoughts were warm and afraid, and annoyed.

She slapped his hand. "I didn't mean to do it," she said, "And you're right. I don't think it was me. I was..." She struggled for the word, and he placed it in her head. "...an instrument," she finished.

She was half relieved and half furious. He looked at her as a little girl, and feared her as some power that he had no words for.

SLEEPING UNDERWATER

There was no love for her there, not of the kind she had for him, a longing that ached and shamed her.

And worse, he was sorry for it, apologizing in her head.

"I'm sorry," he thought, speaking nothing. "You're a child. I care for you in ways I cannot explain to you. You make me feel less alone in the world. I hope you find a man who will feel for you as you feel for me. I am not him. I will be your friend, and your teacher, but I cannot love you. We have discussed this."

She stared into him, angry past words. Her thoughts forged his sympathy into a steel cage wrapped around her heart. She saw the way his body was put together, and under his skin, to the smallest parts of him. She saw twisted ladders winding and coiled up in every small part of him. These told the world how to build him. She knew he would never die. He was not a man like other men. He was some kind of imaginary thing made of flesh, pretending to be real.

She looked at her own hands, and saw she and Nemo were more alike than different. She saw that she would die, and that she had died before. Horrified, she looked deep and saw her own twisted ladders, like a spiral staircase. She imagined standing on the rungs of it. If she looked up the ladder they went up past the end of her, and when she looked down they went back to before her. She could see other people above and below. All of them were different people, but all of them were the same.

Above her was a small, very pretty, dark haired man with sad eyes. He was surrounded by drawings of buildings. He wanted desperately to have just one friend to live in them with him. She waved up at him, and, startled, the man waved back with a sense of recognition.

Nemo shook her, and she found herself back in the world. She stared into his eyes, seeing a purple flame deep inside his pupils.

"Give it back to me," she said quietly.

He looked at her, confused.

"The purple noise is inside you. It's why you're sick. It can't use words like we do. I understand that now."

He shrugged, having no idea how to give it back.

"I'm well again," she said. "It needs me back."

She put her hands on his face, feeling his soft resistance give way. She grabbed the purple voice behind his eyes, and wrapped it in a soft blanket of loving thoughts. She took it back into her own mind and, immediately, it begged for help.

Nemo's eyes rolled back in his head and he collapsed, limbs twitching and kicking. The twitching stopped, his mouth hung slack, the tip of his tongue protruding.

His thoughts were deep and still. She knew that he was only sleeping, and not dead. She felt her anger toward him softening. She felt sorry for him. He did not know what he was, and she realized that there was something in him that had chosen to forget, that would always choose to forget. His mind was like a prison with a thousand small rooms, each of which held memories of a life he could not bear to remember living.

She also knew she had to get home before her mother began to worry, but she couldn't just leave him there in the road alone.

She sat cross-legged beside him and waited for him to wake up. His chest rose and fell, rose and fell, like the slow ticking of a clock that would never stop.

"Your name is Andrew," she said, and kissed his cheek, as though saying good-bye forever.

Carter wept into my shirt and Victor breathed loudly behind us. I tried to imagine what the hell I ought exactly to do next. Everything had taken on the feel of a nightmare. If committing three murders hadn't been enough, this room had pushed me over the edge. I could not, for even an instant, stop wondering what had happened to Des. There was something about the sequence of events that did not seem sensible. Where had he gone? Was he okay? How on earth did I think I was going to get away with any of this come daylight.

"Niles," Carter said at last, "I'm so sorry. I should never have gotten you involved."

"Don't concern yourself with that, all right? What's done is done. You needed help."

I stroked the back of his head, and he mumbled something into my chest I could not understand, his voice still muzzy from the drug.

I tucked the pistol into the back of my trousers, just like on the telly, and gently disentangled myself from him to get a better look at the room. This was made more difficult by the fact that I could not bear to look at Victor in his bed. I was increasingly aware of his smell now, the deeper more pungent smell beneath the spiced scent of the beetles. I moved over to Victor, and pulled back his sheets. He wore what looked like a stolen hospital gown. I could count his ribs, could see, I thought, his heart beating. Recent IV marks were in his right arm, and the sheets beneath him were stained with brown and yellow serum. I rocked him gently and saw the backs of his arms and legs were covered in running bedsores and crushed beetles.

"Sweet God," I said, and choked back gagging, even though I was grateful it hadn't been worse.

I'd expected maggots, truly.

Carter looked at Victor helplessly, with such profound guilt and grief that words, no doubt, were entirely unacceptable.

"Carter," I asked, "do you know how Victor got here?"

He shook his head.

"Was he here when you arrived, then?"

Carter nodded.

"Right. Have you seen a tall man in sunglasses, a little older, looks like a rugby player?"

He blinked, his eyes unfocused, then shook his head hesitantly.

"Okay. Carter, we have to go right now. We have to leave Victor. We'll phone the police from someplace, and get someone sent. I'm sorry, but if we try and take him, it'll only hurt him, and get me caught."

Carter went to the bed, and put his hand on Victor's arm.

"Oh Victor," he said. "I'm so sorry for everything."

Victor turned his head and his mouth moved. A slow croaking rasp caused the hair on my arms to stand up. Carter started in with fresh tears, and I almost followed suit.

"Carter," I said, using my authority voice, "we have to go. Now."

He looked at me, a hint of anger there. I was gladdened by this. Anger is a useful emotional state for survival, far better than grief, not as dangerous as fear. I decided I'd take it.

"Fine," he said.

"Where's the back way? This door?"

"Yes."

I opened the back door and, holding his wrist, walked through it. It led to a dark room filled with empty cardboard cartons. The beetles were in here as well, keeping to the corners of the rooms, and eating the damp cardboard. There were also rats, eating the beetles. Carter stiffened at the sight of the rats as they rushed over the stream of light thrusting into the room from the open door.

"They aren't going to hurt you," I said, but he strained against my arm.

"Come on! Do you want to stay here and get killed?" I asked.

"Yes," he mumbled, and I shook him.

"Bollocks." I jerked him forward.

The rats made way for us, startled, not wanting trouble, and likely stoned. At the end of the room was another door with an old knob and a new deadbolt. I opened it, and immediately felt the cool night air. The door opened out onto a fire escape. I lowered the ladder, and started us down to the alley.

Once I was satisfied that Carter was following me, I reached back to take my gun in hand, fearing I'd need it. I'd missed the weight of it, and my sweat felt like ice in the night air. I was acutely aware of my proximity to death. I could hear the mumbling of a small crowd nearby, likely the assortment of drug fiends I'd displaced in the adventure. I didn't care to walk us into that. I hoped they'd serve as distraction when Jherek's people showed up. I had to believe they knew something was up by now. One of these junkies would have called someone, wanting to curry favour.

Once we were on the street, I led Carter on foot in the opposite direction of the stolen car. If Des was out there somewhere, he was on his own now. I had Carter to worry about, and he was not well. I wondered how much of what was going on he was aware of, and what that drug actually did. It seemed to be some kind of hallucinogen. I didn't like that.

"Well," the inner voice said to me, "how shall we finish the evening? I think a nice stiff drink and then shagging a drugged out trauma victim is a grand way to relax from a triple homicide."

"Christ," I said out loud, and Carter jarred suddenly.

"Can't leave him there."

"Can. Have done," I said, and then saw him start to turn back.

"Stop! Right now!"

Carter stopped.

"You listen to me, Carter Bennet. You will do as I say from this point on, or as God himself is my witness, I will render you unconscious and carry you."

"Fuck you," he said, spinning around, "You have no idea what's going on here, none at all. You don't know who he is, or what he means, or why he's there. You don't know me, and you don't understand any of this!"

"I wonder why, you liar. Now lower your voice."

Carter looked at his feet, and then walked toward me.

"Well done," said the voice, "You've not forgotten. The right sentence can hit like a fist."

I tasted bile, and tried to ignore the voice. It was Andrew's voice.

I had no idea how I'd missed it, all this time.

"Oh," it said. "The penny drops. Finally."

Carter and I walked a few minutes until I was certain we were not being followed. There's a calm relief that comes with walking away from a crime, and almost being able to forget it. It becomes less real to you with each quiet night step, and you focus on moment after new moment, walking away from it like a dream. There I was, out for a night walk with a friend, and that was all. I led us to the nearest tube station. I'd no idea where to go from there.

We couldn't go back to my place. Once word got out, it would be the first place they'd look.

Then I realized I absolutely had to go home. Victor's eyes were in a box on my living room table, where just any thug with the will to break and enter would find them.

I pressed my fists to my eyes.

"Fuck," I said. "Fuck. Fuck Fuck."

Carter looked at me, and asked, "What's wrong?"

"Very nearly everything."

Outside the entrance to the tube, I used a payphone, and rang the police, sending them to pick up Victor. Carter listened intently.

"Best we can do," I said.

"No," he said. "It isn't. But it's something."

"Do you have someplace safe you can get to? For certain?"

He seemed to think, but it was still clear that wasn't something he was good at right now. "No," he said, then, "Yes."

"Right, I need you to go there. Don't tell anyone anything, and just stay there until I come for you. Where is it?"

"Tom's place," he said. "He's a friend."

"I have met him."

"I know," he said quietly.

I looked at him. "I'm not cross about that, I'm worried. It's different. Is he wrapped up in any part of this? Are you sure they wouldn't look there for you?"

"No," he said, "I think they don't know of him at all."

"Do you have the address?" I wrote it on a notepad, and put it back in my pocket.

"Where are you going?" he asked, an edge of panic in his voice.

"I have to go home."

"No, you can't. That's stupid."

"I left Victor's eyes there."

"I'm coming with."

"You aren't," I said. "Final word. Full stop. You'll slow me down."

He looked hurt. I felt a little bad about that. Not very bad. I was a little cross. A little.

"Two draw more notice than one, and you are fucking stoned."

He breathed in raggedly, and let it out. "Fine."

"I will know if you follow me," I said, "and if I find out you have, I will throw Victor's eyes in the Thames. Clear?"

"Yes."

"Go to Tom," I said, shivering, handing him very nearly the complete contents of my wallet. Enough for a taxi, I hoped.

He nodded and turned to go, and then turned back and gave me a hug, his lips brushing my cheek for a quick kiss. Then, too shy for words, he headed across the street and got on the bus.

I took the tube home.

Time passed, and things were no longer the same between Marya and Andrew, who called himself Nemo. He had recovered from his word sickness, and spoke now as just as well as he ever had. She stayed clear of him, half from embarrassment, and half from disdain. The purple noise was her constant companion now, but she had learned to think around it. It was less insistent, she thought, now that it knew it had been heard.

Nemo spent much of his time with M. Findeville. They seemed to have become very close friends. Maya could, therefore, no longer trust him. M. Findeville was an enemy to all things purple. He believed that the island held a sickness that threatened the world. She thought he was the sickness, instead. Men from Europe came and went at his request, and a building had been constructed near the Governor's house. It was a laboratory with large metal drums rolling in and out in the dead of night. Machines droned and thrummed there without rest. Laying in her bed at night, she heard the constant working of the machines.

She had no further recurrence of fever. She had grown slightly taller, and her breasts had become tender, started to swell. Her mother explained this was normal. She knew this was so. She was surprised to find that she was going to miss her childhood.

Some of her friends had already begun to bleed. Her friend Nicola already had a full bosom. Nicola had cried on her shoulder, because her father would no longer let her sit on his knee. She missed the cuddles and kisses, crawling into bed with her parents when she was scared at night. Marya herself feared the loss of simple physical pleasures like that. This made her feel more for Nicola than she had in some time.

Marya's father was aware of the changes in her as well, and seemed to be taking every opportunity left for a quick kiss hello and goodbye. They spent some evenings curled together in their big chair reading, her Mama knitting in the chair next to them. It was a long, sweet farewell to her childhood. She tried to cherish it. Sadness would soon come and then new pleasures and experiences to replace the ones she had now.

She was no longer smitten with Nemo, and was grateful for it. He had proved unworthy of the purple. This had changed her entire feeling for him. She didn't know if she ever would be smitten again and didn't mind, actually. She had seen the way boys chased after Nicola, and didn't want it. Nicola seemed to seek it out as some kind of solace. As Marya understood it, that was a dangerous kind of a game.

Alone in her room, she read by the light of a small lamp. A book about insects. She was trying to find common ground with the purple, to seek some understanding of it. The smell of the burning oil was strong and familiar, though the light was weak and wavered. A strong wind blew in off the sea that was fresh and cold. She found herself reading the same sentence over and again until there was no meaning in it.

She closed her eyes, and set the book down. She should turn down the wick, and let sleep come, but motion was too complicated for her.

The sound of her mother dropping a pot in the other room disrupted the peace. Marya opened her eyes, swung her feet to the cold floor, and ran to look. Her mother stared out the window over the stove. A pot of water was on its side soaking into the dirt floor. Her mother seemed frozen, her eyes still and wide. Marya was frightened, wanted to cry out for her father.

He wasn't home, of course. He was out with the Jherek brothers, making stupid plans, no doubt.

She looked deep into her mother, and saw that her body was healthy, working well, but that it was frightened; she was frightened.

"Mama?" she said, putting a hand on her mother's arm. They were very nearly the same height now, and she noticed the difference a year could make.

Her mother didn't respond. Marya looked out the window. In the darkness outside, the little men were standing, hands and feet clasped in what seemed to be a circle around her house. It didn't scare her, but she found it strange. Her breath caught in her throat. Her mother had begun to shake. Marya squeezed her mother tightly. Suddenly she choked, then gasped as though remembering how to breathe.

Then Marya's mother began to scream.

As if in reply, the little men unfurled their wings, and began to move them. The sound of them rubbing wings together was deep, like a stone had been dropped in a well, but more sustained. She could feel the sound in her chest, ringing her bones like a bell.

She ran to the front door, and verified that they were circling the entire house. She had never seen so many this far from the mounds. People stood in their doorways, and in the road, staring at the sight of it. Many held their ears, looked ill. The sound was deep and loud, and above all insistent. It hurt her deep in the bones.

She had been about to beg them to stop, when they did so all at once. A cracking sound like thunder and a burst of air pushed her back a step. From nowhere, a man appeared. The little men became as passive as ever.

The man was impossibly tall and wide. His eyes were hidden by spectacles tinted black. He was dressed strangely. His shoes were grey and white with thick soles that looked like sponge. They had strange, thick white laces. His pants were blue denim. His black leather jacket was like none she had seen, and he wore a large cotton shirt under it, black and clean. His head was nearly shaved, covered with a fine stubble as though he were a soldier of some kind. He held a strange pistol, short and square, dark black. He looked side to side in a panic and then saw the little men.

"What the fuck?" he exclaimed. His accent was English, which was odd. She knew only a little English. That was one of the words she knew. She blushed.

The strange man spun around to get a sense of where he was. He was clearly frightened. She did not like scared men with guns, and was not sure what to do. He aimed the pistol at the little men. They did not move, or show any sign of understanding at all. He noticed her, and spoke to her over his shoulder.

"What the fuck are those?" he asked. She thought that was at least close to his meaning. She spoke English worse than she understood it. She furrowed her brow.

"Please to not wave with the gun."

He looked at his hand, then lowered the barrel. "You speak French?" he asked, and she almost fainted.

"Yes," she said with relief. "These are the little men of the island. They are strange but not dangerous. They only watch. They won't hurt you."

"Slower, darling," he said, "I only speak a little bit of French."

She nodded, and repeated herself more slowly.

"Where am I?" he asked.

"Salt Mouse," she said. His eyes widened almost comically, and he quickly said something in English that she could not follow.

The little men broke up into groups and started to wander off into the woods together. Whatever they had come to see, they had seen. Whatever they had come to do, they had done. The low shrubs and grass rustled, and they vanished into them.

"What's your name?" he asked, putting the gun in his jacket.

"I'm Marya."

"I'm Desmond."

Still feeling like a total fool, I left the tube station, walking past a group of football fans on their way to the nearest source of chips now that the pubs had let out. They were noisy and joyous and more than slightly drunk. Lost in their own beery world, they

217

didn't notice the pale and empty look I knew was on my face, nor the blood on my cuffs and hands.

The adrenaline had started to turn to poison in my blood, as it always does. I was a bit trembly and ill. Violence is like cocaine without any of the pleasing effects. I felt like hell in a burlap sack. Nobody in view had any idea what life was actually like, that it was so easy to just kill someone and walk away. I knew that it was just a moment's impulse away for me. I felt my pulse in my throat, my shirt binding.

I slipped the gun into a trash bin, as discreetly as I could. I didn't want to hang onto it anymore. The weight of it made me queasy. I knew I might need it, but I also knew that the night could end with me in police custody, and I didn't need to tie myself to every crime I'd done tonight. If I needed a weapon, I'd find another.

I was not sure what I had intended to do when I got home. Jherek would have heard by now what had happened to his people. I gave him enough credit to have looked into my addresses, home and office. I knew that he'd have people waiting for me, at one or the other, or, least happily and most likely, both. I hoped for the best as I turned the corner, and saw two things. A long black car out front of my building, still running, and the lights on in my flat.

I cursed softly to myself. I should have taken the eyes the moment we'd found them, and put them in my office safe. My emotions had taken over, and I'd acted without thinking. My only hope was that Jherek's men expected better of me than that. The eyes were still wrapped up and in amongst the unremarkable junk in boxes on my floor.

I could at least hope they were waiting for me, intending to beat the location of the eyes out of me, never thinking I'd have been so stupid as to have left them where I found them.

I considered my options. I was now unarmed, and physically ill from adrenaline hangover. I was not up for a second go at heroism. I could hide and wait for boredom to set in. I knew they were as likely to search the place as leave in frustration, and that they would, in any case, leave a man behind.

Instead, I walked by the car quickly on the opposite side of the lane, and walked into the chip shop. I asked to use the phone and Rahim's father, Kasr, invited me back around the counter. I called the police and told them that strange men were in my place.

SLEEPING UNDERWATER

I thanked Kasr, and we watched from the street as the police pulled up. A long conversation took place in the street. When they had finished, three of Jherek's men were taken away, glaring at me with no small malice. I was asked a number of questions, and answered them to a mild degree of truthfulness. I then went up to my place. It was a mess. They'd knocked over everything, including the boxes.

My heart sank, but I kneeled down to investigate. The eyes were still there, wrapped in a tangle of scarves, and laying there, halfway under my armchair.

I felt faint with relief and gratitude. I had gotten luckier, by far, than I deserved.

I took a couple of deep breaths, trying to think clearly. Every ounce of me wanted to bolt as quickly as possible. There was no sense in running without a destination, though. I cleared my throat, ran my fingers through my hair, and simply took a series of deep breaths.

These people, as far as I knew, had no interest in Tom. I thought that there was worse I could do than hook back up with Carter, and try and to figure out my next move.

I wrapped the eyes back up in the scarves, slipped them, and the file, into a brown paper bag, and left for the tube. I was very aware of every sound and movement as I left the building, expecting to be jumped by a second crew and beaten to death. That didn't happen.

I made the tube, and headed in the direction of Tom's place. I slumped against the plastic sheet, and my head rested against the glass. It felt cool and soothing. I drowsed there for a few moments. One of the few joys of public transit is that there are no demands upon you.

I was not so relaxed that I dared actually fall asleep. I was too wary of that. I perceived a slight motion from the seat across from me and opened my eyes fully, looking across.

Andrew was in the seat opposite me. There was something not quite real about him, though even now I can't put my finger on what that was. There was no ghostly translucency, no shimmer or wave in the image. He was just very clearly not there even though I could see him as clearly as the hungry fellow in my lap.

"Hello Niles," he said. "I see you're having quite a night." I felt a little itch at the back of my neck, and looked to see if anyone else was close enough to hear.

"You may as well speak to me," Andrew said. "I certainly can't do you any harm from here."

"Go to hell."

"I've tried so many times. Honestly. I've no chance."

"What do you want?"

He smiled with one half of his mouth, the other staying perfectly still. "This really has nothing to do with me. You've called me up from the pit, so to speak. Why don't you figure it out?"

"I did not," I said quietly, "summon you up. I would never summon you up. I put you in a grave for a reason. I am in enough trouble right now without you."

"Would you like some help?"

I swallowed and stared at him. "From you? Hardly. You're a monster."

"That's as may be. In fact, I'll cheerfully acknowledge it. I'm a monster. You, on the other hand, are clearly a dissociative lunatic. I'm just offering you an easy out in all of this."

For a second, something like gratitude surged in me, followed by shame, and anger. And fear. "Go away. If I've summoned you, I now dismiss you. Return to whatever purgatory will have you. Get out of my life."

He stood up and sat beside me. "I'll never leave you, Niles. You are what you are, at least partly, because of me."

He put his hand on my lap. It was cold and wet.

"Don't touch me."

He took his hand back and laughed. "It's too late for that. You're swimming in ghosts. Always were. You've so many people inside you, I'm surprised there was room for me to jump inside."

I closed my eyes. "I'm not speaking to you."

"No, you aren't. I'm dead, my love. Or wishing I was, somewhere in the bottom of that pond. My chest aches from holding my breath all these years. Doesn't yours?"

When I opened my eyes, he was gone.

I leaned back against the bench, and closed my eyes. I could still feel Andrew there watching me, waiting for attention. I waited for my stop to be announced.

I wondered if the eyes in my pocket ever wished they could blink.

SLEEPING UNDERWATER

Desmond and Marya looked at one another in the near darkness. People went back into their houses and stared through their curtains. Her mother came out, looking at Desmond with terror in her eyes, and grabbed Marya's shoulders to pull her back. Marya put her hand on her mother's and told her to stop. Her voice was firm, calm.

She pulled free of her mother, and took a step closer, touched his sleeve. The leather was darker and slicker than any she had ever felt. It was adorned in many places with little interlocking metal clasps that looked like rows of golden teeth locking into permanent grins. It did not belong here. Neither did he. His dark spectacles were made, somehow, from spun oil, and so were parts of his shoes, and his jacket. She no longer wondered how or why she knew these things, anymore. She could see his legs were weak by the way he stood to hide the shaking. She saw fear in the sweat that beaded on his forehead.

"Kid," he said, "quit touching me, right? I'm really wired at the moment, and you're making me even jumpier."

He was speaking English and it was getting easier and easier to understand him, as she kept her hand on him.

"I'm sorry," she said in English, taking her hand back.

"No worries," Desmond said. "You got a phone I could use?"

She saw a "phone" in his mind, and just the concept of it made her mind race. "There's no such thing here. You've come too soon."

Desmond looked at her with a puzzled expression, slowly replaced by alarm. "Sel Souris," he said. "I just now got it. Fuck."

Marya smiled at the naughty word. "This is Sel Souris. Wherever you are from, it is different, far away. I think you come from further up the stairs of time."

"How the fuck? What the fuck?" There was an edge of panic in his voice, of dangerous fear. Marya had seen men this kind of scared. Fists swung, bottles broke. She felt a shiver of fear at this man, of his size and all the ways that danger could flow from him. She needed to calm him, dam off some of these dangers.

"I don't know," she said, softly. "The little men seemed to know you were coming. I don't know how or why they knew. I don't know how or why you came. Perhaps Mr. Nemo would know."

221

"Nemo. Like Captain Nemo?"

"He was only a sailor, I think, not a captain, but he is very old and knows a lot about strange things."

"Look," Desmond said, speaking slowly. "I don't mean to be rude, but back where I am from, my friend is in deep, deep trouble, and needs me. I have to get back."

She furrowed her brow. "Where you're from hasn't happened yet. Not for a hundred years, perhaps more."

Desmond closed his eyes. "What year is it?"

"1880."

Desmond suddenly sat on the grass, elbows on his knees, face in his hands. "I was walking down an alley, and I felt this little pitch in my gut. Nerves, I figured. Then there was this purple flash, and there you were."

Marya said nothing, having nothing to say. The two of them had leaned so close together that their breath mingled in the cold night air. Marya's mother was begging her to come back inside the house, but she could barely hear it. She was too busy staring at the wonder before her. This tall rocky-faced man born so many years after she would die.

Two men came up behind Desmond with long guns. They ordered him, in French, to place his hands on his head. Desmond's nostrils flared.

"All right then," he said, turning around, and raising his hands. He didn't sound scared, so much as cautious.

She stepped between the French soldiers and Desmond and stared them down.

"Don't make me hurt you," she said, and the soldiers laughed at her. Some of the neighbours did as well. Marya's mother didn't laugh. She could hear the weight in her daughter's voice. She was a simple woman, not a blind one, and she knew that her daughter's fever had left her changed in ways she didn't want to think of.

"Kid," Desmond said, from the side of his mouth. "You're gonna get both of us shot. I am okay, here."

Marya paid him no mind, and picked up two small stones, round and blue, and made as if to hurl them. Her face was serious, and not lovely.

One of the soldiers smiled gently. He tipped the barrel of his gun down and stepped forward. "You're clearly a very brave girl to defend this stranger, but you must let us do our work. If he is as good a man as you think, then he shall have no reason to fear. Is this not so?"

She tossed the two stones lightly, one in each hand, and with a faint click they slid directly down the wide barrels. All the adults blinked in surprise. Her aim had been effortless. Marya stepped back and took her mother's hand.

"Control that brat," said the other soldier, fat and blonde, to Marya's mother.

"If you fire those guns," Marya said, to them, "you'll die."

The amusement faded from the soldier's faces, and Marya's mother burst into panicked tears, trying to drag her daughter away.

"Everybody," Desmond said in English, "relax. Please. Be cool."

The fat soldier spat at Desmond. Desmond's face went shock pale, and without thinking, he raised his fist to strike. Both soldiers pulled their triggers, instantly. Two shots rang out, then the sound of shrieking and tearing metal.

When the noise passed, the soldiers laid upon the ground. Blood poured from what remained of their faces like a stream making way to the ocean. The barrels of their guns were bent and blown apart. Desmond stood, smoke staining his trembling face and hands, not so much as grazed.

There was a long moment then, silent, but for the bubbling of blood. Then cheers started from the houses and the lane. Dead Frenchmen were a source of joy, it seemed.

Marya's mother fell to her knees. When Marya turned to look, she saw her father coming up the lane in a hurry. He saw the dead soldiers, the cheering crowd, and his expression transformed to a kind of horror. Behind him were the Jherek brothers. They looked one to another, and headed back down the road in a hurry.

Marya's father stood there as the brothers urged him to follow, and he looked at Marya and his wife, trying to decide. He met his daughter's eyes.

Both knew that something dangerous had just happened, and could not be undone. The neighbours fired their own guns in the air, banged shovels and scythes. They mobbed around Desmond, and around Marya, smiling and cheering. Desmond looked to her for some context. She was as confused and terrified as anyone.

Her father pushed through the crowd, and knelt beside his wife, who shook her head as he tried to raise her up to her feet.

She reluctantly stood, weaving, and then he grabbed his daughter by one hand, and Desmond's arm with the other.

"Follow me," he said in French, "for you are not safe here."

They ran for the Jherek house where there might at least be safety in numbers. Marya knew she had fired the first two shots of many, her actions like a spark to tinder. The island was aflame now, and the purple noise sang to her. It was hard to hear it, smothered by the joy that seemed to come from the people who felt the time had come that the French might be driven away at last.

She thought back to a night when she had been small. Her parents had guests for the evening. Once she had been sent to bed, she was woken up by the sound of loud and drunken laughter. For some reason their lack of control was frightening. She had counted upon grownups not to be silly, to rein her in when her own silliness got out of hand. The noise shook her, and when she walked into the kitchen crying, the laughter stopped, and all the faces softened with worry. It was instantly better.

This was the same fear, but without relief. The grownups had gone silly in a dangerous and bloody way. So had the purple noise. She leaned over as she was dragged down the lane, throwing up, leaving a trail of sick for the beetles to follow.

Tom lived in a six-story condominium much newer than mine. I didn't see anything unusual outside the building, acutely aware that one rarely notices the bullet which kills them. I swallowed, and plunged on.

"You're fine," Andrew said. "I'm not sensing anyone around that cares about you."

"Well," I said, "that's lovely."

I stepped under the black overhang and looked at the rows of little white buttons on the intercom. Tom's was labeled as Occupant. I pushed it, and the buzz was far louder than I would have preferred.

"Yeah?" said a thick northern voice.

"It's Niles."

"Is it?"

The intercom went dead. There was no buzz at the door, no unlocking click. I stood there staring at the panel blankly. I felt terribly exposed, and didn't want, actually, to bring trouble to Tom's door.

A second later, I heard Carter's voice, "Niles, are you still there?"

"Yes."

The door buzzed open and I headed for the lift. The lift had no music, so all I could hear were the mechanisms and my own breathing, which was loud and rapid. When the lift opened onto the fifth floor, I took a deep breath, wanting to keep my face impassive. I stepped out, skin crawling with paranoia. I walked down the hall to Tom's suite.

I knocked on the door, and Tom opened it. If I hadn't known who he was, I'm not certain I would have recognized him. He had gained a stone or more of weight. This was a good thing, as the last time I'd seen him, he'd been a pale and unpleasantly translucent kind of thin. It was a particular look I'd become all too accustomed to seeing since then, as more of my acquaintances and friends had gotten the plague. There was none of that about him now. It took me off guard.

"Are you coming in?" he said, short and annoyed.

I nodded and came inside. Carter was stripped to the waist and sitting on a kitchen chair next to a formica table. On the table was a steel bowl, and he was dipping a brown washcloth in, and wiping himself with the water.

"Thanks," I said to Tom as I came in. He sniffed at me in as manfully a way as can be done, surprisingly manfully, as it happens.

"Is he doing all right?" I asked him.

"He's been fucking beaten on and is drugged up with something. He is as far from all right as I've ever seen."

"He's lucky to be alive."

"It's not his fault," Carter said to Tom.

Tom turned to glare at him, but had no words to say, so he turned back to me and glared at me instead. He was in the mood to shout.

"How the fuck could you send him out onto the tube in his state? Christ!"

Tom slammed his fist into the wall next to my head. I did not flinch, somehow.

Andrew chuckled darkly inside me. "Oh please, let me play with this one."

I put my hand on Tom's shoulder. "Stop it. Or I will restrain you until you calm down."

He pulled his hand back, blood on his knuckles and plaster dust falling. I saw scars on his knuckles. He looked as though he liked to punch walls. He was deciding whether or not he was hard enough to swing on me. I looked him dead in the eyes. By this time Carter had come behind Tom, wrapped both arms around him and was pulling him backwards.

"Stop it," Carter said. "He's not the one you should be hitting."

"Hitting anyone over this would be a waste of effort," I said.

A drop of blood landed on Carter's arm, near a shallow scratch. Tom immediately pulled free and yanked Carter toward the kitchen sink, and washed it off of him. Tom then staggered into his washroom to take care of what he'd done to himself.

Carter turned to look at me. "Sorry."

"He's just taking care of you. You seem like you're doing a bit better."

Carter nodded, and swallowed. I watched his Adam's apple bob up and down in his perfect throat. "Fresh air cleared my head a bit."

I handed him the paper bag. "These are yours."

He didn't open the bag. It was clear that the weight inside was familiar. "Thank you."

"You're welcome."

The silences between us said more than the words had, though exactly what they said was not very clear to me. The last of these silences was interrupted by Tom coming back into the room with a wrap of gauze on his hand, and a spray bottle of bleach. He sprayed it on the wall.

"I'm a walking fucking biohazard, Christ," he said, meaning in some way to be reconciliatory. I had no idea how to respond. Carter did. He hugged his friend from behind in nearly exactly the same way as he had done before, as though nothing mattered less than a drop of blood. Tom closed his eyes, softness coming over his features. Tom patted Carter's arm and let himself be hugged.

"So," I said. "Tom, have you been involved in any of this business with Jherek at all?"

"The mad bastard who had him? No," he said. "Christ. If I'd known that Carter had been involved, I'd have stopped him myself."

"No," Carter said, "you wouldn't have. You'd have told me to stop, and then assumed I'd listen."

Tom pulled free and wheeled on Carter. "You think you know me so well, don't you?"

Carter nodded, his eyes welling with tears. "Yeah," he said. "Think I do."

"You think I learned nothing from what happened to Victor?"

Carter looked down at his shoes. "I don't think people change very much."

"Wrong!" Tom said. "You're wrong there. They do change. It may take a fucking disaster, Christ, but they change."

Carter shrugged.

"Look," I said, a bit sharply, "I realize there is a long history here to which I am only partially privy. I'm trying to respect this. Can we focus on the present for just a tick here? I'd really like to live past sunrise."

Carter seemed vaguely wounded, and Tom was pissed off. I was past feeling either sympathy or malice. Neither of them said anything.

"The situation as it stands is not good," I said. "We have Victor's eyes, and I've left a number of corpses behind me while getting them. The murderous crooks, many of whom are probably family to the dead, are, doubtless, seeking to kill me, Carter, and anyone else who knows either of us, just to be safe. They seem to want the eyes, for whatever reason they have to care, and likely would kill us to get them, even if I hadn't killed several of them, which I have. Now they have revenge as a motive as well."

Carter looked like he was about to interrupt. Tom, on the other hand was rubbing his temples with both hands, seemingly unaware of a large part of this narrative. I held up my hand.

"No," I said, "I'm still summarizing the situation."

Carter closed his mouth, slightly vexed.

"Considering all of this," I continued, "we need to get somewhere safe immediately. Eventually, as you two have a history, they are going to look for us here. I give us a day or two at the most. I recommend the two of you take the train out of town tonight, and a boat to France. From there, I'd say, oh, Australia, though I don't care where you go as long as it is far from here, and so long as you stay there for a couple years."

"What about you?" Carter asked.

"Not your concern," I said. "I'm not telling you where I'm going, and I don't want to know where you'll be, either."

227

"Oh come now," Andrew said from the back row of my mind, "surely you don't mean to run away like a whipped dog?"

I didn't, but I said nothing about that out loud.

"I can't travel," Tom said, "It's not feasible."

Carter looked miserable.

"Well, you'll have to relocate from here, or at least lie your head off. Carter cannot be here when they come looking, and you shouldn't be either."

"I won't be," Carter said.

"Let them kill me." Tom said. "Christ. I'm actually sick of waiting for it at this point."

Carter slapped his arm hard.

Tom looked at Carter as though he'd grown an extra head, and then smiled.

"I should say," I said, "that if you give them the eyes yourself, and disavow further knowledge of me, there is a possibility they might leave both of you alone. It's the sanest option open to you. I assume, therefore, that you'll forgo it."

Carter nodded.

I shook my head. "I thought so."

Tom looked at me, and then at Carter, and then at me. "Christ."

"I don't know how to pay you back," Carter said. "You...well...you know what all you did."

"Forget it," I said. "You needed help and I have a lot of bad karma to work off in this life."

Carter walked over to me, and put his hands on my arms, and looked up at me. "Don't talk to me like you're in a book, and none of this is real. Like none of it matters," he said to me, looking me right in the eyes. "Not if this is goodbye."

Tears came to my eyes suddenly. My cheeks felt hot, and I turned my head, eyes closed. He put his hand on my face, and turned me back toward him. His small soft hands brushed my hair back out of my face.

"I'm very glad we met," I said. "Now get out of here and stay alive."

"You're not the monster that you think you are," he said. "You might be the sweetest man I've ever met."

"I'm a killer, Carter."

"We can't help what we're good at."

I choked from the back of my throat, feeling like his eyes had stripped me bare, and I didn't want to be seen. The only way I was keeping sane here was by keeping myself locked on the mission, and the tactics.

"I have to go," I said.

He pulled my face down to his level and kissed me, his tongue sliding past my lips and brushing mine with such gentleness that it might scarcely been there at all. My body went halfway limp. I kissed him back before pulling away.

"Goodbye, Niles," he said.

I nodded, unable to look at him, as I turned for the door. I went into the hall, and back to the lift. My heart was in sharp, tiny pieces, rattling in my chest like slivers of broken glass.

Nemo sat in an overstuffed chair, waiting for Findeville to come out of the Governor's office. They were discussing the island, what it might be, and the danger it held for the whole of the world. Nemo presumed that Findeville was also explaining his intended plan of action. More than ever, Nemo was convinced that his friend was correct. The mounds, the beetles, the little men, all of them were insidious and dangerous. He'd seen the effect they'd had on Marya, and on his own mind. He was convinced that action of some kind was required.

Findeville's genius for the topic was such that he felt himself straining to keep up. Findeville seemed to have a talent for imagining the world, not as it was now, but as it could be. This allowed him insights that were wild and brilliant. Nemo was grateful he did not need to fully understand. He trusted him, that he knew best, and it was enough. He also hesitated to admit that he felt a deep attraction for the man.

Findeville was unlike other men as well, in that his thoughts were as much a mystery to Nemo as the island was.

Nemo had become increasingly reliant on his ability to, if not precisely read minds, certainly to intuit their wants and desires, and to subtly change them. Findeville's mind was either free of these things, or Nemo could not see them. This was, in and of itself, an intoxicant and a temptation. Whatever Findeville felt about Nemo, he had come to of his own, with no direction from him.

The situation was complicated, however. He had not told Findeville quite everything about himself. He had not explained that he could feel the minds of other people, that he could to some degree influence them. He knew this would likely shake Findeville, undermine his trust. He feared the conclusions Findeville would come to.

Findeville knew that Nemo was, in some way, not as other men were, but that was nearly all Nemo had shared with him. He'd feigned ignorance of anything more, out of a simple fear that he'd no longer have this friendly face, this independent-minded companion.

Nearly a year prior, Nemo had cut his hand deeply on the edge of a broken bottle of Brandy. The both of them had observed that, over the course of an hour, the wound clotted, closed, and healed without a mark. Nemo remembered the expression on his friend's face, somewhere between disdain and awe. He had said a time would come when the talent would have to be studied, but that the island required all of his current attention. Nemo was grateful to be considered so minor a threat, and more than willing to steer the man away from further inquiry.

He had sometimes wondered if he wanted to be studied, to find out what he actually was, how any of this worked.

His present thoughts were derailed by the sound of a loud crashing outside. He moved to the window, and saw a mob in the courtyard outside the mansion. The gathered islanders were hurling bottles of kerosene and rum at the building, and torches after. The building was made of stone and unlikely to burn, but the very act was terrifying. His eyes adjusted, and he saw the island was in total uproar. Torches moved through the night in the distance, and all the world seemed to be one angry shout. Having heard the noise in the night air, his mind took in currents of rage like a single blow that hammered at him over and over.

He was surprised that the revolt had taken so long. It had been simmering since long before he'd arrived.

Findeville burst into the room. "Nemo, the very worst has happened. You must go at once. The Governor and his guests are being taken to boats offshore, lest they be torn apart."

Findeville pulled closed the curtains and interposed himself between them and Nemo himself. "That girl, that Marya, she has incited the mob to action," he continued. "It's said she has slain two soldiers with a wave of her hand. Jherek and his mob are handing out arms, and they mean to take the house."

"Dear god," Nemo said. "What do you intend to do?"

SLEEPING UNDERWATER

"All that I can, before it is too late. The gas is nearly ready, but I don't know if it will be sufficient to burn out the infection at the heart of the island. It must be tried, for it could be our final chance. The infection influences every action of these people. If the mob gains control, we will not be allowed back. This infection could overrun the world in that event!"

"Will you and your men be able to reach the hives safely?"

"We can but try. It matters for nothing but that the colony there be destroyed, if we must all die to do so."

"I agree," Nemo said, "The island has forced this rebellion through Marya. She is its catspaw. It means to delay your work, to thwart you if it can."

Findeville nodded impatiently. "Yes. Go now, to the boats, and stay safe until this is over."

"No. I will stay and help."

His friend stepped closer, laid hands on his shoulders. "Whatever happens here, you must somehow survive. Your gifts could one day cure all human ills."

"I'm not unique," Nemo answered. "An unkillable man can only increase your odds of success."

Findeville's lips tightened. He was resigned that Nemo must flee. "It is shameful enough what I must do to this island. It is marvelous and strange and all too pernicious. I could not bear to think the world lost you as well, my friend."

Calm clear dark eyes looked into Nemo's, and Findeville leaned in, kissed him upon each cheek.

Nemo felt desire and sadness all at once. He felt as though he could be allowed nothing. "I swear that I will live. I always live, my friend. I cannot help but live. If I am to somehow die, I should be pleased to do so at your side."

Findeville let out his breath. "Come then, if you cannot be moved."

Together the two of them ran through the panicked house. They made their way through the frightened people headed to the boat by way of the back exit, and to the sea.

They could hear the mob in the courtyard screaming for justice, or freedom, for something. Nemo could not make out exactly what, if, in fact, there was agreement. The fear and the panic of his hosts, and the rage of those outside, was driving him half mad with reflected emotion. He tried to shut them all out of his mind, and to push down his own feelings.

He focused on the grip of Findeville's strong hand on his wrist. His mind burned with understandings that terrified him. Findeville had described the island as some unwholesome seed out to change the very soil, the air itself. It was a cuckoo's egg for a monstrous and terrible creature. Left to its own devices, the purple would spread across the world, changing it into something rich, strange, and deadly.

Passages of Shakespeare flitted across Nemo's mind. The Tempest had begun.

Without needing to be told, Nemo began to dress in one of the specialized diving suits. Other men were readying large tanks, unhooking hoses and stoppering the ends. The gas, Nemo knew, was nasty stuff. He did not understand it, but did not need to. He knew that it would be far unkinder still to the little men in their hives. It was meant to poison them out forever.

He was at peace with that.

The people here were far too much at peace with the utterly fabulous nature of the island. Tiny winged men, iridescent scarabs everywhere like the ghosts of children. It had, briefly, charmed him. As time passed, it had disturbed him, that life had remained so very normal next to such alien strangeness. This accommodation was dangerous somehow to the people here.

Findeville was speaking to him, but he could not hear. He was too distracted, and the suits dimmed out half the world. All he could hear was his own breath, and the bellows that brought fresh air in and out. There were ten men now, suited up, and they moved the tank into a large rowboat. It rode dangerously low in the water. Findeville, Nemo, and the other men began to row with it into the dark still water, maneuvering around to the western beach of this place, where the hives stood.

They could hear the shouts and gunfire, traveling across the water. They heard cannon in the distance, skirmishing ships perhaps, or French and English vessels warning off local boats as they tried to flee. There was a large fire in the woods, smoke pouring into the night sky.

Nemo was sweating, and saw fear in the eyes of all the others on board with him, staring out the portholes of their helmets.

It was slow, wet work. Men bailed hard as water came over the sides with every wave, large or small. The effort was an excruciation in the thick rubberized suits, but it had to be done. Other men alternated rowing, and working the bellows that filled their suits with safe air enough to breathe for a few minutes. Air near the hives was not safe. It was, to all intents and purposes, another planet, and the air did not suit human lungs.

They passed the nose of the island, and were now moving along the mouse's belly, to the area the islanders called the Heart. It was a lightly grassed area, surrounded by forest and beach. This was where the little winged men lived.

As they drew nearer, he dropped his bucket. He had never seen the hives in their fullness. Even at this distance, they left his mind reeling and grasping for allegory. They were something like termite mounds, but taller, more ornate. They glowed a deep rich phosphorescent purple, which acted as beacon, taking them to the shore.

Lights moved, shimmering and blinking in unfathomable patterns. There was something musical about them.

Findeville grasped and turned him so their faceplates touched. "The devil himself is beautiful."

Nemo nodded, but stared again. Even though he believed in Findeville, believed in what needed to be done for the greater good, he could not deny beauty. He was an easy touch for these pleasures. His heart skipped a beat at this fathomless, strange perfection. He knew that soon it would be shattered like so many cheap glass baubles.

Sometimes it was unbearably ugly to be alive. He returned to his work at bailing.

The men talked amongst themselves fitfully. It was hard to labour in the suits, and breath was precious. They were, to a man, terrified and brave. They likely knew less than he himself did but they plunged on because it was their duty to do so, it was what they had been hired to do, and this was enough.

There was a loud noise, then, as though a thousand sheets of paper had been ripped in half. It echoed over the water, and for a moment all the purple lights of the hive flashed red. All stared for a moment.

Nemo's mind was overwhelmed with sudden, desperate, mindless panic. He screamed and flailed, and set the other men off in panic.

Findeville shouted for calm, and grabbed at Nemo, urging any free hands to do the same until he stopped struggling.

The lights turned purple again.

"What was that?" Findeville shouted, as the others went back to bailing, rowing or pumping.

"It's frightened," Nemo said. "It was screaming for help inside my head."

His friend nodded grimly. "Thank god. I never fully believed it would actually work until this moment."

Nemo stared at the man. He was unshaken and brave, and Nemo was in awe of him, of his certainty.

The boat edged nearer and nearer to the beach, and to the business of saving the world, and the red lights came again.

The night air was cold and still. The wetness on my cheeks was uncomfortable, and I brushed it away with a sleeve. I walked around the building a few times, trying to decide what to actually do now.

Carter and Tom had Victor's eyes. I could be very certain that Jherek and his men would take at least a short while to figure that out. There were a few options for me. The most sensible one was to get the hell out of London for a while. It wasn't really on the table as I had to find out what had happened to Desmond. He was my friend, and had been helping me. I couldn't abandon him.

I found a payphone nearby and dialed his number. His answer phone picked up, but I didn't leave a message. No point, I thought, and then kicked myself, and dialed back. I left a message, non-committal, hoping that he was screening his calls and would pick up. He didn't.

I took the tube to near his home and walked casually by it. The lights weren't on, so I headed to my office. I left the station nearest and did some reconnaissance. The requisite goons were waiting there for me. I froze for a second with indecision. Approach them directly, or run?

I decided to just keep walking as calmly as I could manage. I never looked like anyone special, and I might as well use that. I walked for an hour or so, and then walked into a rather low-rent hotel and went to the counter. The man at the desk was burly and cranky, but looked at me with some concern, rather than suspicion, which earned him points in my eyes. I took the key and went upstairs.

I called the hospitals, looking for Victor, and it didn't take long before I found him. An eyeless man, covered in insects, with full police guard, is something of a spectacle. The police wanted to speak with me, I was told, and so I hung up the phone quickly.

I called Tom's place, and, no surprise, the phone was answered hastily.

"What?" Tom growled into the phone.

"Victor's at the Royal London Hospital," I said. "I thought you should know. He's under police guard, and they're very bloody curious, so you should probably stay away."

"Right," he said. "Thanks."

"Take care."

"I see."

"See what?"

"It's really late," he said.

"If there's something going on in your flat, use the name Paul."

"Sounds lovely, Paul, but I don't think I can be there Friday. Maybe next week?"

"Okay. Understood. Be careful."

"Aye Aye, Cap'n," he said cheerfully.

I put the phone in the cradle and stared at it. I phoned the hospital back, and this time, I asked for the police on the site. "This is D.I. Tyler, who's this?"

"I'm the man who called earlier about Victor Mayhew."

"I see. And who are you, then?"

"It doesn't matter. Look, has he had any visitors? Foreign types. A man named Jherek maybe?"

"That's none of your concern."

"I killed those people, Inspector. The ones you found. I did so to make sure Victor was taken someplace safe. You see the condition he's in? Jherek's people did that."

"You should turn yourself in and come talk to us. It's your best course of action, sir."

"I don't know what my best course of action is, but that isn't it. You know what that place was. You doubtless found enough narcotics onsite to take action. Has he had anyone try to see him?"

"I'm not answering questions for you, Charlie. You're a bloody suspect or a bloody nutter, and either way I'm not playing games. Turn yourself in for questioning."

"Sorry," I said. "Be careful."

I left the hotel by the fire escape next to the window, coming out in the back alley, and trusting in the clerk as an alibi if I had to, for all that was worth. I headed for the nearest tube station. The sun was coming up.

The ride took forever. It felt like I'd spent all night on the tube back and forth, but I got back to Tom's building. There was a familiar black car out front. I walked right to it, and it was empty. I went to the buzzer and buzzed it.

"Hello," said Tom.

"It's me. I'm here."

The door buzzed and I went up in the lift. There was nobody waiting in the hall. I knocked at the door, and a tall black haired man in a cheap shiny green suit answered it. He smiled smugly, and I walked in.

Carter and Tom were on the couch, sitting closely together. Behind them was another man with a gun in his hand. In the chair where Carter had been washing up earlier was Jherek himself. He looked up at me as though he had been expecting an old friend.

"Mr. Townsend," he said. "Nice of you to join us at last."

"Get fucked," I answered, with the grace of royalty.

"You've killed three of my cousins tonight," he said. "You'll notice that your little friends here are quite unharmed. Are you at all curious as to why this may be so?"

"Frankly," I said, "I'm beyond caring, you spooky fucking bastard. You're very impressive and scary. I get it, alright? You seem to know things you shouldn't, and to be everywhere at once. I'm satisfied you have the upper hand. Can we get to the dying part? I'm eager for the tension to be released. I've got a headache from the stress that you would not believe."

Jherek clucked like a disapproving chicken.

"You would remove all the drama from life. In any case, I cannot kill you here, we are going back to my home."

The armed man leaned over Tom and Carter and motioned for them to get up and move to the door. Tom obeyed instantly. I could tell he had had guns on him before, and knew better than to play around. He was doing everything right. Carter, on the other hand, stared with wide eyes, and seemed as though he might do something stupid at any second, out of pure desperation.

"Right," I said.

I walked toward the door of the flat, and was halfway down the hall to the lift when I realized Tom and Carter had been left behind. Jherek and the man with the green suit followed close behind me. The lift doors closed behind us.

"What's going to happen to them?" I asked.

"Nothing," Jherek said. "I've got the object of my desire. Victor, Tom, and Carter have already finished their little part in this story. I need nothing more from, and can give nothing more, to any of them. If you hadn't so foolishly given me cause for revenge, I'd have no more need for you either."

"Fine," I said.

"You face your fate with great bravery," Jherek said, "considering how little you know of what's to come."

"As long as you're done messing about with Carter and his friends, I'm past caring."

"Once there's no chance of them of them disturbing the night's events I will call cousin Kavek and he will leave. If they do not trouble me again, they'll have none from me. You have my word on this"

"It's smashing how seriously you murdering bastards take your honour."

"Without honour, there is only a morass," Jherek said. "Do you not agree?"

"With or without it the world is fucked. And it's largely people like you at fault."

He inclined his head, like a dog the moment before thunder cracks.

"Stop talking," Andrew said to me, "You're feeding him."

Jherek blinked. "How remarkable."

I felt a lurch in my stomach, like I might sick up. "You heard that?" I asked, and then wondered why I'd bothered. Of course he had. He saw and heard everything. He was the nasty second cousin of Father Christmas.

"I did," Jherek said.

I smiled then. It must have been a very disturbing smile, for Jherek himself was taken aback. I saw something there in his eyes that looked like fear.

"Well then," I said. "You're fucked. Because, if you can hear it, then I'm not mad or stoned, after all. But I am very fucking angry, and so very tired of all of this."

I laid back in my own mind. If Andrew wanted to take the reins of me, then let him. The relief of it was like being born without pain. It was like a peaceful first breath, and just how I imagined my last one would someday be.

Marya was lying very still. Her ears were ringing, and the ringing was all she could hear. Her eyes were closed, she was free of thought. She lay in the midst of a group of people. Her father was next to her. His head had opened up like a pomegranate, seeds of black dirt atop the contents deep red and light blue. This mass of flesh had been his mind, and now there was nothing in it but decay. Her father was gone, as if he had never been alive at all.

She was splattered with blood and dirt, but none of the blood was hers except for a little cut on her forehead. A chip of stone had struck her there. If there had been birds, you could have heard them singing. It would have been the only sound but the wind. There weren't any birds on Sel Souris, only wind, and soft weeping.

Desmond was next to her, lying on his back. One of his arms was at his side, the other draped over his belly. His dark glasses were in two pieces beside him. His eyes opened, and tears ran down his lined and bloodied face as he looked up at the sky. It was a deep blue, paling as the sun rose. He was on the verge of madness. Nothing in the last eight hours of his life had made sense and all of it was horrible. He could hear Marya breathing, and knew she was alive. He was grateful because his gut told him he was here for this purpose. There was something in this odd, dark, angry girl that was tied up with Niles and all of the mess back at home.

The distant rumbling thunderous clamour was over. He was grateful, although he knew there was something terrible in the silence.

He sat up and surveyed the situation.

Everyone was on the ground. Some were alive, most weren't. The crude buildings lining the lane were in shambles. It was pretty obvious that they weren't built very well, but anything would have shaken apart the night before. The island itself had seemed to lurch into the air rising and falling over and over, like a worm dropped onto a hot griddle. He was surprised it wasn't much worse to see than it was

Getting to his feet, feeling dizzy as hell, he wondered if he had gotten himself a concussion. He'd not had one before, and wasn't sure what they felt like. He noticed that even the goats and the chickens had fallen over, and stayed down. It reminded him of some old footage he'd seen of an anthrax breakout, the cattle flyblown on the plains of America.

SLEEPING UNDERWATER

His skin crawled and he wondered, again, what the hell he'd gotten himself into. It was probably a dream. Some Jherek cousin or nephew had whacked him on the head, and this was a coma dream.

Marya coughed, wet and unpleasant. He was sure they were all going to die, that it was only a matter of time. Whatever had happened here, they were all going to die from it. He felt okay for now, though, aside from the dizziness, and the bruise on his hip.

He knelt beside her, and put a hand on her face. It was cool and damp with dew.

"Papa," she said, her eyes closed. Desmond wanted to throw up, or shit in his pants, not sure which would be worse. He subdued himself, and picked her up, keeping her face pointed away from what was left of her dad.

"Don't look," he said.

Of course, she looked right away, and saw all the people lying on the ground. She saw all of the blood, but not her parents. She could not let herself see them. She was silent with fear. She realized that the purple noise was gone. She grasped out for it. It wasn't there anymore.

"Where are my parents?" she asked.

"Your Dad's dead, kiddo. I'm sorry. I don't see your Mum. Don't look. I'm getting you the hell away from this. You're too young."

She didn't close her eyes, but did turn her face into his neck. She let him carry her away. He smelled of some strong cologne she had never before smelled. He smelled also of fear and some strange place and time she would never live to see. His arms were strong, and she trusted him absolutely. She tried not to look, not to see. She didn't want to see.

Nemo was still in the boat, lying on his back. The waves lapped against it. The bellows were gone. The tank as well.

He was alone. He was thirsty. He was a monster, and he wanted very badly to die.

He had made the worst mistake he could remember. It had probably been the worst decision of his life, but he could never know for sure. All the memories of his lives beyond number faded as they fell back from him in time. His memories of the night before were the ones he hopes would fade next.

He remembered the convulsions of the hives as the gas spread like dense fog. He remembered the moment when all of the little winged men chose to just lay down and not live anymore. It had been a choice. He'd felt it.

He remembered the sky bending, and vast shapeless shadows through the gaps in the light. They had made his heart and mind and body ache, his eyes and ears bleed. His tongue flicked to his upper lip and he tasted dried blood.

Whatever lived in Sel Souris, whatever the hives had indicated, he knew that it was unique in the world, strange beyond knowing, and that he had helped to murder it. He had felt the presence die in his mind as the very world rippled under him, and the waves surged and fell.

He had run back for the boat and watched the shore recede as Findeville and his men ran for the road in a panic. The last thing he remembered was looking at the island through the mist of torn light, and the terrible noises like god himself choking. The island struggled like a dying beast.

He removed his rubber suit, aching from dehydration. He was soaked in sweat, and the boat had half an inch of seawater in it, but he didn't care. His bailing bucket had washed over, and the boat seemed sound enough for now.

He considered rolling off the side, and letting himself sink in the ocean, to lie there again. This time, perhaps, it would last forever.

He wondered if he had tried this last time, just before washing ashore.

He laid back down in the boat and drifted away.

What would come, would come.

The last thing I remembered from when I was alive was falling into the water, and the desperate need to breathe. I reached out with my mind, desperately, looking for some kind of redoubt. I grabbed onto his.

I had never been able to actually control him before, but something, whether it was desperation or luck, let me inside of him.

I'd like to think that it was, on some level, mercy.

All those years since I'd spent, half aware, floating in his thoughts, I'd been dreaming and remembering. Hazy things. The sort of insubstantial dreams that seem to resolve into a haze upon awakening.

I wasn't sure there was really a me in here at all. I might have just been a memory of myself. I supposed that it could still be true. I chose to think otherwise.

The events of the last few days, the stress, the weirdness of things, they had somehow given me a new sense of myself, of my own existence.

Niles had been running himself like an engine overheating, and if I wished to survive it myself, I needed to try to guide him from rash decisions. I have never been burdened with fear or much doubt. I do not panic. There are drawbacks to this.

I could state this without shame. A larger portion of fear and respect for other people would have meant that I was not a guest in the pleasant plebeian cottage of Niles' mind.

And now, Niles had, exhausted, surrendered to me. I had a body again, for as long as he cared to let me have it.

I hoped that he'd been traumatized enough to stay down there in the dark for a good long time. I resolved to enjoy my time in control as much as I possibly could.

I felt as though I should recognize Jherek, from some other distant time and place. Most of my memories were like that. I had a sense that he'd been trouble then. He was likely trouble now. I looked him right in the eye as he shifted from foot to foot, not sure what had just happened. I reached out with my mind, to take control of him.

Nothing happened. As some were, as Niles largely was, Jherek was immune. Delightful.

I considered my immediate options. Jherek was charismatic, but not my type, and old. His goon was lean and olive skinned, quite attractive in a euro-trash sort of a way. I was outnumbered two to one. I was also inside of Niles. He was older than he'd been, though I could see him in the mirrors of the lift. He was still pretty, if a little more haggard than I remembered. Light brown hair thinning, eyes like milk chocolate. Lines forming at the corners of his eyes. His body wasn't the finely tuned instrument that I would have liked. I wasn't confident of my capabilities. I always kept my own body in a dangerous condition.

Both my mind and Niles' body were desperate for a shag. I reached out for the mind of the thug, and found that he too was immune. This was unheard of. I wondered if my power were biological. Perhaps Niles didn't have the equipment. I'd not met more than a dozen who were immune before, and there were three of them in this elevator.

Pity. I had wanted to use the thug to kill Jherek. After he'd finished, I'd have forced him down with my will so I could shag him, and I'd have made him like it.

Sadly, that wasn't going to be an option. I looked down at my feet.

"For someone so angry," Jherek said, "you seem very calm."

I looked up. "Dreadful mistake to ever assume those are mutually exclusive."

"This is interesting. Do…Do I know you?"

"Do you?"

"Perhaps," Jherek said, his eyes glancing side to side, as though trying to remember. "Though I can't place it."

I nodded and then, without warning, grabbed him. I held him by the throat with my arm, keeping his body between me and the thug. The thug had his gun out and pointed it right at me. At our distance he could easily shoot me in the head without shooting Jherek. I, therefore, did the only thing I could do. I sank my teeth deeply in the side of Jherek's neck as hard as I could and I made eye contact with the thug. He was so startled by my savagery, that his gun hand dropped ever so slightly. Blood trickled down the side of Jherek's neck and I could taste it. I liked it. The thug did not know what to do. I did.

I rammed Jherek's body forward into the other man, who grunted. His gun went off and I heard the ricochet. I was luckier than I was skilled, for the bullet seemed to hit no one. I jerked Jherek back and then forward again. His henchman dropped the gun. I drove my hand forward for his eyes, and raked at them. He screamed, startled more than seriously hurt and clutched at them. I dropped Jherek, who was winded, and he collapsed at my feet, holding his throat, afraid I'd killed him.

I went for the gun, and treasured the weight of it. It was still warm from the thug's nervous, sweaty grasp. He was no career criminal, this one. I shot him in the head twice. He died with a pair of twitches.

I thought that Niles's body count might reach double digits by morning, and I would get to drive. At the very least, I'd watch.

I looked at his face in the mirrored doors again, and saw the blood on my lips and chin from where I'd bitten Jherek. My eyes, his eyes, were clear and focused and beautiful. I reached out and touched finger to finger with his reflection, a little sorry about how it had all gone wrong. The metal was spattered with gore. The lift cage smelled of death. Jherek sobbed on the floor. I pressed the stop button, and there was a two second buzzing sound as the cage lurched still.

"Get up," I said.

Jherek growled like an animal and made as if to lunge for me. I shot him in the left hand. He howled like a wounded beast and sat up against the wall, eyes full of tears.

"You have erred badly," I said. "It's been ten years for me of riding around in this pathetic, whinging, man-boy waiting until something dangerous made him need me. Ten years without form or purpose. That's a lot of desire, and pent up need. Now it's you and me alone in here. Whatever shall I do to you?"

I considered the situation fully.

I felt my pockets for a knife, anything sharp, and I smiled to find that Niles had a little penknife. I opened it one-handed, still pointing the gun at Jherek.

"Which of your eyes should I take first?" I asked him.

Then, before the screaming, and before his world fell into darkness, the dark came for me, pulling me back into a sea of fathomless dreams.

Many days had passed since the island died. Marya and Desmond were in what remained of her little house. It had stood up better than many. This was fair, as her father had worked harder than most on the foundation.

They had not found her Mama. Her father was buried in a plot behind the house, and chickens had already begun to scratch and peck for seeds atop it. Desmond had been all but silent. Marya was comfortable with that.

The whole island was quiet. Many people were dead, and there had been much weeping. People were trying to rebuild their homes. Marya had long since used up her tears. The emptiness in her mind where the purple noise had taken root, ached like a rotted tooth. She could not stop probing for it, which renewed the pain over and over. She missed it, and her family, more than she ever believed she would miss anything.

She believed that Nemo was gone too, that everything strange here had died or left. When she had come home, she'd found six of the little men on her yard, curled up as though they were sleeping. When she touched them, they were dry, too light, like husks and dead grass. They would never wake again, just dry up and blow away.

Well they would have, but Desmond had buried them as well, and hadn't spoken since. He sat in the house and stared. He would answer questions if asked, but would not say anything else.

She had begun to worry about him, but it was just one drop of ink in a sea of curdled milk. It scarcely seemed to matter now. She also wanted to just sit and stare.

She was also, deep under the surface, furious about what had happened. She was sure that Findeville had something to do with it, and she wanted to find a way to make him sorry soon. Right now, she needed to rest. They all did.

There was a knock at the door.

Desmond rose, startling her, and took his gun out. He did not answer the door.

"Who is it?" he asked in French.

"Carl," came an answer from the other side of the door. "Bernor's brother. I must come in."

"You know this guy?" Desmond asked her,

She nodded. "He is…was…a friend of my father. Let him in."

Desmond opened the door, and Carl came in. He was the youngest of the Jherek brothers, and the one she disliked the least. She thought he was trouble, like all the rest, but he was fractionally less unpleasant than the others. He seemed to think things through more carefully. His face was muddy, and he looked as broken as anyone else. With a family the size of his, god only knew how many cousins he had buried. He carried a rifle in his arms. It had been fired recently. She could smell the powder. He was holding it now as if it were a walking stick. There were tear tracks in the grime of his face.

She felt pity for him, for he was close to falling apart. She reached inside him, with her mind, and tried to keep him from falling apart, to shore something up in him. She didn't even know precisely what she meant to do. She felt a sudden falling in the pit of her stomach, because she knew instantly that she had done something terrible.

Something inside of him had changed. He was now more like Nemo, or Andrew, or whatever name he would next use. Carl would never fall apart. She knew she had done this to him, and that it was a mistake, but she was tired. She felt she should try to fix it, but was equally afraid that if she did, she would break him. Before she could even try, she was distracted.

"Marya, "he said, "Bernor is dead, and so is your mother. The French found them in town and shot them up against a wall. We will march on the Governor's house in an hour. We need you there. The island spoke through you, and if you are there, it will give the people strength to drive the French away for good."

"Stop," Desmond said, "Stop right there, mate. This is a little girl. If you people want to play war, you can leave her out."

Carl looked at Desmond, surprised and a bit afraid.

"This has nothing to do with you, old man," Carl said.

Desmond hit Carl quickly with the butt of his gun, but not with much force. Carl grabbed his face, and dropped his rifle.

"You're quite a soldier," Desmond said. "Don't play games. I'm not your enemy, but if you keep back talking me, that's gonna change, right?"

Carl stooped down to pick up his gun, and Desmond let him. Marya crossed the room to look him in the eye.

"There are too many soldiers," she said, "and too many guns. You'll die. We all will. We would have died before, but the island did instead."

"No," Carl said softly, "There is only a small garrison at the House. All the rest have fled, all the Frenchmen, and all the rest. It's just a garrison until the Governor returns. It's now or never."

"I'll go with you," she said.

Desmond picked her up by the waist as though she were a doll, and turned her around in mid-air at eye level.

"Not happening, sweetheart."

She smiled at him. "The French will probably run if we show in force, and if I lead them."

"You're no bloody soldier, darling," he said. "This is for keeps. They'll shoot as they run, and they'll come back with friends. Lots of them."

She shrugged. "Then we'll have to be ready for them, or make them too scared to try again soon.

"What the hell is wrong with you?"

"I know things," she said. "I know what happened to my parents. I know what happened to the island. I know more than you do, more than normal people do... I feel the pain of this place. I am different, and not like other people. I was born to repair broken things, and I know how to take them apart if I have to. I know that I have been born before, and that when I die, I will be

245

born again. Next time, I'll build things instead of only fixing them. I KNOW that this is true. This life I repair. Next life I am an architect."

Desmond swallowed, his Adam's apple bobbing up and down. "I don't know how I got here," he said, "but I know why."

He set her down, and offered Carl a hand.

"No hard feelings?" he said in French. Carl hesitated, then shook it.

"You fought hard for us before, and you've kept her safe. I was rude."

"Truth," Desmond said, smiling, and the smile spread to Carl.

Marya still did not understand how boys stayed friends.

"One hour," Jherek said. "We meet on the road, and walk for the House."

"Yeah," Desmond said. "We'll be there."

Carl nodded and left.

"You had better be right," Desmond said to her.

I was covered in blood. I could taste blood. I held a smoking gun in one hand and my knife in the other. Jherek was bloodied and weeping slightly, his arms up to protect his eyes. I couldn't let Andrew do that, not even to Jherek. I looked down at him and closed the knife, keeping the gun on him. My whole body was still half-drunk on adrenaline.

"I can bring that man back anytime you like," I said. "Or you can deal with me. I recommend me, don't you think?"

I was trying to sound hard, but the smell in here was enough to make me vomit. I reached back and hit the button for Tom's floor, and the elevator lurched.

"Get up," I said.

He did just that. It wasn't easy for him because his one hand was ruined, likely forever. He leaned against the wall of cage and I kept my back bravely to the door. I was breathing hard and so was he. I noticed that the lift music had come on, and had to suppress the sick desire to giggle. I managed it. Jherek was in no danger of laughing, nor was the poor bastard on the floor, the fellow who's blood and brains were soaking my shoes.

The lift bell rang and I heard the doors open. I stepped backward to the sound of a shot in the hall. People opened their doors to look outside. That is the stupidest impulse. I turned to the nearest person. My head just poked outside the doors.

"Go the fuck back inside if you don't want to be shot. I'm a detective. I have this under control."

I turned to Jherek, and motioned him to leave the cage. He staggered forward, and the woman I'd spoke to gaped in horror at the sight of him and slammed her door shut. Another man stepped out, concern on his face.

"Stone me," the man said, "should I call the..."

I fired a round into the empty lift.

"Get back in your fucking flat!"

He did. I waited for the lift door to close behinds us, and turned my back on Jherek, I ran for Tom's door, which was still open. I flung the door open, heedless of danger. A bullet went right by my ear, the crack of it deafening. I fired blind at its source and then everything was quiet. I opened my eyes and Tom and Carter were staring. Tom was holding a gun on me.

He lowered his and I lowered mine, and Carter suddenly screamed out loud at the realization of what might have just happened.

"Everyone is fine," Tom said, taking him by the shoulder.

Carter shook his head side to side, dazed.

"Shit," I said. "That was a fucking miracle."

Tom looked at me, and there was relief in his eyes, and I saw the other one of Jherek's men on the floor in a spreading pool of blood where Tom had clearly shot him.

"Give me your gun," I said.

"Like hell," he said.

"Jesus fuck, you think I'm going to shoot you? I'm not, all right? The other guy is dead, Jherek is unarmed, and only has one sodding hand. Give me your gun. We're short on time."

Carter shook his head forcefully.

"He's right. Give Niles the gun, Tom."

Tom looked at both of us and handed it to me barrel first, which was rude. I let that go. It was possible he didn't know. Possible, not likely.

"Okay," I said. "Here's the deal. Tom, you need to leave in the most discreet way. You get a hotel. This is my card."

I handed him one.

"You call me in two days," I continued. "I'll be able to check these messages. Now go."

"I'm not going anywhere. Christ, why would I?"

Carter turned Tom around to face him. "Because you were never here, and you don't have to be involved in any of this. Niles and I are already involved, but we can keep you out. Give me a key and go. We'll be fine. There's nobody who can put you here when this happened, or there won't be. You need to go. We'll be fine. I've committed no crime, and Niles might be able to call these justified in the name of rescuing me."

"I can testify," he said.

"You don't need to," I said, "and they'll check you for powder residue, and then find it, won't they?"

Tom opened his mouth, then shut it again.

"Are you sure?" he said to both of us.

"No," I said, "but the police are on their fucking way, so will you please fuck off."

Tom ran for his kitchen and tossed a key to Carter, who caught it, and then went out the door without delay.

"Not that quick on the uptake is he?" I said to Carter.

"Shut up," Carter said. "He's trying to be noble,"

"Idiot."

"Yes. I'm sure you've no idea what that's like." He had a half smile on his face.

"Are you clear headed, yet?"

Carter nodded, and he did seem to be.

"Grab your shirt," I said. "The cops will be here in ten minutes, tops. I need to wipe this gun down, to remove Tom's prints. Then I need to make sure my prints and his are on it."

I inclined my head to the corpse as I said the last. Carter grabbed his shirt and pulled it on over his head. I heard a moan in the hall, and then the lift bell.

"Shit," I said, as I was wiping the gun with my shirt and kneeling next to the dead body.

"What should I do?" Carter asked.

"I know what to do," Andrew said, angrily from inside me.

"Look carefully in the hall and tell me what's happening out there."

He took a breath as I put the gun in the dead man's hand and worked his hands a bit. Then I took the gun and put it back in my pocket.

"Jherek's got in the elevator," Carter said.

I nodded.

"He can't get far like that," I said, calmly.

"Idiot!" Andrew shouted.

"Shut up," I said out loud.

Carter blinked.

"Not you. Sorry. Complicated to explain. Carter," I said. "I need to go after Jherek. Can you wait here?"

"Do I need to? I don't want to."

"No," I said, "I don't suppose you do. Come on, then."

We went to the lift and pressed the button, and one opened immediately. It was not the same one with the corpse in it. In a few moments we were in the lobby. Jherek was leaned against the glass of the front door. I walked up behind him, and put the gun in the small of his back.

"You're not leaving, you fucking gobshite. You're lucky I don't blow your guts out."

Jherek made a wet grinding noise in throat. Either he was sick, or it was a chuckle, I couldn't tell.

"Niles," Carter said.

"Yes?" I said, not turning.

"There's a man with a gun to my head."

I raised my hands and turned around.

The man with the gun to Carter's head was terrifying.

His skin was colour of the sky at night, just before the sun fades. It was a rich dark purple. It had to be a tattoo, and the patience that took spoke volumes as to his will. His eyes were bright pale blue, and tattooed around with the kohl lines one associates with old Egypt. His eyes were all wrong for his face. He was tall and thin to a degree that was next to impossible. When he blinked his eyes I saw that his eyelids were the only un-inked part of him. His hair was dyed a rich purple. He wore a long dark trench-coat, with silver painted glyphs on it. He wore sandals, and his toenails were long and curled up. I kept imagining how long it would take for that tattoo, and the degree of agony endured.

The man smiled, and I saw that his front teeth had been studded with little purple gems.

"Hello, Monsieur Findeville," the man spoke, his voice deep, with a flat vaguely southern American accent, monotone. "Please drop your gun so I don't have to hurt this fellow right here."

I dropped my gun at once, not even registering at the time, what he'd called me.

"Now kick it over here, if you please." he said.

I did.

He bent down and picked up my gun, and tossed me his. As I grabbed it, I realized it wasn't a gun at all. It was a piece of black wood you might use on a xylophone as a striker. Looking at it, I found it hard to believe I'd ever thought it was a gun. I felt dizzy.

He shoved Carter lightly at me, and held the gun on us.

"And now, Mister Jherek?" he asked.

Jherek cleared his throat, and sniffed purple powder off his own fist, dropping the vial from his mangled hand.

"The house."

The tall man nodded.

"He's lettin' you live for now," Purple said to us. "Be careful as we get in the car. I could have killed Carter with that little piece of wood. Imagine what I can do with an actual pistol."

The way he spoke, I listened, and Carter and I climbed into the back seat of the car. There were no handles in the back, and the front was sealed with a glass barrier like a taxicab.

"Are you still hurting, boss?" the purple man asked Jherek with genuine concern.

"No," Jherek said. "Thank you."

"I am your servant," he said, "always."

Jherek let a little laugh at that and got in the car, letting the tattooed man drive.

"Idiot," Andrew said. "Fucking fool."

The islanders let out a cry as Desmond and Marya joined them. She knew most of them, of course. They were the fathers and older brothers of her friends, the other children at the school. They smiled at her, reached out to touch her. She didn't like it, didn't like the attention of it, the horrible sense of being worshipped. Desmond stayed right next to her. She pressed in closer to him, a little frightened, but trying to look brave.

Desmond cleared a path through the crowd, and the people fell quiet as she turned to look at them. They all looked at her as though they expected her to make a speech of some kind. She had nothing for them, nothing to say. She felt like a puppet, being forced to finish her part. Somehow she had started a sequence of events that she could not stop, or even slow down.

She turned her back on them, took a breath and started to walk slowly forward. They followed her, almost a march. They began to chant her name, over and over. The sound of it drummed on her chest like a light tap. It seemed to please them, but the sound made her feel ill. She had never wanted this kind of attention. She understood the ways they had come to look at her as their leader, but it made her miserable to consider.

Desmond took her hand, and they started to walk across the base of the Outlook to the eastern shore of the island. They would then turn north toward the hill and House. It was a long walk, and nobody was still chanting by the time they saw the ocean, though many had come forward to squeeze her hand, or tousle her hair, as though touching her brought good luck instead of death.

Desmond stiffened each time but let it happen. He could see she was allowing it, but the whole thing made him as just as sick as it did her.

Just after turning for the north, they heard men talking. Two islanders scouted ahead while all the rest waited as silently as they could. When the scouts returned, they reported that the French were marching to meet them, and there were no more than two dozen of them.

The mob cheered again. Marya saw one of the Jherek brothers hug an Arab from the far southern tip of the island, and kiss him on each cheek. It shocked her, for the Jhereks had always seemed to hate the Muslim newcomers even more than they hated the French.

Carl stood in front of them, and raised his gun high, and shouted. "Death to all French!"

The mob roared and quickened pace. Marya's legs hurt, and she struggled to keep up. At one point she stumbled and fell. Desmond righted her quickly before her own followers trampled her.

They were face to face with the French in moments, the garrison dressed in their faintly ridiculous costumes. They were lined up in one long row, their rifles pointed. One man stood slightly out front.

"Disperse this unlawful assembly," said the French commander, and the mob laughed.

Marya pushed ahead, but Desmond kept a hand on her shoulder.

The Frenchman stepped forward. "Is there a leader among you?"

Marya shrugged off Desmond's hand. "I am her."

The commander smiled, and three of his men laughed. "Ah, so you are the young Jeanne D'Arc of the island trash, of whom I have heard so much talk."

"My name is Marya. Put down your guns, or all of you will probably be killed, and so will some of these people behind me. None of us want to die. Please get on your boat, and go home."

The commander looked at her and drew closer. Some of the islanders pointed guns at him. She raised her hand without looking, and gestured for her to put them down. They mostly did so.

"Girl," the commander said, "Your bravery is to be commended. I have heard of your gift of prophecy. You told two of my men they would die the other night, and they did. Isn't that so?"

It was an accusation, and she looked ashamed. "I wish they'd listened to me."

"As do we all. This has been a bloody few days, has it not?"

She nodded.

"My men and I cannot desert our post here. We have responsibilities to the Governor, and the Governor owes fealty to the government back home. Just as you all have oaths you've sworn to, responsibilities you cannot shirk, so it is for me, and for my men."

She looked at him. He was very polite. She liked him, thought he was doing the best he could, and wished he could be made to understand.

"Sir," she said. "I come because I want to save your life. My people did not need me here for them to have their victory. I came for you. Believe this. If you will see reason, and if I ask them, they will let you go. Please, tell your men to go. Please."

Her eyes were wet with tears as she begged him. She was speaking in earnest, and nobody who heard her could doubt it. She was weeping because she knew it would make no difference.

"Well," he said, "You've been more than honourable, then, my dear. You've been kind. Thank you."

She went back to his men, and the islanders murmured as he spoke to them. For a just a moment she felt a surge of hope, until he saw the grim cast of the commander's face.

"Disperse or be fired on," he said. Then he added, quietly, but not quietly enough, "Aim for the girl. That should take the fight out of them."

SLEEPING UNDERWATER

By the time he had finished speaking, the islanders had growled like one furious creature, and the shooting began. The noise around her was terrible. Her horror at his words had paralyzed her. She saw a soldier take aim for her, and she knew the path was true. She heard the crack, but the bullet had missed her. She was shoved to the ground. Desmond had landed on her. His weight was considerable, but she squirmed free. The islanders were on top of the French then. She heard could hear screams. Two of them were already dead, one had an arm torn out by the roots.

Desmond had a small hole in his chest, and a much larger one in the back of him. She screamed as she understood what he had done for her.

"It was for me!" she shouted. "It was supposed to be the end of me! I would be back! I do not matter. I live and live and live no matter what! I cannot stop."

He lifted his hand, meaning to pat her on the cheek, but he wasn't strong enough. Instead he smiled, his big uneven teeth slick with blood. He could not speak, the blood that ran over his lips was full of tiny bubbles. She looked into him, and tried to tell his body how to put itself together. He was losing himself faster than she could put him back, and he shook his head at her in wonder, somehow feeling what she was doing.

"No wonder Niles loves you," Desmond thought, and the thought was so bold and pure and strong that it rang in her mind. Desmond went out like a candle and he was gone. Now there was just a body, and the mystery of him, of where he'd come from, was as dead as the little winged men, the island itself.

The battle was over, and she was left beside the body, crying in the way a child should be allowed to. She was, after all, just a child. The islanders looked on quietly.

"Did he have family that you know of," Carl asked, kneeling beside her.

"No."

"Do you know where he was from?"

"Tomorrow and tomorrow after." she said. "Thousands of tomorrows."

He nodded as though he understood, but he didn't.

He rose, and spoke to the crowd, saying that Desmond had died for the sake of tomorrow and a thousand tomorrows. The battle was only half over, as long as the Governor's house still stood.

Marya was furious. "Let's go."

The crowd shouted assent and all but four marched on.

Those four stayed behind to bury the stranger who had died for her, and the five men who had taken bullets in the charge.

Carter leaned against me in the back seat as we were driven out to god only knew where actually, Jherek's house, if I could take his word for it. I put my arm around Carter. There was no reason to act any differently. We were at the mercy of Jherek and his purple man. I was exhausted from adrenaline overdose and from disappointment. There had been a moment when I honestly believed that by letting Andrew out, I had taken control of the situation, and everything would be fine.

Now I was once again realizing there were situations that simple violence could not resolve.

"No," Andrew said, "Violence was more than sufficient. You got squeamish and weak and stopped short. That's what happened."

I sighed, trying to ignore him. He was right, of course, although I believed that the tall, dark, and terrifying man in the flamboyant coat would have come to trouble us sooner or later.

"I tried to tell you he wasn't alone," Andrew said. "If you recall."

I ignored him, and Carter sighed beside me.

"Sorry," he mumbled.

"Sorry?"

"For getting us both killed."

"We're not dead yet," I said quietly. "Obviously he wants us alive for some reason."

"I think you'll find that what he probably wants is privacy," Carter said.

"You might be right," I said, "but I've learned that hope is something to cling to until the last possible second."

I felt a sudden sharp pain in my chest. It felt like a piece of me had been torn away, and blood was pouring to fill the hole. I gasped at the shock of it.

Carter sat back for a second. "Niles? What's wrong?"

I looked into his eyes and he looked into mine. I started to cry. His own face mirrored mine, and tears flowed.

"What's wrong?" he asked me again.

"Desmond," I said, "he's dead."

He blinked. "I'm sorry," he said, and it was clear that he didn't know who Desmond was. Why would he?

"You didn't know him," I said, wiping my eyes. "And I'm being silly. I don't know anything about it for sure. It's just one of those stupid feelings you know? I'm upset is all. He's likely fine."

"He's not," Jherek said, loudly. "You're quite right. He's dead."

I pounded the glass with my fist and shouted. "Fuck you! You murderous fucking antichrist!"

"Settle down, now," said Mr. Purple, "or I'll settle you down, and you won't care for it much."

"Fuck you as well!"

Carter put his hands on my shoulders. "You're feeding them." I spun around. "What?"

"Bullies feed on that kind of reaction. You know that."

"He's right," Andrew said. "You know he is."

I took a deep breath.

"By my count, Mr. Townsend," Jherek said softly, "you, or spirits in control of you have killed five men, and maimed one tonight." He lifted his hand for emphasis. "I've killed none, maimed none."

"Fuck you!" I said, shrugging Carter's hands off me, and he patted my back slightly. "What have you done with Desmond?"

"I've done nothing. He was shot to death by the French in 1880 on the Island. I was there. I've no idea why you are so entangled with my past. I have no idea how you do not know your part in it, Monsieur Findeville. This is why you still draw breath."

I had no response to that, to any part of it. I sat back in the seat and inclined my head to Carter. "Did that make sense to you?"

Carter shrugged, but there was a faraway look in his eyes, a dawning realization of something that I didn't care for.

"What the fuck are you on about?" I said to Jherek.

"You honestly don't know, do you?" Jherek laughed and elbowed his companion.

"I told you so, boss," Purple said with an unnatural grin, teeth and eyes glittering with something like joy.

"It's such an interesting world," Jherek said. "I will never be bored."

"Yes," I said, "I'm just in love with it."

"Where I come from we have some understanding of people who hear voices, and of familiar faces that seem to be born time and again. The night that you showed up in my home, I recognized you for who you were. I let it pass. I had assumed that you yourself knew."

I blinked.

"Knew what?" I asked, my stomach churning, waiting for Andrew to chime in, to mock my ignorance.

Andrew was notably quiet, and then he said, "To my great surprise, I've no more idea than you, love."

"Then what are you for, damn you!"

"Don't worry," Jherek said, "his voice will stop soon. When we get home, my friend here will capture him in a little jar. Also several other pieces of your soul. Once that's done, I'll put a bullet in your head."

Carter leaned forward and wrapped his arms around my chest from behind.

"Am I talking out loud in more than one voice?"

"No," Carter said. "Not out loud."

I felt tears rising up in me again and I cried, leaning back into Carter. I didn't understand any of this, and yet I felt broken.

"It's okay," Carter said.

It wasn't, but I understood why he felt the need to tell me that, and it was kindness.

"Listen to me," Andrew said. "I don't know if that creature driving is a genuine wizard or if he isn't. If he is, there's every reason to think he can get rid of me. I'm not in favour of that, and I don't think you should be, either."

"Why not?" I said quietly.

"Because I'm a part of you now. Also, because I'm more than willing to kill these people for you."

"Do you know what he's talking about where Desmond is concerned?"

"No."

Jherek tsked in the front, and Purple laughed. I barely noticed. I was dizzy with confusion.

"What did you do to Desmond?" I asked Jherek, "What did you mean when you said he was shot by the French?"

Jherek shook his head. "I also recognized him the night you came to my home to meet me. I assumed it was some kind of gambit. I watched him die on the island a hundred years ago."

"But how?" I yelled.

Jherek shrugged his shoulders. "I do not know. It is a mystery as so very much is. Perhaps some part of your many-bodied soul will tell us."

I leaned back into Carter. He kissed the top of my head.

"What do you want me to do?" Andrew said, with the sense that he was straining at his lead, desperate to be unleashed. He seemed scared and off balance to me.

"Nothing," I said.

"Don't talk to it," Carter said.

I nodded.

I closed my eyes and didn't open them again until the car stopped. Andrew screamed and raged and pouted deep in my mind, and hammered at the bars of his cage until he realized it was getting him nowhere. Not one to waste energy, he stopped.

My own actions in the world had been proven irrelevant. Nothing I did mattered, so I stopped doing. I simply sat still.

The governor's house had been half in ruins, since the island's death throes. It had been the biggest and most impressive building on the island, made mostly of stone and some real brick. There were beams of dark wood brought from the continent before Marya was born. Even now, the building looked like it would be able to recover and stand forever, wounded, but not dead.

There were loose stones, and slats fallen from around the eaves that lay in a near circle around the house. She had never seen the inside of the house but suspected she soon would. There were no soldiers on the front lawn, as they approached, no soldiers here at all any more.

This was good, for they were all tired and half sick from the slaughter earlier.

It was very quiet, and all she heard were the footsteps of the islanders. Her heart pounded in her ears. She wanted to sleep. She did not let herself lag. The pace was slower now, in any case.

Her head ached from the anger and sadness of the crowd, and the tired resignation that the island had to be made free of Europe. She was sad for so many reasons, and this was one more. They wanted so desperately to feel joy in the victory, in their freedom. There was too much killing in it, and too much death and sadness for any satisfaction in it.

There was a shout from a window in the House.

"Put down your weapons and surrender, or we'll fire at the crowd." It was a French soldier, and she saw the two cannons leveled through the windows.

"Burn in hell, pigs," Carl yelled. "Come out with hands empty or we'll burn you out!"

The soldier laughed, as the building was made of stone.

"Stone may not burn," Carl yelled, "but kerosene does, and it'll be hot enough in there to roast you!"

Marya shuddered, and the islanders ran for the barrels of kerosene at the sides of the building. Others dropped to a knee, taking aim.

There was a momentary pause, and then it was clear what would happen. She saw potential moving at the mouth of the cannons, and then all the potential coalesced and the air was full of pieces of lead the size of the quotation marks in her mother's bible. She could see them coming for the crowd, moving fast. She knew where not to be, as they moved past her into the bodies of her people, and through them, moving flesh aside, and taking blood out with them as they left. The life flew out from people like air from a bellows.

There was still another cannon.

She looked at the building, shaken half to pieces. She looked at the design of it and in a moment saw the weakness at its heart. There was one loose brick on the front eastern corner that currently held the entire building up. The house was so strong, yet so fragile, just like everything.

She ran for the house with empty hands, still hearing the screams of the islanders pierced by metal. She heard the shots they fired in return. The second cannon fired. There was nowhere for her to be that did not hold pain for her. She twisted as a piece of metal burned into her arm. She felt it stop against the bone, still so hot.

She did not fall down, and did not run. Two men came forward to pull her back, and the soldier shouted in French, firing from the windows as his two companions tried to reload the cannons.

She slid from their arms, and saw Carl Jherek holding his guts inside his body and wondering how he was not dead. There was no pain in his eyes, just fear and awe. She had no time to explain and pushed forward.

SLEEPING UNDERWATER

She was cold, and the pain pounded in her arms like a thousand hot needles. An ache burrowed inside her bones.

"Marya!" Carl shouted, a wet edge of blood on his tongue.

She heard more men call as the cannon fired again. The islanders were mostly on their bellies, and all had slowed firing, for fear of hitting her.

Everything swam before her, tears blurring the world. She hurt very badly, and wanted her Mama to pick her up, kiss her, and hold her close. She wanted to curl up with Papa and read, and, for all the world, she wished to be innocent again.

She was nearly to the brick, and turned to look back. The sound of the guns echoed until she did not know what was happening, really.

She gritted her teeth, and knelt at the corner of the house. The loose brick was hard to budge, and using her injured arm was possible, but the pain flared up until she saw coloured lights and nearly dropped dead from the pain. She fell on her back and kicked at the loose brick with the heel of her shoe.

It came free and dropped to the grass. She held her bad arm, and wept.

The house groaned, and something settled deep inside. There was another deeper sound like a grunt, and the wall bulged out in her direction. The men in the House began to panic. The islanders had been divided into three groups. Some stared, some ran, and some were dead. The latter was the largest of them.

She saw the house was going to fall right then and there. It could no longer stand. The only uncertainty was whether it fell in on itself, or down and out into the crowd, onto her body.

She stared at the potentials, thought of Desmond, and of her parents. She let out just a little puff of air from her lips, blowing at the trembling wall. It is enough for all the possibilities to condense into one and the building to tumble in on itself.

It's been a long strange night, and on into morning now, and Carter is aware that his mind is still not entirely as it should be. His thoughts are tinged with the same strange purple quality that he had been drowning in at Victor's bedside until Niles came to rescue him.

Niles leans against him in the car. Jherek and the purple man speak quietly to each other, or maybe to him. It is just noise to Carter right now. He can't make out the words in it.

He is lost in the feel of Niles against him, the smell of his shampoo, and his aftershave, the stronger smell of sour sweat and stress in his hair, the blood on his skin and clothes.

This man, a stranger more or less, has gone through hell for him with no tangible expectation of payment and for reasons that Carter could only hope were founded in love. He puts his hand on Niles's forehead and it is too warm. Niles is fever slick and his eyes move under the lids, his breathing deep, even. He is asleep. Carter presses a soft kiss to his forehead.

Niles looks calm, but the motion of his eyes means that his mind is working, whether dreaming, or locked in conversation with the voice that haunts him, and the pieces of him that cannot be reconciled with who he wants to be. Carter sighs. People never see themselves as the miracles they are and the greater miracles they could be. Like tongues to missing teeth, all they find are faults, and Carter himself knows he is no different.

Carter wishes he had left Niles out of this mess or, barring that, had told him the truth. He assumed Niles would never have believed the strangeness of all his truths. It was a mistake he'd have forgiven anyone else, so he tried to forgive it in himself.

The last of the water he'd wrung out from the washcloth at Tom's table is long gone. He wishes that he'd accepted Tom's offer of the shower instead of sticking his nose in the air because there was no tub to lie in. His body aches for the soft surrounding touch of cool water. He has seen more of violence in the last several hours than in this whole life so far. He looks back to try and remember things from before his birth this time around. Only hazy fragments come. He seems to remember a time when he knew of more than structure and pattern, but could see deeper into things.

In this life, he is less than he had sometimes been, but in this life he is able to know love, to feel it strongly. He feels tears on his face, because he is scared of the end of this particular life, and scared of the end of Niles.

He does not truly wish he had left Niles out. He wishes he could wish that. That would be the noble thing. If he is honest with himself, he could never have traded this. Out of all of this came one thing. He knows Niles, trusts him, sees in him the kind of simple perfect honesty of good intent that he has always wanted in his own behaviour. Carter knows that he thought too much, or too little, to ever just do anything from the gut.

Niles does what he thinks he should, does so with knowledge of consequences. He has more courage than Carter had thought possible, and is not even aware of it. He will do, always, what needs to be done, no matter the cost.

It is all Carter can do, most days, just to speak to people. He never knows what to do, or say, or even what to feel, most of the time. He watches. Niles moves through the world without hesitation, and there is a price he pays.

Carter wishes he could look behind Niles's sleeping eyes and see inside him. He wants to know all of him, to talk with him forever, or at least to listen to him. He knows that he is never going to be a talker.

The car stops, and when Carter looks up, Jherek and the purple man are not in the front seat. They are out front of a house that he has seen before. It's Jherek's house, the place he was taken before they dragged him to the beetles and his mind went purple. Before he saw Victor again, in that terrible bed.

He breathes in hard, trying to banish the image of Victor, emaciated and blind and mad and is assisted by the fact that he is being jerked from the back by three strong men who don't seem to like him, or, possibly, anyone.

Niles is slapped and his eyes open. The two of them are frog-marched into the front door, through the beetle infested hall and down a narrow staircase. Niles mumbles as they go, and Carter can make out only snatches of words. He is torn between fear for his own life right now, and fear for Niles, and what he must feel.

He is shoved down, and Niles is dropped beside him. The dirt floor is crawling with beetles, but none are touching him. He blinks tears of pain from his eyes, and sees that he and Niles are inside a circle made of purple sand that sits on top of the dirt. The beetles do not climb over that sand.

He realizes that it isn't sand. The dust of it tingles when he breathes. Jherek sits in a white high back chair. He has a beetle on his good hand, and as it crawls to the edge, he turns it, so that it keeps crawling on a little loop that never ends. He looks at it with fondness.

The dark man has removed his trench-coat, and his shirt. His chest is free of hair and is the same dark colour as the rest of him, but there are scars cut in his chest. They are symbols of some kind, but Carter does not know them. In this way, he is incompletely educated, and the realization of that brings instinctive shame, which he beats back with some annoyance. Why must he demand of himself that he know everything?

Niles is awake, staring at the purple man. There is no fear there, but neither is there any defiance. Carter is horrified, and strokes his face. "Niles?"

"Hello," Niles answers. "Sorry about this, Carter. I think it possible that I have fucked up the rescue plan. You know, it was going really well up to a point."

Niles smiles at him like a sheepish child and Carter laughs and kisses him. "It really was, but who accounts for things like all of this?"

"Andrew tried to warn me. I didn't listen."

"I wouldn't have either."

"Niles brushes an errant lock of hair off Carter's face.

"Very touching," Jherek says. "It almost makes me want to leave the room for what is to come."

Carter looks at Jherek and his face burns hot and he realizes that he is angry.

"What's that exactly, then?" Niles asks him.

Jherek smiles as the dark man lights candles and snorts up thick lines of purple dust.

"My friend here is going to trap your souls, however many you have between you, in little bottles. Then we're going to kill you and I will go home to my Island."

"Oh," Niles says with no passion.

Carter is afraid, his heart pounding. He looks at the purple man, who is either magical or insane, if not both. He sees Jherek in much the same way. It's all pain and need in this room disguised as rage. Nobody here is truly wicked.

He stands up, and he sees that on the altar before the circle are Victor's eyes looking at him.

"What do you need his eyes for?" he asks Jherek. "Why are they worth so much to you?"

"They matter," Jherek answers, "because they are what it took to grant Victor his wish, and because they are mine."

"His wish?"

Niles reaches up and takes his arm. "Don't talk to him. You're feeding him."

Carter swallows. "His wish?"

"Yes. He came because he wanted a cure for his lover's disease. The price was his eyes. He got the cure for his friend, and the Island needs his eyes."

Carter nods, feeling numb. "You have them then, why did you take Victor, and why kill us?"

Jherek looks at him, and for a moment there is a hint of a real human there. "Victor came looking for us when we arrived here. He wanted to be with people who understood him, people who could hear the deep purple at the heart of the island."

Jherek took in a deep breath and let it out before continuing. "As for your deaths, those are called for by simple revenge. Nothing has happened here that could not have been solved by you leaving the eyes to me after my men took them back from you. Think on that as you die."

Niles leans over, and blows on the circle. The dust scatters, and beetles clamber into the circle. The dust is light and Carter is breathing in and the tingling spreads through him. He starts to hear the faint whispering of the purple noise.

It was Findeville who found her, laying in the middle of a circle of bricks at the edge of the rubble. She had curled up, and lay there sleeping, her face calm. The Governor's house had collapsed inward on itself almost too neatly. There was, in it, something uncanny, as there had been with the whole island since the day he arrived.

Findeville had torn himself free of his rubberized suit, had been wandering the island, sick and worn. His light brown hair was falling out in clumps. His teeth were rotting in his head. His suit had failed and he had been exposed to the gas as they pumped it deep into the hives. The gas had been caustic, and full of heavy metals, had eaten holes in the fabric, and one by one, his men had succumbed. He was the last alive that he knew of.

His mind was in disorder. He felt a deep horror at what he had done. The island itself had flailed and pitched like a dying animal, as though it had, itself, been alive. There was something in that that affected him, far more than those hives, those unnatural creatures that sought to change the very air itself.

The locals had told him the air was bad there, but they had also made it clear that it had always been thus, and had not ever

263

grown larger or more aggressive. He did not believe it could remain so.

It is not the way of nature for the alien to simply co-exist. Over and over had it been shown thus. And still, and still, and still, he felt sick to his stomach at what he had accomplished. Nemo was nowhere to be seen. God only knew if he had died, or fled, or gone mad from shame. Findeville wished deep to the centre of his bones that he had listened to Nemo when the man began to express doubt.

Findeville had wandered the island for days, unsure of where he was, precisely, the present and the past blurring in his mind. He recalled memories of being dandled on his father's knee, of being told stories of the monsters that lurked in the woods, of the dangers of dealing with fairies.

He had grown older and put such stories aside, had fancied himself a man of science. He had become the inestimable Louis-Napoleon Findeville, much respected for his wit and his knowledge and his inquisitive mind.

Yet, when he had been summoned here, and confronted with something truly exotic and in need of understanding, he had reacted like the villain in a fairy tale. He had assumed the worst of something different, and burned it clean out of the world with poison.

And now, he would die for it.

Everywhere on the island people were dead, crushed by fallen buildings, shot at, torn apart by mobs. The survivors had the look of men found adrift at sea, hollow-eyed and desolate. In time, they might recover. For now, all they could do was stare at the distance and wonder what had happened.

Violence, he had discovered, was all to simple to desire in theory, and much harder to stomach once completed.

He knelt beside the girl, Marya. It was clear the stones had fallen around her, as if they could not dream of hitting her. She was strange, had been strange from their first meeting. The little men had no fear of her, no hesitation in touching her, as though she were part of their colony.

He touched her shoulder, and her eyes stirred open. She looked at him, and it took her moments to recognize him. His face was ruined, his eyes themselves burned and yellowed. When she did, her eyes narrowed, and he felt his heart seize. She was staring inside of him, and holding his heart in her mind's eye. He could feel her hatred in the centre of his chest.

"Please," he begged. "Mercy."

His voice was slurred, his tongue poking through gaps in his crumbled teeth. She closed her eyes, and tears slipped from the lids. The pressure in his chest eased, and he dropped to his rear end, legs splayed.

She sat up and looked at him. "Why do I have pity for you? Explain this to me. Explain all of this to me. Look at my home. Look what you have done with your poison. You have killed the island. Why? Why did you do this? Why do I not have it in me to demolish you as I did this stupid hateful house?"

She rose to her feet, shaking, and he tried to rise, stumbling and falling to his knees twice before managing.

"I should hope," he said quietly, "that you give mercy because you know that there is nothing that can be done to me that is worse than the fate that lies before me. I think this is why. Look at me."

She did, and she could see as clearly as he could, more-so, he suspected, that his body was falling apart like rotted wood.

"As to why I did it," he said, "It is because I was wrong, and I was afraid, and because I could. I wish that I had a better answer. I did not truly understand, I think, that any of this was real until it was too late. Far too late. It was like a strange and frightening dream, and I acted in accordance with that."

Marya closed her eyes. "Sometimes," she said, "we do things because there is no choice. All the things that came before lead us to choices, and those choices to other choices. It is much like a bad dream."

"So it is," he said. "But I have made another choice. You must come with me."

Her head slumped down on her shoulders, and she shook it side to side. "Please, I am too tired, and too sad to do more than pity you. Do not ask for more."

"I must," he said. "For this dream, this story demands it. I am now nothing but ruined flesh, and regret, and its instrument."

As the beetles swarm, and the purple dust rises, Carter loses his grasp on flesh in the same way water takes away his aches and his fretting. Relaxed and still, free from the encumbrance of it. He realizes in this instant how much tension he always carries in his body, and how carefully he holds it.

Now, his body is at his command, he feels a strange disconnection from it, a strange pull toward the other people in the room. The purple whispers in the back of his mind are soothing. It is like being softly stroked with velvet. He understands why people pay for this feeling. He can't be afraid of it, even now, just as he had not been scared of it while being held prisoner. He loves it. He feels it loves him back.

Niles is laughing, like a little child, at the mess he's made of the light feathery particles of purple dust. The grains of it hang in the air, impossibly fine. Carter can feel the rush in Niles, the warmth that creeps up his limbs. Perhaps Niles can hear the whispers too, perhaps not. Carter is never quite sure how much of what he perceives is real to other people, and how much is real only to him. He knows he should be acting, doing something, because Jherek has risen to his feet, seemingly in a panic that his magic circle has been broken. Time, for Carter, has slowed to a crawl. This is new for him. He wonders if he is thinking faster, or if time itself has changed. He wonders if this is some new part of him, or some old one risen to the foreground, as needed. He feels ridiculous for taking time here to speculate, but time seems to be something he has.

The panic on Jherek's face is curious. Carter cannot understand the urgency. With or without the purple man and his magic, there is no danger to Jherek. Bullets are everywhere in this place, and all of them belong to Jherek and to his men.

Panic comes from fear, and fear he can understand. Carter doesn't understand who or what Jherek could fear. The purple man is on Jherek's side. Carter is certain that this can only be a temporary alliance because the man is mad in ways that are not just frightening but sad. Every inch of him has the beetle's purple pushed into his very skin. He is dyed head to toe with this drug, or these creatures, whatever they are. It suffuses the purple man, and the pain of the tattoos, the dose of the drug, it has pushed his mind past real understanding. The purple man is in pieces, no person there anymore, just an assembly of parts.

Niles is beyond his endurance and broken right now. Between the violence and the adrenaline, the loss of his friend, and the struggle inside his own head, he has nothing left to fight with.

Carter is distracted. He feels so badly for Niles, and he understands only part of Niles, what he is going through. It has not seemed strange to him until this moment that he feels such an affinity for Niles. He feels as though he knows what Niles is thinking, though not in any direct way. Still he has known that Niles was not entirely alone in his thoughts since that first night they sat in his place eating fish and chips, pretending that everything was fine for a while so they could enjoy one another. At that time it was just an inkling, a sense of things that seemed out of place, or a sense that Niles was complicated, and had many facets to him.

When Niles had come to rescue him, and Carter was still freshly high on the purple, he had seen inside Niles, somehow, and sensed more than the one man there.

And of course, Carter does not see any way that he himself might be dangerous.

Jherek is closer now, nearly at the circle itself. The purple man has a gourd in his hand, and has turned calmly to repair the circle with its contents.

The purple suddenly rushes over him, and he feels the room swim. He is standing on a ladder that loops around another like the twin strands of DNA. He turns the image around in his mind, and knows exactly how, and what he will build it out of. He begins to realize the ladder belongs in a library that reaches up and down infinitely. He hears a noise from below. On the other ladder, many rungs below him, is a girl, not quite a teenager, in a simple brown dress. She looks at him with deep earnest eyes. He knows her, remembers pieces of her, and knows he has seen her before. She waves.

He smiles, in spite of himself, and raises a hand to wave back.

She speaks to him, hands cupped to her mouth like a megaphone.

He cannot not hear her. She is just that little bit too far away.

She drops her hands and says something again, and he can make out what she's saying between the dim murmur of sound and by lip reading. She is saying, "Desmond found me."

He nods vaguely, not understanding, and looks up the staircase. He sees a pair of feet in strange shoes that look like they were pressed as one piece from some kind of warm looking glass. The sight of it reassures him, because it implies continuity.

He is back in the room, and his eyes fall on Niles's face. Niles is looking up at him, eyes wide, and mouth open, beetles crawling up into it. The purple man looks at him, and he sees the man for what he is, a pretender. He has no more power in him than a strong force of will, sleight of hand, and a well stocked medicine cabinet. Jherek looks to him with awe because, for him, the purple man represents power and hope. Jherek has lived a long time, much too long, it seems, without any hope at all.

Jherek meets Carter's eyes and Carter sees him not as a thief, or an enemy, or some other terrifying villain. He is, instead, a not very complicated man, and a victim of fate. He and Jherek are both trapped in a world that seems arbitrary and mean. Jherek holds so much anger in him, so much of his past that he cannot move forward. He is frozen forever in one moment of time. Anger, loss, and horror at the death of his Island. He has been holding his own guts in for a hundred years.

Carter feels that pain like a pulse in his own soul, and knows there is some piece of it that is his own. Jherek is as lost, as alien to this world as Carter is, has always been.

He steps forward to meet Jherek, and puts one hand on his face. "Carl. Please stop."

The tattooed man points one bony finger at him, and starts to mumble some kind of a curse. Carter turns his head to look at him, and does all that he needs to do to protect himself.

He laughs. His head falls back, as he laughs. The purple moves through him, and he sees that life is ridiculously complicated. Even on this night, horrible as it has been, everything is a comedy of errors and tragic misunderstandings.

He does not deny that magic is real, that the world is stranger than anybody knows. How could he? He walks through his life with snatches and memories of so many who walked in it before him. Even now, he is gloriously high on a magic powder from a mysterious island nobody has heard of. What he does not believe in is the power of a pointed purple finger and mumbled words meant to harm him.

Jherek shoves Carter's hand off of his face. "Don't you touch me. I'll have you killed."

"It won't matter. I'd be back, and it wouldn't make you any happier."

"Don't presume you know me, English fuck."

The tattooed man pulls Carter back, furious, both hands on Carter's shoulders, and then one of his hands reaches for a knife. Carter believes he may die. Jherek steps back and smiles darkly.

"Fuck their souls," Jherek says, "Kill them. End this."

Two of Jherek's men step into the room, with guns drawn, moving quickly. The tattooed man is just about to thrust the curved dagger into Carter's back when there is a sudden impact. Niles is on top of him, raining blows down onto purple skin. Niles pauses for a breath, and Carter sees that is not him. It is that other piece of him, his other self, smiling. Niles's face is pulled back in a terrible grin. He seems to have far too many teeth, like some nightmare thing. Jherek screams in anger.

Carter turns to the gunmen, and seeing the beetles crawling on his own forearms now, he turns, and flicks his wrists. A beetle lands neatly in the barrel of each gun. The gunmen rear back and, on reflex, pull the triggers. The guns explode in their hands. Carter knows this must be impossible, but it feels like practiced dancing. Every motion of his body is at perfect sync with the music of the purple in his head. He whirls around and smiles at Jherek, who is staring now with no kind of anger, and little fear.

The Person Who Is Not Niles stands up, looking at Carter with terrible lust, and then panic.

Niles returns to himself confused and off balance. Carter moves forward to the altar of bricks and grabs the edge of one in his strong fingers. For a moment, his hand seems too small. Then he pulls back hard, and with one slight brush of his hip the entire wall on which the altar is built dances itself to pieces, as though this single brick was a hidden capstone supporting all the others. The room opens up onto the one next to it, bare simple concrete, and boxes. There is a lone man smoking. He sees the bricks falling at his feet, and jumps back, surprised and gawping.

The noise of bricks is all there is for a moment. Then there is a silence broken only by breathing, and the moaning of the gunmen. Carter feels alive, alive, alive, and the music is in his head, like a nightclub made of light and strange bent spaces. He comes to rest on his knees, looking up at Jherek. Carter can see something in Jherek crumble and fall, and the man drops to his knees in front of him, sagging. Carter wraps arms around him and holds him from falling.

"Help me," Jherek says in French, "It's been so long. I'm very tired."

Carter kisses the hair of this tired old man, and whispers kind words to him.

Niles is quiet, and steps forward. "We should really go."

Carter looks at him, and shakes his head.

"We don't have to," Carter says, and offers Niles a hand.

Niles looks at his hands. "I have blood on me."

"That's life, all right," Carter says.

269

Niles takes his hand, and the warmth of it is soothing. Carter is ready for Niles, because all of this with Victor will soon be over, and he understands that now.

Jherek has dropped Victor's eyes, and they are in amongst the rubble of brick and plaster looking up at the ceiling. Carter picks them up, and puts them into Jherek's hands. He reaches inside Jherek's body with his mind, wanting to fix his endlessness, and finds, to his surprise, that the job was done.

"Take them home," Carter says. "however you tried to fix yourself, it worked. Victor doesn't need them any more, and they don't matter."

Jherek blinks, and looks at Carter, who nods.

Carter looks at the tattooed man, crumpled on the floor, no longer alive, and wishes that he were still able to see this. The purple man had wanted so badly to be a real magician. If it would have made him feel better to know that somehow he truly had traded Jherek's forever for Tom's death, that would have been fine.

Carter could feel that time had taken a hold of Jherek, and had begun to pull him forward again. He would keep getting older now and, in time, even that would stop, and he would sleep in the ground of the Island, with all his brothers and cousins who died there trying to save it.

Of course, Carter believed in magic. It was, all of this, magic. So many things had needed to happen to draw him here to this place, to this moment where all the pieces connected.

Niles squeezes his hand slightly. "What are you doing? We killed for those."

"They're not important," Carter says, and wraps his arms around Niles, breathing him in, the purple making everything sharper.

"But…"

"I needed them back before, but I don't anymore."

Niles looks at Jherek, and his face is calm. "Go home to wherever the hell you come from, and stay there. If you do that, I'll go home, and that will be the end. Do we have an understanding?"

Jherek looks at Niles, and there is a moment of confusion. He says nothing.

"There's one more thing," Carter says. "Take the purple home with you. It doesn't belong here."

Jherek nods.

Niles clears his throat. "Carter, we have to leave."

Carter takes Niles' hand again, and they turn to go up the stairs.

"Desmond saved her," Carter says to him. "She asked me to tell you."

Niles looks at him and doesn't understand, but Carter can see his mind working on it.

Niles is busy at the moment. His mind is alert for bullets from behind. As they walk into the living room, the beetles clear a path, and the islanders in the house look at the two of them with something like religion in their purple clouded eyes.

The morning air outside is cool, and Niles begins to shake, wet with fresh blood from the Purple man. Carter turns to him and kisses him softly on the mouth as sirens draw closer. They stand there, not caring as their lips touch. Niles stops thinking for these few moments. It's a mercy to them both, sweet and brief.

They are kissing when the cars stop, and when the people get out, and point guns at them.

"Put your hands in the air," a man yells, "right fucking now."

Carter and Niles turn, smiling for no good reason considering the circumstances, and do exactly that.

Marya and Findeville stood amidst the ruined green and purple mounds. The little men were still there, dried husks, blowing away in pieces like leaves in autumn. Marya saw blurrily through the tears in her eyes. This place is dead, she thought, and now the island is no more than so many rocks and plants. It is just another place.

They could now breathe there, though she knew they shouldn't. The grass was dying, all the plants were dying. Findeville had explained that for the next hundred years or more, this place would be poisoned sand, and salted earth.

She could feel the poisons in her body, and see them working in Findeville. She could see deep into Findeville, and knew he was coming apart. His gas was like a saw that cut through every rung on his own twisted ladders, and his body did not know how to repair itself. She did not know how to fix him. She did not want to try.

"Please," he said, "tell me, for I know you have always been connected to it, if any part of it still lives, if there is any part of this that we can save."

She was hopeless at the sight of this place. She closed her eyes, and reached into the mounds, searching, feeling for any sign of purple. All she found were poisons and chemicals that undid life. She felt cracks forming in the rungs of her own ladders, and she opened her eyes again.

"No," she said, "You have killed it."

Findeville looked at her in disbelief.

"I've been so wrong so often in this place, I was sure you'd show me that I was wrong again."

Marya looked at Findeville, and could no longer manage to hate him. Hate had always been the hardest emotion for her to hold in her mind. She knew too well the ways in which things fit together. Perhaps, in all the complication of the world, nobody was to blame, truly, for anything. She wondered if it were possible that there were no choices in the world at all. It was a scary thing to consider.

She had made a choice to defend Desmond with two small stones, and she could not feel sorry for it. Yet, that single choice had led to all this death. What might have happened on the night the island died if she had not done it?

But then, how had Desmond come to be here? Had the purple called him from tomorrow, and if so, why? They could have done nothing to stop the gassing. Did they act out of revenge? Did the purple use her in this way? She could not believe that were true. If it were, then perhaps M. Findeville was correct to be scared of them.

She didn't think so. She couldn't think so.

M. Findeville didn't think so either. His confession had been an elaborate one.

Both of them had acted according to their fears and hopes the best they could, and it had become a nightmare for each of them.

He was not a wicked man. He was a good man ruled by fear.

And she could not hate him.

She reached over and took his hand. "Monsieur Findeville," she said, "it is an impossible thing to be human sometimes, and it is best that I do not die hating you for it."

He fell to his knees, then, partially from weakness, and partially in relief, and looked into her eyes with his own that seemed to barely function. His pupils were different sizes, and pointed in different directions.

"I pray I do better next time. I want," he said, "so badly to do the right thing."

His heart was quivering in his chest, the even beat had become irregular and then stopped. He took in a deep breath, and let it out. Something had burst inside of him, and his blood emptied out inside his chest and he was gone.

She sat beside his body for a long time, holding his hand. feeling poisons chipping at her.

She listened to her own breathing, slow and soft and regular, and tried to think of nothing at all. She looked up at blue skies, clouds drifting above. The waves rolled in against the sand at the water's edge. She could hear people in the distance, talking loudly. She could not make out a word of it.

She felt something across her legs, and looked down to see a dozen purple beetles as they crawled over her shins. As they did, there was just the faintest hum of purple across the underside of her thoughts. There were no words, not even feelings, just a spark that, given time, might become something.

She closed her eyes, and let go of the entire world.

Andrew tried to convince me that I could kill all of them and get out of there, that I should leave Carter to take the heat as he was a trouble-making bastard anyway. His voice was insistent and annoying, but I could cope with it. I could still feel the warmth of Carter's hand in my own as I raised my hands and turned to face what I presumed was the police.

They weren't uniformed. There were five of them, in suits, with guns. There was a woman there as well, and as she stepped forward, I recognized her. It was Janice Featherstone. I stared.

"Doctor Featherstone?" I said, stammering.

"Mr. Townsend," she said. "Glad to see you're alive and well. I presume that isn't yours."

I cocked my head, then realized she meant the blood I was soaked in.

"Um. No. No, it isn't."

"It's fresh," she said. "Most of it."

"Um. Yes."

She turned to the man nearest her and said, "You and McCabe go inside. We need that powder above all else. If any of them give you any trouble, arrest them."

"They won't," Carter said, and he was likely right.

"Do you know a Tom Bradstreet?" Featherstone asked.

"Yes," I said, not sure why I was trusting her, but I felt a strong compulsion to do so as Andrew seethed inside of me.

"Do you know if he's alright?" she asked.

"He's fine, I presume. We were borrowing his place for a while."

"Are we arresting these two or not?" asked a nervous, pale little man, cockney, with bright green bugged out eyes.

"I don't know," she said, looking at me. "Am I?"

"I didn't even know you were with the police," I said.

"I'm not. I'm with MI-13."

Carter laughed beside me, a quick sudden snort. I looked at him, then at her.

"I beg your pardon."

"We deal in the sort of affairs that people like Mr. Matheson bring about. We deal," she said, "frankly, with monsters. Like Mr. Matheson."

Carter stiffened, and fear overtook him, and I leaned into him slightly.

"I see," I said.

"Obviously," she said, "I'm going to need a full accounting of what happened here. In any case, do tell me, am I arresting you or not?"

I swallowed. "Carter hasn't broken any laws that I'm aware of. Not of his own free will anyway. So no for him. I, on the other hand, have killed several people, so I suppose you had better at least question me."

Two hours later I was in an interrogation room, and Carter was outside waiting for me.

Dr. Featherstone and two of her people were there, and she sat down opposite me. Her question was simple.

"So," she said, "how's your life has been going since we last spoke. Tell me every little thing."

I told her everything, including the parts about Desmond's disappearance and Andrew being inside my head, and, therefore, how crazy I actually was. I told her about the killings, and falling in love. I told her about the way Victor had stared up at me sightlessly from the bed in that back room. I told her about Carter knocking the walls down in Jherek's basement and Jherek's sudden change of heart. I told her about letting Andrew out again to stop that purple man, even after all he'd done already.

When I was done, she put her hand on mine and smiled.

"You did fine," she said. "You were maybe a little hasty with violence, but you did fine."

I blinked, because, by this time I was more or less crying out loud, and all I wanted was to get into my bed and lie beside Carter for a long time.

"The truth is," she said, "that this all has to more or less vanish anyway, just as Andrew did back when you took care of that for us. This fucking drug has got to go. That's our main priority. People have been having psychic meltdowns all over the country since that poison showed up. Anything else is incidental to that, as far as public order is concerned."

"It's the beetles," I said. "The drug comes from them."

"We know. They won't survive the winter here, fortunately."

"I killed people," I said. "They died. Foot soldiers, mostly."

"You certainly did. And the real horror is that it doesn't matter. You already know that, of course, and you'll have to live with it. I can't help you there. That's yours to carry. This country owes you gratitude for what you did to stop Matheson the first time, and probably for your part in this, as well. Jherek and his people are being deported because trying to keep them here for trial would be complicated and messy, and we don't want that drug to be any more than a rumour. They seem happy to go. Case closed."

I didn't know what to say, though I did now fully understand how I had gotten away so cleanly with Andrew's murder. I didn't care for this truth. I did not trust the government. I wondered how much of a coincidence it was that I'd consulted her on the killings, and how much I had been somehow handled, manipulated by fate or magic or something like it. My skin came over in gooseflesh.

"What do I do now? I shouldn't be out on the streets, should I? I'm out of my fucking mind. I still have Andrew, or a convincing memory of him in there screaming for me to kill you right now."

She shrugged. "You'll notice you aren't killing me. I notice you haven't killed anyone in this mess who wasn't a threat to you and yours. It seems you have it under control. In fact, it sounds to me as though you've been figuring all this out, on some level, for a while now, and let yourself use it. Is that Andrew in there?

Possibly? Is it just you allowing yourself to disassociate? Also possible. In the end, what matters is what you do. You are in control of that voice, and not the other way around."

I started to protest, but she raised a hand to stop me.

"Go forth my son," she said, "and sin no more. You have a little magic in you. How much? Who knows, but it's there. Nothing to be done for it. It rubs off on people. You do alright, and you're certainly someone I'd rather have on the streets doing good work than in a cell half a mile underground."

I looked down at my shoes. The fluorescent light was yellow and sad.

"Congratulations, by the way," she said. "Carter seems like a very sweet man."

"He is," I said, standing up. "I'll go now."

She smiled and nodded. "I hope I don't see you again soon. I hope you have a quiet life."

I hoped that as well.

Carter stood up to hug me when I came out, and asked me to take him home. We called a taxi, and went back to my place. It was still a mess, but I didn't care. The beetles in the shoebox were all dead. Carter smiled at me.

"Don't mean to be antisocial," he said, "but I want to take a bath in your incredibly beautiful tub." He walked towards my bathroom, stripping as he went, as unashamedly as a small child.

I breathed in deeply, hoping for a whiff of Desmond's cologne. It wasn't there. Neither was the cigarette lighter he'd left on my table a month ago. He was gone from my place as though he'd never existed. I had no idea where he'd gone. I wondered if I ever would.

"You know," Andrew said, in the quiet. "I want out of you as badly as you want me gone."

"Well," I said, "it's a shame that nobody ever gets what they want."

"Take me to my body," he asked.

"I don't think you'd want it," I said. "In the condition we left it."

"Oh, you might be surprised," he said.

"In any case," I said, "you are a fucking monster. I'm not unleashing you on the world."

I heard a splashing noise as Carter got in the tub and settled in. It was a nice sound. It made the place feel like a home.

SLEEPING UNDERWATER

"If you give me my body I will leave and you will never hear from me again. I swear."

"So you say. Of course, you lie like other people breathe."

"You're immune," he said, "and you can keep your gun at the ready. I am more than willing to let you be if it means I can have my life back."

He was probably telling the truth as he perceived it. I shut him out, until he was just a whimper. I closed my eyes. A long time had passed, how long exactly I don't know. When I woke up it was nearly dark.

I stretched a little, sleeping sitting up having been a mistake. It was very quiet in my place. I wondered if I were alone, and went into the bathroom.

Carter was, of course, asleep, completely under the water except for his nose, and that tiny ridge that runs to his lip. I sat on the closed toilet and looked at him, not dreaming of waking him up.

His eyes opened.

"Hullo, lovely," he said, and I took his hand.

I was not alone. Not ever again.

PART FOUR:

EPILOGUE

C arter and Niles are on a stone bridge over a pond in the country. They have long poles with hooks, and have been poking the bottom of it for over an hour. Carter is completely focused in a way that Niles has become accustomed to, and still finds fascinating. He has, however, given up hope of finding the bag they're looking for. Most likely MI-13 had long since cleaned up the scene.

He is here at Carter's insistence. In the last year, the two of them have gradually talked about every part of the strangeness of their lives. Carter has explained as much as he himself understands about what happened with Jherek and the people of Sel Souris. It is a sad, beautiful story. They have not told Tom everything about what Victor managed to do. Carter decided he does not need to carry that kind of guilt. Tom will eventually realize that he is in no danger of death from his disease, or probably any disease, and maybe then he'll ask questions on his own. In the meantime, Tom has been happy to know that Victor is back at home with his family. Carter is fine, and more than fine. He is happy.

Carter insisted they come out here, on a hunch. He believes that Andrew is not wrong, that they will find his body unmolested after years underwater. It seems like madness to Niles, but he does not doubt the possibility of anything at all any longer.

Carter makes a satisfied grunt.

"Got it," he says.

"You're mad," Niles says, "You haven't."

Carter smiles his little half smile and cocks his head at the water.

"How much?" Carter asks.

Niles rolls his eyes.

"Five billion pounds," he answers.

"You're on."

Carter hands him the pole, and Niles holds it as Carter dives into the filthy water. Carter makes his way to the pole, sucks in a breath and makes his way under. A few moments pass, and he surfaces.

"You owe me!" Carter says. "And you used too many bloody rocks!"

He dives under again, and pops back up, and then under, and then comes back up, again, this time dragging the black bag behind him, holes torn in it where he pulled away the stones. Niles rushes to the shore to help him, and the two of them pull the bag onto the grass and start tearing at the plastic.

The body inside, Andrew's body, is pale and cold, and bent. The hands and feet are still bound. Niles cuts the bonds with his knife, and there is a crunching sound as they fall to the grass. He is not even slightly rotten. His skin is cold, but soft. Carter looks a little queasy.

"I'm wishing you'd won the bet," he says to Niles, "for what that's worth."

Carter never bets if it isn't a sure thing. Niles still hasn't fully internalized this, perhaps never will.

They are both startled a second later when the body opens its eyes, and sucks in air.

Niles, in particular, is shocked to see the clear blue eyes looking at him. His face is so filled with contradictory emotions that it is hard to guess at what he's feeling. Carter, conversely, is looking at the body intently.

"I told you," Andrew says inside Niles's head. "Now just let me out, and I'll take my body back."

The body on the grass looks at Carter. "Where is this place?"

"You're in England," Carter says, "near London."

"Really? I have the feeling I've been here before. Do I know you?"

"No," Carter says, "but I have one of those faces."

The man nods, and looks at Niles, who is horrified to hear Andrew speaking, and who is dealing with the shrieks of the dead man inside of him.

"Are you all right," the man says to Niles. "You look upset."

"I…" Niles has no words, and Carter puts a hand Andrew's arm. His clothes have long since rotted to shreds on him.

"Do you know your name?" Carter asked.

The man considered, then smiled. "No. Call me Nemo, if you like."

Carter covers his mouth with his hand.

"Oh my God," Carter says.

"Give me the body!" Andrew rages, "Do it now or as god is my witness, I will destroy you somehow. I will destroy him somehow!"

Nemo stands up, and takes a step closer to Niles.

"Please, let me help you," he says, "I don't know why I know this, but I know I could help you."

Niles steps back hastily. "Don't even try to look inside my head. Stay out."

Nemo has his turn now at surprise. How could this man know what he can do when he himself has only just begun to remember small pieces of it.

Carter takes in a breath. "What's the last thing you recall?"

"There was a storm," Nemo says, "like nothing I've seen. I know I was sad, and I felt…"

Nemo's face is pensive and he stops.

Carter nods slightly, prodding him to continue.

"I felt responsible somehow for the storm. Isn't that strange? I felt like I'd hurt God himself, plucked the wings off of an angel."

Carter wiped a tear from his face and looked to Niles, then back to Nemo.

"Nemo," Carter says, "please stay right here a moment, okay?"

Nemo nods, then Carter takes Niles by the arm and leads him a short ways away.

Andrew sulks and kicks his legs in Niles's mind. Niles is distracted by him for a moment and has to shake his head to focus on Carter.

"I don't know why," Carter says, "but somehow all of the crazy part of Andrew isn't in there anymore."

"It's in me," Niles says indignantly, "that's bloody why!"

"I know," Carter says, putting a calming hand on Niles's arm. "But look at that. He's still alive. He doesn't remember me but I kind of remember him."

"You remember him?"

"From before I was born. From the island, last time. He meant well."

Niles sighs. "I don't know what must have happened to him between then and when I met him to turn him into a monster," Niles says, "but I admit, it's not in there anymore. Two minutes alive, and it's clear he only wants to help me."

"I know," Carter says.

Niles is quiet. "So what do we do?"

"We take him home to the island," Carter says. "He wasn't crazy there. Perhaps his powers are weaker there, and he's not as likely to be corrupted. Maybe it's the beetles. Maybe it's just magic there."

"Take him home?" Niles says, "to Sel Souris, where they gouge the eyes out of English visitors?"

"He's not English."

That was true, Niles realizes. Whatever he was, he had never been English.

"We are, though," Niles says, "and I like my eyes inside my head."

"I like your eyes too," Carter says.

Niles smiles. After a full year he still goes a bit soft when Carter flatters him. He is slightly resentful of the damage it does to his cool and cynical charade.

"Well that's very nice," Niles says, "but it doesn't change anything."

Carter takes his hand and walks back to Nemo.

"Can you swim?" he asks the new, naked man with Andrew's eyes

Nemo thinks on it for a moment.

"Yes. I'm quite good."

"Solved, then." Carter says.

SLEEPING UNDERWATER

Niles looks at Carter as though he is a lunatic on a day pass. This happens twice a day.

"I'll kill Carter," Andrew says. "I'll do it, and then I'll find a way to make you relive it over and over. You can't keep me down forever. This is your last chance."

"No," Niles says to Andrew, and Carter turns to pay attention. "I'm stronger than you. I was stronger than you when you were alive, and it's only more true now that you're dead. I'm not listening to your shit anymore. Shut up."

Andrew struggles inside of him, but the noise gets quieter and quieter.

"Sel Souris?" Niles asks.

"Yeah," Carter says.

"What's a salt mouse?" Nemo asks.

Carter puts an arm around Nemo, with easy affection, as they head to the car. They look like old friends.

Nemo has, he thinks, seen a car before, but hesitates to ride inside of one. After brief assurances that all will be well, he gets in. Nemo has no reason to distrust these kind strangers. They seem familiar. Looking at them fills him with a sense of home, and of missing something he cannot quite remember.

I stood on the deck of the rental boat, looking at Carter as he stood on the bow, leaning into the salt spray of the early morning. He was dressed in a striped black and white sweater and khakis and an actual white Captain's hat. I had mocked him about that all the way from Spain, but he was having none of it. Carter was without pretension, and had a sense of fun that could not be smothered or restrained.

Nemo was reading one of the number of history books he'd been working at all month. He wasn't interested in the water. I couldn't blame him. He'd seen enough of water for even his lifetime, I was sure.

I liked Nemo, though he was enough like Andrew that I'd still be happy to see him go. I wanted him safe and happy, but far away from me. Carter felt sure that he would be all three in Sel Souris.

We had just spotted the northeast coast of the island, and were headed in close to one of the harbours. As Englishmen, we weren't allowed to visit, but Nemo could easily swim ashore. This was also fine with me, as I didn't want to see Jherek, or any of his people, ever again. Nor did I wish to see the beetles I presumed swarmed this island in numbers beyond imagining. We took the east coast because Carter did not want, ever again, to see the beach on the western side, where Victor's eyes stood watch, a monument to what had once lived there.

I didn't either.

Victor had been mad. The cost of what he'd done had stolen from him even the power of speech, but he was happy. He had saved Tom, somehow, and in doing so had saved Carter and Jherek. Carter understood this only as a vague shape off in the distance. I didn't really get it, only that Jherek had somehow been able to swap his curse of long life to Tom for whom it probably was no curse at all. There was more to the complicated setup of dominoes that had been set up and knocked over, I was sure. I was happy to dwell in ignorance. I still am.

Magic is all well and good, but it's no substitute for a man to hold, and a hot cup of tea, and the thousand small comforts of bog standard human existence.

The captain spoke to Carter, who understood Spanish, because, of course he did, and explained. Carter translated that they were as close as it was likely safe to go. The people on Sel Souris, he said, liked to shoot at boats, and were notorious pirates in what they perceived as their own waters.

Nemo's ears pricked up.

"Are we there?" he asked. "My God."

His English was perfect, and Carter laughed at the tone of surprise in his voice.

"Yes. As near as we can be."

"I don't think I'll ever be used to the speed of things in this day and age," Nemo said.

"You will," I said, "but then you'll get more and more impatient."

"It's true," Carter said. "I'm fairly sure, actually, that's how the world ends."

Nemo looked at Carter, not sure if he was kidding. I, myself, was only mostly sure.

The captain barked something at us, and I didn't need translation to understand it. Carter hugged Nemo, and handed him the small waterproofed bag they'd packed, and Nemo stripped to his bathing suit, which was as brightly coloured and ludicrous as any number of peacocks. I smiled. He did not try to hug me. He probably had figured out there was no hostility in my desire to be untouched by him.

"Thank you both," he said, and stepped close to me. "And especially you."

I looked at him.

"Carter told me what you've done for me, what you've taken on. Don't be cross with him. I'm very good at cajoling."

I looked most of the way at him.

"Good luck," I said.

"Good bye, my dear Napoleon," he said.

He then impulsively kissed my cheek, and before I could say a word, was over the side. We watched him swim, until we couldn't see him, or the yellow neoprene bag on his wrist.

"Déjà vu," Carter said.

"All over again," I said, and put my arm around him.

And that was the end of Sel Souris for me and him, except for one package several weeks later, filled with photographs.

The island was run-down, but you could see a sense of community. The people, who were of a wide variety of ethnic groups, had united themselves against the outside world, and it was probably a very supportive place to grow up, as long as you were okay with hating all outsiders as though it was a matter of religious conviction.

Nemo sent us pictures of the little house in which a girl named Marya had lived her life. She was a hero there, a little girl who led a revolution. Carter explained that I had met her once, and we were both quiet.

There was also a photo of Marya's grave, which had a small statue on it, and an inscription in what turned out to be Basque. Nemo had scrawled a translation on the photo in felt marker. It read, "She heard the noise first."

The last was a photo of another grave. This was not in the cemetery, but at the meeting place of two small roads. The grave simply said, "Desmond. He Died For Strangers." There was a place sign there at the crossroads. It read, in English, "Desmond Fell".

I cried when I saw it, and sometimes I still cry. It makes no sense to me.

I don't know how Desmond disappeared, and I don't know how he landed in that time or place, and I am certain that I never ever will.

Money is not a problem. Desmond's flat was full of bags of cash, which I found instead of him. I took it into my care, and when he was finally declared dead, it stayed with me. If he had any friends or family to speak of, I never found them.

I wondered if he had ever been entirely real, or if he'd just been some other person until Andrew needed a killer.

I'd have asked Andrew, but we don't speak anymore.

I didn't like how the money had been made, or how I'd gotten it, but it was mine, or close enough. I kept some, donated a lot of it to charities I knew he would have loved, and donated the flat to a battered women's support group.

I also found that I was receiving a modest pension from Her Majesty's government. My country's gratitude had a dollar figure it seemed. Either that, or it was a retainer in disguise. If Dr. Featherstone expects anything in return for the money, she's never said a word.

Carter and I still live in my old flat. He putters, and makes improvements. We talk endlessly, which is to say that I do, and he mostly listens. We have discussed what we'd like to do with the rest of our lives. Maybe he'll start making buildings again. We don't know, and don't have to.

We sleep in a bed that we picked out together, except on those nights where it just has to be the tub for him. When he lies beside me, he fits there like he was built to. He always sleeps before I do, and more than I do, which gives me ample time to be grateful for his existence, and to listen to the sound of his breathing. This is a source of nearly infinite comfort.

Some nights though, his dreams are troubled, and his breathing changes speed. It reminds me of the sound of waves against the shore. It reminds me of Victor,

lying in his sick bed in Northhampton, smiling, while, a thousand miles away, his eyes watch the tide roll in over and over on the poisoned beach on the western coast of Sel Souris.

LINER
NOTES

My editor has asked that I write a little introduction to explain how this book came to be.

Before I get into that, though I have to address something sad. During the midst of preparing this novel for publication, global warming took a toll in the world that was very personal for me. The rogue island nation of Sel Souris was smashed by hundred foot waves, and when the storm was over, so was Sel Souris. My family there had, by pure luck, ben elsewhere when it hit. My niece Faiza was away at school at Cambridge. My brother Landers, and his wife Mirat were on their way to visit her. Landers was to guest lecture there on C. Souria, a beetle endemic only to the island.

It's likely extinct now.

It's a horrible thing, what's happened to the island, first of all for the few hundred people who lived there, and as of this writing, I have to assume most of them have been killed. It's also just deeply sad in ways that are hard to explain to people without more space than this introduction allows.

Whether you know it or not, you've encountered Sel Souris before. The Beatles (you'll have a new understanding of their name when you've finished), Jimi Hendrix, Prince, William Burroughs, Antoine de Saint-Exupéry, Wilhelm Reich, and Austin Osman Spare were all influenced by their brushes with Sel Souris.

All through the twentieth century Sel Souris inspired artists and musicians and occultists, and has left a huge, but largely unnoticed impression on our culture.

So why has nobody heard of it? Well, that's part of the mystery of the thing, and I don't have an answer. Google Sel Souris, and you'll probably not find a thing I didn't write about it. I've found myself, as Gayleen has said, the unofficial historian of the place.

Everything I know about the place I found out first hand, and by time spent in libraries, looking for casual references to the place in old books and magazine articles. But no books on the island itself. Utterly baffling.

The truth is that I've obsessed and written about Sel Souris for most of my adult life now, and I'm deeply unsettled to find that it's gone. I've enough to write about for the rest of my life, frankly, and it's a bit selfish in any case to think about the effect of this loss in terms of my piddling little artistic career.

What I find myself wondering is what happens to the rest of us now that it's gone?

But as to why I wrote this particular novel, the story is not that interesting, not really. I met Tom Bradstreet, who you'll see is a character in this novel, at a pub near where I live. I heard him talking about Sel Souris to one of the other drinkers, and was shocked. So I struck up a conversation with him. Over the course of several years, we became friends. He moved from Edmonton two years ago, and I miss him. He tends to move a lot, though, and I understand why. This story, obviously, was pieced together from our conversations. I'm telling it with his blessing.

Is it all true? Well, I have my doubts. Tom exaggerates a lot. But I've been to the island, and I've seen things.

So maybe?

Ryan States, November 24, 2018

M E N T I O N S

Thanks to Gayleen Froese, as always, for everything

Thanks to the Souris Swarm, the literally dozens of incredibly generous people who have given me notes on this book. There are too many of you to thank individually. To be honest, I've even lost track. Dear GOD, though, am I grateful for your help in making the book work.

Thanks to John Darnielle, who gave me his permission to open the book with the lyrics to his beautiful song, and for the inspiration all the way through this book.

Thanks to the Pet Shop Boys, for being splendid

Thanks to Rob Bose for his editing

Above all, thanks to Tom Bradstreet and Landers, Faiza, and Mirat Somerset for putting me onto this story, and leaving me with skin in the game

And, of course, I dedicate this book to the people of Sel Souris, with the hopes that they someday find a new home.

ABOUT
THE
AUTHOR

Ryan States, was born in Calgary in 1971, and raised in Saskatoon. He spent huge numbers of hours at the library reading old books, studying cryptozoology, UFOs, the occult, and film history. He also watches far far more movies than anyone should. He knows the "real names" of virtually every hero and villain in the history of DC Comics, but is iffy on his own phone number.

Currently, he lives in Edmonton, Alberta with author Gayleen Froese, his platonic life partner, and their three dogs. He is inordinately sentimental about all of them.

He puts food on his table working as a public servant. His retirement plans include winning the lottery, hoping for sudden unexpected literary success and/or working until he dies.

He is the author of two other self-published books, *Silver Bullets* and *Souria.*

But he assumes you already knew THAT....
Right?

COFFIN HOP PRESS

NEW CRIME. NEW WEIRD. NEW PULP.

Visit us online at
www.coffinhop.com